BETTY NEELS

A Valentine for Daisy
& The Awakened Heart

HARLEQUIN® SPECIAL RELEASE

ISBN-13: 978-1-335-04509-6

A Valentine for Daisy & The Awakened Heart

Copyright © 2018 by Harlequin Books S.A.

The publisher acknowledges the copyright holder
of the individual works as follows:

A Valentine for Daisy
Copyright © 1993 by Betty Neels

The Awakened Heart
Copyright © 1993 by Betty Neels

Recycling programs
for this product may
not exist in your area.

Printed in U.S.A.

Praise for beloved romance author Betty Neels

"Neels is especially good at painting her scenes with choice words, and this adds to the charm of the story."
—*USATODAY*.com's *Happy Ever After* blog on *Tulips for Augusta*

"Betty Neels surpasses herself with an excellent story line, a hearty conflict and pleasing characters."
—*RT Book Reviews* on *The Right Kind of Girl*

"Once again Betty Neels delights readers with a sweet tale in which love conquers all."
—*RT Book Reviews* on *Fate Takes a Hand*

"One of the first Harlequin authors I remember reading. I was completely enthralled by the exotic locales… Her books will always be some of my favorites to re-read."
—*Goodreads* on *A Valentine for Daisy*

"I just love Betty Neels!… If you like a good old-fashioned romance…you can't go wrong with this author."
—*Goodreads* on *Caroline's Waterloo*

Romance readers around the world were sad to note the passing of **Betty Neels** in June 2001. Her career spanned thirty years, and she continued to write into her ninetieth year. To her millions of fans, Betty epitomized the romance writer, and yet she began writing almost by accident. She had retired from nursing, but her inquiring mind still sought stimulation. Her new career was born when she heard a lady in her local library bemoaning the lack of good romance novels. Betty's first book, *Sister Peters in Amsterdam*, was published in 1969, and she eventually completed 134 books. Her novels offer a reassuring warmth that was very much a part of her own personality. She was a wonderful writer, and she is greatly missed. Her spirit and genuine talent live on in all her stories.

CONTENTS

A VALENTINE FOR DAISY

Chapter 1

The hazy sunshine of a late July afternoon highlighted the steady stream of small children issuing from one of the solid Victorian houses in the quiet road. It was an orderly exit; Mrs Gower-Jones, who owned the nursery school and prided herself upon its genteel reputation, frowned upon noisy children. As their mothers and nannies, driving smart little Fiats, larger Mercedes and Rovers, arrived, the children gathered in the hall, and were released under the eye of whoever was seeing them off the premises.

Today this was a small, rather plump girl whose pale brown hair was pinned back into a plaited knot, a style which did nothing for her looks: too wide a mouth, a small pert nose and a determined chin, the whole redeemed from plainness by a pair of grey eyes fringed with curling mousy lashes. As Mrs Gower-Jones so often complained to the senior of her assistants, the girl had no style although there was no gainsaying the fact that the children liked her; moreover even the most tiresome child could be coaxed by her to obedience.

The last child seen safely into maternal care, the girl closed the door and crossed the wide hall to the first of the rooms on either side of it. There were two girls there, clearing away the results of the children's activities. They were too young for lessons but they spent their day modelling clay, painting, playing simple games and being read to, and the mess at the end of the afternoon was considerable.

They both looked up as the girl joined them. 'Thank heaven for Saturday tomorrow!' exclaimed the older of the girls. 'Pay day too. Ron's driving me to Dover this evening; we're going over to Boulogne to do some shopping.' She swept an armful of coloured bricks into a plastic bucket. 'What about you, Mandy?'

The other girl was wiping a small table clean. 'I'm going down to Bournemouth—six of us—it'll be a bit of a squeeze in the car but who cares? There's dancing at the Winter Gardens.'

They both looked at the girl who had just joined them. 'What about you, Daisy?'

They asked her every Friday, she thought, not really wanting to know, but not wanting to be unfriendly. She said now, as she almost always did, 'Oh, I don't know,' and smiled at them, aware that though they liked her they thought her rather dull and pitied her for the lack of excitement in her life. Well, it wasn't exciting but, as she told herself shortly from time to time, she was perfectly content with it.

It took an hour or more to restore the several play-rooms to the state of perfection required by Mrs Gower-Jones; only then, after she had inspected them, did she hand over their pay packets, reminding them, quite unnecessarily, to be at their posts by half-past eight on Monday morning.

Mandy and the older girl, Joyce, hurried away to catch the minibus which would take them to Old Sarum where they both lived, and Daisy went round the back of the house to the shed where she parked her bike. It was three miles to Wilton from Salisbury and main road all the way; she didn't much like the journey, though, for the traffic was always heavy, especially at this time of the year with the tourist season not yet over even though the schools had returned. She cycled down the quiet road and presently circled the roundabout and joined the stream of homegoing traffic, thinking of the weekend ahead of her. She went over the various duties awaiting her without self-pity; she had shouldered them cheerfully several years earlier when her father had died and her mother, cosseted all her married life, had been completely lost, unable to cope with the bills, income tax and household expenses with which he had always dealt. Daisy had watched her mother become more and more depressed and muddled and finally she had taken over, dealing tidily with the household finances and shielding her mother from business worries.

In this she had been considerably helped by her young sister. Pamela was still at school, fifteen years old, clever and bent on making a name for herself but understanding that her mother had led a sheltered life which made it impossible for her to stand on her own two feet. She knew that it was hard luck on Daisy, although they never discussed it, but she had the good sense to see that there was nothing much to be done about it. Daisy was a darling but she had never had a boyfriend and it had to be faced—she had no looks to speak of. Pamela, determined to get as many A levels as possible, go to college and take up the scientific career she had decided upon, none the less intended to marry someone rich who would solve all their problems. She had no doubts about this since she was a very pretty girl and knew exactly what she wanted from life.

Daisy wove her careful way through the fast-flowing traffic, past the emerging tourists from Wilton House, and turned left at the centre of the crossroads in the middle of the little town. Her father had worked in the offices of the Wilton estate and she had been born and lived all her life in the small cottage, the end one of a row backing the high walls surrounding the park, on the edge of the town. She wheeled her bike through the gate beside the house, parked it in the shed in the back garden and went indoors.

Her mother was in the kitchen, sitting at the table, stringing beans. She was small like Daisy, her hair still only faintly streaked with grey, her pretty face marred by a worried frown.

'Darling, it's lamb chops for supper but I forgot to buy them...'

Daisy dropped a kiss on her parent's cheek. 'I'll go for them now, Mother, while you make the tea. Pam will lay the table when she gets in.'

She went back to the shed and got out her bike and cycled back to the crossroads again. The butcher was halfway down the row of shops on the other side but as she reached the traffic-lights they turned red and she put a foot down, impatient to get across. The traffic was heavy now and the light was tantalisingly slow. A car drew up beside her and she turned to look at it. A dark grey Rolls-Royce. She eyed it appreciatively, starting at the back and allowing her eyes to roam to its bonnet until she became aware of the driver watching her.

She stared back, feeling for some reason foolish, frowning a little at the thin smile on his handsome face. He appeared to be a big man, his hair as dark as his heavy-lidded eyes…it was a pity that the lights changed then and the big car had slid silently away before she was back in the saddle, leaving her with the feeling that something important to her had just happened. 'Ridiculous,' she said so loudly that a passer-by on the pavement looked at her oddly.

Pamela was home when she got back and together they set about preparing their supper before sitting down in the pleasant little sitting-room to drink the tea Mrs Pelham had made.

'Been a nice day; have you enjoyed it?' asked Pamela, gobbling biscuits.

'It's not been too bad. The new children seem all right. I've got four this term—that makes fifteen. Two of the new ones are twins, a girl and a boy, and I suspect that they're going to be difficult…'

'I thought Mrs Gower-Jones only took children from suitable families.' Mrs Pelham smiled across at her daughter.

'Oh, they're suitable—their father's a baronet or something,' said Daisy vaguely. 'They're almost four

years old and I think they'll drive me mad by the end
of the term.'

Pamela laughed. 'And it's only just begun...'

They talked about something else then and after supper Daisy sat down at the table, doling out the housekeeping money, school bus fares, pocket money, and
then she put what was over—and there wasn't much—
into the old biscuit tin on the kitchen mantelpiece. They
managed—just—on her wages and her mother's pension; just for a while after her father's death they had got
into difficulties and her mother had appealed to her for
help, and ever since then Daisy sat down every Friday
evening, making a point of asking her mother's advice
about the spending of their income. Mrs Pelham always
told her to do whatever was best, but all the same Daisy
always asked. She loved her mother dearly, realising
that she had had a sheltered girlhood and marriage and
needed to be taken care of—something which she and
Pamela did to the best of their ability, although Daisy
was aware that within a few years Pamela would leave
home for a university and almost certainly she would
marry. About her own future Daisy didn't allow herself to bother overmuch. She had friends, of course,
but none of the young men she knew had evinced the
slightest desire to fall in love with her and, studying
her ordinary face in her dressing-table mirror, she
wasn't surprised. It was a pity she had no chance to
train for something; her job was pleasant enough, not
well paid but near her home and there were holidays
when she could catch up on household chores and see
to the garden.

She was a sensible girl, not given to discontent, although she dreamed of meeting a man who would fall in love with her, marry her and take over the small burdens of her life. He would need to have money, of course, and a pleasant house with a large garden where the children would be able to play. It was a dream she didn't allow herself to dwell upon too often.

The weekend went far too quickly as it always did. She took her mother shopping and stopped for coffee in the little town while Pam stayed at home studying, and after lunch Daisy went into the quite big garden and grubbed up weeds, hindered by Razor the family cat, a dignified middle-aged beast who was as devoted to them all as they were to him. On Sunday they went to church and, since it was a sultry day, spent the rest of the day in the garden.

Daisy left home first on Monday morning; Mrs Gower-Jones liked her assistants to be ready and waiting when the first of the children arrived at half-past eight, which meant that Daisy had to leave home an hour earlier than that. The sultriness had given way to thundery rain and the roads were wet and slippery. She was rounding the corner by Wilton House when she skidded and a car braked to a sudden halt inches from her back wheel.

She put a foot to the ground to balance herself and looked over her shoulder. It was the Rolls-Royce, and the same man was driving it; in other circumstances she would have been delighted to see him again, for she had thought of him several times during the weekend, but now her feelings towards him were anything but friendly.

'You are driving much too fast,' she told him severely. 'You might have killed me.'

'Thirty miles an hour,' he told her unsmilingly, 'and you appear alive to me.' His rather cool gaze flickered over her plastic mac with its unbecoming hood framing her ordinary features. She chose to ignore it.

'Well, drive more carefully in future,' she advised him in the voice she used to quell the more recalcitrant of the children at Mrs Gower-Jones's.

She didn't wait for his answer but got on her bike and set off once more, and when the big car slid gently past her she didn't look at its driver, although she was sorely tempted to do so.

She was the first to arrive and Mrs Gower-Jones was already there, poking her rather sharp nose into the various rooms. As soon as she saw Daisy she started to speak. The play-rooms were a disgrace, she had found several broken crayons on the floor and there were splodges of Play-Doh under one of the tables. 'And here it is, half-past eight, and all of you late again.'

'I'm here,' Daisy reminded her in a matter-of-fact voice, and, since her employer sounded rather more bad-tempered than usual, she added mendaciously, 'and I passed Mandy and Joyce as I came along the road.'

'It is a fortunate thing for you girls that I'm a tolerant employer,' observed Mrs Gower-Jones peevishly. 'I see that you'll have to make the place fit to be seen before the children get here.'

She swept away to the nicely appointed room where she interviewed parents and spent a good deal of the day 'doing the paperwork', as she called it, but Daisy, going in hurriedly one day over some minor emergency, had been in time to see the *Tatler* lying open on the desk, and she was of the opinion that the paperwork didn't amount to much.

The children started to arrive, a thin trickle at first with time to bid a leisurely goodbye to mothers or nannies and later, almost late, barely stopping to bid farewell to their guardians, running into the cloakroom, tossing their small garments and satchels all over the place and bickering with each other. Mondays were never good days, thought Daisy, coaxing a furious small boy to hand over an even smaller girl's satchel.

The morning began badly and the day got worse. The cook, a local girl who saw to the dinners for the children, didn't turn up. Instead her mother telephoned to say that she had appendicitis and was to go into hospital at once.

Daisy, patiently superintending the messy pleasures of Play-Doh, was surprised when Mrs Gower-Jones came unexpectedly through the door and demanded her attention.

'Can you cook, Miss Pelham?' she wanted to know urgently.

'Well, yes—nothing fancy, though, Mrs Gower-Jones.' Daisy removed a lump of dough from a small girl's hair and returned it to the bowl.

'Mandy and Joyce say they can't,' observed Mrs Gower-Jones, crossly, 'so it will have to be you. The cook's had to go to hospital—I must say it's most inconsiderate of her. The children must have their dinners.'

'You want me to cook it?' asked Daisy calmly. 'But who is to look after the children? I can't be in two places at once.'

'I'll stay with them. For heaven's sake go along to the kitchen and get started; the daily girl's there, and she can do the potatoes and so on...'

Daisy reflected that if she were her employer she would very much prefer to cook the dinner than over-see a bunch of rather naughty children, but she didn't voice her thought, merely handed Mrs Gower-Jones her apron, advised her that the children would need to be cleaned up before their dinners and took herself off to the kitchen.

Marlene, the daily help, was standing by the kitchen table, doing nothing. Daisy wished her good morning, suggested that she might put the kettle on and make a cup of tea and said that she had come to cook the dinner. Marlene, roused from daydreaming, did as she was asked, volunteered to peel the potatoes and the carrots and then observed that the minced meat had just been delivered.

'Beefburgers,' said Daisy; mince, offered as such, never went down well—perhaps the beefburgers would. Marlene, brought to life by a mug of tea, saw to the potatoes and carrots and began to collect cutlery ready to lay the tables. Daisy, her small nose in and out of store cupboards, added this and that to the mince, thumped it into shape, rolled it out and cut it into circles with one of Mrs Gower-Jones's best wine glasses, since there was nothing else handy. She would have liked to do chips but there wasn't time, so she puréed the po-tatoes with a generous dollop of butter and glazed the carrots. By half-past twelve she was ready to dish up.

Mrs Gower-Jones took over then, drawing hiss-ing breaths at the nicely browned beefburgers and the mounds of buttery potatoes. 'And really,' she protested crossly, 'there is no need to put parsley on the carrots, Miss Pelham.'

Which was all the thanks Daisy got.

There was a temporary cook the next day, an older woman who spoke little English, and who, in Daisy's opinion, didn't look quite clean. She served up fish fingers and chips with tinned peas. Daisy thought that she wasn't a cook at all but probably all Mrs Gower-Jones could get at a moment's notice.

When she went into the kitchen the next morning to fetch the children's mid-morning milk the sight of the woman preparing dinner in a muddle of dirty saucepans, potato peelings and unwashed dishes made her glad that Mrs Gower-Jones's meanness stipulated that her assistants should bring their own lunches. Unwilling to disparage a fellow worker, all the same she went in search of her employer.

'The new cook seems to be in a bit of a muddle,' she ventured. 'The kitchen…'

'Attend to your own work,' commanded Mrs Gower-Jones. 'She is perfectly capable of attending to hers.'

The children ate their dinner—what Mrs Gower-Jones described as a wholesome stew made from the best ingredients, followed by ice-cream—and Daisy, Mandy and Joyce took it in turns to eat their own sandwiches before arranging the children on their little camp beds for their afternoon nap, a peaceful hour during which they prepared for the hour or so still left before the children were collected. Only it wasn't peaceful; before the hour was up every child—and there were forty of them—was screaming his or her head off, clasping their small stomachs in pain and being sick into the bargain.

Daisy, rousing Mrs Gower-Jones from the little nap she took after lunch while the children were quiet, didn't mince her words. 'All the children are vomiting and worse—something they've eaten. They'll have to go to hospital. I'll phone...'

She sped away to dial 999 and then to join the hard-pressed Mandy and Joyce. The place was a shambles by now and some of the children looked very ill. They wiped hands and faces and comforted their wailing charges and had no time for Mrs Gower-Jones, who had taken a look and fled with her hands over her mouth, but she appeared again when the first of the ambulances arrived, asserting her authority in a shrinking fashion.

'I shall have to notify the parents,' she uttered to no one in particular. 'Miss Pelham, go to the hospital and let me know immediately how the children are. Mandy, Joyce, you can stay here and clear up.'

It took some time to get all the children away; Daisy, squashed in with the last of them, looked down at herself. She smelt nasty for a start and the state of her overall bore witness to that fact; she felt hot and dirty and very worried. Food poisoning—she had no doubt that was what it was—was no light matter with small children; she remembered the new cook and shuddered.

Casualty was full of screaming children although some of them were too quiet. Daisy, making herself known without fuss, was led away to wash herself and remove the overall and then she was given a plastic apron to take its place. Feeling cleaner, she was handed over to a brisk young woman with an armful of admission slips and asked to name the children. It took quite a while for she stopped to comfort those who weren't feeling too bad and bawled to her to be taken home. The brisk young woman got a little impatient but Daisy, her kind heart torn by the miserable little white faces, wasn't to be hurried. The last two children were the twins, no longer difficult but greenish-white and lackadaisical, staring up at her in a manner so unlike their boisterous selves that she had a pang of fear. Disregarding her brisk companion's demand for their names, she bent over the trolley where they lay one at each end.

'You'll be all right very soon,' she assured them, and took limp little hands in hers. 'The doctor will come and make you well again…'

Two large hands calmly clasped her waist and lifted her to one side. 'He's here now,' said a voice in her ear and she looked up into the face of the owner of the Rolls-Royce.

Katie and Josh spoke as one. 'Uncle Valentine, my tummy hurts,' and Katie went even greener and gave an ominous heave. Daisy, a practical girl, held out her plastic apron and the man beside her said,

'Ah, sensible as well as sharp-tongued.' He looked over his shoulder. 'Staff Nurse, these two are dehydrated; get a drip up, will you? Dr Sims will see to it. Where's the child you told me couldn't stop vomiting? I'll see him next.' He patted the twins on their sweaty little heads, advised Daisy in a kindly voice to dispose of her apron as quickly as possible and, accompanied by one of the casualty sisters, went away, to disappear into the ordered chaos.

The brisk young woman showed her where to dump the apron, took a look at her overall and found her another plastic pinny. 'If I could have their names,' she said urgently. 'They called Dr Seymour Uncle Valentine...'

'Thorley, Katie and Josh, twins, almost four years old,' Daisy told her. 'They live along the Wylye valley—Steeple Langford, I believe. If I could see one of the sisters just for a minute perhaps she could let me know if any of the children are causing worry. Mrs Gower-Jones told me to phone her as soon as possible so that she can warn the parents.'

Her companion gave a snort. 'I should have thought it was Mrs whoever-it-is who should have come here with the children. Still, I'll see if I can find someone for you.'

A nurse and a young doctor had arrived as they talked and they began to set up the saline drips, no easy task for the twins took exception to this, screaming with rage and kicking and rolling round the trolley.

'Well, hold them still, will you?' begged the doctor impatiently. 'What a pair of little horrors...'

'Well, they don't feel well,' said Daisy with some spirit, 'and they're very small.' She leaned over the trolley, holding the wriggling children to her, talking to them in her quiet voice.

Dr Seymour, coming back to take another look, paused for a moment to admire the length of leg— Daisy had such nice legs, although no one had ever told her so. He said breezily, 'They need a ball and chain, although I have no doubt they prefer to have this young lady.' As Daisy resumed a more dignified position, he added, 'Thanks for your help—my nephew and niece are handfuls, are they not?' He ignored the young doctor's stare. 'You work at the nursery school? You may telephone the headmistress or whatever she is called and assure her that none of the children is in danger. I shall keep in some of the children for the night—Sister will give you their names. Run along now...'

Daisy, mild by nature, went pink. He had spoken to her as though she were one of the children and she gave him a cross look. If she had known how to toss her head she would have tossed it; as it was she said with a dignity which sat ill on her dishevelled appearance, 'I'm not at all surprised to know that the twins are your nephew and niece, Doctor.'

She gave him a small nod, smiled at the children and walked away; fortunately she didn't see his wide grin.

She was kept busy for quite some time; first getting a list of the children who would be staying for the night and then phoning Mrs Gower-Jones. That lady was in a cold rage; the nursery school would have to be closed down for the time being at least—her reputation would suffer—'and you will be out of a job,' she told Daisy nastily.

Daisy realised that her employer was battling with strong emotions. 'Yes, of course,' she said soothingly, 'but if you would just tell me what you want me to do next. Shall I stay until the children are collected?'

'Well of course,' said Mrs Gower-Jones ungratefully, 'I've enough to do here and Mandy and Joyce are still clearing up. I have never seen such a frightful mess; really, I should have thought you girls could have controlled the children.'

A remark which Daisy thought best not to answer.

She phoned her mother then went back to organise the children who would be fetched as soon as their parents had been told. Anxious mothers and nannies began arriving and in the ensuing chaos of handing over the children fit to go home Daisy lost count of time. They all, naturally enough, wanted to see Mrs Gower-Jones, and since she wasn't there several of them gave vent to their strong feelings, bombarding Daisy with questions and complaints. No matter that they had already had reassuring talks with Sister; they could hardly blame her for their children's discomfiture, but Daisy, unassuming and polite, was a splendid target for their indignation. She was battling patiently with the last of the mothers, a belligerent lady who appeared to think that Daisy was responsible for the entire unfortunate affair, when Dr Seymour loomed up beside her.

He had been there all the time, going to and fro with his houseman and registrar, making sure that the children were recovering, but Daisy had been too occupied to see him. Now he took the matter smoothly into his own hands.

'A most unfortunate thing to happen; luckily, none of the children is seriously affected.' He glanced down at the wan-faced small boy clutching his mother's hand. 'This little chap will be fine in a couple of days—Sister has told you what to do, I expect? This young lady is an assistant at the nursery school and is not to be blamed in any way. The matter will be investigated by the proper authorities but it is evident that the cause was either in the cooking or in the food. I suggest that you take the matter up with the principal of the school.'

Daisy, listening to this, reflected that he had a pleasant voice, deep and unhurried and just now with a hint of steel in it. Which might have accounted for the ungracious apology she received before the small boy was borne away.

'The last one?' asked the doctor.

'Yes. Only I'm not sure if I'm supposed to stay—there are the children who are to remain here for the night; their mothers are here but they might want to ask questions—the children's clothes and so on.'

'What's the telephone number of this nursery school?'

She told him, too tired to bother about why he wanted to know. She would have liked to go home but first she would have to go back and get her bike and very likely Mrs Gower-Jones would want a detailed account of what had transpired at the hospital. She yawned, and choked on it as Dr Seymour said from behind her, 'Mrs Gower-Jones is coming here—she should have been here in the first place. You will go home.' It was a statement, not a suggestion and he turned on his heel and then paused. 'How?'

'I have my bike at the school.' She hesitated. 'And my purse and things.'

'They'll be there in the morning; you can fetch them. The place will be closed as a nursery school at least for the time being. Did you come like that?'

She frowned. 'Yes.'

'I'll drive you to your home. Come along.'

Daisy, a mild girl, said, 'No, thank you,' with something of a snap. But that was a waste of time.

'Don't be silly,' advised Dr Seymour, and he caught

her by the arm and marched her briskly out of the hospital and stuffed her into the Rolls while she was still thinking of the dignified reply she wished to make. No girl liked to be told she was silly.

'Where to?'

'Wilton.'

'Where in Wilton?'

'If you put me down by the market square…'

He sighed. 'Where in Wilton?'

'Box Cottage—on the way to Burcombe. But I can easily walk…'

He didn't bother to answer as he drove through the city streets and along the main road to Wilton. Once there, within minutes, he turned left at the crossroads by the market. 'Left or right?' he asked.

'On the left—the last cottage in this row.'

He slowed the car and stopped, and to her surprise got out to open her door. He opened the little garden gate too, which gave her mother time to get to the door.

'Darling, whatever has happened? You said the children were ill—' Mrs Pelham took in Daisy's appearance. 'Are you ill too? You look as though you've been sick…'

'Not me, the children, Mother, and I'm quite all right.' Since the doctor was towering over her she remembered her manners and introduced him.

'Dr Seymour very kindly gave me a lift.'

'How very kind of you.' Her mother smiled charmingly at him. 'Do come in and have a cup of coffee.'

He saw the look on Daisy's face and his thin mouth twitched. 'I must get back to the hospital, I'm afraid; perhaps another time?'

'Any time,' said Mrs Pelham largely, ignoring Daisy's frown. 'Do you live in Wilton? I don't remember seeing your car...?'

'In Salisbury, but I have a sister living along the Wylye valley.'

'Well, we don't want to keep you. Thank you for bringing Daisy home.' Mrs Pelham offered a hand but Daisy didn't. She had seen his lifted eyebrows at her name; Daisy was a silly name and it probably amused him. She wished him goodbye in a cool voice, echoing her mother's thanks. She didn't like him; he was overbearing and had ridden roughshod over her objections to being given a lift. That she would still have been biking tiredly from Salisbury without his offer was something she chose to ignore.

'What a nice man,' observed her mother as they watched the car sliding away, back to the crossroads. 'How very kind of him to bring you home. You must tell us all about it, darling—' she wrinkled her nose '—but perhaps you'd like a bath first.'

When Daisy reached the nursery school in the morning she found Mrs Gower-Jones in a black mood. The cook had disappeared and the police were trying to trace her, she had had people inspecting her kitchen and asking questions and the school was to be closed until it had been thoroughly cleaned and inspected. A matter of some weeks, even months. 'So you can take a week's notice,' said Mrs Gower-Jones. 'I've seen the other girls too. Don't expect to come back here either; if and when I open again parents won't want to see any of you—they'll always suspect you.'

'I should have thought,' observed Daisy in a reasonable voice, 'that they would be more likely to suspect you, Mrs Gower-Jones. After all, you engaged the cook.'

Mrs Gower-Jones had always considered Daisy to be a quiet, easily put-upon girl; now she looked at her in amazement while her face slowly reddened. 'Well, really, Miss Pelham—how dare you say such a thing?'

'Well, it's true.' Daisy added without rancour, 'Anyway I wouldn't want to come back here to work; I'd feel as suspicious as the parents.'

'Leave at once,' said her employer, 'and don't expect a reference. I'll post on your cheque.'

'I'll wait while you write it, Mrs Gower-Jones,' said Daisy mildly.

She was already making plans as she cycled back to Wilton. She would have to get another job as soon as possible; her mother's pension wasn't enough to keep all three of them and Pamela had at least two more years at school. They paid the estate a very modest rent but there were still taxes and lighting and heating and food. They relied on Daisy's wages to pay for clothes and small extra comforts. There was never any money to save; her father had left a few hundred pounds in the bank but that was for a rainy day, never to be spent unless in dire emergency.

Back home, she explained everything to her mother, carefully keeping any note of anxiety out of her voice. They would be able to go on much as usual for a week or two and surely in that time she would find a job. It was a pity she wasn't trained for anything; she had gone to a good school because her father had been alive then and the fees had been found, although at the cost of holidays and small luxuries, and since she had done well the plan had been to send her to one of the minor universities, leading to a teaching post eventually. His death had been unexpected and premature; Daisy left the university after only a year there and came home to shoulder the responsibilities of the household and take the job at the nursery school.

Her mother reassured, she went out and bought the local paper and searched the jobs column. There was nothing; at least, there was plenty of work for anyone who understood computers and the like and there were several pigpersons wanted, for pig breeding flourished in her part of the world. It was a great pity that the tourist season would be over soon, otherwise she might have enquired if there was work for her in the tearooms at Wilton House. Tomorrow, she decided, she would go into Salisbury, visit the agencies and the job centre.

It was a bad time of year to find work, she was told; now if she had asked when the season started, no doubt there would have been something for her—a remark kindly meant but of little comfort to her.

By the end of the week her optimism was wearing thin although she preserved a composed front towards her mother and Pamela. She was sitting at her mother's writing desk answering an advertisement for a mother's help when someone knocked on the door. Pamela was in her room, deep in schoolwork; her mother was out shopping. Daisy went to answer it.

Chapter 2

Daisy recognised the person on the doorstep. 'Lady Thorley—please come in. The twins are all right?'

'Quite recovered,' said their mother. 'I wanted to talk to you…'

Daisy led the way into the small sitting-room, nicely furnished and with a bowl of roses on the Georgian circular table under the window, offered a chair and then sat down opposite her visitor, her hands folded quietly in her lap, composedly waiting to hear the reason for the visit. It would be something to do with the nursery school, she felt sure, some small garment missing…

'Are you out of a job?' Lady Thorley smiled. 'Forgive me for being nosy, but Mrs Gower-Jones tells me that she has closed the place down for some time at least.'

'Well, yes, she has, and we all had a week's notice…'

'Then if you are free, would you consider com-

ing to us for a while? The twins—they're a handful,
more than I can cope with, and they like you. If you
hear of something better you would be free to go, but
you would be a godsend. There must be other nursery schools, although I don't know of any. I thought
that if you would come while I find a governess for
them…only I don't want to be hurried over that—she
will have to be someone rather special. Would you
give it a try?'

'I could come each day?'

'Oh, yes. We're at Steeple Langford—about three
miles from here. Is there a bus?'

'I have a bike.'

'You'll give it a try? Is half-past eight too early for
you? Until five o'clock—that's a long day, I know, but
you would have Saturday and Sunday.' She hesitated.
'And perhaps occasionally you would sleep in if we
were about to go out for the evening? We have some
good servants but I'd rather it was you.' And when
Daisy hesitated she added, 'I don't know what you
were paid by Mrs Gower-Jones but we would pay the
usual rate.' She named a sum which sent Daisy's mousy
eyebrows up. Twice the amount Mrs Gower-Jones had
paid her; heaven-sent, although she felt bound to tell
her visitor that it was more than she had earned at the
nursery school.

'By the end of the week you will agree with me
that you will have earned every penny. You have only
had the twins for a few days, diluted with other children. Full-strength, as it were, they're formidable.' She
smiled charmingly. 'You see, I'm not pretending that

they're little angels. I love them dearly but because of that I'm not firm enough.'

'When would you like me to start?' asked Daisy. 'Only you'll want references.'

'Oh, never mind those,' said Lady Thorley breezily, 'Valentine told me that you were a sensible girl with an honest face and he's always right.'

Daisy blushed and Lady Thorley thought how pleasant it was to find a girl who still could, happily unaware that it wasn't a blush at all, just Daisy's temper, seldom roused, coming to the surface. Even if that was all he could think of to say about her, it would have been far better if he had kept quiet—honest and sensible indeed; what girl wanted to be called that?

For a moment she was tempted to change her mind and refuse the job, but then she remembered the marvellous wages… 'How kind,' she murmured, and agreed to cycle over to Steeple Langford the next morning.

Lady Thorley went presently and Daisy tore up her reply to the advertisement for a home help and then did cautious sums on the back of the writing paper. The job wouldn't last forever—a month, six weeks perhaps—but the money would take care of the phone bill and the gas and electricity as well. There would be enough left over for her mother to have a pair of good shoes ready for the winter, and Pamela to have another of the baggy sweaters she craved, and she herself— Daisy sucked the end of her pen—torn between high-heeled elegant shoes she would probably never have the chance to wear and a pair of sensible boots; last winter's pair had had their day and were beyond repair.

She was still brooding over this when her mother and Pamela came back, and, much heartened by the news, Mrs Pelham fetched the bottle of sherry they hoarded for special occasions and they all had a glass. 'I mustn't forget Razor,' said Daisy. 'I'll get some of that luxury catfood he enjoys and perhaps a tin of sardines.'

The road along the Wylye was quiet, used mainly by local people, winding from one small village to the next one with glimpses of the river from time to time and plenty of trees. It was a splendid morning and Daisy cycled along it trying to guess what the job would turn out to be. Hard work, no doubt, but the money was good...

The Thorleys' house was on the further side of Steeple Langford, a roomy place typical of the area, with plenty of large windows, a veranda and a wide porch. It was surrounded by nicely laid-out grounds with plenty of trees and as she went up the short drive she could see ponies and a donkey in the small adjoining field.

The front door was opened as she reached it and the two children and a black Labrador dog spilled out noisily. Daisy got off her bike. 'Hello,' she said cheerfully, 'what's your dog's name?'

'Boots. Have you got a dog?' They had crowded round her, all three of them.

'No, though we had one when I was a little girl. We have a cat; he's called Razor.'

'Why?'

'He's very sharp...'

The twins hooted with mirth. 'May we see him?'

'Perhaps one day your mother will let you come and see him. We'll see.'

'Why do all grown-ups say "we'll see"?'

Daisy was saved from answering this by the appearance of Lady Thorley, wearing the kind of thin jersey dress that Daisy coveted.

'Good morning. May we call you Daisy? Come on inside and have a look round. We've just finished breakfast but there's coffee if you'd like it.'

Daisy declined the coffee, propped her bike against the porch and, with a twin on either side of her, went into the house.

It was as nice inside as it was out; comfortably furnished with some good pieces, a great many comfortable chairs, flowers everywhere and a slight untidiness which one would expect in a house where there were children and dogs. The nursery was on the first floor overlooking the back lawn, a large room with a low shelf around its walls to accommodate the various toys the twins possessed. There was a low table too and small chairs and also a comfortable chair or two for grown-ups.

'They prefer to be out of doors,' said their mother. 'They're very energetic, I'm afraid. I'll show you the garden and then leave you, shall I?' She led the way downstairs again. 'The children have their milk about half-past ten and Jenny will bring your coffee at the same time. They have their lunch just after twelve, with me—and you, of course—and they have their tea at five o'clock before bed at six o'clock.' Lady Thorley hesitated. 'I'm sometimes out to lunch…' She looked doubtfully at Daisy.

'I'm sure Josh and Katie will keep me company when you are,' said Daisy matter-of-factly and watched their mother's face light up with relief.

'The children had a nanny until quite recently,' confided Lady Thorley. 'She—she was very strict.'

'I don't know if I'm strict or not,' said Daisy cheerfully. She beamed down at the children. 'We'll have to find out, won't we?'

She spent the rest of the morning in the garden with the twins and Boots, pausing only long enough to drink her coffee while they reluctantly drank their milk. At lunch they were difficult, picking at their food, casting sly glances at their mother as they spilt their drinks, kicked the rungs of their chairs and upset the salt cellar. Lady Thorley said helplessly, 'Darlings, do behave yourselves.' She spoke in a loving voice which held no authority at all and they took no notice of her.

'I wonder,' observed Daisy pleasantly, 'if it would be a good idea, Lady Thorley, if Josh and Katie were to have their lunch in the nursery for a few days—by themselves, of course…? I'll sit in the room with them, naturally.'

Lady Thorley caught Daisy's look. 'What a good idea,' she said enthusiastically. 'Why didn't I think of it before? We'll start tomorrow.'

The twins exchanged glances. 'Don't want to,' said Josh, and was echoed by Katie. They had stuck their small lower lips out, ready to be mutinous.

'Well,' said Daisy, 'if you really don't want to, will

you eat your lunch like grown-up people with your mother and me?'

'You're strict…'

'Not a bit of it. While you're having your rest I'll read whatever story you want.'

It had seemed a long day, thought Daisy as she cycled back home, but she had enjoyed it. The twins were nice children, spoilt by their mother and probably too strictly brought up by the nanny. She began to plan a daily regime which might, at least in part, correct some of that. They were very bright for their age; she would have to win their confidence as well as their liking.

By the end of the week she felt reasonably sure that she had done that; the twins were about the naughtiest children she had had to deal with while she had worked for Mrs Gower-Jones, and so charming with their large blue eyes and innocent little faces that it was sometimes difficult to be firm, but they seemed to like her and since she ignored their small tantrums she felt that she was making progress. She liked the job too, and enjoyed the cycle ride each day and the long hours spent out of doors with the children. The weather was delightful too, dry and warm with no hint of autumn. Of course, the ride wouldn't be so nice in rain and wind, but she would be gone by then, although Lady Thorley hadn't mentioned the likelihood of a governess yet.

Lady Thorley was going out to lunch, Daisy remembered as she pedalled along the quiet road, and since it was such a fine day perhaps she and the twins could have a picnic in the garden; she was good friends with the cook and the elderly housemaid and surely between them they could concoct a picnic instead of the usual meal indoors.

The twins were waiting for her with faithful Boots and she went up to the nursery with them for an hour's playschool—Plasticine and wooden blocks, crayons and large sheets of scribbling paper—and they were tidying up when their mother came to say that she was going out to her lunch party and would be back by tea-time. She looked elegant and pretty and Daisy had no doubt in her mind that her husband must adore her. The twins were kissed and told to be good, and Daisy was to be sure and ask for anything she might want. The three of them escorted her to the door and waved as she drove away in her smart little Mini, and Katie began to sniff sorrowfully.

'Who's coming to help get our picnic ready?' asked Daisy, and whisked the moppet out into the garden with Josh and Boots. 'Look, Cook's put a table ready; let's put the plates and knives and things on it and then we'll go to the kitchen and fetch the food.'

She was leading the way back to the garden, laden with a tray of dishes—hard-boiled eggs, bacon sandwiches, little sausages on sticks and a mushroom quiche—when she saw Dr Seymour sitting on the grass leaning against the table. The children had seen him too; the dish of apples Josh had been carrying went tumbling to the ground and Katie, close behind him, dropped the plastic mugs she held as they galloped towards him with shrieks of delight. He uncoiled his vast

person in one neat movement and received their onslaught with lazy good humour. 'May I stay to lunch?'
he asked Daisy and, since he quite obviously intended
to anyway, she said politely,

'Of course, Dr Seymour. Lady Thorley is out but
she'll be back at teatime.' She put down her tray. 'I'll
fetch the rest of the food...'

She started back to the house and found him beside
her, trailed by the twins and Boots. 'Quite happy here?'
he wanted to know.

'Yes, thank you.'

'Pleased to see me again?'

What an outrageous man, thought Daisy, and what
a colossal conceit. She said pleasantly, 'Should I be,
Dr Seymour?'

'Upon reflection, perhaps not.' They had reached the
kitchen and found Cook, who had seen his car, cutting
a mound of beef sandwiches. 'You'll be peckish, sir,'
she said comfortably. 'Hard-boiled eggs and sausages
on sticks aren't hardly fitting for a gentleman of your
size, if you don't mind me saying it.'

He took a sandwich and bit into it. 'When have I
ever disputed an opinion of yours, Mrs Betts? And if
I can't finish them I'm sure Daisy will help me out.'

So she was Daisy, was she? And she had no intention of eating his beef sandwiches. She didn't say so
although she gave him a chilly look.

It was impossible to remain chilly for long; the
twins, on their best behaviour because their favourite
uncle was going to share their picnic, saw to that. The
meal was an unqualified success; Josh ate everything

he was offered and, since Katie always did as he did, the usual patient battle to get them to eat didn't take place; instead, the doctor kept them entertained with a mixture of mild teasing and ridiculous stories in the face of which it was impossible to remain stand-offish; indeed Daisy enjoyed herself and found herself forgetting how much she disapproved of him. That was until he remarked, as the last of the lemonade was being drunk, 'I hope Meg has got you on a long lease.'

She gave him a puzzled look. 'A long lease…?'

'It would seem to me that you have all the makings of a family nanny, handed down from one generation to another.'

Daisy, a mild-tempered girl, choked back rage. 'I have no intention of being anything of the sort.' Her pleasant voice held a decidedly acid note.

'No? Planning to get married?'

'No, and if I may say so, Dr Seymour, I must remind you that it's none of your business.'

'No, no, of course it isn't; put it down to idle curiosity.'

Josh, for nearly four years old, was very bright. 'You're not married either, Uncle Val; I know 'cos Mummy said it was high time and it was time you thought about it.'

His uncle ate a last sandwich. 'Mummy's quite right; I must think about it.'

Daisy began to collect up the remains of their meal. 'Everyone carry something,' ordered the doctor, 'and no dropping it on the way to the kitchen. What happens next?' He looked at Daisy.

'They rest for an hour—I read to them.'

'Oh, good. I could do with a nap myself. We can

all fit into the hammock easily enough—not you, of course, Daisy. What gem of literature are you reading at the moment?'

'Grimm's fairy-tales; they choose a different story each day.'

She wasn't sure how to reply to the doctor's remarks; she suspected that he was making fun of her, not unkindly but perhaps to amuse himself. Well, she had no intention of letting him annoy her. 'Perhaps you would like to choose?' she asked him as, the picnic cleared away, they crossed the lawn to where the hammock stood under the shade of the trees.

He arranged a padded chair for her before lying back in the hammock with the twins crushed on either side of him. '"Faithful John",' he told her promptly.

She opened the book. 'It's rather long,' she said doubtfully.

'I dare say we shall all be asleep long before you've finished.'

He closed his eyes and the children lay quietly; there was nothing for it but to begin.

He had been right; Josh dropped off first and then Katie, and since he hadn't opened his eyes she supposed that the doctor had gone to sleep too. She closed the book on its bookmark, kicked off her sandals and sat back against the cushions. They might sleep for half an hour and she had plenty to occupy her thoughts.

Dr Seymour opened one eye. He said very softly, 'You don't like me very much, do you, Daisy?'

She was taken by surprise, but Daisy being Daisy she gave his remark thoughtful consideration. Presently she said, 'I don't know anything about you, Dr Seymour.'

'An indisputable fact. You haven't answered my question.'

'Yes, I have—I don't know you well enough to know, do I?'

'No? Personally, I know if I like or dislike someone the moment I set eyes on them.'

He would have disliked her on sight, she reflected, remembering the cold stare at the traffic-lights in Wilton and the short shrift he had given her, almost knocking her off her bike. She said primly, 'Well, we're all different, aren't we?'

The mocking look he gave her sent the colour into her cheeks. The doctor, watching her lazily, decided that she wasn't as plain as he had thought.

The twins woke up presently and they played ball until their mother came back. The twins fell upon her with shrieks of delight, both talking at once. 'Val— how lovely to see you—I wanted to talk to you...' Seeing Daisy, she turned to her. 'Do go home, dear, you must be exhausted—I know I am after several hours of these two.' She unwound her children's arms from around her neck. 'Take Daisy to the gate, darlings, and then go to the kitchen and ask Mrs Betts if she would make a pot of tea for me.'

Daisy got to her feet, reflecting that Lady Thorley's airy dismissal had been both friendly and expected; she was the daily mother's help and was treated with more consideration than she had ever had with Mrs

Gower-Jones. All the same, she wished that Dr Seymour hadn't been there.

Her goodnight was quietly said. 'I'll be here at half-past eight, Lady Thorley,' and she left them without further ado, taking the twins with her.

The doctor watched her go. 'What do you want to tell me, Meg?' he asked.

'Hugh phoned—such news—the man at the Hague is ill—jaundice or something—and he's to replace him until he's fit again. Hugh says there's a lovely flat we can have and he wants us to go there with him—he'll be home this evening but I wanted to ask your advice about the twins. I'll go with Hugh, of course, but what about them? I did wonder if they had better stay here with Daisy—that is if she would agree to come…'

'Why not take the children with you and Daisy as well?'

'Well, that would be marvellous—she's so good with them and they like her, but she might not want to come…'

'Why not ask her and find out? What does Hugh say?'

'He told me I could do whatever I thought was best as long as it won't upset the twins—going to live somewhere else—foreign too…'

'My dear girl, Holland is hardly darkest Africa, and it's only an hour away by plane.' He stood up. 'I must go back to town. You're quite satisfied with Daisy?'

'Oh, yes. How clever of you to tell me about her, Val. She's so sensible and kind—it's hard to find girls like her. Plain, of course—such a pity for she'd make a splendid wife.' She walked round the house to where his car was parked before the door. 'I suppose you wouldn't find the time to visit us while we're at the Hague?'

'Very likely—I'm lecturing at Leiden Medical School and there's a seminar for paediatricians in Utrecht—I'm not sure of the dates.' Lady Thorley tip-toed to kiss his cheek.

'Lovely. I'll talk to Daisy—better still I'll get Hugh to do that.'

'Why not? When does he go?'

'Two weeks—at least, he's to go as soon as possible; he thought it would take me two weeks to pack up and so on.' She stopped suddenly. 'Oh, what shall I do about Boots? We can't leave him here just with Mrs Betts...'

'I'll have him.' He glanced at his watch. 'I must go, my dear—give me a ring when you have things settled.'

Daisy, unaware of the future being mapped out for her, cycled home and thought about Dr Seymour. She wasn't sure if she liked him but she was fair enough to admit that that was because he was a difficult man to get to know. He was splendid with the children, prob-ably he was an excellent paediatrician, but he was ar-rogant and, she suspected, used to having his own way. Moreover, he had this nasty habit of mocking her...

She was surprised to find Sir Hugh at home when she reached Steeple Langford the next morning. He was still young but he had a serious manner which made him seem older.

'If we might talk?' he suggested, coming to the

nursery where the twins were running riot with the Plasticine under Daisy's tolerant eye.

Daisy's heart sank. He had come to tell her she was no longer needed, a governess had been found, and she was mentally putting her name down at several agencies in Salisbury when he went on. 'I'm about to be posted to Den Haag for a time; we wondered if you would consider coming with us to look after the children? I'm not sure for how long; I'm to fill in for a colleague who's on sick leave.'

'Me?' said Daisy.

'If you would. We're to take over an apartment in the residential part of the city, with a garden, I believe, and there are parks close by, so I'm told, and of course it is close to the sea.'

'I don't speak Dutch,' said Daisy.

He smiled faintly. 'Nor do I. I believe that almost everyone speaks English—there are certainly a good many English people living there—there would be other children for the twins to play with, and I'm sure there are young Englishwomen living there—you wouldn't be lonely.' When she hesitated he added, 'I'm told it will be for a month or six weeks.'

'If I might have time to talk to my mother? I could let you know in the morning if that would do?'

'Certainly, I shall be here for a good part of tomorrow.' He got up. 'My wife and I do so hope that you'll see your way to coming with us! You'll let me know in the morning?'

'Yes, Sir Hugh. For my part I should like to come, but I must tell my mother first.'

She thought about it a good deal during the day with mounting excitement; it would mean that she was sure of the job for at least another month besides the added pleasure of seeing something of another country. She would have to talk to Pam and make sure that she could cope with the various household demands. She wouldn't be able to add to the housekeeping money each week while she was away, but there was enough in the bank to cover them and she could pay that back when she eventually returned. All in all she was sure that everything could be arranged with the minimum of trouble for her mother and sister.

Her news was received with pleased surprise; there was no doubt at all, declared her mother, that they could manage very well while she was away. 'It's a marvellous opportunity,' said Mrs Pelham happily. 'Who knows who you will meet while you are there?' she added enthusiastically. 'Sir Hugh is something to do with the Foreign Office, isn't he? There must be clerks and people…'

Daisy said, 'Yes, Mother, I'm sure there are.' There was no harm in letting her mother daydream. Daisy, well aware of her commonplace features and retiring disposition, thought it unlikely that even the most lowly clerk would give her as much as a second glance.

Not a girl to give way to self-pity, she spent the evening combing through her wardrobe in search of suitable clothes. The result was meagre; it was Pamela who remembered the raspberry-red brocade curtains some aunt or other had bequeathed to their mother. They were almost new; they spread them out on the sitting-room floor and studied them. 'A skirt,' said Pamela. 'We'll get a good pattern, and Mother—there's that white crêpe de Chine blouse with the wide collar you never wear.'

'But will I need them?' asked Daisy doubtfully.

'Perhaps not, but you must have something, just in case you get asked out. There's your good suit and we can get your raincoat cleaned…'

So when Daisy saw Sir Hugh in the morning she told him that she would go to Den Haag with the twins, and was rather touched by his relief. His wife's relief was even more marked. 'I hardly slept,' she told Daisy, 'wondering what we should do if you decided not to come with us; Josh and Katie will be so happy. I should warn you that I shall have to be out a good deal—there's a lot of social life, Hugh tells me—you won't mind, will you?'

Daisy assured her that she didn't mind in the least and Lady Thorley gave a sigh of relief. 'You'll have a day off each week, of course, though I dare say it will have to be on different days, and an hour or two to yourself each day. Hugh wants us to go in ten days' time. We'll see to the travel arrangements, of course. There's just your luggage and passport.' She smiled widely. 'I think it's going to be great fun.'

Daisy agreed with her usual calm. Looking after the twins wasn't exactly fun; she liked doing it but it was tiring and keeping the upper hand over two small children determined to be disobedient was taxing both to temper and patience. But she truly liked Lady Thorley, and the twins, naughty though they were, had stolen her affection.

It was impossible not to be excited as preparations got under way for their journey: clothes for the twins, their favourite toys carefully packed, and a good deal of over-time because their mother needed to go to London to shop for herself. Daisy assembled her own modest wardrobe, wrapped the crêpe de Chine blouse in tissue paper, dealt with the household bills and with Pamela's help made quite a good job of the skirt. Trying it on finally and eyeing it critically, she decided that anyone not knowing that it had been a curtain would never guess...

It wanted two days to their departure when Dr Seymour turned up again. Lady Thorley was packing and Daisy and the twins, housebound by a sudden bout of heavy rain, were in the nursery. He came in so silently that none of them was aware of him until he spoke in Daisy's ear.

'An artist as well as a nanny?' he wanted to know, studying the variety of drawings on the paper before her.

Her pencil faltered so that the rabbit's ear that she had been sketching didn't look in the least like an ear. She said evenly, 'Good afternoon, Dr Seymour,' and rubbed out the ear while Josh and Katie rushed at their uncle.

He pulled a chair up beside Daisy, picked up a pencil and added a moustache and beard to the rabbit.

'Ready to go?' he asked her.

'Yes, thank you. Would you like me to fetch Lady Thorley?'

'No. I came to see these two. Being good, are they? Not turning your mousy locks grey or causing you to lose weight?'

How could he know that she detested her soft brown hair and was shy about her slightly plump person? A good thing she wouldn't see him for at least six weeks for she didn't like him.

'No,' said Daisy, 'they're good children.' Which wasn't in the least true but Katie, hearing it, flung her arms round her neck.

'We love Daisy; we think she is beautiful and kind like a princess in a fairy-tale waiting for the prince to come and rescue her.'

'And why not?' said her uncle idly, getting up from his chair. 'I'm going to see your mother but I'll say goodbye before I go.'

Josh climbed on to a chair beside her. 'Draw a bear,' he ordered. 'I'm going to be just like Uncle Val when I grow up.'

'So am I,' said Katie, and was told not to be a silly little girl by her brother. Threatened tears were averted by Daisy's embarking on a description of the party dress Katie, being a girl, would be able to wear when she was grown up.

Josh curled his small lip. 'Girls,' he said scornfully.

The doctor was still there when Daisy went home; she cycled past his car in the drive, unaware that he was watching her from the drawing-room window.

Two days later she said goodbye to her mother and Pamela, gave Razor a cuddle and went to the gate where Lady Thorley and the twins were waiting in their car. Her case was stowed in the boot and she got in the back with the children. They were strangely subdued and their mother said, 'Val came for Boots last night and they miss him—he's to stay with my brother while we're away.'

So Daisy spent a good part of their journey explaining how very much Boots would enjoy a holiday. 'And think of all the things you can tell him when we get back,' she pointed out.

'We wouldn't let anyone else have him, only Uncle Val,' said Katie tearfully.

'Well, of course not. He's family, isn't he? And Boots knows that he belongs to all the family as well as you two. You might send him a postcard from Holland...'

A suggestion which did much to cheer the children up.

Sir Hugh had made sure that his family need have no worries on their journey. They were met at Gatwick, the car was garaged and they were guided through the business of checking tickets, baggage and Customs and seen safely aboard the plane. The children were a little peevish by now and Daisy was relieved to see lemonade and biscuits and, for herself, coffee.

Lady Thorley was on the other side of the aisle and the first-class compartment was only half-full; Daisy drank her coffee while the twins munched and swallowed, grateful for the short respite. Afterwards there were comics to be looked at and the excitement of visiting the toilets, small enough at the best of times but needing a good deal of side-stepping and squeezing, much to the delight of the children.

By then the plane was coming in to land, something

the twins weren't quite sure if they liked or not. Daisy
wasn't sure if she liked it or not herself.

They were met by a well turned-out chauffeur at
Schiphol and shepherded through Customs and into
a gleaming, rather old-fashioned car and driven away.
A little over an hour's drive, the chauffeur told them,
joining the stream of traffic.

The twins, one on each side of their mother, on the
back seat, stared out of the windows and had little to
say beyond excited 'oh's and 'ah's. Daisy, sitting beside the chauffeur, gazed her fill too; she mustn't miss
anything for she had promised to write every detail to
her mother.

Presently the car left the busy streets around the airport and picked up speed along the motorway. There
wasn't much to see here—occasional patches of quiet
meadows, but it seemed to her that there were a great
many factories lining the road and she felt vague disappointment. Not for long, however; soon the factories
dwindled and died away to be replaced by trees and
charming houses, set well back from the road which
in turn gave way to the outskirts of the city.

The streets were busy here and the chauffeur had
to slow down, so that she had a chance to look around
her. It looked delightful—old gabled houses, canals,
imposing buildings, a splendid place to explore on
her free days… They left the heart of the city, driving down a straight road with parks on either side
and then large, solid houses, set well apart from each
other, before they turned off into a side-road, wide
and tree-lined. There were blocks of modern flats on

either side and here and there town mansions in their own grounds. Halfway down they stopped before the wide entrance of a solid red-brick block of flats and the chauffeur got out, opened their doors and led the way across the pavement as a concierge came hurrying to meet them.

'I do hope,' said Lady Thorley, 'that someone has put the kettle on; we need a cup of tea.' She smiled at Daisy, 'You must be tired; I know I am.'

Daisy had the twins by the hand, dancing with excitement. She thought it unlikely that she would have time to be tired until they were given their tea and put to bed, but that didn't worry her. 'I'd love one,' she said cheerfully.

Chapter 3

The concierge led them inside, across a wide hall to an ornate lift. She was a tall, bony woman with a hooked nose and a cast in one eye and the twins stared at her with growing delight. 'Is—is she a—?' began Josh.

'No, dear,' began Daisy before he could utter the word, 'this is the lady who looks after these flats…'

'Juffrouw Smit.' She ushered them into the lift which took them to the first floor. The landing was as wide as the hall below with a door on either side, one of which she now opened. 'The apartment,' she announced, and ushered them inside.

The flat was large, with lofty ceilings, large windows and a balcony overlooking a sizeable garden. There was a staircase at one end of it leading to the garden and Juffrouw Smit waved a generous arm. 'It is yours, the garden.'

'Oh, how nice,' said Lady Thorley uncertainly. 'The people in the flat below?'

Juffrouw Smit shrugged. 'A very small apartment; he is but a clerk.'

Daisy peered over the balcony balustrade. There were iron railings separating the flat from the garden; it seemed hard on its occupant.

It was obvious that Juffrouw Smit was preparing another speech in her very basic English. 'The cook and the serving maid wait in the kitchen.'

She led the way through two handsome reception-rooms, a small sitting-room and down a short passage and opened a door.

The kitchen was a good size and, as far as Daisy could see at a glance, well equipped. There were two women there, stoutly built and well past their first youth, with pleasant round faces and white aprons over dark dresses. They smiled and nodded, shook hands and said, 'Welcome,' several times. The elder of them pointed to herself. 'Mien,' she said and then pointed to her companion and said, 'Corrie—we speak English a little and understand.'

She beamed at everyone. 'I make tea? I make good English tea…'

'Oh, splendid,' said Lady Thorley. 'Please—in the sitting-room?' She turned to Juffrouw Smit. 'Thank you for your help.'

'At your service, Lady Thorley. I will help at any time.'

She stalked away and Lady Thorley said, 'Well, we'd better go to the sitting-room and have tea and then we can get unpacked. Hugh will be here soon. Daisy, I shall leave you to see about the children's suppers and get them to bed. I must say this is rather a nice flat. You like your room?'

Daisy had had no time to more than glance at it; it was next to the children's room and what she supposed would be the play-room while they were there. There was a bathroom too; all were tucked away at the end of a passage at one end of the flat. She said now, 'It seemed very nice and the twins' room is a nice size.'

'Oh, good.' They were all in the sitting-room now, a comfortably furnished room obviously meant for family use, and Lady Thorley was leafing through the little pile of envelopes on the small desk under the window. 'Heavens, invitations already; I only hope I've brought the right clothes with me...'

They had their tea while the children drank their milk and presently Daisy took them with her to do the unpacking, a lengthy business as they wanted to help, and by the time it was done and she had put away her own modest wardrobe it was almost bedtime for them. There was no sign of Lady Thorley although there was a distant murmur of voices from the other end of the flat. Daisy, with a twin on either hand, found her way to the kitchen.

Mien was at a table putting the finishing touches to a salad.

'Could the children have supper?' Daisy asked.

'You tell, I make,' said Mien obligingly.

'Milk?' She glanced at the twins who were scowling horribly. 'Buttered toast?' she suggested. 'Coddled eggs? Yoghurt?'

She was rewarded by Josh's glare. 'Noodles—buttered noodles?' Daisy asked hopefully and saw

Mien nod. 'These I have, with buttered toast and a special sauce. In fifteen minutes, miss, it will be brought to you in the play-room.'

Daisy heaved a sigh of relief. Mien's English was excellent; her accent was terrible but who cared about that? She smiled widely at the cook, went back to the children's room and got them ready for bed. They had had their baths and were cosily wrapped in their dressing-gowns when their supper was put before them.

The play-room had a door on to the balcony; moreover it boasted a piano, several small comfortable chairs and several shelves and cupboards. The children were hungry and the noodles were almost finished when their parents came in.

'Daisy, how clever of you. The children look at home already. How did you make Cook understand?'

'She speaks good English and is so helpful. The children are ready for bed when they've finished their supper; I thought an early night...'

'Quite right. As soon as you've tucked them up come to the sitting-room and we will have dinner.' The Thorleys stayed for a while, talking to the children, and presently went away, leaving Daisy to coax them to their beds. They were disposed to be fretful but she tucked them in firmly, picked up a book and sat between their beds until they slept and then went away to tidy herself for dinner.

Her room was small but comfortably furnished and the bathroom she was to share with the twins was more than adequate. She did her face and hair, changed her dress and went along to the sitting-room.

'We thought we would dine here this evening,' said

Lady Thorley, 'as it's just the three of us. Hugh says that we shall entertain a lot, Daisy, so you won't mind if you have your dinner in the play-room from time to time?'

'Not at all,' said Daisy. 'I'm quite happy to have it there every evening. It's near the children if they should wake, too.'

Lady Thorley looked relieved. 'You wouldn't mind? You will have lunch with me, of course, unless there are guests. Now, we have to decide your free time too.'

Of which there was none, it seemed, during the day, although she was free to take the children out to the beach at Scheveningen whenever she wished. There was a car with a driver she might use if Lady Thorley wasn't free to drive them, and there was a park close by where she would meet other English girls and could chat while the children played together. 'You must have one day a week to yourself,' declared Lady Thorley. 'One of Hugh's colleagues has a nanny who is free on Wednesdays and he suggests that his wife and I should join forces and take it in turns to spend the day at each other's houses with all the children. If you would get the children up and dressed I'll see to their breakfasts and there is no need for you to come back until late evening.' She added apologetically, 'I know that compared with other jobs, you won't get much free time, but you can arrange your days to suit yourself, as long as I know where you are. The children will love the beach… Oh, and some Sundays we'll take the children out and you will be able to go to church…'

'Thank you, that sounds fine, Lady Thorley, and I'll

let you know each day where we shall be going. The twins love to walk and there'll be a lot to see.'

She drank her coffee and excused herself on the plea that she would like to write home…

'There's a phone in the lobby leading off the hall,' said Sir Hugh. 'Telephone your mother now and there won't be such an urgent need to write at once.'

It was a temptation to have a good gossip with her mother and Pamela but she confined her news to the fact that they had arrived safely and that everything was quite perfect, promised to write as soon as possible and took herself off to bed.

The Thorleys were still in the sitting-room with the door half-open. As she went past, Lady Thorley's rather high voice reached her clearly. 'Val's coming over quite soon. There's heaps of room for him to stay here; we must invite some people to meet him…'

Daisy, getting ready for bed, allowed her thoughts to wander. She wasn't sure if she wanted to meet Dr Seymour again; on the other hand she had to admit that she found him interesting. Not, she reflected, that she was likely to have much to do with him even if he was a guest in the flat; she could see that any social life she might see would be from the outside looking in. Not that she minded, she told herself stoutly and, being a sensible girl, went to sleep at once.

The next day was largely taken up with finding their way around. They went into the garden after breakfast and then walked to the nearby park, although there wasn't time to do more than give it a brief visit before they went back to have their lunch with Lady Thorley; and, since they were nicely tired by now, the twins con-

sented to lie down for a while, giving Daisy a chance
to get her letter home started. In the afternoon they
went out again, this time to watch the trams at the end
of the road. These went to Scheveningen and back and
Daisy decided that going to the beach by tram might be
much more fun than driving there in a car. She would
have to ask Sir Hugh if that was allowed. Tucking the
children in that evening, she considered that their first
day had been quite successful. The twins were taking
everything in their stride, Mien produced exactly the
right food for them and Corrie hadn't seemed to mind
the extra work when Daisy had asked if she might have
her dinner in the play-room. Perhaps there had been
a nanny before her and it was the normal thing to do.

They spent most of the next day at Scheveningen,
driven there by a morose man from the British embassy
and collected by him during the afternoon. Daisy's request that they might use the trams had been received
by Sir Hugh with sympathy, but he wished to take advice from his colleagues first... All the same, they had
a lovely day. The sand stretched as far as the eye could
see in either direction and there was a great deal of
it. They built sandcastles, paddled in the rather chilly
water and ate a splendid lunch of sandwiches and buns
and potato crisps and went very willingly to bed when
they were home again. Lady Thorley had joined them
for nursery tea. 'Such a busy day,' she had declared. 'I
would have liked to be on the beach with you. You must
be tired, Daisy. We're going out to dinner this evening,
but when you have had yours, do watch television in
the sitting-room or go into the garden for an hour.'

It was a splendid evening, the first hint of autumn

in its creeping dusk and faint chill, much too nice to
sit and watch an indifferent TV programme which she
couldn't understand anyway. The twins already asleep
and her dinner eaten, Daisy pulled a cardigan around
her shoulders and went down the staircase to the garden. The sun had set but the wide sky reflected its rays
still and the garden, carefully tended, smelled faintly
of lavender and pinks with the faintest whiff of roses
along the end wall. She wandered along its length and
then back again to be brought up short by a voice from
behind the iron railings before the ground floor apartment.

'I saw you yesterday but you had the children with
you.' A cheerful face peered at her through the bars.
'Philip Keynes—I live here. It's a very small flat but
I'm a clerk at the embassy and on my own. It's nice to
have someone in the flat above… Are you a daughter?'

'Me? No. I'm a temporary nanny—Daisy Pelham—
just until they can find a governess for Josh and Katie.'

They faced each other through the bars, liking what
they saw.

'You're not lonely?' he asked.

'No, no, I don't have time; the twins keep me busy
all day.'

'You get time off?'

'Not during the day and in the evening Sir Hugh
and Lady Thorley get asked out a good deal, I believe.'

'But you get a free day?'

'Oh, yes—Wednesdays. There's a lot to see here,
isn't there? I hope I stay long enough to see everything…'

He said diffidently, 'I'd be glad to show you round

if you'd like that; I can always get an afternoon off. Next Wednesday perhaps?'

'Well, that would be nice…'

He heard the doubt in her voice. 'Sir Hugh knows me…' He grinned suddenly. 'I mean, I'll get him to introduce us properly if you like.'

Daisy laughed. 'No need. I would be glad of someone to show me round the Hague.'

'Good. I'll be free at half-past twelve. Do you think you could meet me? There's a brown café just across the street from the Bijenkorf—that's the big department store in the shopping street—you can't miss it.'

'Yes, of course. I must go and make sure that the children are all right.'

She bade him goodnight and went back up the stairs to the balcony where she paused to look down into the garden. It was somehow comforting to see the reflection of a lamp from his sitting-room window.

During the next few days she met some other English girls when she took the twins to the park. They were friendly, giving her useful tips—where to find the nearest hairdresser, the best shops to go to for humdrum things like toothpaste and tights, the cafés which served the cheapest food. They wanted to know if she had a boyfriend and gave her faintly pitying looks when she said that no, she hadn't. They considered that she was badly treated when it came to time off, too. 'You should have at least two evenings a week as well as a whole day; some of us get weekends…'

'I wouldn't know what to do with them,' said Daisy, 'and anyway I'm only here until Lady Thorley finds a governess.'

They smiled at her with faint patronage. A plain little thing, they told each other when she had left them.

Wednesday came with pleasing swiftness. Daisy had seen very little of Lady Thorley for there was a constant stream of visitors and she was out a good deal. True to her promise, she came to the play-room in good time for the children's breakfast this morning. 'I asked Corrie to take a tray to your room,' she told Daisy, 'and you go just as soon as you like. Will you be out late this evening?'

Daisy thought it unlikely; Philip Keynes hadn't mentioned any kind of evening entertainment. 'I don't think so, not this evening. Some of the girls I met in the park suggested that we might all go to a cinema on Wednesday evening but I expect I'll come back once the shops have shut.'

'Then I'll ask Mien to leave a tray for you in the kitchen. Have a pleasant day, Daisy; we shall miss you.'

Daisy gobbled her breakfast as she got ready to go out. She was a little excited; she had a week's pay in her purse and the prospect of a morning's window-shopping and then the unknown pleasures of the afternoon. She boarded a tram at the end of the road, thankful that it was a cool day so that the good suit didn't look out of place.

The shops were absorbing; she gazed into elegant boutique windows, shuddering at the prices, had coffee and spent the rest of her morning in de Bijenkorf, rather like a small Selfridges and more suited to her pocket. Not that she bought much but it was fun to go round the departments deciding what she would take home as presents, and at half-past twelve she crossed the road to the brown café and found Philip Keynes waiting for her.

She had felt a little shy of meeting him again but there had been no need; he was friendly, full of enthusiasm at the idea of showing her round the Hague, but it was a casual friendliness which quickly put her at her ease. He came from Bristol, he told her, and knew her home town quite well. Over coffee and *kaas broodjes* they talked about the West Country and its pleasures. 'I don't care much for cities,' he told her, 'but this is a good job and once I'm promoted I'll get a posting back home. What about you, Daisy? Do you want to travel before you settle down?'

'Not really. I'm glad I've had the chance to come here but when I get back home I'll find a local job.'

They didn't waste too much time over their lunch. He had the afternoon planned and kept to it. They visited the Ridderzaal and after that the Mauritshuis with its famous paintings. Daisy would have liked to have lingered there but she was urged on; the Kloosterkerk was a must, he told her; never mind that they could spend only a short time there—she would know where to go when next she went exploring and from there there was a glimpse of the eighteenth-century Kneuterdijk Palace. They stopped for tea then, this time in a café in Noordeinde, and it was as they emerged from it that Daisy came face to face with Dr Seymour. The pavements were crowded with people hurrying home from work, and since they were going in opposite directions it seemed unlikely that he had recognised her, but all the same she had been surprised at the sudden delight she had felt at the sight of him, instantly followed by the hope that she wouldn't meet him while he was in Holland. A good thing, she reflected, that she dined alone each evening; there would be no chance of meeting him if he came to see his sister...

She was recalled to her present whereabouts by her companion. 'I say, will it be all right if I put you on a tram? I've got to get to one of these official gatherings at the embassy. It's been a delightful afternoon; we must do it again.' He added anxiously, 'You hadn't any plans for this evening?'

'No, and I said I'd be back some time after tea, I've all kinds of odd jobs I want to do.' She saw the relief in his nice face. 'And you don't need to come with me to the tram; I know which one to catch.'

He wouldn't hear of that; they walked through the narrow streets together and he actually saw her on to a tram which would take her to the end of the road where the Thorleys were living. It was still early evening, but she had letters to write and her hair to wash and an hour or so just sitting with a book would be pleasant. She told herself this as she wished him goodbye, doubtful if he would repeat his invitation; she thought that she was probably rather a dull companion... All the same she had enjoyed the afternoon and she thanked him nicely for it and was surprised when he said, 'I meant it when I said we must do it again. A cinema, perhaps?'

'I'd like that.' She nipped on to the tram and was borne away at high speed down the Scheveningen-scheweg, to get out at her stop and walk the short distance to the house.

The concierge admitted her with a muttered 'good evening' and Daisy, ignoring the lift, skipped up the stairs to the Thorleys' apartment and rang the bell. Corrie opened the door, bade her a cheerful hello and told her, in her peculiar English, that her dinner was ready whenever she liked to have it. Daisy thanked her and crossed the hall, to be stopped by Lady Thorley's voice from the half-open door of the drawing-room.

'Daisy?' she called. 'Come in here and tell us if you've had a nice day.'

The drawing-room was a grand room, rather over-furnished in a handsome way. Daisy crossed the parquet floor to the group of people sitting together at the far end by the open windows. She was halfway there when she saw that Dr Seymour was there too, standing leaning against the wall, a drink in his hand. There was a woman sitting there, a strikingly handsome woman in her early thirties and dressed in the kind of clothes Daisy, not given to envy, envied now.

'You know Dr Seymour already,' said Lady Thorley in her friendly way, 'and this is Mevrouw van Taal.'

Daisy said, 'How do you do?' and wished the doctor a good evening.

'You enjoyed your day?' Sir Hugh wanted to know. 'The Hague is a most interesting city. Of course you would have enjoyed it more if you had had a guide…'

Daisy glanced at the doctor. He was looking at her and smiling, a rather nasty little smile, she considered. So he had seen her after all. It was on the tip of her tongue to tell him that she had spent most of her day with Philip Keynes, but that might sound boastful and besides, he might not like that. She agreed quietly that it was indeed a most interesting city and it would take several days to explore it thoroughly.

There was a little silence and the *mevrouw* said in a sugary voice in faultless English, 'Well, I suppose if you have nothing better to do it passes the time.'

'Most agreeably,' said Daisy. 'Goodnight, Lady Thorley, Sir Hugh.' She smiled in the general direction of the doctor and Mevrouw van Taal and walked tidily out of the room, shutting the door gently behind her.

'I wish him joy of her,' she muttered as she went to her room.

The twins were asleep; she wondered what sort of a day their mother had had—she would hear in the morning, no doubt; in the meanwhile she would enjoy her dinner. She had been only a few minutes in the play-room when Corrie came in with a tray. Cold lettuce soup with a swirl of cream in its delectable greenness, chicken *à la* king, asparagus and game chips and a chocolate mousse to finish. Coffee too, brought by Corrie just as she had polished off the last of the mousse. Really, she thought, life couldn't be more pleasant. The unbidden thought that she was lonely crossed her mind, to be dismissed at once. It would have surprised her if she had heard the doctor, sitting at the dinner-table, waving away the chocolate mousse in favour of some cheese. 'Does Daisy not have her meals with you?' he asked idly.

'We almost always have lunch together—the two of us and the children. Of course Daisy could dine with us if she wished but she thought it would be better if she stayed in the play-room in case the children should wake.'

Lady Thorley sounded apologetic and then frowned when Mevrouw van Taal spoke. 'Well, one would hardly expect the nanny to dine, would one? Besides, it is likely that she has no suitable clothes. They have a garish taste in cheap clothes, these au pairs and nannies.'

Dr Seymour's face was inscrutable. He said mildly, 'One could hardly accuse Daisy of being garish.' He thought of the times he had seen her; mousy would be a more appropriate word, and that terrible plastic mackintosh...

The conversation became general after that and presently Mevrouw van Taal declared that she would really have to go home, smiling at the doctor as she said it. 'If someone would call a taxi?' she asked. 'Since my dear husband died I have not dared to drive the car.'

The doctor rose to his feet at once. 'Allow me to drive you back,' he said; his voice held nothing but social politeness. 'I have to go back to the hospital.'

An offer which Mevrouw van Taal accepted with rather too girlish pleasure.

Unaware that the doctor was spending the night at the apartment, Daisy slept peacefully; she still slept when he went down into the garden very early in the morning. There was a decidedly autumnal chill in the air but it was going to be another fine day. He strolled around and presently became aware that there was someone watching him—the occupier of the downstairs flat, leaning against the wall, behind the railings.

The doctor caught his eye, wished him good morning and was sure that he had seen him before—with Daisy yesterday afternoon. 'Are you not allowed to share the garden?' he enquired pleasantly. He held out a large well cared-for hand and thrust it through the railings. 'Valentine Seymour—Lady Thorley's brother—

over here for a few days. I saw you yesterday with Daisy.'

Philip shook hands. 'Philip Keynes—I'm a clerk at the embassy. Yes, I showed Daisy something of the Hague. She's nanny to the children, but of course you know that.'

'Yes. She must have been glad of your company; it's hard to find one's way around a strange city.' The doctor leaned up against the railings. 'Have you been here long?'

'Almost a year; I'm hoping for promotion so that I can go back home! You're not at the embassy, are you?'

'No, no. I'm a paediatrician; I'm over here lecturing and seeing one or two patients that they've lined up for me. I live in London, but I have beds at Salisbury and at Southampton.' He glanced at his watch. 'I must go—I have to be in Utrecht soon after nine o'clock. I dare say we shall meet again.'

He went back upstairs to the balcony just as the twins, dressed and released to let off steam before breakfast, tore on to the balcony, screaming with delight at seeing him and followed at a more sedate pace by Daisy.

She stopped at the sight of him, uttered good morning in a small cool voice and added, 'They must have their breakfast.'

'So must I; shall I have it with you?'

He had spoken to the children and their shouts had drowned anything she might have wanted to say. Not that he would have taken any notice. He went into the play-room with them and found Corrie there, putting boiled eggs into egg-cups. She received the news that he was breakfasting with his nephew and niece with smiling nods, laid another place at the table and went away to get more eggs and toast. She came back presently with a plate of ham and cheese, a basket of rolls and croissants and a very large pot of coffee.

Daisy sat the children down, tied their bibs and poured cereal and milk into their bowls while the doctor leaned against a wall, watching, before pulling out her chair for her and seating himself opposite.

Daisy, pouring coffee and beakers of milk, had to admit to herself that he was good with children. They were, she suspected, a little in awe of him, and upon reflection she supposed that she was too but she found herself at ease and laughing with the children over the outrageous stories he was telling them. Daisy stopped abruptly at his quiet, 'You should laugh more often, Daisy, it turns you into a pretty girl.'

She went very pink. 'If that's meant to be a compliment I can do without it, Dr Seymour.'

'No, no, you mustn't misunderstand me; I was merely stating a fact.'

He spoke mildly and she felt a fool, her face reddening at his assured smile.

He passed his cup for more coffee. 'I had a talk with young Keynes—a sound young man—pity he's caged up behind those iron railings. Did you enjoy your afternoon with him, Daisy?'

'Yes, he knows where everything is...how did you know?'

'Well, I saw you, didn't I? Besides, I asked him this morning.'

Her small nose quivered with annoyance. Before

she could speak he added, 'None of my business, is it? How do you like being a nanny?'

She said sedately, 'Very much, Doctor.' She got up to wipe the twins' small mouths and untie their bibs. 'And now if you will excuse us…?'

'Being put in my place, am I?' He got up too, tossed the children into the air, promised them sweets next time he came and made for the door, to turn and come back to where Daisy was standing, lift her firm little chin in his hand and stare down at her, his eyes, half hidden by their lids, studying her face.

'Kiss Daisy goodbye,' shrieked Katie, who, being female, was romantic even at four years old.

'Not this time,' said her uncle, and went unhurriedly from the room.

Daisy swallowed all the things she would have liked to utter; the twins were remarkably sharp for their age and they might repeat them to their mother and father. She urged the children along to the bathroom to wash teeth, faces and hands, vowing silently that if she saw Dr Seymour again she would run a mile, or at least go as quickly as possible in the opposite direction. Perhaps there would be no need to do that; hopefully he would be going back to England soon.

It was with relief that she heard Lady Thorley tell her that her brother had gone to Utrecht; she wouldn't have felt that relief, though, if Lady Thorley had added that he would be with them again that evening.

She spent the day on the beach with the children; there wouldn't be many more days in which to do that, she reflected. There was a distinct nip of autumn in the air now; October wasn't more than a few days away and already the beach kiosks and little seaside shops selling buckets and spades and postcards were putting up their shutters. Then it would be the park and, should they still be there, carefully planned hours to be spent in the play-room. She doubted, though, if she would be called upon to do that; long before then she would be back in Wilton, and if a governess had been found she would be looking for another job.

She took the children home in time for tea, and they had it with their mother in the play-room, and, much to Daisy's astonishment, Lady Thorley asked her if she would dine with them that evening. 'Just us,' she said. 'It will be nice to have a quiet evening. There's a reception tomorrow evening so we shall be out again—you've been very good and patient, Daisy, staying with the children; I'm sure I don't know what we should have done without you. Mrs Perry was telling me about Katwijk-aan-Zee—it's no distance away and she says it's so much nicer than Scheveningen—I thought I might drive you and the children there before it gets too chilly. I don't think I can spare the time to stay all day, but I could pick you up during the afternoon.'

Daisy agreed because she saw that Lady Thorley expected her to. One of the girls she had met in the park had told her it was a nice little seaside town and it would make a change.

She put the children to bed, read to them until they were sleepy and then changed into the blouse and skirt, did her face and hair with rather more care than usual and went on to the balcony to wait for the dinner-gong. It had been another fine day, now fading into a golden dusk, and the garden below looked inviting. She leaned on the balustrade and wondered if she had time to go down there, and decided against it just as Dr Seymour ranged himself alongside her.

He ignored her gasp of surprise. 'A delightful evening,' he observed pleasantly. 'There's a great deal of wide sky in Holland, isn't there?'

'Haven't you gone back to England yet?' asked Daisy, not bothering with the sky.

'Now that's the kind of encouraging remark I suppose I should have expected from you, Daisy.'

He turned his head to smile at her and she thought how very good-looking he was and so very large. 'You surprised me,' she told him.

'I'm relieved to hear that.' He smiled and this time it was kind. 'You're looking very smart this evening— Margaret tells me that you're dining with us.'

He had seen the beautifully washed and pressed blouse, certainly not new and decidedly out of date, and the skirt—a pretty colour which suited her and made, unless he was much mistaken, from what looked suspiciously like a curtain...

'Yes, Lady Thorley invited me, but perhaps now you're here—I mean, if she didn't know you were coming...'

'Oh, but she did—it will be an opportunity to talk about the twins; they seem very happy and they're fond of you.'

'They're very nice children.' She couldn't think of anything else to say, so that the faint sound of the gong came as a relief.

They went down together and he waited for her

while she went to take a quick look at the twins, and, to
her surprise, once they were downstairs sipping sherry
before they went in to dinner, she forgot to feel shy,
happy to find that Lady Thorley was wearing a blouse
and skirt too—rather different from her own—oyster
satin with a filmy black skirt and a jewelled belt. All
the same Daisy felt at ease because she was wearing
the right clothes.

They dined splendidly at a table covered with white
damask, shining silver and gleaming glass; lobster
bisque, guinea fowl with sautéd potatoes, artichokes
and asparagus followed by profiteroles with a great
deal of cream, all nicely helped along with a white Bor-
deaux and then a sweet white wine she didn't much like
to go with the pudding. There was brandy served with
the coffee but she declined that. It seemed to her that
nannies shouldn't do that; anyway, she wasn't sure that
she would like brandy. She had maintained her part in
the conversation very well and, since she was a good
listener, Sir Hugh declared after she had said goodnight and gone upstairs that she had been a much more
interesting table companion than Mevrouw van Taal.
'Nice manners too,' he observed. 'Do you agree, Val?'

'Oh, indeed, you have found yourselves a treasure—
if a temporary one.'

'That reminds me,' said his sister, 'I was talking to
Mrs Ross today—her husband's been posted to Brussels and her governess wants to go back to England. It
seems she's a marvellous woman, splendid with small
children and able to give lessons until they're old
enough for school. Would it be a good idea if I found

out a bit more about her? Personal recommendation is so much better than advertising.'

'That sounds promising,' Sir Hugh agreed. 'Make quick work of it, darling—I'll be here for another month at the outside; this paragon could take over when we get back home.' He paused. 'I'll be sorry to see Daisy go.'

'So shall I; she's so nice and gentle and kind. She should get a good job, though; I'll give her a splendid reference.'

To all of which conversation the doctor listened without saying a word; and, as for Daisy, blissfully unaware of what the future held in store for her, she put her head upon the pillow and went to sleep.

Chapter 4

Daisy woke with a pleasant feeling of excitement which, upon investigation, and to her surprise, was due to the fact that she would see the doctor again. She expected him to come and say hello to the twins—perhaps stay to breakfast—but there was no sign of him, nor did Lady Thorley mention him when she came to wish her children good morning after that meal. It wasn't until lunchtime, after she had taken the twins for a walk in the Scheveningse Bos, where there was plenty of open space in which they could tire themselves out, that Lady Thorley mentioned that her brother had gone back to England. 'He works too hard,' she complained. 'I tell him that he should marry, but he says he has no time for that. Such nonsense; one day he'll fall in love and then he'll find the time.'

As long as he didn't fall in love with someone like

Mevrouw van Taal, reflected Daisy, and wondered why she disliked the idea so much; after all, she still wasn't sure if she liked him and he was surely old and wise enough to take care of himself.

The days unrolled themselves smoothly, each one rather like the last, until it was Wednesday again and Daisy, released from her duties, took the tram into the Hague. She had seen Philip Keynes on the previous evening and he had arranged to meet her at four o'clock for tea and then take her to the cinema. She was looking forward to it and now that she had some money in her pocket she would spend the morning looking for something for her mother and Pamela. Coffee first, she thought happily, as the tram deposited her at the stop nearest to the Bijenkorf.

She found a silver brooch for her mother and a silk scarf for her sister, both costing rather more than she could afford, so that her lunch was sparse, but in any case, she reminded herself, eating took up precious time and she planned to spend the afternoon, map in hand, getting some idea of the town. She lingered for some time along the Korte Vijverberg and the Lange Vijverberg, admiring the old houses with their variety of gabled roofs, and from there she walked to Lange Voorhout, pleasantly broad and tree-lined with its small palaces and embassies and luxurious Hotel des Indes. It must be pleasant working in such surroundings, she decided, thinking of Philip, even in the capacity of a clerk. She looked her fill at the patrician houses around her—a far cry from her own home; the thought of it made her feel homesick for a moment; it would be nice to see her mother and Pam again, but not just yet. Each week she was adding to her small nest-egg; a month, six weeks even, would allow her to put by more money than she had earned in months of work at the nursery school.

She strolled back to the café where she found Philip waiting for her. His pleasure at seeing her added to her enjoyment of her day and he was an easy person to talk to. They drank their tea and ate the rich creamcakes so temptingly displayed and then made their way to the cinema.

It was a good film and there was time for a quick cup of coffee before they boarded the tram for home. Saying goodnight in the entrance to the flats, Daisy reflected that she hadn't enjoyed herself so much for a long time. Philip was the kind of man she would like to marry: easy to get on with, not given to sarcastic remarks and quite lacking in arrogance—unlike Dr Seymour, the sight of whose well-tailored appearance caused her instant annoyance.

She went indoors, spent ten minutes with the Thorleys describing her day and then went to her room, wondering if it was too late for her to get some supper. Tea had been delicious and the coffee after the cinema equally so but her insides were hollow.

She hadn't been in her room five minutes before Mien tapped on the door, bearing a tray. Soup in a pipkin, ham and a salad and coffee in a Thermos jug. A most satisfactory end to her day, she thought, gobbling her supper and then, after a last look at the twins, tumbling into her bed.

The weather changed, a mean wind blew and there was persistent rain. The twins reacted as might have been expected—tantrums, a refusal to do anything asked of them and a steady demand to go to the beach.

Lady Thorley finally gave way to their persistent small rages. 'Could you bear to go with them?' she asked Daisy. 'Perhaps if they went just once and got soaked they wouldn't want to go again—just for an hour or two?'

So Daisy buttoned them into their small mackintoshes, tied their hoods securely, stuffed their feet into wellies and then got into her plastic mac, tucking her hair under its unbecoming hood. They took a tram to the promenade and then, with buckets and spades, went down to the beach. Deserted, of course, and in a way Daisy liked it. The sea was rough and coldly grey and the wide sky was equally grey with the sandy shore below stretching away on either side as far as the eye could see. Lonely and magnificent and a bit frightening...

Daisy dispelled such a fanciful thought and got on to her knees the better to help build the sandcastle under Josh's shouted instructions.

They were to go back home for lunch, Lady Thorley had said, but there was time enough to build a dozen sandcastles. Daisy, fashioning a wall around the last of them, was startled by Katie's piercing shriek. The two children, shouting with delight, were hurtling up the beach towards Dr Seymour, making his leisurely way towards them. She got to her feet then, dusting the sand off her damp knees, looking just about as unglamorous as it was possible to look; the hood, never flattering, had slipped sideways so that a good deal of damp hair had escaped and her face was as damp as her knees.

She watched him coming towards her, a twin on either hand, wished him a good morning and stood quietly under his scrutiny, aware that she looked an absolute fright and hating him for it.

He smiled at her. 'Hello, Daisy, what marvellous sandcastles—I haven't made one for half a lifetime.' Unnoticing of the drizzle, he squatted down to inspect their work, fashioned a drawbridge, added an imposing tower, invited Daisy to admire them and got to his feet.

'Want a lift back?' he wanted to know. 'It's a bit early for lunch, but you'll all need a wipe down first, won't you?' His glance swept over Daisy and she lifted her chin. If he dared to smile... But he didn't. They went back up the beach to the promenade with the children happily hopping and skipping between them, making so much noise that there was no need to talk. A good thing, for she could think of nothing at all to say.

The Rolls was at the kerb and sitting in it was Mevrouw van Taal.

'You know each other, don't you?' observed the doctor easily as he stuffed the children into the back of the car. 'Hop in between them, Daisy.'

Mevrouw turned an elegant shoulder to look at them. 'What a very strange way in which to spend the morning,' she said acidly, 'but of course I suppose it doesn't matter to you when you do not need to bother with your appearance.'

Daisy thought of several things to say and uttered none of them; it was the twins who yelled rudely at her, protesting that the beach in the rain was the nicest thing they knew of, a sentiment echoed by their uncle, who had got into the car, taken a quick look at

Daisy's outraged face and smoothly taken the conversation into his own hands, so that the twins, hushed by Daisy, subsided, allowing him to carry on a desultory exchange of remarks with Mevrouw van Taal. When they arrived at the house she whisked them upstairs to be washed and tidied for their lunch, and they were so pleased with the idea of their uncle having lunch with them that they forgot all about Mevrouw van Taal. But, when they were led into the dining-room, faced with the sight of that lady sitting by their uncle, sipping sherry, their small faces puckered into scowls.

'Why—?' began Josh, and was hushed by Daisy.

'Tell Mummy about the castles we built this morning,' she urged.

He went obediently but his lower lip was thrust out in an ominous manner. It was Katie who spoke in her shrill voice. 'I thought Uncle Val was having lunch with us, not with her,' she observed.

'Well, we are all having lunch together,' observed Daisy. 'Do tell Daddy about that crab you found.' She caught the doctor's eye and saw that he was laughing silently. Let him, she thought savagely, and looked away from his mocking glance.

Mien came to the door then to announce that lunch was ready, which was a good thing—the children had a look on their faces which boded no good. She prayed silently that they would behave themselves at table.

The prayer wasn't answered; it was unfortunate that Mevrouw van Taal was seated opposite them, and Daisy, sitting between them, knew without looking that they had fixed their large blue eyes upon her and at any moment would say something outrageous...

'Which reminds me,' said Dr Seymour apropos of nothing at all, 'I have something for you two—you may have it after lunch if your mother says you may, on condition that you're extra-good.'

Daisy let out a relieved breath and then drew it in again sharply when the doctor winked at her from a bland face. Really, the man was simply impossible. She busied herself attending to the children and was thankful that they were behaving like small angels. Their father paused in the middle of a sentence to ask if they were sickening for something. 'You must have performed a miracle on them, Daisy,' he said kindly. 'Let us hope…' he caught his wife's eye '…that it lasts,' he ended tamely. He had forgotten for the moment that Daisy hadn't been told that the new governess would be taking over very shortly—something which would have to be broken to the children at the proper time, which wasn't now.

Mevrouw van Taal could be charming in the right company. Daisy had to admire her—she had good looks, the right clothes and a helpless-little-girl manner which Daisy felt simply certain would appeal to any man. She was an amusing talker too; Daisy allowed her rather high-pitched voice to go over her head while she thought about the doctor. Was he here for a long stay, she wondered, or a lightning visit? She frowned; it was no concern of hers anyway, only it would be nice to know…

The twins were allowed down from the table once the pudding had been eaten; they kissed their parents, stared stonily at Mevrouw van Taal as they muttered what Daisy hoped was a polite goodbye.

'Run along with Daisy, darlings,' begged their mother. 'We'll have coffee in the drawing-room, shall we?' she said to the others.

Dr Seymour got up to open the door and bent his massive person to whisper to Josh, 'Wait in the hall; I'll be out in a moment.'

He went back into the room, leaving the door half-open so that Mevrouw van Taal's voice was very audible to Daisy, waiting at the foot of the stairs with the twins.

'Charming children,' she declared, 'and so well behaved. That girl—their nanny—is the quiet sort, isn't she? Plain with it too.' She gave a tinkle of laughter. 'Let us hope she is as quiet and kind when she is alone with the children...' Daisy, rigid with rage, heard the Thorleys protest as the woman went on, 'Oh, I didn't mean to upset you, I'm sure she is a very good young woman, but one does hear such tales.'

'Not about Daisy.' It was the doctor, speaking in such a cold voice that Daisy shivered. 'I'm sure you meant no harm, Rena, but it is perhaps a little unwise to give an opinion of someone of whom you know nothing, is it not?'

He came into the hall a moment later, shutting the door behind him.

'I'm sorry if you heard that; I'm sure Mevrouw van Taal meant nothing personal.'

'I don't care what she means,' said Daisy in a stony voice. 'Pray don't bother to make excuses for her. If you would be good enough to give the children their present I can take them upstairs so that I may be discussed at your ease.'

'Spitfire,' said Dr Seymour mildly and added, 'You have very lovely eyes.'

'Ah—you forget, a plain face...'

'We'll discuss that some time.' He smiled very kindly at her and she felt tears crowding her throat, which made her crosser than ever.

'There's a small box on the hall table,' he told the children. 'Will you fetch it, Josh?'

It was actually quite a big box; he opened it and took out two smaller boxes and gave them to the children. 'Not to be opened until you're lying on your beds.' He bent down and kissed their excited faces and then, in an afterthought, kissed Daisy too.

'I'm going away directly,' he told her. 'You'll be glad, won't you?'

'Yes,' said Daisy, not meaning it. She urged the twins upstairs and didn't look back.

The boxes contained musical boxes, the sort which, when wound, displayed a group of dancing figures on their lids. The twins were enchanted with them and quite forgot to be difficult about taking their afternoon nap, so that Daisy found herself with nothing to do until they woke again. It was still raining and she turned her back on the dismal weather, got out her pen and writing pad and began a letter to her mother, anxious to occupy her thoughts with something other than dwelling on the kiss Dr Seymour had given her. It was exactly the same kind of kiss as those he had bestowed upon his small relations, and she hoped that it hadn't been bestowed in pity; she hoped too, with quite unnecessary fervour, that he would be gone by the time she went downstairs with the children again.

Fate always answered the wrong prayers; there was no sign of him when the children went down to have tea with their mother; moreover he was already on his way back to England, Lady Thorley told her. 'He will be back, though, for a few days shortly,' she continued, 'some meeting or other in Leiden.'

All memories of the summer were being washed away by a persistent fine rain, and the twins' high spirits, because they were largely confined to indoors, were rapidly turning to fits of sulks and displays of childish rage. Daisy took them out each day despite the wind and rain and the three of them, swathed in mackintoshes and hoods and sensible shoes, went to the park, empty of people now, where they ran races and then went home, sopping-wet and tired, but by the afternoon their energy was firmly restored, and Daisy was glad when it was bedtime and she could tuck them up. Of course, they were reluctant to sleep and she read to them until she was hoarse…

It rained on her day off too, which was a pity, for Philip had borrowed a friend's car and had promised to drive her to Apeldoorn then down to Arnhem through the Hoge Veluwe National Park and then back to the Hague. All the same they went, making light of the weather, and Philip, who prided himself on the knowledge he had of the Dutch countryside, took pains to point out everything interesting in sight. Even in the rain Apeldoorn was pleasant; they had their soup and a roll in a small café on the edge of the town and then set off for Arnhem. The road ran through wooded country and stretches of heath, the villages were small and infrequent and here and there they caught glimpses of large villas half-hidden by trees, and when they reached Arnhem he took her round the open-air museum where Holland's way of life was portrayed by farms, windmills and houses from a bygone age. Despite the rain, Daisy would have lingered for hours but it was quite some distance back to the Hague and they simply had to have tea…

Back at the house they parted like old friends. 'I'll get the car next week,' Philip promised, 'and we'll go north to Alkmaar and Leeuwarden. You're not going back home yet, are you?'

'No, I don't think so yet; I heard Sir Hugh saying that he expected to be here for another month or even longer.'

'Good. I'll see you next week.' She rang the bell and watched him get into the car to drive it back to his friend's flat. It had been a lovely day and Philip was an undemanding companion, always ready to agree with her suggestions. He would make a nice brother, she thought, as Mien opened the door and she went inside.

Mien took her wet things and nodded her head upstairs where small cross voices could be heard. 'It is good that you are back. Lady Thorley is weary. The children…' She raised her hands and rolled her eyes up to the ceiling.

Daisy sped upstairs and found Lady Thorley attempting to get the twins quiet. They were bellowing and screaming and quite out of hand but they paused long enough to shout at Daisy.

'If you're quiet,' said Daisy, 'I'll tell you where I've been today, so say goodnight to Mummy and lie down, there's dears.'

Lady Thorley gave her a thankful look, kissed them and went to the door. 'I'll tell Mien to send you up a tray in half an hour, Daisy.' She asked belatedly, 'You had a nice day?'

'Delightful, thank you, better than yours.'

Lady Thorley made a face. 'They need a dragon to look after them. I'll say goodnight, and thank you, Daisy.'

Getting ready for bed a few hours later, Daisy prayed once more, this time for fine weather; much more of the twins' naughtiness would make even her stout heart quail; at least out of doors they tired themselves out.

This time her prayers were answered; the really heavy rain ceased and although the wind was chilly and the sky overcast at least they could get out. Three days passed in comparative peace and on the fourth morning, just as they had finished their breakfast, Dr Seymour walked into the play-room.

The twins were delighted to see him and, although she wouldn't admit it to herself, Daisy was too. Disentangling himself from the twins' embrace, he addressed himself to her. 'I'll keep an eye on these two—Margaret would like you to go down to the sitting-room; she wants to talk to you.'

There had been some talk of buying warmer clothes for the children; Daisy, nipping smartly along the passage, rehearsed in her head the various garments which would be necessary.

Lady Thorley was at the breakfast table and Sir Hugh was still there too. Daisy, her mind engaged in the choice of Chilprufe as against Ladybird vests, wished them both good morning and, when bidden to sit, sat.

'We wanted to talk to you,' began Lady Thorley, and looked at her husband, who coughed and said,

'Er—well, it's like this, Daisy…' and coughed again. 'You know, of course, that we engaged you on a temporary basis; indeed, we had intended that you should stay with us until we returned to England in a few weeks' time. However, a colleague of mine is being posted and the governess he employs for his children does not wish to stay with them but wants to return to England. We thought at first that she might take over from you when we go back there but it would make it much easier for everyone concerned if she were to come straight to us here. We think that if she were to join us here in two days' time you might spend a day with her—show her the ropes—and return to England on the following day. We will, of course, arrange your journey and, needless to say, a very good reference.'

Daisy said in a polite voice, 'That seems a very sensible arrangement, Sir Hugh. I'm glad you've found a governess; it's so much better to have someone recommended, isn't it?'

She heard herself uttering the words she felt sure her companions wished to hear while inwardly she fought unhappy surprise. She had felt secure at least for another month, which had been silly of her, and she was quite unprepared for such a sudden decision on the part of the Thorleys. Something of her thoughts must have shown on her face for Lady Thorley said quickly, 'You do understand that we have never been less than absolutely satisfied with you, Daisy. You've been splendid with the twins; I don't know how I would have managed without you…'

'I've enjoyed looking after them, Lady Thorley. If there's nothing else I'll go and get the children ready for their walk.' Daisy got up. 'I expect you know that Dr Seymour is with the twins?'

'Yes. He's due at the hospital this afternoon; he'll be going back home some time this evening.' Lady Thorley smiled at Daisy. 'Run along, then; if I don't see you at lunch, I'll be here in good time for the twins' tea.'

The doctor was sitting on the table, the breakfast things pushed to one side, and the children were beside him; the three heads were close together but they looked up as she went in.

'If you go to the hall,' said the doctor, 'you might find something in the umbrella stand by the door; if you do, take it to your father and mother and ask if you may have it.'

When they had scampered off he got off the table and went to stand before her. 'Surprised?' he asked.

'You knew? That I'm going back to England?'

'Yes. Hugh asked me what I thought about it some time ago when he first heard of this governess. I think it's a splendid idea; they need a female sergeant major to look after them. You're a splendid nanny, I should suppose, but you're too kind and forgiving, my dear; they'll be twisting you round their thumbs in a few months.'

'That's an unkind remark to make,' said Daisy coldly, 'but I suppose only to be expected of you. I know your opinion of me is low…' She added with a snap, 'Not that I care about that.' She drew a sustaining breath. 'I shall be sorry to leave the twins but nothing will give me greater pleasure than the thought that I need never see you again.' She went to the door. 'Now if you will excuse me, Dr Seymour, I will go to the children.' Her hand on the doorknob, she turned to look at him over her shoulder. 'I do hope Mevrouw van Taal manages to catch you; you deserve her.'

She didn't exactly sweep out of the room—she was too small for that—but she managed a dignified exit.

The doctor stood there where she had left him, the outrage on his face slowly giving way to a wide grin.

Daisy buttoned the children into their outdoor things and took them for their walk. She would have liked time to sit down and think about the turn of events; she had known that the job was temporary but she had expected to have a longer warning of its finish so that she could have made plans about getting work when she got home. Now there would be no time to do that and although she had saved up almost all of her wages it might be weeks before she found another job. There was no time to worry about that now, though; the twins, intent on reaching the park to see if any of their small friends were also there, hurried her along, both talking at once, leaving her no time at all for her own thoughts. Which was just as well.

Nothing was to be said to the children until the new governess arrived; Daisy, carrying on with their usual routine during the next two days, wondered if they would like her. Dr Seymour had described her as a sergeant major... She wished she could stop thinking about him; he had gone as swiftly as he had come, and presumably he was back in England. She reminded herself that she had no wish to see him ever again and, once the children were in their beds, began to get her clothes ready to pack.

The sergeant major arrived after breakfast as Daisy was arranging painting books and paints on the play-room table; the dull morning had made it easy to per-suade the twins that a walk later in the day would be a better idea so that when their mother and the new governess came into the room they were engaged in quarrelling amicably together as to who should have the bigger paintbox.

Daisy put a jar of water in the centre of the table out of harm's way, smiled at Lady Thorley and said good morning to her companion. The woman was a good deal older than herself, tall and thin and good-looking, but she looked kind and when Lady Thorley said, 'This is Amy Thompson, Daisy,' she held out her hand and gave Daisy a firm handshake.

The children had come to stand by Daisy, eyeing the stranger with suspicion; it was their mother who said coaxingly, 'Come and say hello to Miss Thomp-son; she's going to spend the day with us…'

'Why?' asked Josh and then, urged by Daisy, of-fered a small hand.

'Well,' began his mother, 'Miss Thompson is going to live with us and be your governess; you're going to have lessons at home, which will be much more fun than going to school…'

Katie shook hands too, eyeing the newcomer. 'We'd rather keep Daisy,' she observed.

Josh's bottom lip was thrust forward in an omi-nous manner and Daisy said quickly, 'The thing is, my dears, I do have to go home and live with my mother and sister...'

Katie burst into tears and Josh flung himself on to the floor, where he lay kicking and shouting. Daisy got down beside him. 'Look, Josh, we'll still see each other; I live very close to your home, you know—perhaps Miss Thompson will invite me to tea sometimes and allow you both to come and see Razor.'

He opened an eye. 'Promise?'

Daisy glanced at Miss Thompson who nodded and smiled. 'Promise,' said Daisy, 'and now if you will get up and Katie will stop crying we can have some fun showing Miss Thompson where everything is and what you wear when you go out and just how you like your eggs boiled. She will really depend on you both for a little while, just as I had to when I first came to look after you.'

It took time to coax the children to calm down, something they did unwillingly, but Miss Thompson was a veteran at the job; by lunchtime they were on good terms with her, with only the occasional suspicious look. She went away at teatime with the assurance that she would return the following morning.

With Josh and Katie in bed, Daisy packed, washed her hair, checked the contents of her handbag and went downstairs to dine with the Thorleys. Sir Hugh gave her her ticket. 'One of the drivers will take you to Schiphol,' he told her. 'We thought if you took the late morning flight—Miss Thompson will be here at ten o'clock, and it might be easier if you go shortly afterwards, in case the children...'

He paused, and Daisy said, 'Yes, of course, I quite understand.'

'You'll go home by train? You'll find travelling expenses in that envelope—you'll have to go up to London from Gatwick unless you can get a bus to Basingstoke.'

'Either way will be easy,' said Daisy; she sounded as though she knew what she was talking about although she had only the vaguest idea about the train service to Salisbury from London; but there were bound to be several and she would be at Gatwick by one o'clock at the latest.

Sir Hugh said thankfully, 'Oh, good, it should be quite simple. Do telephone your mother if you wish to…'

She decided against that; she wasn't sure what time she would get home and her mother would worry. They went in to dinner and she joined in the conversation in her quiet way, all the while not quite believing that in twenty-four hours' time she would be home again and out of a job once more.

She hated leaving the twins; she was quite sure that Miss Thompson would be kind as well as seeing to their education, but all the same it was a wrench and all the harder since she had to keep a cheerful face on things when she said goodbye. It was a wet morning; the last she saw of them was two small faces pressed against the play-room windows. She waved until the car turned into the street, and since the driver was disinclined for conversation she spent the journey to the airport musing over a choice of jobs. Another nanny's post perhaps? Or a mother's help? Failing those, how about working in a shop? But wouldn't she have to know something about selling things? How did one start? she wondered. She was still wondering when they reached Schiphol and the driver fetched her case from the boot and carried it to the desk for her. She thanked him, gave him a tip and joined the queue of passengers being processed towards their various flights.

The flight was uneventful; she collected her case from the carousel, went through Customs and to the entrance, borne along on a stream of people intent on getting home as quickly as possible. There were taxis there and, some distance away, a bus. She picked up her case, to have it taken from her at the same time as Dr Seymour said quietly. 'The car's over here.'

She turned round and gaped up at him. 'That's my case,' she told him sharply. 'And I'm not going by car; there's a bus...' She drew breath. 'How did you get here, and why?'

'How you do chatter.' He took her arm. 'I'm on my way back to Salisbury. Margaret rang me this morning and mentioned that you would be on this flight; it seemed only good sense to collect you on my way.'

They had reached the car and he had opened the door and stuffed her inside and put her case in the boot; now he got in beside her. She was still thinking of something to say as, with the minimum of fuss, he drove away from the airport.

'Had a good trip?' he asked casually.

'Yes. Thank you.' She had remembered that she had never wanted to see him again and she sounded waspish.

'Still peeved?'

Hateful man. 'I don't know what you mean, and

please don't feel that you have to—to entertain me
with conversation; I have no wish to come with you.
Probably you mean it kindly but I thought I had made
it clear that I didn't want to see you again…'

They were away from the airport and the big car
surged silently forward.

'Yes, yes, I know that, and if you're bent on keeping to your rigid principles I won't say another word;
you can sit there and pretend I'm not here.'

And he didn't. They went down the M3 at a spank-
ing pace, slowed to go through Salisbury and ten minutes later slowed again as they reached Wilton. He
stopped outside her home, got out, opened her door,
fetched her case and banged the knocker on the door.

'Thank you for the lift,' said Daisy. 'Would you like
a cup of coffee or—or something?' She looked as far
as his tie and then gave him a quick glance. He was
looking down at her, an eyebrow raised to mock her.

'My dear Daisy, is this an olive-branch?' He turned
to the door as it opened and Mrs Pelham gave a small
shriek of delight.

'Daisy, darling—how lovely.'

She looked enquiringly at the doctor and Daisy
said, 'Hello, Mother. This is Dr Seymour, who kindly
brought me home…'

'That's twice,' said her mother, and smiled at him.
'Come in and have a cup of tea.'

'I should have liked that, Mrs Pelham, but I've an
appointment.'

Mrs Pelham nodded sympathetically. 'Well, of course,
you doctors don't have much time to spare, do you?'

He had nice manners; his goodbyes weren't to be

faulted but the eyes he rested upon Daisy were as cold and hard as granite.

They waited until the Rolls had reached the end of the street before they went indoors.

'Such a lovely surprise,' said her mother. 'I thought you wouldn't be home for another few weeks, dear.'

'Well, so did I, Mother, but there was a governess who'd been with friends of the Thorleys and she's taken over the twins.'

'Well, I'll put on the kettle and you shall tell me all about it. Pam will be home soon; she will be pleased.'

Mrs Pelham led the way into the kitchen. 'That nice doctor driving you back like that. Did he meet you at the airport?'

'He was on his way to Salisbury and the Thorleys did tell him which flight I'd be on.'

'Now that is what I call kind; you must have had a delightful journey together.'

Daisy took off her jacket. 'Oh, yes, we did, indeed we did.' She uttered the lie so heartily that she almost believed it herself.

Chapter 5

Pamela came home when Daisy was halfway through the account of her stay in Holland, so she would have to begin all over again, but before she had a chance to start her sister said, 'Do tell; this Philip you wrote about, is he nice? Will you see him again?'

'Perhaps, if he comes home on leave and he hasn't forgotten me. He had planned to take me to the north of Holland but I've come home instead—I only had a few minutes in which to say goodbye.'

Her mother said, 'There, I knew you'd meet someone nice.'

'He was just a friend, Mother; I think he felt lonely and he enjoyed showing me round the Hague.'

Her mother looked disappointed. 'Yes, well, dear… did you meet anyone else while you were there?'

Daisy refilled the teapot from the kettle. 'Friends of

the Thorleys—there are a lot of English people living there—and Dr Seymour; he's abroad a great deal and he came to see them while I was there.'

'He didn't bring you all the way home?'

'No, I told you, he was on his way from London to Salisbury and Lady Thorley had told him I would be coming back on the late morning flight.'

'So kind,' commented her mother. 'It's lovely to have you home, Daisy.' She glanced at Pamela. 'We've managed quite well, I think.'

'I knew you would. I've almost all of my wages; I'll go to the bank tomorrow and pay them in.'

'Yes, dear. Now I'm going to get us a nice supper while you unpack.'

It was much later, after Pam had gone to bed and her mother was sitting contentedly knitting, that Daisy took a look at the housekeeping purse and then leafed through the chequebook. Even in those few weeks while she had been away the money seemed to have melted away alarmingly; she would have to start looking for a job as soon as possible.

She spent a couple of days at home, sorting out the small problems her mother had, paying one or two bills which had been overlooked, catching up with the local news and tidying the garden. After the weekend, she promised herself, she would start looking for a job.

There was nothing in the local paper on Saturday so she cycled into Salisbury on Monday morning, bought all the magazines which advertised work and visited two agencies. Neither of them had anything for her; there was, it seemed, no demand for mother's helps, nannies or unqualified kindergarten teachers. 'Now if you had simple typing and shorthand,' suggested the brisk lady at the second agency Daisy went to, 'I could offer you several good jobs. I suppose you haven't had any experience in a shop? There's a good opening for an experienced sales girl in a fancy goods shop.'

Daisy shook her head; she wasn't sure what fancy goods were anyway, and the lady gave her a scornful look. 'Well, dear, all I can suggest is that you take a course in something and then try again—there's always domestic work or work for early morning office cleaners...'

It might even come to that, thought Daisy. How fortunate it was that there was a little money in the bank, enough to keep them all for several weeks, although the uneasy thought that she would have to order coal for the winter very soon haunted her... There was no point in getting pessimistic, she told herself; after all, she had only just started to look for work.

She spent the week applying for various jobs she found in the magazines but they were few and none of the advertisers bothered to answer her applications. So she sat with Razor on her lap, writing an advert to put in the local paper, and had to admit that her skills were too limited to attract more than the casual eye. All the same, she sent it off and went along to the job centre.

There wasn't anything there, either; it seemed that she was unemployed. But things could have been worse; the local bakery needed part-time help—Friday mornings and Saturday afternoons for two weeks only. It was quite hard work and she didn't get on very well with the till but the money was a godsend, little though it was. She received her wages for the last time and started to clear up in the shop before she went home. The manageress was totalling the day's takings and was disposed to be friendly.

'Well, you've not done too badly, love,' she observed, 'though I can see it's not quite your cup of tea; still, anything's better than having no work, isn't it?'

Daisy, wiping down the counter, agreed. 'I've liked working here. I dare say something will turn up soon.'

However, it didn't, and September was nudging its way into October. Daisy ordered the coal; paying for it left a hole in the bank account, a hole which would have to be filled. She cycled to Salisbury again and tried the two agencies once more; the first one had nothing at all, the second offered her work as a mother's help in a family of six children living on a farm at Old Sarum; she would have to live in and the wages were low. Daisy said that she would think about it and despite her lack of money went and had a cup of coffee. If only something would happen, she reflected as she drank it.

It was as well that she was unaware that Dr Seymour was drinking coffee too—in her mother's kitchen. He had called, he told Mrs Pelham, on the spur of the moment. 'I know my sister will want to know if Daisy has found a good job and I shall be seeing her shortly.'

Mrs Pelham gave him a second cup of coffee and offered biscuits. 'Daisy's gone to Salisbury to see those two agencies again; there's nothing, you know, and you have no idea how difficult it is to find work, and the dear child isn't trained for anything—you see, my husband died and there was such a lot to see to and I'm not very businesslike and then we found that there wasn't enough money so she took that job with Mrs Gower-Jones—it was just enough with my pension.'

'So Daisy has no work yet?'

'Well, she helped out at the local bakery for two weeks, just for two half-days a week.' Mrs Pelham paused. 'I really don't know why I'm bothering you with all this…'

'Perhaps I can be of help. I happen to know that the hospital is short of ward orderlies—not domestics but they help with all the small tasks so that the nurses have more time for their own work.' And since Mrs Pelham was looking bewildered he explained, 'Helping with the meals, tidying beds, arranging flowers and so on. I believe that the hours are reasonable and the pay is adequate; at least it might tide her over until she finds something more to her taste.'

'She wouldn't need any training?' asked Mrs Pelham eagerly.

He said gently, 'No, just common sense and kindness, and she has both.'

'I'll tell her the moment she gets in…'

'Why not? But I think it might be a good idea if you don't mention that I've been to see you or that I've told you of the job; I think Daisy might resent anything which smacks of charity and it might seem like that to her. Could you not say that you've heard of work at the hospital from some friend or acquaintance?'

'Well, yes, I can do that; we know a great many people in the town—I could have heard about it from a dozen people. And I see what you mean about not telling Daisy that you called and told me about it; she is a dear girl but very independent.'

They had another cup of coffee together and parted on the best of terms and Mrs Pelham sat down and rehearsed what she would say to Daisy when she got home, pausing to regret that the doctor seemed to have no interest in Daisy; his voice had been impersonal when he had talked of her, and why should it have been otherwise? Daisy was no beauty and she had a way of saying exactly what she thought which could be disconcerting; perhaps she had annoyed him in some way, in which case it was kind of him to put himself to the trouble of finding her a job and in all probability he was only doing what his sister had asked him to do.

Daisy, despondent at her lack of success, listened eagerly to her mother's news when she returned home. 'I met Mrs Grenville—remember her, dear? She lives somewhere in Salisbury. She was at the market and we got chatting. She told me that they need these orderlies at the hospital; they're going to advertise but if you went along you might stand a chance before it gets into the paper.'

'I'll go in the morning; I can at least apply if there really are vacancies.'

It wasn't until she woke up in the middle of the night that she remembered Dr Seymour worked at the hospital. Unfortunate, she thought sleepily, but that was a small hindrance compared with the possibility of a secure job.

She telephoned the hospital the next morning and was told that yes, applicants were to be interviewed for several vacancies for ward orderlies and if she cared to present herself at two o'clock that day, bringing with her two references, she would be seen some time during the afternoon.

It was rather daunting to find that she was one of many and one of the last to be interviewed.

She hadn't much chance of getting a job, she reflected, answering the questions the severe woman behind the desk was asking her, unaware that the severe lady had been discreetly told that, should a Miss Daisy Pelham present herself for an interview, Dr Seymour would vouch for her personally. Thoroughly reliable, hard-working and trustworthy, he had said, previously employed by his sister and leaving only because the children had grown too old for a nanny.

The severe lady did not mention this for the simple reason that she had been told not to; she merely told Daisy that she would be notified if she was successful.

'I'm not very hopeful,' said Daisy as she had supper with her mother and sister that evening. 'There were dozens of us there and most of them looked frightfully efficient.'

'We'll have to wait and see,' sighed her mother placidly.

They didn't have to wait long; there was a letter the next morning confirming her appointment as a ward orderly, starting on the following Monday. She was to report for work at half-past eight each morning except for Saturdays and Sundays, but she would be expected to work one weekend in four. The wages were adequate; there would be no money to spare but they would be solvent. They had a rather excited breakfast and Pamela said, 'I'm glad you've got a job, Daisy, but you're not to stay a ward orderly a day longer than you must—if something better turns up... Will the work be rather beastly? Cleaning up after patients and fetching and carrying for the nurses?'

'It will be interesting,' said Daisy stoutly.

When she presented herself in a wrap-around pink overall on Monday morning she really found it more than interesting—thoroughly bewildering. She was to work on Women's Medical with another orderly, a woman in her thirties, who, Daisy quickly discovered, did her work with a kind of dogged thoroughness, disregarding the occupants of the beds—indeed, they might as well have been empty for all the notice she took of them. Daisy, friendly by nature, smiled at the patients, moved their glasses of water where they could reach them, picked up their knitting dropped on the floor and unreachable, and exchanged magazines and papers.

'You'll never get your work done while you waste your time with them,' observed Mrs Brett sourly. 'Just you collect up them empty cups and take them out to the kitchen. The trolley's on the landing.'

So Daisy collected cups, wiped locker-tops, collected water jugs and ran errands for Sister, who, beyond asking her her name and telling her to do whatever Mrs Brett told her to do, had had nothing more to say to her. Mrs Brett, relishing her superiority, told her to do a great deal: carry round the trays at lunchtime, help frail elderlies to the loo, change sheets in the beds of those who had had unfortunate accidents and hurry with bowls to those who felt sick. It was all very muddled and Daisy wasn't sure if she was going to like it; Mrs Brett was far too bossy and the nurses were too busy to see it...

She was sent to the canteen for her lunch at half-past twelve and was much more cheered to find several girls of her own age at the table, orderlies like herself and prepared to be friendly, and when she told them where she was working a comfortably plump girl with a pleasant country accent observed kindly that it was hard luck having to work with Mrs Brett, who had been at the hospital for a long time and behaved as though she ran the place. 'A pity that once you get a ward you stay on it, though you might be lucky and get moved.'

Daisy went back for the afternoon's work feeling more cheerful; it was, after all, her first day and probably Mrs Brett would be nicer when they got to know each other. Mrs Brett, however, wasn't disposed to be friendly; indeed if anything she became more sharp-tongued as the afternoon wore on. Daisy, her day's work done, went home and presented a cheerful face to her mother and sister; the work was interesting, she was sure she was going to like it, and to her mother's enquiry as to whether she had met any of the doctors on the ward she said no, not yet, not wishing to disappoint her parent with the fact that the doctors, even the young housemen, didn't so much as cast a glance in her direction and weren't likely to either; an orderly was a domestic after all.

By the end of the week she had come to the conclusion that Mrs Brett, for all her bossiness, wasn't organised; there was a great deal of time wasted over their various jobs and far too much to-ing and fro-ing. Besides, she didn't much like the way Mrs Brett tossed knives, spoons and forks on to the patients' beds ready for their meals, so that some of the less agile patients had to wait until someone bringing their lunch- or tea-tray scooped them up and handed them over. Daisy knew better than to say anything and, uncaring of Mrs Brett's cross voice, nipped around arranging things within reach, and tidily too, and when Mrs Brett wasn't looking cutting up food and filling water glasses. She got the sharp edge of her colleague's tongue several times a day but she ignored that. One day, she promised herself, she would tell Mrs Brett just what she thought of her. It was a great pity that she was allowed to do more or less what she liked on the ward but to Sister she presented an appearance of hard-working efficiency, ready with the tea-tray when that lady sat down in her office to do the paperwork and running errands for the nurses. The patients didn't like her; indeed, some of the elderlies who depended on a helping hand were a little afraid of her.

Daisy, going home at the end of the first week with her pay packet in her pocket, decided that even if she didn't much like being an orderly the job provided her family's bread and butter and gave her the chance to help some of the patients.

'Have you seen anything of Dr Seymour?' her mother asked that evening.

'Him?' Daisy had washed her hair and was winding an elaborate turban around her head. 'No, but he works in London as well, you know. Probably he only comes to Salisbury when he's needed.'

'A pity, but at least you'll see something of the Thorleys when they come back, won't you?'

'I expect so. I promised the children I'd go and see them.'

She had been happy with Josh and Katie, she reflected and, despite the fact that she never wanted to see Dr Seymour again, she had been unable to forget him. He would have forgotten her already, of course.

Halfway through the next week she met him face to face on her way back from her lunch; there was no one else in sight and she debated whether to stop and speak to him—a wasted exercise for he gave her a wintry smile, nodded briefly and walked past her. She stood, watching him go out of sight; she still wasn't sure just how important he was; if the young housemen ignored the domestic staff, she supposed that the more senior medical staff were hardly aware of any but the senior nursing staff. All the same, he could have said something—hello would have done...

Gobbling bread and butter and drinking strong tea with some of the other orderlies during her brief tea break, she suddenly realised that they were talking about him.

'Marvellous with the kids,' said a voice, 'a pity we don't see more of him; comes twice a week for his outpatients and ward-rounds; ever so polite too—says good morning as affable as you like, more than some I know...'

There was general laughter. 'Well, what do you expect? No one's going to look twice at the likes of us. He's different, though—a real gent.'

'Married, is 'e?' asked one of the girls.

'Well, I don't know him well enough to ask...' There

was a good deal of good-natured laughter as they got up to go back to their wards.

It must be that he didn't like her, reflected Daisy, hurrying along corridors and up stairs; if he had said good morning to the other girls, why couldn't he have done the same to her? She had quite overlooked the fact that she told him in no uncertain terms that she had no wish to see him again.

That afternoon, when she was cycling home after work, the Rolls whispered past her. The doctor was looking straight ahead and there was a good deal of traffic on the road; he wouldn't have seen her. All the same, she wished most unreasonably that he had at least lifted a hand in salute.

When she got home her mother said in a pleased voice, 'Lady Thorley phoned, love. They came back today and the children want to see you. I told her you were only free at the weekends—she said she'd ring again.' She glanced at Daisy's face. 'You've had a horrid day, haven't you? Come and sit down; I'll have supper on the table in no time. It'll be nice for you to have an outing and go and see those children again—she said that they still miss you.'

Lady Thorley phoned after supper; the children were well and getting on famously with Miss Thompson but they did want to see her again. Daisy agreed to go to tea on Saturday and was relieved and at the same time disappointed to be told that Lady Thorley would be on her own. 'Hugh won't be home until Sunday—we can have a nice gossip and I know Miss Thompson will be glad to see you again.'

Daisy put down the phone; the doctor would have

got back to London by then, of course. A good thing too, she muttered to Razor as she gave him his supper.

She woke to rain on Saturday morning, not that she minded overmuch; for two days she was free of Mrs Brett's grumbling voice. She got the breakfast, saw Pamela off to spend the day with friends, made a shopping-list with her mother and walked to the centre of Wilton; doled out carefully, there was money enough to buy all the right sort of food; she visited the butcher, the grocer and the post office, bought bread still warm from the oven, and carried the lot home, had coffee with her mother and, since there were only the two of them, settled on soup and bread and cheese for lunch. While her mother got them ready, she went up to her room and changed into a navy blue jersey dress she had bought in the January sales. It was elegant, well cut and well made, and it fitted her nicely, but the colour did nothing for her. A well-meaning friend had once told her in the kindest possible way that unless a girl was pretty enough to warrant a second look it was wise to wear clothes which didn't draw attention to herself. Daisy, aware of her shortcomings, had taken her advice. Besides, one didn't get tired of neutral colours; at least, in theory one didn't. That she was heartily sick of them was something she never admitted to herself.

The twins would have been happy to see her wearing an old sack; they gave her a rapturous welcome and the welcome from Lady Thorley and Miss Thompson was equally warm. There was a good deal of talking before everyone settled down—Lady Thorley to go back to her drawing-room and Miss Thompson and the children, taking Daisy with them, to the nursery where she was shown the twins' latest craze. They had discovered the joys of Plasticine, which they had not been so keen on when Daisy had looked after them—not just small quantities of it, but large lumps which they were modelling into a variety of large and obscure objects.

'I'm no good at making things,' confessed Miss Thompson as they sat down at the table. 'I can just about manage a dog or a cat but Josh wants a model of Buckingham Palace.' She handed Daisy a hefty lump. 'They tell me that you're very good at making things…'

So Daisy embarked on the royal building while the twins, their tongues hanging out with their efforts, started on their various versions of the Queen and Prince Philip, all the while talking non-stop. Presently Miss Thompson said quietly, 'Daisy, I've some letters to post; would you mind very much if I go now? Josh and Katie are happy with you—if it weren't raining so hard we could all have gone…' Daisy didn't mind. At Josh's request she had stopped her modelling to make a drawing of Razor and she had no worries about keeping the children amused. The village post office wasn't too far away; Miss Thompson would be back in plenty of time for tea. Daisy glanced at the clock; she had promised to be home as soon after six o'clock as possible, but that was three hours away.

One drawing of Razor wasn't enough; she embarked upon a series of this splendid animal, handing over each sketch for the children to colour, Katie in her favourite pink, Josh with large spots and stripes. It was a good thing that Razor, a dignified animal, wasn't there to see.

She was putting the finishing touches to Razor's

fine whiskers when she heard the twins give a kind of whispered shout, but before she could look up two large, cool hands covered her eyes.

'Guess who?' asked a voice she had done her best to forget.

There was no need for her to reply—the twins were shouting with delight, 'You don't know, do you, Daisy? You must guess—we'll help you...'

She should have been feeling annoyance but instead she felt a pleasant tingling from the touch of his hands and a distinct thrill at the sound of his voice. Which simply would not do. Besides, the children would be disappointed.

'Father Christmas?' she suggested, a remark hailed by peals of laughter from Josh.

'Silly Daisy, it's not Christmas yet,' and,

'Two more guesses,' said Katie.

'Mr Cummins?' She had heard all about him from the twins; he had been in the nursery all day repairing the central heating.

'One more,' shouted Josh.

'Dr Seymour.' Her voice was quite steady.

'You mean Uncle Val. You've guessed; now you don't have to pay a forfeit.'

'What a pity,' remarked the doctor and dropped his hands to let them rest on Daisy's shoulders, which she found even more unsettling. 'I don't mind being taken for Father Christmas but I'm not so sure about this unknown Mr Cummins.'

'The plumber,' said Daisy and wished he would take his hands away.

However, he didn't; indeed he began to stroke the

back of her neck with a thumb, which, although wholly delightful, she soon put a stop to by getting up quickly; and, since she had no idea what she was going to do next, it was a relief when Miss Thompson, followed by Lady Thorley, came into the room.

'Shall we all have tea here?' asked Lady Thorley, and didn't wait for an answer.

'I'll tell Cook,' said Miss Thompson, leaving Daisy to clear the table of the lumps of Plasticine, fend off Boots's delighted caperings and find a cloth for the table. The doctor, sitting with a twin on either knee, listened to his sister's idle talk and watched Daisy.

Tea was noisy, cheerful and leisurely, and Daisy, despite the doctor's unsettling presence, enjoyed herself so much that she forgot the time, and, her eye lighting on the clock, she saw that it was already past six o'clock.

She caught Lady Thorley's eye. 'I really have to go,' she said. 'I said I'd be home by six…' She lifted Boots's great head off her lap and stood up as the twins raised a roar of protest. 'Look,' she told them, 'if your mother and Miss Thompson will allow it, you can come and have tea with me and meet Razor.'

'When?' asked Josh.

'Any Saturday.' She paused. 'No, not next Saturday; I have to work that day.'

She began her goodbyes, long-drawn-out on the part of the children, brisk and friendly from Miss Thompson, and was politely cool towards the doctor.

'I'll see you to the door,' Lady Thorley said comfortably and they went down the hall, lingering for a moment while Daisy got into her plastic mac and uttered suitable thanks. She had her hand on the door-knob when the doctor joined them, took her hand off the knob and opened the door.

'Ready?' he asked briskly, and to his sister said, 'I'll be back shortly, Meg.'

Daisy swept out into the porch, then found her voice. 'My bike's here—I'm cycling home—I can't leave it here, I need it...'

He had opened the car door and she found herself inside without quite knowing how she had got there. 'Your bike will be delivered to you at the latest by to-morrow afternoon, so stop fussing.'

He got inside the car, fastened her seat belt as well as his own and made no effort to start the car.

'Enjoying your new job?' he asked.

She said peevishly, 'Oh, so you did see me the other day—you looked at me as though I weren't there. Thank you, I quite like the work; I like the patients too...'

'But?'

His voice was beguilingly encouraging and for a moment she forgot that she wanted nothing more to do with him. 'Mrs Brett—the other orderly—she's been there a long time and she's a bit set in her ways; I suppose she's seen so many patients she doesn't really notice them any more.'

'And what do you intend to do about that?'

'Me? Nothing. I've only been there for a few weeks and I want to keep the job; and besides, who am I to criticise her? Only I can see that the patients can reach their water jugs and cut up their meat and pick up their knitting.' She stopped and went a bright pink. 'That sounds priggish; I can't think why I'm telling you about it—it's not important.'

He said casually, 'Why not get a transfer to another ward?'

'Orderlies are sent to a ward and stay on it until they're moved somewhere else.' She stared ahead of her. 'I think we're called ancillary workers but we're domestics. When are you going back to London?'

The sound which escaped his lips might have been a chuckle. 'Very shortly; that's a relief, isn't it? We shan't need to ignore each other if we should meet at the hospital.'

There didn't seem to be a reply to that.

He drove her home then, carrying on the kind of conversation which meant nothing at all but sounded pleasant. He got out when they reached her home, opened her door and held the gate as she went through it.

She thanked him as he shut it behind her, making it obvious that if she had invited him in he would have refused anyway, so she wished him goodbye and went into the house.

'Is that you, darling?' called her mother from the kitchen. 'Are you very wet?'

'I got a lift,' said Daisy, getting out of the hated mac, 'and my bike will be brought back some time tomorrow.'

'Who brought you back?' Her mother had poked her head round the door to ask.

'Dr Seymour came to tea and brought me back.' She added quite unnecessarily, 'It's raining.'

Her mother gave her a thoughtful look. 'Yes, dear.

I've started supper.' She opened the door wider. 'But I thought you might like to make the pie—all those apples and they won't keep.'

Daisy, rolling pastry ten minutes later, wondered if Dr Seymour was staying with his sister, and if not where was he? He must live somewhere. In London? He worked there too, didn't he? Perhaps he had a house there as well as living in Salisbury; but perhaps he didn't live there either.

She frowned, reminding herself that she had no interest in him.

Much refreshed by a weekend at home, Daisy went back to work on Monday, full of good resolves: not to allow Mrs Brett to annoy her, to carry out her orders even if she found them unnecessary—locker-tops didn't need to be washed twice a day, whereas water jugs, sitting empty, needed to be filled… She bade her superior good morning and had a grunted reply, followed by a stern request to get on with the cleaning since it was the consultant's round, 'And don't you hang around wasting time picking up knitting and such like, and see that the ten o'clock drinks trolley is on time; I don't want no 'itch.'

Daisy didn't want a hitch either; all the same she contrived to unpick a row of knitting and take two lots of hair curlers out while Mrs Brett had gone to have her coffee.

Her hopes of a better relationship between herself and Mrs Brett came to nothing; it seemed that she couldn't please that lady. Whatever she did was found fault with, and as the week progressed it was apparent that Mrs Brett had decided not to like her and nothing

Daisy could do would alter that. They parted company on Friday evening with Mrs Brett full of foreboding as to how Daisy was going to manage over the weekend.

'You'll get no 'elp,' she warned her. 'You'll 'ave ter work for two, and lord knows what I'll find when I gets 'ere on Monday morning.'

Daisy said, 'Yes, Mrs Brett,' and 'Goodnight, Mrs Brett,' and cycled home, the prospect of two days without her surly companion quite a pleasing one.

Without that lady breathing down her neck every ten minutes or so, Daisy found herself enjoying her work; she had common sense, speed and a kind nature that, she discovered for herself, was what her job was all about. No one bothered her; she got on with her chores and found time to satisfy the needs of those patients who were not in a fit state to look after themselves. She went off duty on the Saturday evening feeling pleased with herself even though her feet ached abominably.

Sunday was even better, for Sister wasn't on duty until one o'clock and there was a general air of leisure on the ward so that there was time to listen to titbits of news read aloud by those patients who had the Sunday papers and pause to help with the odd crossword puzzle. She went down to the canteen feeling that life was quite fun after all.

She was going off duty that evening, crossing the main entrance hall, inconspicuous in her good suit, when she saw Dr Seymour watching her from one corner. He was talking to one of the house doctors, staring at her over the man's shoulder. She looked away at once and whisked herself out of the door and over to the bicycle racks and presently pedalled home as though the furies were after her, but no Rolls-Royce sped past her, and she arrived home out of breath and feeling foolish. What, she asked herself, had she expected him to do? Speak to her? Open the door for her? A thin-lipped smile perhaps?

She was free all day on Monday, a splendid opportunity to help her mother around the little house, tidy the garden before the weather worsened and change the library books. As she biked to work on Tuesday morning she allowed herself to wonder if she would see the doctor.

Scrambling into the pink overall in the small room the orderlies used, she was accosted by one of them. 'Lucky you,' said the girl, 'you're being sent to Children's—Irma told me—it's on the board outside. You'd better look for yourself.'

'Me?' said Daisy. 'But I thought you never got moved…'

'Someone off sick, I dare say—make the best of it, Daisy, it's the best ward in the whole place.'

There, sure enough, was her name—to report to the children's unit forthwith. She skipped along corridors and in and out of swing doors with a light heart; no more Mrs Brett… She was opening the last of the swing doors when she remembered that Dr Seymour was a consultant paediatrician.

Chapter 6

After the quietness of the women's medical ward, the children's unit gave forth a steady roar of sound: shrill cries, shrieks, babies crying and cheerful voices, accompanied by background music just loud enough to weld the whole into a cheerful din. Daisy paused just inside the doors, not sure where to go; there were doors on either side of the wide hall leading to the ward. She supposed she should report to Sister...

A very pretty young woman put her head round one of the doors. 'Our new orderly?' she asked in a friendly voice. 'Come in here, will you, and I'll give you a few ideas...?'

Sister Carter was as unlike Sister on Women's Medical as chalk was from cheese. Not much older than Daisy, with curly hair framing a delightful face, she looked good enough to eat. Daisy, bidden to sit, sat and said politely, 'Good morning, Sister. I'm the orderly; my name's Daisy.'

'Nice—the children will love it.' She glanced at a folder on her desk. 'I see you've been working in a nursery school, just the kind of person we need here.' She smiled at Daisy. 'Lots of dirty work, though.'

'I don't mind that, Sister.'

'Good. Come and meet Maisie—our other orderly.'

Maisie was on her hands and knees clearing up a toddler's breakfast porridge which had been hurled away in a fit of childish pique. She came upright, beaming from a round and cheerful face. ''E's at it again, Sister,' she observed without rancour.

'Naughty boy,' said sister. 'Maisie, here is Daisy, your new partner.'

''Ello, love, am I glad to see you—one pair of 'ands don't go far with this lot.' She looked Daisy over in a friendly way. 'Like kids?'

'Yes,' said Daisy.

'You and me'll get on fine,' declared Maisie. ''Elp me clear the breakfast things and I'll tell you what's what as we go.'

Daisy had never been so content; the ward was a happy place despite the sick children in it and she had spent the day clearing up messes, sorting clean linen and bagging mountains of soiled sheets and small garments, going to and fro with meals, making Sister's coffee and listening carefully to Maisie's advice. Maisie was a treasure with a heart of gold and endless patience. The nurses were nice too; she might not be one of them but she had been made to feel that she was part of the team. Daisy blessed the unknown authority who had seen fit to send her to the children's unit. Going down to her short tea break, she wondered who it was.

The unknown authority was sitting in Sister Carter's office, going over his small patients' case-sheets and drinking strong tea from a mug. Presently he glanced up. 'The new orderly—she'll settle down?'

'Daisy? Oh, yes, sir. A nice little thing. You recommended her, didn't you? Not quite our usual sort of girl but she has a way with the children and our Maisie assures me that she's a good worker. She's at tea—did you want to see her?'

'No. My sister employed her as nanny to her children and she needed to have a job near home. Now, what are we going to do with baby George? He had better have another X-ray. I have to go back to town this evening but I'll speak to Dr Dowling before I go—I shall be away for the rest of this week.' He got up to go. 'Thanks for the tea.' As he went through the door he saw Daisy's pink-clad person disappearing into the ward.

It was late evening when he left the hospital and drove himself through the city, through the medieval gates of the cathedral close and parked before his house. It was a very old house, but like many of its neighbours had a Georgian front with an important pillared door and a charming transom over it. He let himself in and was met in the hall by a tall, bony woman of uncertain years, whose sharp-nosed face lighted up at the sight of him.

'There you are, sir. And there's your dinner waiting for you, and eat it you must before you go to Lon-

don… I've packed your case and there's messages for
you—' She was interrupted by a deep-throated barking. 'That's Belle, in the garden with all the doors shut,
but she knows it's you.'

'Sorry I'm late, Mrs Trump. Give me five minutes,
will you? Thanks for packing my bag; I'll join Belle
for a moment—I could do with some fresh air.'

The doctor opened a door at the back of the square
hall and went into a fair-sized walled garden behind the
house, to be greeted with ecstasy by a golden Labrador.
He bent to fondle her ears and then strolled round the
small garden still bright with autumn flowers until his
housekeeper called from the door and they both went
inside to the dining-room, its walls panelled, the mahogany table and sideboard gleaming with polished
age, silver and glass gleaming in the soft light of the
wall-sconces. He ate his solitary, deliciously cooked
meal without waste of time, had coffee at the table and,
accompanied by Belle, went to his study to collect up
those papers he wished to take with him. It was a pleasant room at the back of the house, its walls lined with
books, its leather chairs large. His desk was large too,
every inch of it taken up with case-sheets, folders and
a mass of reading matter. It looked a splendid muddle
but he put his hand on what he wanted without hesita-
tion, put it into his briefcase and went up to his room
to fetch his bag.

Downstairs again, he went through the door beside
the graceful little staircase and found Mrs Trump load-
ing the dishwasher. He let Belle into the garden and
addressed himself to his housekeeper.

'I'll be away for the best part of the week,' he told

her. 'I'll ring you later.' He smiled at her. 'Take care of yourself.' He whistled to Belle and presently got into his car and drove himself away. It would be late by the time he got to London but the drive would give him time to think. Rather against his will he found he was thinking about Daisy.

Daisy was thinking about him too. She had been on tenterhooks all day expecting to see him on the ward, but there had been no sign of him, nor had his name been mentioned. 'And a good thing too,' she muttered to herself. 'The less we see of each other the better; he unsettles me.'

Luckily, when she got home her thoughts were happily diverted by a letter from Philip, home on leave in Bristol and asking if he might drive down to Wilton and see her. A day out together, he suggested in his neat handwriting, or failing that could they meet for a meal? If she would like that could she phone him and perhaps something could be arranged.

Her mother and Pamela, apprised of the contents of the letter, were enthusiastic. 'Phone him now,' urged Pamela. 'You're free this weekend, aren't you? Well, say you'll spend the day with him. Wear the good suit. Debenhams have got a sale on; see if you can get a top to go with it—one of those silk ones, you know, short sleeves and a plain neck; you can borrow Mother's pearls…'

Philip sounded pleased when she phoned. Saturday, he suggested with flattering eagerness. They could drive out into the country and have lunch. He assured her that he was looking forward to seeing her again and to exchanging their news. Daisy put down the receiver feeling a faint glow of pleasure.

Before she slept that night she lay thinking about Philip; it would be nice to see him again—he was a very pleasant companion and they got on well together, which thought somehow reminded her that she and the doctor didn't get on well at all. Surprisingly, it wasn't Philip in her sleepy thoughts, but Dr Seymour, his handsome face vivid under her eyelids.

Naturally enough, she saw no sign of him during that week. There were a number of children under his care and a youngish man with a friendly face came each day to see them. Daisy, cleaning the bathrooms with Maisie, asked who he was.

''E's Dr Dowling, registrar to Dr Seymour—keeps 'is eye on the kids when 'is nibs isn't here.' Maisie gave her a sidelong glance. 'Got a boyfriend, 'ave you, Daisy?'

'Me? No...'

'Go on with you, a nice girl like you.'

Daisy thought of Philip. 'Well, it's true, though I'm going out on Saturday with someone I met a little while ago in Holland. Just for lunch.'

'Holland, eh? Been to foreign parts, 'ave you? I've always fancied a bit of travel meself. Is 'e a Dutchman, then?'

'No, he just works there; he's on holiday.'

Maisie was mopping the floor. 'Our Dr Seymour, 'e goes over to Holland once in a while—very clever, 'e is, with the kids. Tells other doctors what to do.'

That sounded like him all right, thought Daisy, arranging the tooth-mugs in a neat line on their appointed shelf. She squashed an impulse to talk about him and instead suggested that she should go to the kitchen and get the trolley ready for the dinners. 'Unless there's something you'd like me to do first, Maisie?'

'You run along, Daisy, and get started, then, and lay up a tray for Sister at the same time, will you? She likes her pot of tea after her own dinner.'

Saturday came at last. Daisy got up early and dressed carefully. She had found a plain silk top to go with the suit, very plain, round-necked and short-sleeved, but if they were to go to the kind of restaurant where she would be expected to take off her jacket it would pass muster. The pearls gave it a touch of class, or so she hoped. Carefully swathed in one of her mother's aprons, she got the breakfast, saw to Razor's food and sat down with her mother and Pamela to boiled eggs and bread and butter.

'Let's hope you get a smashing lunch,' said Pam with her mouth full. 'Any idea where you're going?'

'Not the faintest. If he hasn't been to Salisbury before I dare say he'll want to look round the cathedral.'

Pamela looked horrified. 'But that's not romantic.'

'I'm not expecting romance,' said Daisy. She had the ridiculous idea that if it were Dr Seymour and not Philip it would have been romantic in a coal hole. She frowned; really she was allowing the most absurd ideas to run through her head. She helped clear the table, made the beds and did her hair again and then went downstairs to wait for Philip.

He arrived punctually, greeted her with pleasure, drank the coffee her mother had ready and led the way out to his car. It was a small, elderly model, bright red and nice but noisy. Daisy got in happily enough. Philip had no wish to see the cathedral; instead he had planned a trip down towards the coast, through Fordingbridge and Ringwood. A friend of his had said that there was a good pub in Brockenhurst where they could have lunch. 'We could go on to Beaulieu but I don't suppose there would be time for that; I have to get back this evening.'

'Yes, of course; come home to tea, though.'

They were almost on the outskirts of Salisbury when the doctor, driving the other way, passed them. Neither of them noticed the Rolls slide past them but he, even in the few seconds allowed him, had a clear view of them both laughing.

Less than ten minutes later he drew up before her home, got out and banged the knocker. Mrs Pelham came to the door, beaming a welcome.

'How very nice to see you again!' she exclaimed. 'Did you want to see Daisy about something? Such a pity you've just missed her.' She opened the door wider. 'Do come in and have a cup of coffee; I've just made some.'

'That,' said the doctor at his most urbane, 'would be delightful. I'm on my way to see my sister.'

Mrs Pelham looked past him. 'Is that a dog in the car? Yours? Bring him in, do. Razor won't mind.'

'Her name's Belle; she's very mild. You're sure—er—Razor won't mind?'

'Our cat. He has a keen brain, so Daisy says, but he's bone-idle.'

They sat over their coffee, with Belle at her master's feet and Razor sitting on the corner of the mantelpiece for safety's sake, and since the doctor was at his most charming Mrs Pelham told him all about Philip coming to take Daisy out. 'All the way from Bristol,' she observed. 'They've gone down towards the coast—I told Daisy to bring him back for tea. He seemed a nice young man.'

'Indeed, yes,' agreed the doctor, at his most amiable. 'I met him while I was at the Hague—a sound young man.' He put down his coffee-cup. 'I must be on my way.'

It was only as he was at the door saying goodbye that he asked casually, 'Daisy is happy at the hospital?'

Mrs Pelham said happily, 'Oh, yes, and now she's been moved on to the children's ward—your ward?— I dare say you'll see her.' She hesitated. 'But of course she's an orderly; I don't suppose you talk to them.'

He said gravely, 'Well, I don't have much contact with anyone outside the medical or nursing profession. I must look out for her, though.'

'Yes, do,' said Mrs Pelham. 'I'm sure she'll be delighted to see you again.'

He agreed pleasantly, reflecting that delight was the last thing he expected to see on Daisy's face.

In the car, he assured himself that it was because Daisy was so unwilling to like him that he found her so often on his mind. She appeared to have got herself a possible husband too. There was nothing wrong with young Philip; he would be an ideal husband in many ways, reliable and hard-working with little time for romantic nonsense. 'Well, if that's what she wants…' he muttered so savagely that Belle lifted an enquiring ear.

It might have been a relief to the doctor's feelings

if he had known that Daisy had never once thought of
Philip as a husband. If she had had a brother she would
have liked him to be just like Philip—easygoing and
cheerful, a good companion. She was enjoying herself enormously; there was a great deal to talk about,
mostly about his work in the Hague and his hopes for
the future, and at Brockenhurst they had found the
pub without difficulty and had a ploughman's lunch,
and presently drove on to Lymington, parked the car
on Quay Hill and walked the length of the High Street
and then down to the shore to look at the sea.

'We must do this again,' said Philip as he drove
back later. 'I've got two weeks. Are you free every
weekend?'

'I have to work every fourth weekend. That'll be in
two weeks' time—I've been sent to another ward and
the off duty's different.'

'I'm going to Cheshire to spend next weekend with
friends and I'll be gone before you get your next free
weekend. Could I come and see you at the hospital?'

'Heavens no. I mean, not just like that—I suppose if
something really urgent happened and someone needed
to see me about something.' Daisy shook her neat head
firmly. 'Otherwise not.'

'I'll be home for a few days for Christmas; we must
see each other then.'

He gave her a brotherly grin and she said, 'Yes, that
will be nice.'

They had a splendid tea with her mother and Pamela, and Mrs Pelham, if she hoped for signs of a
romance, was very disappointed; nothing could have
been more prosaic than Daisy's manner towards Philip,

and he, thought Mrs Pelham sadly, was behaving like a brother.

He left soon after tea, unknowingly passing the doctor's Rolls once more in one of Wilton's narrow streets, happily unaware of the frowning scrutiny that gentleman gave him as they slowed, going in opposite directions. The doctor had spent several hours in his sister's company, had a civil conversation with his brother-in-law, obligingly played a rousing game of snakes and ladders with his nephew and niece and had pleaded an evening engagement as soon as he decently could, and now he was driving himself back to his house in the close. He had a consultation at the hospital on Monday morning and there was no point in going back to London. He had no engagement; at the back of his mind had been the tentative idea that it might be pleasant to take Daisy out to dinner and use his powers of persuasion to stir up her interest, even liking, for him. Only an idea and a foolish one, he told himself and greeted his housekeeper with tight-lipped civility so that she went back to the kitchen to cook an extra-splendid meal. 'To take his mind off things,' she explained to Belle, who was eating her supper under the kitchen table.

She might just as well have served him slabs of cardboard although he complimented her upon the good food as he went to his study, where he sat, Belle at his feet, doing absolutely nothing but think about Daisy.

It was a waste of time thinking about the girl, he reasoned; cold facts proved that. She had disliked him on sight, and she had even told him so, hadn't she? He was far too old for her and he was quite sure that if she were to discover that it was through his good offices that she had got work at the hospital she would quite likely throw up the job at once. As far as he knew, she had never discovered that it was he who had asked his sister to take her on as a nanny, nor did she know why she had been moved to the children's ward or who had arranged that. He hoped she never would. What had started as a kindly act towards a girl who had intrigued him had become an overwhelming desire to make life as easy as possible for her.

He went up to bed at last, long after midnight, resolved to put her out of his mind. There was more than enough to occupy it; he had his work, more than he could cope with sometimes, many friends and family; he would find himself a wife and settle down. The doctor, a man with a brilliant brain, a fund of knowledge and priding himself on his logical outlook on life, had no idea how foolish that resolve was.

As for Daisy, she had enjoyed her day. They had reminisced about the Hague, and she had listened to Philip's light-hearted criticism of his job, pointing out in a sisterly fashion that however dull it might be at the moment it could lead to an interesting post.

'Well paid too, I shouldn't wonder,' she had added.

'Oh, yes,' he had agreed. 'I don't do too badly now. They like married men for the more senior jobs, though the thing is to get promotion and find a wife at the same time.'

They had laughed together quite unselfconsciously about it.

She had settled down nicely on the children's ward; it was hard work and at times extremely messy but Sister Carter was a happy person and the ward and its staff took their ambience from her; the nurses were treated fairly and if there were any small crises—and there very often were—and it was necessary for them to work over their normal hours, she worked with them. Daisy, going about her lowly tasks, wished that she could be a ward sister. She was happy enough, however; she was on good terms with the nurses and Maisie and the children had accepted her as a familiar face.

The week went by without a glimpse of Dr Seymour and she didn't know whether to be pleased or vexed when she went back after the following weekend to hear from Maisie that he had been to the ward several times during the weekend but had now returned to London.

As casually as she could, Daisy asked, 'Does he only come at weekends?'

'Lord bless you, no—'e comes when there's something needs sorting out, too much for 'is registrar; 'e comes regular like, for 'is rounds and out-patients and that. Busy man, 'e is.'

It was her turn to work at the weekend and she couldn't entirely suppress a feeling of expectancy as she cycled to work. Maisie had said that the doctor sometimes visited on a Saturday or Sunday and there was a chance that he might as there were several ill children on the ward...

There was no sign of him on Saturday; the registrar had been to the ward several times, obviously worried about some of the children, and Sister, who was on duty for the weekend, had spent a long time at their cotsides. Daisy longed to know what was the matter with them and if Sister hadn't been so busy she would have asked. As it was, she was busy herself, managing to do Maisie's work as well as her own. Sunday was just as hectic too but in the early evening the children seemed better and the ward was quiet. Daisy could hear the distant continuous murmur of visitors on the floors below; in another hour she would be going home… She picked up the tray of tea she was taking to Sister's office and, pausing at its door, came face to face with Philip.

He said breezily, 'Hello, is this where Sister lives? I've come to see you—I'm sure she won't mind just for a few minutes; I brought a friend down from home to visit his granny—she's had an operation.'

'You can't…' began Daisy, but it was too late; he had tapped on the door and she heard Sister's nice voice telling whoever it was to come in.

Afterwards she tried to understand what had happened. Sister had looked up from her desk and she and Philip had just stared at each other; they looked as though they had just discovered something they had been searching for all their lives and for the moment she had been quite sure that neither of them had any idea of where they were or what they were doing. She had waited for a moment for someone to say something and then put the tray down on Sister's desk. Sister had moved then and so had Philip.

Philip spoke first. 'I brought someone to visit and I wondered if I might have a few minutes with Daisy—we met in Holland.' He held out a hand. 'Philip Keynes…'

Sister blushed. 'Beryl Carter. You're a friend of Daisy? It's not really allowed to visit staff, but since you're here…'

'It's not at all important,' said Philip, summarily dismissing Daisy from his mind and life without a second's thought, so that Daisy slipped away and fetched another cup and saucer. She was in time to hear Sister say,

'Do sit down, Mr Keynes; have you come far?'

Daisy had never quite believed in falling in love at first sight, but now she knew better. They would make a nice pair, she reflected as she helped a hard-pressed nurse to change cotsheets. Philip would have to get a larger place in which to live, of course—if he had a wife he might get his promotion. She was deep in speculative thought when Sister came to the ward door.

Philip was standing by the swing doors, ready to leave. He said in a bemused kind of voice, 'I say, Daisy, I'm so glad I came to see you.' Then when she agreed pleasantly he went on, 'She's got a day off tomorrow; I'm coming to take her out for the day...'

'What a splendid idea,' said Daisy. 'I'm sure you'll have a lovely time. She's so very nice, Philip.'

'Nice? She's an angel—I knew it the moment I set eyes on her.'

He was, she saw, about to embark on a detailed description of Sister Carter's charms. Daisy cut him short in a kindly way. 'Good for you; I must go. Let me know what happens next, won't you?'

She went back into the ward; there was still almost an hour before she was free to go home.

Sister was in the ward checking one of the ill children when Dr Seymour came quietly in. Daisy, going down the ward with an armful of nappies for one of the nurses, slithered to a halt when he came towards her. He gave her a cold look and she wondered why; she hadn't expected a smile but his eyes were like grey steel. Naturally enough, if she had but known, for he had seen Philip leaving the ward only seconds before he himself entered it. The young man hadn't seen him; indeed, he was in such a state of euphoria that he was in no shape to see anything or anyone. The doctor, his face impassive, entered the ward in a rage.

He was still there when it was time for Daisy to go off duty. She bade Sister goodnight, and whisked herself away. It was a pity that she was free the next day—Dr Seymour might still be at the hospital, although, if he was going to look at her like that, perhaps it was just as well that she wasn't going to be there. She frowned; the last time they had met they had been quite friendly in a guarded sort of way. She shook off a vague regret and fell to planning what she would do with her free day.

It was nice to have a day at home, to potter round the garden, help her mother around the house; do some shopping. After supper she sat down at her mother's desk and carefully checked their finances. There was very little in the bank but at least they were paying the bills as they came in and putting by a little each week into what she called their 'sinking fund', which really meant schoolbooks for Pamela, and for having shoes mended and what she hoped would be a winter coat for her mother. She went back to work on the Tuesday morning feeling that life wasn't too bad; a few months' steady work and it would be even better; further ahead than that she didn't care to look. The thought of being an orderly for the rest of her working days made her feel unhappy.

She was cleaning out the older children's lockers by their small beds when Dr Seymour came in. Sister was with him; so was Staff Nurse, his registrar, a young houseman and one or two persons hovering on the fringe whom Daisy couldn't identify. He brought with him an air of self-assurance nicely timed with a kindly, avuncular manner—very reassuring to his patients, reflected Daisy, getting off her knees and melting discreetly into the nearest sluice-room. Maisie had dinned it into her on her first day that orderlies kept off the wards when the consultants did a round.

Maisie was having her coffee break and the sluice-room was pristine; Daisy wedged herself near the door and watched the small procession on its way round the cots. It was a leisurely round; Dr Seymour spent a long time with each occupant, sometimes sitting on the cotside with a toddler on his knee. He had a way with children, Daisy admitted, making them chuckle and undisturbed when they bawled.

The group moved round the ward and crossed over to the other side to where the older children were and Daisy, getting careless, opened the sluice-room door a little wider just as the doctor came to a halt and looked up, straight across the ward and at her. His look was impassive so why did she have the feeling that he was laughing behind that blandness? She stared back, not sure whether to shut the door or melt into the sluice-room out of sight, or perhaps stay well out of sight where she was.

The problem was solved for her, for he moved away, his head bent to hear what Sister was saying.

She had been at home for half an hour that evening when the doorknocker was soundly rapped. Pamela was in her room doing her homework, her mother was making a shopping-list and said vaguely, 'The door, dear,' so Daisy, spooning Razor's supper into his saucer, put the tin down and went to see who it was.

Dr Seymour stood on the doorstep and at her startled, 'Oh, it's you,' wasted no time on polite preliminaries.

'I should like a word,' he told her, and since he expected to be invited in she stood on one side.

'Come in, Dr Seymour.' Her voice was tart for she saw no reason to be anything else. Why he should want to come and see her was a mystery—surely if she had needed a reprimand for something she had done wrong on the ward it should be Sister who administered it?

She opened the sitting-room door but he brushed past her. 'You're in the kitchen?' he said, and before she could answer he had stalked in, to wish her surprised mother good evening with just the right degree of apologetic charm.

Mrs Pelham put down her pencil. 'Dr Seymour—how nice. Do you want to talk to Daisy? I'll make a cup of coffee.' She smiled at him in her gentle way. 'Do sit down.'

He sat, refusing the coffee at the same time. 'I've come to ask a favour of Daisy.' Since she was still standing just inside the door, he got up again. Lovely manners, reflected Mrs Pelham and told Daisy quite sharply to sit down. It would be easier to talk to him sitting down; he loomed rather large on his feet...

'My sister asked me to come and see you; she's unable to leave the children. Miss Thompson has had to go home to look after her sick mother and she thinks that I can explain matters more easily than if she spoke to you on the telephone. She and her husband have to attend some function or other next Saturday evening. There is no one she cares to leave the children with; she'll have to take them with her. She hopes that if you're free you might be persuaded to go with her and look after them—just for Saturday and Sunday. They'll take you up in the car and bring you back, of course.' He looked at Daisy. 'Of course we realise that it is an imposition; you have little enough free time. But the children like you and Meg trusts you, Daisy.'

Daisy opened her mouth to say no and then closed it again. After all, he was only passing on a message from his sister; it was really nothing to do with him, and Lady Thorley had been very kind to her. She glanced at her mother who smiled faintly at her. 'Why not, dear?' asked her parent. 'It will be a nice little change for you, and Lady Thorley has always been so kind to you.'

Daisy still hesitated, though; indeed she might have refused if Pamela, hearing voices, hadn't come down to see who had called. Her hello was casually friendly. 'I bet you want to borrow Daisy,' she said, and pulled up a chair to the table. 'Do tell. What is it this time? Measles?'

The doctor laughed. 'Nothing to do with me; I'm only the bearer of a message. My sister wants Daisy to go with her and the children to London for the weekend—their governess has had to go home for a few days.'

'Good idea; will you drive her up?'

'I—no, no. I shan't be here. My sister would fetch Daisy if she's willing to go.'

'Of course she'll go,' said Pamela, 'won't you, Daisy?'

Daisy, unable to think of any reason to refuse, said that yes, she would.

He got up to go presently, saying all the right things before going to the door with Daisy. As she opened it he asked carelessly, 'Have you seen any more of young Philip?'

He gave her a friendly smile and she quite forgot that she had no wish to be friendly too. 'Oh, yes, he came to see me the other evening; he met Sister Carter, though.' She forgot for the moment to whom she was speaking. 'It was really very strange—I mean, they just looked at each other as though they had known each other all their lives. I've never believed in love at first sight, but now I do.'

She glanced at him and saw the little smile and felt her cheeks grow hot. 'Goodnight, Dr Seymour,' she said coldly and opened the door wide.

His, 'Goodnight, Daisy,' was uttered with great civility and he said nothing else. She stood at the door, keeping still and not looking as he got into his car, and as he drove away closed it with deliberate quiet. Otherwise she would have banged it as hard as she was able; she had made a fool of herself talking to him like that. He would be sitting in his car, smiling that nasty little smile...her face was scarlet at the thought.

The doctor was indeed smiling, a slow, tender smile

which made him look years younger. He drove to his sister's house, whistling softly under his breath, and Belle, sensing that he found life very much to his satisfaction, sat on the back seat and thumped her tail happily.

Chapter 7

There was no sign of the doctor when Daisy went to work in the morning and she wasn't sure whether to be relieved or disappointed. Dr Dowling did a ward-round with the housemen and staff nurse, since Sister Carter had a day off—out with Philip, no doubt of that. Daisy wondered where they would go—somewhere romantic, she hoped. Maisie, bustling up and down the ward, gave her opinion that Sister was far too pretty to be stuck in a hospital. 'Ought to 'ave a 'ome of her own with kids.' She gave a hoarse chuckle. 'And that won't be no trouble to 'er—she's 'ad enough practice 'ere.'

At home, Daisy combed through her wardrobe again. She supposed it didn't really matter what she wore when she went to London, and it was only for two days anyway. It would have to be the good suit once again; she could travel in a blouse and take the silk top, spare undies and night things and her small collection of make-up. They could all go easily enough into the roomy shoulder-bag, which would leave her arms free for the twins.

'You don't suppose you might get asked out?' asked her mother hopefully.

'No, love. I shall be with the twins while the Thorleys go to this banquet or whatever it is. I dare say I shall take them for a walk in the morning and we'll come back here in the afternoon. I shall enjoy the trip there and back,' added Daisy in her sensible way.

'Where will you stay?'

'Don't know. In a hotel, perhaps, or they may even have a flat or house in London—that's the most likely, I should think.'

'It sounds rather dull to me,' observed Mrs Pelham. If Daisy agreed with her parent she didn't say so.

Sister Carter was on duty the next morning, starry-eyed and looking prettier than ever. During the morning she sent for Daisy to go to her office, and when she tapped on the door and was bidden to enter she was told to sit down.

Daisy sat composedly while she beat her brains trying to remember if she had done something worthy of a talking-to. So it was all the more surprising when Sister Carter said cheerfully, 'Philip was telling me about you yesterday. You really shouldn't be an orderly, you know, Daisy. Can't you train as a nurse?'

It was so unexpected that Daisy didn't answer at once. When she did her voice was as quiet as usual. 'I think I might like to do that, Sister, but until my sister is through school I do need to have a job; a student nurse's pay wouldn't be quite enough…besides, I—I need to live at home.'

'For how long would that be?' asked Sister Carter kindly.

'Another three years. There would still be plenty of time for me to train as a nurse—I'm twenty-two—I wouldn't be too old…'

She was uttering a pipe-dream—her mother couldn't be left alone and Pamela would be miles away at some university, but there was no need to burden Sister with that.

'A pity. Still, there doesn't seem to be anything we can do about it at present, does there? As long as you're happy here?'

'I am—very happy, Sister.' That at least was true, thought Daisy.

'Well, we'll have to see,' said Sister Carter vaguely. She smiled suddenly. 'I don't suppose I'll be here in three years' time, but I'll make sure that you have a special splendid reference when I go.'

She hesitated. 'Did you have no opportunity to train for anything, Daisy?'

'No, my father died.'

'I'm sorry. Anyway, you can count on me if ever you see the chance to start training.'

Back in the ward, bagging the endless nappies, Daisy thought it unlikely.

Saturday came, bringing with it chilly blue skies and a sunshine without much warmth. Just the right weather for the suit, decided Daisy, getting up early.

Lady Thorley arrived late, explaining worriedly that the twins had been troublesome at the last minute.

'If you wouldn't mind sitting in the back with them, Daisy?' she asked. 'They're cross because we haven't brought Boots with us.' She added hopefully, 'They usually listen to you.'

At first they weren't disposed to listen to anyone, even Daisy whom they liked, but presently they decided to be good and the rest of the journey was made in comparative harmony. All the same Daisy was relieved to see the outskirts of London closing in around them; there was so much more to see and the children, rather excited now, were kept busy pointing out everything which caught their eye. Daisy was excited too although she appeared serene enough, as Lady Thorley drove along Millbank and the Victoria Embankment until she turned off at Northumberland Avenue, skirted Trafalgar Square and turned into Pall Mall, and after that Daisy was lost—she didn't know London well; all she knew was that they had crossed Piccadilly and were driving through streets of dignified mansions opening out from time to time into quiet squares encircling a railed-off garden. Very pleasant to sit there under the trees on the wooden seats, thought Daisy, and indeed there were small children and mothers and nursemaids doing just that. Living in such surroundings it would be hard to remember that the busy London streets were close by.

Lady Thorley drove past another square and turned into a tree-lined street where the houses were smaller, although to Daisy's eyes they looked of a handsome size, and presently stopped halfway down the terrace.

'Well, here we are,' Lady Thorley observed. She

looked over her shoulder to the twins. 'You've both been very good—are you tired, Daisy?'

'Not in the least, Lady Thorley. Would you like me to see to the cases or mind the children?'

'The children, please; Trim will take the bags inside.'

The house door had opened and an elderly man, very spry, crossed the pavement.

'Trim, how nice to see you again. Will you see to the luggage for us? This is Miss Daisy Pelham who has kindly come with me to look after the children.'

Trim greeted her with dignity, exchanged a more boisterous greeting with the children and took the car keys from Lady Thorley. 'Nice to see you again, my lady,' he said. 'Mrs Trim will be waiting for you.'

The door opened on to a small vestibule which in turn led to a long wide hall. Daisy, following Lady Thorley indoors, saw that the house was a good deal larger than it appeared to be from the outside but she had little time to look around her. Advancing to meet them was a stout middle-aged woman with improbable black hair and eyes to match. She had a round face which crinkled nicely when she smiled and the children rushed towards her with shouts of delight.

'There, my darlings—you've grown, I declare.' She embraced them and swept towards Lady Thorley. 'Welcome, my lady. Your usual room and I've put Miss Pelham next to the children.' She turned a beady eye on Daisy and smiled largely. 'You'll be wanting to see to them. If you, my lady, would go to the drawing-room while I show Miss Pelham their rooms? There will be coffee in a few minutes and lunch is at one o'clock.'

She bustled Daisy and the children up the elegant staircase at one side of the hall, along a narrow passage and into a room at its end. 'The children usually sleep here.'

It was a large room with two beds and white furniture geared to suit a small person and a big window overlooking a surprisingly long, narrow garden at the back of the house. 'You will be here, Miss Pelham.' The housekeeper opened a door and Daisy walked past her into a charming room, the bed and dressing-table in maplewood, a comfortable little chair by the window and a matching tallboy against one wall. The bedspread and curtains were in a faint pink and the carpet underfoot was a deep cream and very soft.

'The bathroom is here,' said Mrs Trim, throwing open another door, 'if you won't mind sharing it with the children.'

Daisy nodded wordlessly and Mrs Trim trotted to the door. 'You'll want your coffee. It'll be downstairs in the drawing-room; the twins know where that is.'

Left with the children, Daisy made haste to see to their wants, brush their hair, apply handkerchiefs to small noses, and urge them to good manners when they went downstairs while she tidied her already neat head, powdered her prosaic nose and added lipstick. That done, she led the way downstairs again. In the hall she said, 'Josh, dear, which is the drawing-room?'

He took her hand and the three of them opened the door to which he led them. Lady Thorley was sitting there comfortably by a small fire in a handsome Adam fireplace but for the moment Daisy only had eyes for the room. It was of a comfortable size, its bow window overlooking the street and it was furnished with what she recognised as antiques. Beautiful cabinets, lamp tables, a long sofa table and in one corner a long-case clock was tick-tocking in a soothing monotone. The chairs were large, upholstered in wine-red velvet, and there were two sofas, one each side of the fireplace.

'There you are,' said Lady Thorley. 'Daisy, come and have some coffee; you must be parched. Josh, Katie, Mrs Trim has made some lemonade especially for you. Sit down by Daisy and drink it up.'

Over coffee Lady Thorley voiced her plans for the evening. 'This banquet is at nine o'clock but there's a reception first and that's at eight o'clock. We shall have to leave here about a quarter past seven. Would you see that the children have their suppers and go to bed? Mrs Trim will have a meal ready for you about eight o'clock. We shall be very late back so go to bed when you want to. In the morning would you give the twins their breakfasts and have yours at the same time and perhaps take them for a walk for half an hour or so? I expect lunch will be at one o'clock and we'll leave about three o'clock. Hugh's coming back with us, so he'll drive, thank goodness.'

Daisy took a sip of coffee. It was delicious. 'Very well, Lady Thorley. I could have supper with the children if that would be more convenient.'

'No, no. You deserve an hour or two of peace and quiet. Trim will look after you.' She glanced at the clock. 'Lunch must be almost ready.'

She looked across at the children, one each side of Daisy, drinking their lemonade with deceptive meekness. 'Now you must behave nicely at table...'

'If they don't,' said the doctor from the door, 'I shall throw them into the garden—not you, of course, Daisy.'

He strolled into the room, kissed his sister's offered cheek, suffered an excited onslaught from his nephew and niece and wished Daisy a bland good-day. 'You had a good trip?' he asked. 'Hugh should be here at any minute; I'll tell Trim to serve lunch ten minutes after he gets here—that will give us time for a glass of sherry.'

Daisy hadn't uttered a sound. She was surprised and delighted and at the same time puzzled; he had spoken as though he owned the place...

He caught her eye. 'Welcome to my home, Daisy,' he said and smiled with such charm that she blinked her lovely eyes and went pink.

'You've gone all red,' said Josh but before his mother could reprimand him Sir Hugh joined them and in the general hubbub and the handing of drinks Daisy was able to regain her normal colour and during lunch she was far too busy seeing that the children ate their meal and behaved themselves to feel self-conscious. The doctor's manners were impeccable; whenever possible he included her in their conversation but beyond polite answers she took little part in it, which gave her the chance to look around.

The dining-room was behind the drawing-room, overlooking the back garden. Here again was a bay window with a door leading to a covered veranda. The walls were panelled and hung with paintings, mostly portraits, and the table and sideboard were mahogany of the Regency period. The table had been decked with a damask cloth, crested silver and crystal glasses. The soup was served in Worcester plates, as was the ragout of chicken, and, as a concession to the children's presence, the trifle, with glacé cherries and whipped cream. The twins spooned their portions up without any urging and were bidden by their uncle to sit still while Daisy had her coffee. She didn't linger over it; she felt sure that the three of them had plenty to talk about. She excused herself, removed the children from the table and bore them off upstairs where they were prevailed upon to lie on their beds while she told them a story. They were asleep within ten minutes, looking like two cherubs, leaving her to sit by the window with nothing to do. Presently, lacking anything to keep her awake, she closed her eyes and dozed off.

She woke to find the doctor sitting on Josh's bed, a twin on either side of him. All three of them were watching her with unnerving intensity.

'You were snoring,' said Josh.

'I never snore,' declared Daisy indignantly, very conscious of being at a total disadvantage.

'No, no, of course you don't.' The doctor was at his most soothing. 'Josh, no gentleman ever tells a lady that she snores—it's bad manners.'

Daisy sat very upright. 'I'm sorry I went to sleep…'

'No need to be sorry. I expect you were up early and two hours or more of these children, mewed up in a car, is sufficient to make anyone doze off. But we're glad you're awake. We wondered if you would like to come with us—we're going to take a quick look at the zoo.' He glanced at his watch. 'It's not yet three o'clock—we could have an hour there and come back for a late tea.'

He didn't wait for her to agree. 'If you could get these

two ready, and yourself, of course, and come downstairs in ten minutes or so, I'll have the car outside.'

He had gone before she had said a word.

For once the twins were both quick and helpful; with a minute to spare they were downstairs in the hall where they found the doctor talking to his sister.

'Splendid, you're ready. Meg, we'll be back around five o'clock—tell Mrs Trim to have tea ready for the children, will you? Ask for yours when you want it.'

He ushered his party outside, shovelled the children into the car and told Daisy to get in beside him. 'A pity Belle can't come too...'

'Oh, is she here? I haven't seen her.'

'She has been with me all the morning—she's in the garden now; you'll see her when we get back.'

The streets were comparatively empty, and the distance wasn't great; beyond the excited chatter of the twins, little was said. Once there, they lost no time in deciding what had to be seen in the time they had.

'Snakes and scorpions, sharks and man-eating tigers,' demanded Josh, to be instantly contradicted by his twin.

'Bears and elephants,' she demanded, 'and a camel.'

'Well, I dare say we shall have time to see all of them, provided you don't hang around too long. Let's get the snakes and scorpions over first, shall we?'

Daisy, annoyed at the high-handed way in which the doctor had arranged her afternoon without so much as a by your leave, found her annoyance melting in the face of the children's happy faces and his whole-hearted enthusiasm for the afternoon's entertainment. The snakes and scorpions duly shivered over, the bears admired, the camels marvelled at, there was time to have a ride on an elephant. The twins weren't faint-hearted; they needed no one with them, they assured their uncle and Daisy watched the great beast with its burden of small people plod away.

'They'll be all right,' she breathed anxiously. 'They're so small, though…'

'Well, of course they're small; they're children, aren't they?' The doctor sounded testy. 'Do you suppose I should allow them to go unless I was quite certain they would come to no harm?'

'Well, no,' said Daisy placatingly, 'I'm sure you wouldn't.'

He looked down at her. 'How's the job going?'

'Very well, thank you.' She considered telling him that Sister Carter had mentioned her training to be a nurse, but decided not to—it might sound a bit boastful.

'I suppose you won't be there long,' he said airily, a remark which sent her into instant panic.

'Oh, why not? Aren't I suitable? I know I'm not as quick as Maisie…'

'Suitable? Oh, you're that all right. I was merely uttering my thoughts aloud.'

He said no more, leaving her to wish that he would keep his thoughts to himself.

The children came back then and there was no chance to ask him what he had meant. With the promise that they should come again next time they came to London, the twins were stowed in the car and, with a silent Daisy beside him, the doctor drove back to his house. It was a crisp winter evening and Daisy thought longingly of tea and was delighted to find that Mrs

Trim, mindful of the twins' bedtime, had set out a splendid meal in a small room at the back of the house. It was a very cosy room, with a bright fire burning, plenty of bookshelves and comfortable chairs as well as the round table loaded with the twins' favourite food, a pot of tea for Daisy and a dish of little cakes.

Lady Thorley joined them for a moment. 'I'm just off to dress,' she told Daisy. 'We shall have to leave in an hour or so—you'll be all right? I know Val has told the Trims to look after you. We shall be late back, I expect.'

She embraced her children. 'I'll come back and tuck you up before we go,' she promised, 'and so will Daddy.'

The children were nicely tired and, after a splendid meal, sleepy. Daisy led them away upstairs, undressed them, and urged them, rather reluctantly, to their baths. They were emerging from these noisy and damp activities, the twins with shining faces and smelling of the best kind of soap, and Daisy dishevelled and damp, when their parents and the doctor came to say goodnight. Lady Thorley, in sequinned black chiffon, looked superb, as did Sir Hugh in his white tie and tails, but it was the doctor who stole the show; he wore his evening clothes with ease and elegance, his broad shoulders enhancing the inspired cut of his coat, the very size of him meriting a second or even third glance. Daisy took one look and turned her head away because he was watching her with that small smile which she found so disconcerting. There was no need to look at him again; she was fully occupied in keeping the twins from embracing their mother too fervently.

'If you get into your beds,' she suggested in her calm fashion, 'I dare say everyone will kiss you good-night.' She added artfully, 'And there'll still be time for another chapter of *The Rose and the Ring*.' This was a book to which they were passionately devoted and which Lady Thorley had had the presence of mind to bring with her.

Soothed by their favourite story, the children presently slept and Daisy went down to the quiet dining-room and found Trim waiting for her.

'A glass of sherry, miss—little Josh and Katie can wear you out.' When Daisy hesitated he added, 'The doctor said you should have a glass before your dinner, miss.'

'Oh, did he?' asked Daisy. 'How kind of him. In that case I'd like one.'

Presently Trim led her to the table. At the sight of the damask and silver and crystal, for all the world as though the table had been decked out for a dinner-party, Daisy exclaimed, 'Oh, but you shouldn't have gone to all this trouble! I could have had something on a tray.'

'The doctor wished it, miss,' said Trim, 'and I must add it is a pleasure for us. Mrs Trim has cooked a meal which she hoped you will enjoy.'

He disappeared and returned presently with vichyssoise soup, and Daisy's small nose wrinkled at its delicious aroma. It tasted good too—this wasn't something out of a tin, it was the real thing, made with cream and eggs and chicken stock nicely mingled with the creamed leeks. It was followed by a perfectly grilled sole, sautéd potatoes and braised celery, and when Trim

offered her white wine she accepted, quite carried away
by the unexpectedness of it all.

'Mrs Trim's special sweet,' murmured Trim, remov-
ing her empty plate and offering a chestnut soufflé with
chocolate cream, 'and I shall serve your coffee in the
drawing-room, Miss Pelham.'

When she hesitated again he added, 'The doctor
hoped that you would keep Belle company for a little
while.'

'Well, just for a short time,' said Daisy, 'and do
please thank Mrs Trim for that delicious meal.'

Belle was delighted to see her and accompanied her
on a tour of the room. There was a lot to see: fine porcelain and silver in their display cabinets and a great
many paintings, mostly portraits. She supposed that
they were of the doctor's ancestors, for several of them
had his dark hair and heavy-lidded eyes, even the suspicion of the smile which made her feel so uneasy.

An hour passed quickly and when the case clock
chimed a tinkling half-hour she bade Belle goodnight
and went into the hall. Should she go to bed without
telling Trim? she wondered. Would he mind if she went
in search of him through the baize door at the end of
the hall? As if in answer to her problem Trim appeared
silently from the dining-room, asked if there was anything she required, wished her goodnight and informed
her in a fatherly way that should the children wish to
get up early either he or Mrs Trim would be about in
the kitchen should they require a drink of milk before
their breakfast.

Daisy thanked him, wished him goodnight and went
to her room. The twins were fast asleep; she bathed in

peace, got into her own deliciously comfortable bed
and closed her eyes. Before she dozed off she wondered what the doctor was doing and whom he might
be with. Some lovely young woman, she thought forlornly, dressed with the same expensive taste as Lady
Thorley. She was too tired to wonder why the thought
made her unhappy.

She was wakened by the twins who had climbed on
to her bed and were whispering into her ear, urging
her to wake up. 'We want to go into the garden with
Belle,' Josh explained.

Daisy sat up in bed, tossing back her mousy curtain
of hair. 'Isn't it a bit early? Wouldn't it be nice if you
got under the eiderdown and I read a bit more of *The
Rose and the Ring*?'

Katie liked the idea but Josh thrust out his lower lip
and shook his head. 'I want to go into the garden...'

'So you shall presently, love, but it's only just after
six o'clock; it isn't even quite light...'

'Belle wants to go too.' He fixed her with a very determined eye. 'We're going home today and she won't
see us again.'

'Oh, I'm sure she will; your uncle often goes to see
you. You stay here with Katie like a good boy and I'll
fetch your book.'

The house was pleasantly warm and the carpet was
soft under her bare feet when she got out of bed and
went in search of the book—a matter of a minute or
so, but when she got back Josh wasn't there.

'Josh says he's going out into the garden,' said Katie.
'I think I'll go too.'

'We'll all go,' said Daisy desperately, 'only give me

time to get some shoes on his feet and his dressing-gown on. Stay there, darling—I promise we'll all go if you do.'

Katie had made a tent of the eiderdown and was prepared to stay. Daisy flew out of the room and down the stairs, guided by the murmur of Josh's voice, to be halted at the bottom step by the doctor's voice. He was leaning over the banisters watching her with interest.

'Good morning, Daisy,' he observed in the mildest of voices. 'A pleasant surprise so early in the day...'

'Oh, be quiet, do,' said Daisy waspishly. 'Josh is going into the garden and he's only in his night-clothes...' It was borne in upon her that she was in a like state and she wasn't wearing sturdy winceyette pyjamas.

The doctor had come down the stairs, wearing a rather splendid dressing-gown and soft slippers. He hadn't been told to be quiet for a very long time and certainly not by a small girl in her nightie; he found it intriguing. He said, with a glance which reassured her that he hadn't even noticed what she was wearing, 'I'll get him out of the kitchen and bring him back to you. Get the pair of them dressed and we'll all go into the garden.'

Daisy was already halfway up the stairs but she turned round to whisper fiercely, 'But aren't you tired? Don't you want to go back to bed?'

'Yes to both questions. Just do as I say, there's a good girl.'

She opened her mouth to tell him that she wasn't his good girl but thought better of it and he went on down the hall to the baize door.

Katie was delighted as Daisy told her of the prospect of a walk in the garden with her uncle. 'I'll dress you in a minute,' declared Daisy, tearing into her clothes, washing her face and cleaning her teeth and tugging a comb through her hair. She looked a fright but at least she was decent… Katie, for once, was only too glad to be dressed too; Daisy was fastening her shoes when the doctor, bearing a tray of tea and two mugs, closely followed by Josh and Belle, appeared silently at the door.

He had them all organised within minutes. The children were to drink their milk and Josh was to get into his clothes as far as he was able, 'And Daisy and I are going to enjoy a cup of tea.'

Belle had got on to the bed beside Katie and since the doctor didn't seem to mind Daisy said nothing but meekly took the cup of tea she was offered and drank it.

'Put on something warm,' advised the doctor, finishing his tea. 'I'll be with you in ten minutes.'

Daisy still said nothing; it was hardly an occasion for aimless conversation and she was feeling shy because of the inadequacies of her nightie. The doctor took his vast person silently away and she set about rearranging Josh's clothes in the right order—jersey back to front, shoes on the wrong feet and childish hair standing up in spiky tufts all over his small head.

She had time to tie her hair back before the doctor returned and they all crept downstairs and, with Belle in close company, out into the garden through the kitchen door. It was chilly with a hint of frost still in the air but the sun had almost risen by now and the birds were singing. No one, thought Daisy, would know that they were in the heart of London, standing in the quietness.

She wasn't allowed to stand for long. The doctor took her arm and urged her along the flag-stoned path between a wide border—herbaceous in the summer? wondered Daisy, being whisked briskly past—and a strip of lawn which took up the whole of the centre of the garden. The path disappeared behind shrubs and ornamental trees, ending in a charming little rustic hut with an arched door and tiny windows on either side of it.

'The witch's house,' explained the doctor as the children tumbled inside. He pushed her gently before him and then followed her so that they were a bit crowded. There were benches built along its walls and he sat her down and then folded his great size into the space beside her. The children had no intention of sitting; they were exploring the little place as they always did, finding plates in a shallow opening in the wall. Everything was taken down, examined and put back again until presently Josh came to stand by Daisy.

'She's a good witch,' he explained; 'she's kind to animals and children and if she casts a spell it's a nice one.'

'She sounds a very good sort of witch; does she have her meals here?'

Josh, carried away on childish imagination and with Katie playing dutiful chorus, went into some detail while the doctor watched Daisy's face. It was alight with interest and the practical suggestions she offered as regards the witch's diet showed that she was entering whole-heartedly into the children's world. He sat back, enjoying himself.

Presently he said, 'We'd better go back for our breakfasts.' So the children put everything neatly back in place and they all went back into the garden, out of the shrubs and the small trees, on to a similar path on the opposite side of the lawn with an identical flower-bed against one high brick wall. The sun was up now but held little warmth and the children danced to and fro with Belle weaving between them.

'You have a very charming garden,' said Daisy, for something to say.

'A bonus in London. The house has been in the family for many years—George the Fourth's time, I believe, and in those days gardens were considered small. Be that as it may, it's secluded and quiet.'

She took the children upstairs to wash their glowing little faces, brush their hair and tidy them for breakfast, a meal they shared with the doctor and their father. Lady Thorley was having hers in bed.

The two children, perched each side of Daisy, ate their meal in an exemplary fashion, calling forth praise from their parent. 'We're going home directly after lunch,' he told them. 'What do you want to do this morning?'

'A ride on the top of a bus,' said Josh, as usual speaking for Katie as well as himself, and when neither gentleman reacted with enthusiasm to his suggestion it was Daisy who said,

'Oh, what a splendid idea. If you tell us which bus to catch and what time we're to be back here...'

She was disappointed that the doctor had made no

offer to go with them. Their father, she guessed, would want to remain with his wife, but surely the doctor could have spared an hour or so...

'There's a sightseeing bus goes from Trafalgar Square—I'll drop you off,' said the doctor casually. 'I won't be able to pick you up when you get back but take a taxi, Daisy.' He glanced at her. 'Have you enough money?'

She flushed. Somehow he had made her sound like a servant.

'I've no idea what it will cost, but I don't expect I have.'

Sir Hugh took out his wallet, found some notes and handed them over. 'That should cover it. If you're short, we can settle with the cab when you get back.'

The two men sat back, looking as though they had settled the matter to their satisfaction, and since the children were getting restless Daisy excused herself and them and took them upstairs to get them ready for their trip. Ten minutes later, without seeing anyone, the three of them left the house. The doctor had said he would give them a lift to the bus, but she hadn't believed him; it shouldn't be too difficult to find a bus stop and get to Trafalgar Square.

He was leaning against the car's gleaming side, obviously waiting for them. Belle was already on the back seat and the children lost no time in joining her; unlike Daisy, they had had no doubt in their minds that if their uncle had said he would do something it would be done.

The doctor opened the car door. 'You didn't believe me, did you?' He sounded mildly mocking as she went pink.

'Well, no. You must have got home very late in the night and you were up early this morning.'

He had got in beside her. 'And how very worthwhile that was,' he observed softly. And she, remembering, blushed.

An episode to be forgotten, she told herself as the three of them sat perched on the top deck of the bus and she pointed out the House of Commons, Westminster Abbey, Buckingham Palace, the Tower of London and all the other sights on the route. The children looked when bidden but like all small children were far more interested in the people on the pavements and the other traffic. Culturally, the trip hadn't been very successful although they had enjoyed every minute of it and at lunch they gave colourful accounts of people they had seen: the policeman, the horse guards, several ambulances, flashing blue lights and racing through the traffic, plenty of policemen on motorbikes, and a small crowd surrounding a man who had fallen down in the street. Their sharp eyes had missed nothing.

'Did you see Buckingham Palace?' asked their father.

'Where's that?' asked Josh.

'Anyway, they enjoyed their morning,' said their mother comfortably.

The doctor had little to say; only when his sister put a low-voiced question to him did Daisy realise that he had been at the hospital. He would be glad to see the back of them, she reflected. She stole a look at him and decided that he looked tired; the twins, as she knew to her cost, could be exhausting and they had begun their day very early.

She repacked their bags after lunch, dressed the children in their outdoor things once more and collected her own possessions while the Thorleys stowed everything in the boot and made their farewells. No mention was made of the doctor returning to Salisbury; he took leave of them cheerfully on his doorstep, his hand on Belle's collar, and his polite, 'It was a pleasure,' was the only answer Daisy got to her thank-you speech.

She got into the car between the twins, telling herself that she never wished to see him again.

Chapter 8

The twins were peevish and inclined to quarrel and Daisy breathed a sigh of relief as Sir Hugh drew up before her home. She bade the twins a brisk goodbye, assuring them that they would see each other again, responded suitably to Sir Hugh's thanks and Lady Thorley's heartfelt gratitude and got out of the car.

'We will keep in touch,' declared Lady Thorley. 'We won't stop now—the twins...'

'I quite understand, Lady Thorley.' Daisy saw ominous signs of temper in the children's small faces and felt sympathy for their mother. They would be a handful by bedtime. She went through the gate and watched the car drive away and then went indoors.

There was no one at home, only Razor, who lifted a welcoming head and went to sleep again. Her mother, said the note on the table, had gone to church and Pamela was spending the day with her best friend and wouldn't be back until eight o'clock. Daisy took her bag upstairs, took her coat off and then made herself a cup of tea and laid the table for supper. Her mother would have had nothing much to eat since Pam hadn't been at home; she poked her nose into the fridge and set about gathering the ingredients for a Spanish omelette.

'You're back,' said Mrs Pelham, letting herself in half an hour later. 'Darling, I couldn't remember when you said you'd be home so I thought I'd go to Evensong. Have you been in long?'

She sniffed the air. 'Something nice for supper? What a dear you are; what would I do without you?'

Over the meal Daisy told her about her weekend; it didn't amount to much when all was said and done and her mother listened eagerly. 'Dr Seymour seems such a kind man; tell me some more about his home—it sounds lovely.'

Pamela came in presently, wanting to talk about her day with her friend and for the moment the doctor and his house were forgotten; only later, as Daisy got ready for bed, she allowed her thoughts to dwell on him.

She didn't see him until the end of the next day. She had been to tea and when she returned to the ward he was there, standing halfway down it talking to his registrar and Sister. His back was towards her, his hands in his pockets, crushing his long white coat, looming head and shoulders above his companions. Daisy paused just inside the door, staring at his vast back; she didn't know why, but she was sure that he was bone-weary although there was no sign of that, and she had a great urge to do something about it—a sen-

sation which welled up inside her and left her feeling
breathless, and what breath she had left her entirely
when he turned his head and looked at her. She knew
what the feeling was then. It was love, catching her un-
awares, and it couldn't have been at a more awkward
or inappropriate time, nor could she have been more
surprised. She wanted to smile with the sheer delight
of it but his look was grave and thoughtful, reminding
her that just for a moment she had imagined herself in
a fool's paradise, so that she looked away and hurried
down the ward to the far end to where she could see
Maisie stuffing the day's dirty laundry into sacks. She
felt terrible; a quiet corner, preferably in the dark with
the door locked, where she could have a good weep in
comfort, would have been just the thing. As it was she
picked up an empty sack and began on the cotsheets.

Maisie didn't pause in her work. 'What's eating
you?' she wanted to know. 'Look as though you've
'ad a nasty dream—white as them sheets, you are.'

'I'm fine,' declared Daisy. 'I've a bit of a headache...'

''Eadaches is useful things sometimes,' said Maisie.
'Make an 'andy excuse. Dr Seymour's back. Looks
tired, 'e does too. All this to-ing and fro-ing don't do
'im no good. Can't think why he wants ter do it—
'e's got 'is nice 'ouse in the close—what more could
a body want?'

'Oh, I didn't know he lived in Salisbury as well as
London.'

'Got a posh 'ouse there too, so I've heard. Not that
I grudge 'im that. Does a lot of good, 'e does.' Maisie
tied the strings of the last sack. 'I think 'e's gone—
good. We'll get rid of this lot and go 'ome.'

Leaving the hospital presently, Daisy peered cautiously around her; there was no sign of the Rolls-Royce, nor its owner. The doctor had parked it behind the hospital and was standing at a ward window, watching her. He grinned tiredly, for she was craning her neck in all directions before getting on to her bike and pedalling way out into the busy street. He had wanted to walk down the ward and take her in his arms but even if that had been possible he was sure that she was still not quite certain of her feelings.

He turned away from the window and dismissed her from his mind.

As for Daisy, she cycled back home, her head in the clouds; it was one thing to find herself in love and quite another thing wondering what to do about it. Common sense dictated that to find work which would take her as far away as possible from the doctor was the thing to do but the very thought of not seeing him again sent such a strong shudder through her person that she wobbled dangerously on her bike. On the other hand, would she be able to bear seeing him at the hospital? Not speaking to him, of course, not even smiling, and probably in the course of time he would marry...

She wheeled her bike through the gate and into the garden shed behind the house and went in to find her mother rolling pastry.

Her, 'Hello, darling,' was cheerful. 'Pasties for supper and the gas bill came this morning, not nearly as much as we expected. I must say life is much easier now that you've got this job. You should be doing something better, I know—perhaps later on...'

Daisy kissed her mother, took off her outdoor things

and gave Razor his supper. She said cheerfully, 'That's great about the gas bill. I'll pay it as I go to work—put it through the door; it'll save postage.'

'Had a nice day, dear?' asked Mrs Pelham.

Daisy gave the answer expected of her and reflected that unless she could find a job as secure with the same wages as she now had she would have to stay at the hospital. She would talk to Pam and see if she would look for a part-time job during the Christmas holidays. If only they could save a little money...

'You're very quiet, love,' observed her mother. 'Perhaps you're tired?'

It was Pamela, while they were washing up the supper things, who asked, 'What's up, Daisy? Is that job awful? Shall I leave at the end of term and get a job? It's so unfair that you should have to keep us going.'

'Don't you dare suggest such a thing—another couple of years and you'll be well on the way to a career and then it'll be your turn. And the job's not bad at all; in fact I quite enjoy it—the children are fun and the nurses are friendly.'

'Yes? All the same, you look different. Are you sorry about Philip?'

'Heavens, no. I liked him but that was all. He and Sister are so exactly suited to each other. I'm hoping to hear any day now that they're engaged.'

Pamela piled the plates neatly. 'All the same, there's something.'

Daisy wiped the bowl and wrung out the dishcloth. 'There's some money to spare—the gas bill's much less than we reckoned. There's the end-of-term disco... would you like something to wear?'

'No—you have it.'

'Shall we take Mother to Salisbury next Saturday and let her choose?'

'Is it enough for a dress?'

'Afraid not—a blouse from Marks and Spencer, or some slippers—hers are worn out...'

'OK,' said Pamela wistfully. 'Do you suppose there'll ever be enough money for us to go into a shop and buy something without looking at the price ticket?'

Daisy had picked up Razor and he lay across her shoulder, purring. 'Well, of course—just give me time to find a millionaire and marry him.'

Pamela laughed with her but she looked at her thoughtfully at the same time; Daisy's laugh had sounded a little hollow.

There was no Maisie when Daisy came to work the next morning. 'It's not like her,' commented Sister. 'I've never known her miss a day. I hope she's not ill—she's not on the phone.'

It was Staff Nurse who said, 'Probably she's overslept or been to a party...'

As the day wore on there was still no sign of her. Towards the late afternoon Sister sought out Daisy.

'I've got Maisie's address—I ought to go and see her myself but Philip's coming this evening.'

Daisy looked at the pretty worried face and said at once, 'I'll go on my way home, Sister. Probably it's nothing to worry about. I've got my bike and it won't take me long.' At Sister's relieved sigh she asked, 'Where does she live?'

It wasn't far out of her way—one of the little streets she passed each day turning off Fisherton Street. 'If

I could ring my mother and tell her that I'll be home later?'

'Yes, yes, of course. Daisy, I'm so grateful.'

Maisie lived in a row of terraced houses at the very end of a narrow street, dwindling into a kind of no man's land of abandoned houses, old sheds and broken-down fences. She leaned her bike against dusty iron railings and thumped a dirty brass knocker.

She had to wait before someone came to the door—a young woman with her hair in pink plastic rollers, in a T-shirt and leggings and with a grubby baby under her arm.

'Good evening,' began Daisy politely and remembered that she had no idea what Maisie's surname was. 'I've called to see Maisie—she does live here?'

'Course she does. Miss Watts. Front room upstairs. 'Aven't seen her all day.'

The narrow hall was dark, so were the stairs. There were three doors on the small dark landing; Daisy knocked on the one facing the street and when no one answered tried the handle. The door opened under her touch and she found herself in a small room, surprisingly light and airy and smelling strongly of furniture polish.

'Maisie?' Daisy crossed the room to the bed along one wall where Maisie was sitting up against her pillows; she looked flushed and ill and took no notice of Daisy. There was a tabby cat curled up beside her and a small, scruffy dog on her feet. The dog growled as Daisy bent over Maisie and bared elderly teeth but Daisy was too concerned at the sight of Maisie to worry about that.

'Maisie,' she said urgently, 'what's the matter? Do you hurt anywhere? Did you fall down?'

Maisie opened her eyes. 'Pain in me chest,' she mumbled. She put out a hand and touched the cat. 'Look after 'em, Daisy...'

A doctor, thought Daisy, or better still get her to hospital where everyone knew her. 'And the animals... they need their suppers,' muttered Maisie.

There was a curtained-off alcove where Maisie had her kitchen; Daisy found cat and dog food kept there, piled it into bowls, filled a dish with water and gave Maisie a drink. 'I'm going to get a doctor,' she told her. 'I must go away for a little while and phone. I'll be back.'

There was a phone box further up the street and she rang the children's ward because she wasn't sure what else to do and since Maisie worked there surely someone would get her into hospital.

Sister was still on duty; Daisy didn't waste words. 'Sister, I'm so glad it's you. Maisie's ill. She has a pain in her chest; she looks awful. What shall I do?'

'Stay with her, Daisy; I'll get an ambulance organised as quickly as I can. Has she had a doctor?'

'No, I don't think so...' She rang off and hurried back, to find Maisie lying exactly as she had left her. The dog and cat had eaten their food and got back beside her, and Daisy rather warily picked up one of Maisie's limp, sweaty hands and found her pulse. It was very rapid and faint and Maisie seemed to be asleep even though from time to time she coughed painfully.

Daisy pulled up a chair, wiped Maisie's hot face with a damp cloth and sat down to wait. Sister would send help but it might take at least ten minutes, perhaps longer than that, before an ambulance arrived. Perhaps she should have dialled 999 first...

The door behind her opened quietly and she turned round; if it was the young woman who had let her in she might know who Maisie's doctor was.

Dr Seymour came hurriedly into the room. 'I was with Sister when you phoned,' he said in his calm voice which instantly soothed her worst fears. 'The ambulance is on its way. Has Maisie a doctor?'

'I don't know. There's a woman downstairs who let me in; she might know.'

'Don't bother. We can sort that out later.' He was bending over Maisie, taking her pulse, talking gently to her and getting a mumbled response.

'You're going to be all right, Maisie,' he assured her with calm matter-of-factness. 'You're going to hospital presently and we'll look after you.'

Maisie opened her eyes and caught at his arm. 'Milly and Whiskers—' she stopped to cough '—I can't leave 'em.'

'I'll take them home with me until you're well again.'

'Promise.' Her eyes sought Daisy. 'You 'eard what 'e said, Daisy? They're all I've got...'

'Don't worry, Maisie; if Dr Seymour says he will look after them, he will. All you have to do is get well again.'

The ambulance came then and after a brief delay while the doctor took the cat and dog out to his car and shut them in Maisie was borne away to hospital. The doctor had gone down with the ambulancemen and presently as she tidied the room and stripped the bed of its bedclothes Daisy heard it drive away. The room needed to be cleaned and there was food in the cupboard which would have to be either given or thrown away and she had better see the woman downstairs and then lock the door.

The doctor came soundlessly into the room. 'Maisie will go to the women's medical ward—virus pneumonia—I've warned them.' He looked round the room. 'We must do better than this when she's well again. Leave it all now, Daisy. I'll see that someone comes in in the morning to clear up. Perhaps you'll be good enough to come with me and give a hand with those animals?'

'My bike's here. And where are they to go?'

'To my house, of course. God knows what Belle will say when she sees them.' He took the key from the door. 'Come along, there's nothing more you can do here.'

He ushered her out on to the landing, locked the door and followed her downstairs, to knock on the nearest door. The young woman opened it, eyeing him with a slow smile. 'Got rid of 'er, 'ave you? Poor cow…'

'Miss Watts,' said the doctor evenly, 'has been taken to hospital; she is a much liked member of the staff there. We're taking her cat and dog with us and will care for them and in the morning someone will come and clear out Miss Watts's room. One more thing—is there someone here capable of riding a bicycle to Wilton? This young lady will be going back there by car later but she'll need the bike in the morning.'

He put a hand in his pocket and took out a note.

'Me 'usband'll do it—give us the address.'

The doctor was writing in his notebook and tore out the page. 'Your husband...he's here?'

A young man came to the door. 'OK, I 'eard it all. I'll ride the bike back—I've 'ad an 'ard day's work too.'

'Perhaps this will compensate for that,' said the doctor, handing over the note and the address. 'It's very good of you and I'm much obliged.'

'A doctor, are you?'

'Yes, indeed I am.'

The man laughed. 'A good idea to keep on the right side of the medics; you never know.'

'Be sure if ever you or yours should need our attention, you shall have the best there is,' said the doctor gravely and bade the pair of them goodnight before ushering Daisy out to the car.

The animals were sitting on a blanket on the back seat, looking utterly forlorn, and the sight of them was just too much for Daisy. Two tears trickled down her cheeks as she sat rigidly staring ahead of her while the doctor drove back into the heart of Salisbury and in through the entrance to the cathedral close. She hadn't said a word; she was beyond words—everything had happened so quickly and she seemed no longer capable of doing anything for herself.

The doctor hadn't spoken either although she knew he had seen the tears, but as he drew up before the house he handed her a beautifully laundered handkerchief, and waited while she mopped her face. Without looking at her he said in a matter-of-fact voice, 'Will you carry the cat? We'll take them straight to the kitchen and see if Mrs Trump can find them some food; Maisie has obviously cared for them but I suspect that she hasn't felt up to feeding them since she fell ill.'

Daisy said in a watery voice, 'I gave them something—Maisie was so worried about them.'

'Very sensible.' His manner was nicely detached and the brief glance he gave her was somehow reassuring. Perhaps she didn't look quite as frightful as she felt.

He got out of the car, opened her door and reached for the cat. It wriggled half-heartedly as Daisy took it in her arms and the dog, tucked under the doctor's arm, made no sound although it quivered. 'Poor little beast,' said the doctor and fished in his pocket for his keys.

His housekeeper came through the baize door as they went in and he said at once, 'Good evening, Mrs Trump. We have two lodgers to keep Belle company for a few days. Their owner is ill.'

Mrs Trump's sharp nose quivered but she said in the mildest of voices, 'I dare say they'll want a bite to eat, sir...?'

She glanced at Daisy, standing tidily beside the doctor, and he said, 'And this is Miss Daisy Pelham whose sensible help led to the patient being admitted to the hospital.' He swept Daisy forward, a great arm on her shoulders. 'Daisy, this is Mrs Trump, my housekeeper and long-standing friend.'

Daisy offered a hand and smiled and Mrs Trump smiled back, shook the hand firmly and asked, 'What about your dinner, sir?'

'Oh—stretch it for two if you can, Mrs Trump. Miss Pelham will be dining here before I take her home.'

A piece of high-handedness which Daisy had her mouth open to censure, to be stopped by his casually friendly, 'You will, won't you, Daisy? We must discuss what's to be done with Maisie. You shall telephone your mother in just a moment.'

He took the cat from her with the remark that he would only be a moment, and went through the baize door followed by his housekeeper, to return almost immediately, which gave her no time to gather together her scattered wits.

'Let me have your jacket.' He unbuttoned it and threw it over a chair before she could speak. 'Now come into the drawing-room and phone your mother.'

His large gentle hand propelled her through the door and into a room which took her breath away. There were tall windows and a door leading to the garden at the back and a wide arch opposite leading to the dining-room at the front of the house. There was a brisk fire burning in a burnished steel grate with a massive sofa on either side of it and a satinwood sofa table behind each of them. The walls were hung with burgundy silk and the ceiling was strapwork. There was a William and Mary winged settee by the window with a tripod table with a piecrust edge beside it and above a hanging cabinet with a delicate lyre pattern. At the other end of the room was a small grand piano, several winged armchairs grouped around a Regency library table and in the corner a wrought-iron stand holding a great bowl of chrysanthemums.

Daisy revolved slowly, taking it all in. 'What a very beautiful room,' she observed. 'Your London house is grand and beautiful too but this is like home...'

'As indeed it is.' He picked up the phone and dialled her home number and handed it to her, walked to the door to let Belle in from the garden and stood there with his back to her.

'Mother,' said Daisy and waited patiently while Mrs Pelham asked a great many agitated questions. 'No, I'm quite all right; Dr Seymour will bring me back presently. Yes, I know a man brought my bike home—I shall need it tomorrow. I'll explain when I get home; I'm quite all right—really. Now bye.' She hung up and the doctor came back from the window and offered her a seat on one of the sofas. He sat down opposite her with Belle's great head on his shoes.

'I'll drive you home when we've had dinner,' he told her. 'I'll take a look at Maisie later on once she has been settled in bed and tomorrow I'll get Dr Walker to look her over. If it is virus pneumonia—and I'm sure that it is—she can have a course of antibiotics and a week or ten days in hospital and then some sick leave. But you must agree with me that some other place must be found for her. That room was terrible.'

'It was spotlessly clean,' said Daisy. 'Bed-sitting rooms cost an awful lot of money, you know.'

He got up and went to a side-table with a tray of drinks on it. 'Will you have a glass of sherry?' He turned to smile at her. 'You look as though you could do with it.'

She felt her cheeks grow hot; she must look awful, hair anyhow and probably a red nose from crying. 'Thank you,' she said primly, and he hid a smile.

'I'll ask around; I'm sure there must be somewhere more suitable than her present room. You don't know if the furniture is hers?'

'No, I don't, but I think perhaps it is, because it was

all so beautifully polished...' She sipped her sherry. 'What about Milly and Whiskers?'

'Oh, they can stay here. Mrs Trump has a heart of gold, Belle will be delighted to mother them and they can enjoy the garden.'

'But you're not always here.' She wished she hadn't said that because he smiled and didn't reply and that made her feel as though she had been nosy. The silence went on for a little too long and she was racking her brains for a suitable remark when Mrs Trump came to tell them that she had put the soup on the table. 'Those two poor creatures are asleep in front of the Aga,' she told them. 'Fair worn out, they are.'

The table was decked with the same elegance as that of his house in London; the doctor seated her, took his own chair at the head of the table and politely offered salt and pepper. They weren't needed; Mrs Trump was quite obviously the kind of cook whose food needed nothing added. The soup, served in Worcester china, was a creamy blend of leeks and potato with a hint of sorrel; Daisy, who cooked very nicely but of necessity dealt with the plainest of food, supped it with delight and wondered what would come next.

The plates were removed and the doctor engaged her in small talk and offered her white wine. Fish or chicken, she decided, agreeing pleasantly that Salisbury was a lovely city. It was roast duck, something she had never tasted before and it was delicious. She had known about the orange sauce but there was a delicious tang to it as well; if ever she had the chance, which wasn't likely, she would ask Mrs Trump what it was...

It was followed by castle puddings, served with a

custard so rich that it must have been made almost entirely from cream. She refused a second helping and said rather shyly, 'That was the most delicious meal I've ever tasted.'

'Mrs Trump is a splendid cook and I must agree with you—what's the food like at the hospital?'

'Really very good—of course, cooking for several hundred people can't be the same as cooking for one, can it?' She thought for a moment. 'Besides, it's cabbage and mince and boiled potatoes, though we do get fish on Fridays and sometimes roast meat.'

She stopped then, afraid that she was boring him. 'If you don't mind I think I should go home…'

The doctor hadn't been bored; he had been sitting there, watching her nice face, listening to her pretty voice and thinking how delightful she looked sitting at his table, but he allowed none of this to show.

'Coffee? We'll have it in the drawing-room, take a quick look at Maisie's animals and then I'll drive you back.'

Daisy had had a long day; her eyelids dropped as she drank her coffee and the doctor bent forward gently and took the cup and saucer from her. She looked exactly right, sitting there in a corner of the sofa. Her small nose shone, the lipstick had long since worn off and her hair needed a good brush; moreover her gentle mouth had dropped very slightly open so that what sounded very like a whispered snore issued from it. Nevertheless her small person had an endearing charm. He touched her shoulder gently and she opened her eyes.

'I went to sleep,' said Daisy prosaically. 'I'm so

sorry—it was the wine and the sherry. Whatever must you think of me?'

She sat up very straight and the doctor decided not to answer that. Instead he said soothingly, 'You must be tired. I'll take you home—are you on duty in the morning?'

'Yes. Please may I see the animals before we go so that I can tell Maisie how well cared-for they are?'

'Of course. We'll go now.'

Milly and Whiskers were curled up in front of the Aga in the kitchen—an apartment which Daisy considered to be every woman's dream. They eyed their visitors warily for a moment but Daisy got down on her knees and stroked their elderly heads and mumbled comfortingly and they closed their eyes again. 'I'll take care of them, don't you worry,' Mrs Trump assured her.

The doctor drove Daisy back in a comfortable silence, got out and knocked on her door, assured Mrs Pelham that there was nothing to worry about and wished Daisy goodnight.

She put out her hand. 'You've been awfully kind, sir. Thank you for my dinner and for seeing to the animals. Will Maisie be all right?'

'Yes. I can promise you that. Goodnight, Daisy.'

He had gone and she went indoors and sleepily told her mother and Pamela what had happened. It was Pamela who told her to go to bed. 'You're tired out, aren't you, Daisy? And I suppose you've got to go to work in the morning?' When Daisy nodded she added, 'Do go to bed now—I'll see to laying the table for breakfast and feeding Razor. You would have thought they would have given you a day off...'

'Well, if Maisie's not there there's only me,' said Daisy and went thankfully to her bed.

She went to see Maisie the following morning during her coffee break. Feeling a good deal more self-possessed than on the occasion of her first visit to the women's medical ward, she tapped on Sister's door.

That lady said grudgingly, 'Ah, Daisy. I've been instructed to allow you to visit Maisie whenever it's convenient.' She lowered her head over the papers on her desk. 'She's at the end of the ward.'

Daisy met Mrs Brett halfway down the ward. 'And what are you doing here?' demanded her erstwhile colleague.

'Visiting,' said Daisy sweetly and walked past.

Maisie was sitting up in bed, looking a lot better than she had done the evening before. All the same, she was a shadow of her former cheerful self.

'Hello, Maisie,' said Daisy cheerfully, 'you look better already. I may come and see you whenever I have the time. I thought you'd like to know that Milly and Whiskers are fine. Dr Seymour's housekeeper is such a nice person and I'm sure she'll look after them.'

Maisie nodded her head. ''E came ter see me last night. I wasn't feeling too good but 'e said 'e'd look after 'em. What about me room?'

'Dr Seymour told me that he'd see about it so I shouldn't worry about it. Is there anything you want?'

'Me nighties and me 'andbag.'

'I'll get them for you this evening as I go home. Will it be all right if I bring them in the morning?'

'Yes, ducks.'

The unbidden thought crossed Daisy's mind as she

left the ward that it would have been nice to see the doctor, but there was no sign of him. She went back to her work, doing her best to do Maisie's share as well and a little to her surprise getting some willing help from the nurses. All the same she was tired when she finished work for the day and got on her bike. It wasn't until she was knocking on the door of the house where Maisie had been living that she remembered that the doctor had locked the door of her room and probably there wasn't another key. She would have to ask the young woman if there was another one.

There was no need. 'Go on up,' said the young woman wearily, 'the door's open. Any more of you, are there? I don't aim to be opening the door all night.'

Daisy murmured apologetically and went up the stairs and opened Maisie's door. The doctor was there, sitting in one of the chairs, doing nothing.

'Oh,' said Daisy, aware of a rush of feeling at the sight of him. 'I didn't know—that is, Maisie asked me to get her handbag, only when I got here I remembered that I hadn't a key…'

He had got to his feet and took the key out of his pocket. 'I went to see her this afternoon and she told me and since I have the key I thought I'd better come along with it. By the way, Mrs Trump tells me that one of her friends is a widow living in Churchfields Road. She wants to let part of her house; I thought we might go along and see her. Tomorrow evening?'

'Me?'

He was lounging against the back of a shabby arm-chair, watching her. 'I feel certain that you know better than I what kind of a place Maisie would like.'

'Does she know? I mean, will she mind?'

'I suggested that it might be nice for her to move from this place, somewhere where there was a garden for Milly and Whiskers. She'll be in hospital for ten days; if we could get her settled before then she could go there and have some sick leave.' She was surprised when he said unexpectedly, 'How are you managing, Daisy?'

'Me? Oh, fine, thank you; the nurses are being marvellous and I believe there's someone coming to help part-time until Maisie's back.' He nodded and she went on, 'Don't let me keep you; if you'd let me have the key...'

'Anxious to be rid of me?' he said, but he said it kindly and smiled so that she found herself smiling back. 'Pack up whatever she needs and I'll take them back with me.'

She had found a large plastic bag and was collecting things from the chest of drawers; she put in all the things she thought Maisie might want and laid the handbag on top. 'But you haven't got the car here.'

'Ten minutes' walk.' He took the bag from her and opened the door. Locking it behind him, he said, 'I'll be outside tomorrow evening. We'll go in the car for I have an engagement later on. Leave your bike at the hospital—you can come in by bus in the morning?'

'Yes.' She had followed him down the stairs and the young woman poked her head out of a door and demanded to know how many more times they intended coming. 'The rent's paid until the end of the week—I shall let the room unless I get it by Saturday.'

'The furniture is Miss Watts's?'

'Yes, but not the carpet or the lights. Moving out, is she? I shan't be sorry—her and her animals. Don't know why I've put up with them all this time.'

'Someone will come here tomorrow to remove the furniture. Perhaps you would be good enough to be present when that is done. Good evening to you.'

He propelled Daisy out on to the pavement and the door banged shut behind them. 'You're never to come here alone, Daisy,' said the doctor firmly. 'I'll attend to whatever has to be done. Now get on your bike and go home.'

He waited while she unlocked the bicycle. 'Goodnight, Daisy.' His kiss was unexpected so that she almost fell off her bike. She muttered something and pedalled away from him at a furious rate. She heard him laugh as she went.

Chapter 9

Daisy worried about that laugh all the way home. What had there been to laugh about? Did she look comical on a bike? Had she said something silly? With an effort she dismissed it from her mind. His kiss was harder to dismiss but then by the time she had reached her home she had convinced herself that it had been a casual gesture of kindness, rather like patting a dog or stroking a cat. She wheeled her bike into the shed and went in through the kitchen door.

Pamela was at the kitchen table, doing her home-work, and her mother came from the sitting-room as she took off her jacket.

'Darling—you're so late again, I was getting worried.'

'I'll be late for the next few days, until we get some help instead of Maisie, Mother. I had to go to Maisie's room and get something for her.'

'You never went all the way back to the hospital?'

'No, Dr Seymour was there; he took it back for me.'

She saw the pleased speculation on her mother's face and sighed soundlessly; her parent was indulging in daydreams again. Such hopeless ones too.

'What a kind man he is and you see quite a lot of him, don't you, love?'

'No,' said Daisy matter-of-factly, 'only if it's something to do with Maisie. He's asked me to go and look at a room to rent for her—she can't possibly go back to that awful place. I thought I'd go tomorrow after work.'

She wasn't going to mention Dr Seymour again; it would only add fuel to the daydreams.

Pamela was watching her thoughtfully. 'Lady Thorley phoned. She's asked you to go to tea on Saturday. I said you'd give her a ring.'

'Then I'd better phone her now...'

'Your supper's in the oven; I'll have it ready when you've done that.' Her mother peered anxiously at the cottage pie. 'We've had ours.'

'It's Miss Thompson's birthday—we thought we would give her a tea party. I'll come for you about three o'clock,' said Lady Thorley when Daisy duly phoned her. She had taken it for granted that Daisy would go and she agreed readily. It would be nice to see the twins again, and the proposed shopping trip to Salisbury with her mother and Pamela could wait.

She left the ward half an hour later than usual the next day—there was still no help and she had tried her best to do the work of two. Besides, she had gone to see Maisie in her dinner-hour, which had meant gobbling down Monday's mince and carrots and missing the pudding. She was in no mood to go anywhere but she had promised the doctor, and she wasn't a girl to break a promise lightly.

He was standing by the entrance, talking to the senior consultant physician, but they broke off their conversation to watch her cross the hall. Both gentlemen greeted her politely and the other man wandered away, leaving Dr Seymour to urge her through the door and into the car.

'Busy day?' he wanted to know.

'Yes,' said Daisy baldly.

'You've seen Maisie?'

'Yes. She's better, isn't she?'

'Yes. You went in your dinner-hour?'

'Yes.' Daisy felt that her conversation hardly sparkled but she was too tired to bother.

'You're bound to be hungry.' He picked up the car phone. 'Mrs Pelham, I'm just taking Daisy to look at rooms for Maisie—I dare say you know about that?' He was silent for a moment and Daisy wriggled with embarrassment; her mother would be explaining that her dear daughter, while mentioning that she would be late, hadn't said that he would be with her.

Dr Seymour's voice took on the soothing tones so effective with his small patients. 'I'll bring her back in the car, Mrs Pelham, you've no need to worry.'

He put the phone down and started the car without speaking and Daisy looked out of the window and wished that she were anywhere but there.

The drive was a short one; the quiet street he stopped in was lined with neat terraced houses with front gardens and well-kept front doors. He got out of the car and opened her door, remarking easily, 'This looks more like Maisie, doesn't it? We shall see…'

The door was opened the moment he knocked and the plump middle-aged woman said at once, 'Dr Seymour? Mrs Trump told me. Come on in.'

She looked enquiringly at Daisy, and the doctor said, 'This is Miss Pelham, who works with Miss Watts—I thought that perhaps she might know better than I…?'

He smiled gently and Mrs King smiled back. 'Of course.'

She nodded at Daisy in a friendly fashion and led the way into her house. The room they were shown into was exactly right, thought Daisy, and a door at its end led into a small conservatory which opened out on to quite a long garden, well-fenced. There was a gas fire and a very small gas cooker and a washbasin in one corner.

'Before my husband died he was ill for quite a long time, so we had this room specially done for him—there's a shower-room at the end of the hall. I never use it so it could go with the room. She's got her own furniture?'

The doctor had gone to look at the conservatory; obviously he expected Daisy to arrange things. 'Yes, she has. She has a dog and a cat too, both used to living indoors. You wouldn't mind?'

'As long as they don't bother me. A good dog would be quite nice to have—I'm a bit nervous, especially at night.'

'It's a very nice room,' said Daisy. 'I'm not sure if Maisie could afford it…'

'At the hospital, isn't she? Mrs Trump told me what

she earned. Would she consider…?' She paused and then mentioned a sum a good deal less than Daisy had expected.

'I should think she could manage that. Could I let you know tomorrow? I shan't see her until then.'

The doctor didn't turn his head. 'Never mind that, Daisy. Would a month's rent in advance be acceptable?'

Driving back to Wilton presently, Daisy asked, 'Wasn't that a bit high-handed, Dr Seymour? How do you know that Maisie will like the room?'

He said placidly, 'If you were Maisie, would you like the place?'

'Oh, yes…'

'There's your answer.'

He stopped the car outside her home and got out to open her door.

'Thank you for bringing me home,' she told him and opened the gate.

'Your mother asked me if I would like a cup of coffee,' he said at his most placid, giving the knocker a brisk tattoo.

Pamela opened the door. 'Come on in,' she invited; she stood aside to allow him to pass her. 'The coffee's ready and Mother's bursting with curiosity.'

Her mother had got out the best china and there was a plate of mince pies on the table. The doctor took off his jacket and sat down, very much at his ease, answering Mrs Pelham's questions with every appearance of pleasure. Anyone looking at them sitting around the table, thought Daisy, would have considered him to be an old friend of the family.

Presently he got up to go and somehow it was Daisy

who saw him to the door. 'I'll see Maisie in the morning but I'd be glad if you'd visit her if you can spare the time, convince her that she'll have a comfortable home and that it'll be much better for Milly and Whiskers. Once she has agreed I'll arrange to have her furniture moved in.'

'Very well,' said Daisy sedately, anxious to appear detached but willing. It was disconcerting when he patted her on the shoulder in an avuncular manner and observed that she was a good girl before bidding her a brisk goodnight and getting into his car and driving away.

'Such a delightful man,' declared her mother, collecting the coffee-cups. 'Supper's all ready. Do you suppose he enjoyed the mince pies?'

'Well, he ate almost all of them, so he must have done,' said Pamela. 'It's hard to think of him as a well-known man in his own particular field of medicine.'

Daisy turned to stare. 'Whatever makes you say that?' she asked.

'Well, he is, you know. I looked him up in the medical *Who's Who*. He's got a string of letters after his name and there's a whole lot about him.' She peeped at Daisy. 'Aren't you interested?'

'Not really,' said Daisy mendaciously.

Maisie was sitting up in bed looking better when Daisy went to see her during her lunchtime the next day, and there was no need to persuade her to do anything; the doctor had been to see her and everything was what she termed hunky-dory.

'Bless the pair of you,' declared Maisie, 'going to

all that trouble; me and Milly and Whiskers are that grateful. Me own shower too and a bit of garden. I'm ter go 'ome in a week and just take things easy, like. 'Ow are yer getting on, ducks?'

'Just fine, Maisie. We've been promised part-time help for a day or two and the ward isn't busy.'

'Yer looking peaky. Working too 'ard, I'll be bound. P'raps you'll get a bit of an 'oliday when I get back.'

Daisy went back to the ward and started on the endless chores, glad of something to occupy her thoughts. At the end of the day when she went to tell Sister that she was ready to go, that young lady greeted her with the news that she and Philip were engaged. 'I'm going to tell everyone tomorrow morning, but I wanted you to know first, Daisy. Philip and I hope you'll come to our wedding.'

Daisy offered suitable congratulations, admired the diamond ring, hanging on a gold chain round Sister's neck under her uniform, and went off home. She was glad about Philip and Sister Carter; they would make a splendid pair. She must remember to write and congratulate him. It was to be hoped that someone as nice as Sister Carter would take over the ward; surely Dr Seymour would have a say in the matter?

She hadn't seen him that day and she guessed that he was back in London; indeed as she was leaving the hospital at the end of the day the hall porter handed her a letter addressed in an almost unreadable scrawl. It was from the doctor and very brief and to the point. Would she be so good as to go to Maisie's new home and make sure that everything was suitably arranged? It took a few minutes to decipher and it ended as abruptly as it had begun, with his initials.

'Written with the wrong end of a feather and with his eyes shut,' said Daisy to the empty hallway. All the same she tucked the missive safely away until she could put it under her pillow when she went to bed that night.

She could find no fault when she went to Maisie's new home that evening. It had been furnished with care, Maisie's bits and pieces polished, the bed made up. There was nothing for her to do but compliment her new landlady on the care which she had lavished upon her new lodger's room.

'Me and Mrs Trump,' she was told. 'Dr Seymour said as we were to make it as home-like as possible.' She beamed at Daisy. 'He's a real gentleman.'

Daisy had to work on Sunday for there was no one to relieve her but she was free on Saturday and she cycled to Lady Thorley's house in the afternoon. She had taken pains with her face and her hair, telling herself that since it was a birthday tea party it behoved her to make the best of her appearance. It was a pity that Lady Thorley had phoned in the morning to say that the car was being serviced and could she find her own way, but it was dry even if it was cold and she could wear her good shoes… And if at the back of her mind she was hoping that the doctor would be there she wasn't going to admit it.

He wasn't there. She was greeted rapturously by the twins, more soberly by Lady Thorley and their governess and informed that Sir Hugh wouldn't be home until evening. 'And Valentine, of course, is still in London— probably catching up on his social life.'

Despite her disappointment, Daisy enjoyed her afternoon; tea was a splendid meal and the birthday cake was magnificent and she had been led away to look at the presents, the best of which, Miss Thompson assured her, were a bead necklace threaded by Katie and a cardboard box containing Josh's model of Belle in Plasticine. These needed to be admired at some length before Miss Thompson, asked what she would like to do since it was her birthday, diplomatically opted for a rousing game of snakes and ladders.

Daisy, promising to return in the not too distant future, went home a few hours later.

Salisbury was quiet when she went to work the next morning—a few people either going or coming from church, an infrequent car and several workers like herself. Even the hospital seemed quiet as she went up to the ward after changing into her pink pinny in the cloakroom used by the orderlies.

It wasn't quiet in the ward, of course. Most of the children were convalescing and making a fine racket, and since Sister had a weekend off and Staff Nurse was in charge they were noisier than usual; Staff Nurse was a splendid nurse but she lacked Sister's authority.

Daisy plunged into her day's routine, buoyed up by the news that there would be help in the morning. During her lunch break she went along to see Maisie and found her sitting by her bed, looking almost her old self.

'Can't wait ter get out of 'ere,' she confided to Daisy. 'The nurses are all right but that Sister—she's an old dragon. I wouldn't work 'ere for a fortune.'

'Well, you won't have to,' said Daisy. 'Sister can't

wait to get you back.' She glanced at her watch. 'I must go—we all miss you, Maisie, really we do.'

Maisie looked pleased. 'Go on with you. Mrs Trump came ter see me yesterday—nice of 'er, weren't it? Thought I might like ter know about Milly and Whiskers. Very 'appy, she says.' She added wistfully, 'I'll be glad ter see them…'

'They'll be glad to see you too, Maisie, and it won't be long now. You're all going to be so happy…'

The children were unruly that afternoon; mothers and fathers had come and they had become over-excited. They were allowed to visit any day they liked, of course, but the fathers were mostly at work and most of the mothers had other children or jobs, so Sunday afternoons saw an influx of mothers and fathers who stayed for the children's tea, so that they wouldn't eat, because they were excited or, worse, ate too much of the various biscuits and sweets which should have been handed over and very often weren't.

The last reluctant parent was ushered out finally and the nurses set about getting the children washed and ready for supper and bedtime, Daisy trotting to and fro with clean sheets, collecting up used bedlinen and bagging it, carrying mugs and plates out to the kitchen where an impatient maid, doing double duty since it was a Sunday, waited to wash up.

Stacking mugs and wiping down trays, Daisy became aware of a distant rumble. It wasn't thunder; it sounded like a vast crowd all talking at once but a long way off.

'Kids on the rampage,' said the maid crossly when

Daisy mentioned it. And presently when the noise got nearer Staff Nurse made the same remark.

'A protest march or a rally, I dare say, marching through the town. Daisy, will you go down to the dispensary and get that Dettol Sister ordered? It didn't come up this morning and Night Nurse might need some during the night.' She picked up her pen to start the report. 'I've only got Nurse Stevens on and she's still feeding baby Price.'

Daisy made her way down two flights of stairs and along several corridors; most of the wards were at the back of the hospital and it was suppertime, early on Sundays. There was a pleasant smell of cooking as she nipped along, and her small nose twitched. As usual she had cut short her midday meal in order to have more time to spend with Maisie and now she was empty.

The dispenser on duty was on the point of going home and grumbled a good deal as he handed over the bottle. 'I don't know what this place is coming to,' he observed to no one in particular so that Daisy felt it unnecessary to answer him. She bade him goodnight and started on her way back.

It would be quicker if she used the main staircase from the entrance hall—strictly forbidden but there was no one around and it would save quite a few corridors. She reached the entrance hall, aware that the noise of a lot of people was growing louder by the minute; they sounded rather out of hand too. It was to be hoped that they would go past the hospital quickly.

She had her foot on the bottom stair when she realised that they weren't going past; the shouts and yells were very close now—they must be in the forecourt. Even as she thought it the double doors were flung open and a dozen or more youths came through them. They were laughing and shouting and ripe for mischief and she looked towards the porter's lodge. There was always someone on duty there; they could telephone for help—get the police…

It was apparent to her after a moment that there wasn't anyone there. The corridors on either side of her were empty, the rooms which led out of them would be empty too—the consultant's room, Matron's office, the hospital secretary's, and on the other side the committee room which took up almost all of one side of the corridor.

The youths had hesitated at the sight of her but now they were dribbling in, two and three at a time. Some of them had what looked to her like clubs and one of them, bolder than the others, was chipping the bust of a long-dead consultant of the hospital; he was the first in a row and Daisy felt sick at the idea of the damage he could cause. He had a knife; she shook with fright—she was terrified of knives. Her mouth had gone dry too and she clasped her hands in front of her to stop them trembling; all the same she stayed where she was.

'Go away at once,' she called in a voice which wobbled alarmingly; 'this is a hospital…'

The hooligans hooted with raucous laughter. 'An' you're the matron?' yelled someone. 'Try and stop us…' Those behind surged forward and the leaders came nearer, taking a swipe at a second bust, this time of the hospital's founder, as they did so.

Daisy had put the Dettol bottle down when she had

turned to see what the commotion was; now she picked it up and held it clasped in both hands in front of her. It wasn't exactly a weapon but if she threw it… First she tried again; rage had swallowed at least part of her fear. 'Get out,' she bawled, 'you louts. The police will be here any moment now.'

This was greeted by jeers and bad language, a good deal of which she didn't understand, which was a good thing, although she had an idea that it was unprintable.

The lout who had been swiping at the marble busts edged nearer and her shaking hands tightened on the bottle…

A great arm encircled her waist and lifted her gently, to push her with equal gentleness behind Dr Seymour's vast back.

'Just in time,' said the doctor placidly. 'I do believe you were going to waste a bottle of Dettol.'

Daisy got her breath back. 'Valentine,' she muttered before she had stopped to think, and heaven alone knew what she might have said next if he hadn't said in a quite ordinary voice,

'Get help, my darling, and ring the police, just in case they don't already know…'

'They'll kill you,' said Daisy into the fine cloth of his jacket. 'I'm not going to leave you…'

'Do as I say, Daisy, run along.'

There was no gainsaying that voice; she turned and flew up the staircase and tore along the corridor until she reached the men's medical ward.

The charge nurse at the other end of the long ward looked up as she raced down its length.

'Mr Soames—there's a mob of hooligans in the hall;

Dr Seymour's there, he needs help, and I'm to ring the police.'

Mr Soames was already walking up the ward, beckoning two male nurses to follow as he went. 'Ring the police then the porter's room and the housemen's flat. The numbers are by the phone on my desk.' He paused for a moment by a student nurse. 'You're in charge until we get back.'

He opened the ward doors and Daisy heard Dr Seymour's voice quite clearly. It wasn't particularly loud but it sounded authoritative and very calm. She went into Mr Soames's office and dialled 999. The police were already on their way, she was told; she hung up and dialled the porters' room and then the housemen's flat and a few minutes later heard feet thundering down the staircase. She still had the bottle of Dettol with her; she picked it up and carried it carefully up another flight of stairs to the children's ward and gave it to Staff Nurse.

'There's a frightful racket going on,' said that young lady, 'and you've been ages, Daisy.'

'Some hooligans broke into the hospital, Staff.' For the life of her she couldn't say any more, only stared at the other girl from a white face.

'A cup of tea,' said Staff. 'Sit yourself down. Did you get caught up in it?' When she nodded Staff added, 'A good thing it's time for you to go off duty.' She fetched the tea. 'Sit there for a bit—it must have been upsetting.' She eyed Daisy's ashen face and decided that she would wait to find out what was happening. There was a good deal of noise now, loud men's voices and heavy feet tramping around, luckily not so close as to disturb the children.

Daisy drank her tea. Everything had happened rather fast and she was terribly bewildered, but one thing she remembered with clarity. She had called the doctor Valentine and he had called her his darling. 'Get help, my darling,' he had said, but perhaps he had said that just to make her listen…

The phone rang and she supposed she had better answer it.

'Stay where you are until I come for you,' said the doctor in her ear. 'In the children's ward?'

'Yes.' She suddenly wanted to cry.

The phone went dead and she sat down again and presently Staff Nurse came back to write the report.

'Feeling better?' she asked kindly. 'Dr Cowie was in the ward just now; he said they'd cleared those louts away. You were very brave, Daisy, standing there all alone, telling them to go away. Weren't you scared?'

'I've never been so frightened in my life before; I think I would have run away if Dr Seymour hadn't come.'

'He said you were magnificent.' Staff glanced at Daisy's face. 'If it had been me I'd have cut and run.'

'I was too frightened,' said Daisy. 'I don't suppose I could have moved.' She smiled at the other girl, who reflected that Sister had been right—Daisy wasn't the usual sort of orderly; she wondered why she had taken the job…

The door opened and Dr Seymour walked in unhurriedly. 'Get your coat,' he told Daisy, 'I'll take you home. Feel all right now?'

Daisy frowned; he had made it sound as though she had had the screaming hysterics. 'I'm perfectly all right, thank you, Doctor.'

'Good. I'll be in the entrance hall in five minutes.' He held the door open for her and she bade Staff Nurse goodnight and went past him, her chin lifted.

In the car she asked presently, 'What happened to all those hooligans?'

'The police carted some of them off, the rest ran away. Very few of them were locals.'

His voice was casual; he couldn't have been more impersonal. She felt too discouraged to say anything else. As he stopped outside her home she made haste to get out, to be stopped by his hand on the door. 'Not so fast. I'm coming in.'

'There's no need,' she assured him but that was a waste of breath; he got out, opened her door and urged her through the gate as the door opened.

Before she could say a word her mother said, 'Oh, my dear—are you all right? What a dreadful thing to have happened—were you very frightened? And how can I ever thank you, Dr Seymour, for rescuing her as you did?'

'Hardly a rescue, Mrs Pelham.' He had pushed Daisy gently ahead of him so that they were all standing in the little hall. 'I happened to be passing—I'm sure Daisy would have coped very well on her own.'

'Well, of course, she's a very sensible girl,' agreed her mother. 'Nevertheless, I do thank you.' She hesitated. 'I dare say you're a busy man, but if you would like a cup of coffee...?'

'That would be delightful.'

Daisy hadn't said a word; he still had a hand on her shoulder, and now he turned her round, unbuttoned her coat and took it off, pulled the gloves from her hands and propelled her briskly into the kitchen where he sat her down in a chair, took a chair himself and fell into cheerful conversation with Pamela. It wasn't until Mrs Pelham had handed round the coffee and offered cake that Pamela asked, 'Were you scared, Daisy?'

Daisy put her cup down carefully, burst into tears and darted out of the room. Mrs Pelham looked alarmed, Pamela surprised and the doctor undisturbed.

'No, Mrs Pelham, leave her alone for a while. She'll be all right but she had a nasty shock and the reaction has set in. She was remarkably brave—you would have been very proud of her. Tomorrow she'll be quite herself again; bed is the best place for her now and perhaps a warm drink before she sleeps.' He added kindly, 'You mustn't worry.'

Mrs Pelham said faintly, 'She's such a dear girl...'

'Indeed she is,' agreed the doctor, and something in his voice made Pamela stare at him.

'Are you in love with her?' she asked, and ignored her mother's shocked indrawn breath.

'Oh, yes,' said the doctor blandly and smiled at Pamela. 'I must go. The coffee was delicious, Mrs Pelham.' He said his goodbyes and Pamela went to the door with him.

'I won't tell,' she told him. He smiled then and dropped a kiss on her cheek before he went away.

He had been quite right, of course; Daisy slept like a baby all night, ate her breakfast and cycled to work, quite restored to her normal sensible self. She felt

ashamed of her outburst in front of the doctor and as
soon as she saw him she would apologise. It was a great
pity that she had called him Valentine to his face like
that, but he would surely realise that she had been upset
at the time. She rehearsed a neat little speech as she
cycled and presented herself in the ward nicely primed.

It wasn't until the end of the day that Sister mentioned in Daisy's hearing that he had gone to Holland.
'Lectures or something,' she explained to Staff Nurse.
'He does get around, doesn't he? I should have loved
to see him telling those louts where they could go…'

Daisy, collecting the sheets and listening with both
ears, wondered forlornly if she would see him again.

Sooner than she expected. It was two days later
as she was collecting the children's mugs after their
morning milk that one of the nurses told her that she
was wanted in Sister's office. Daisy put down her tray,
twitched her pink pinny into neatness and knocked on
the office door, and when there was no answer poked
her head round it. Her eyes met Dr Seymour's steady
gaze and since she could hardly withdraw without saying something she said, 'Oh, I'm sorry, sir, I was told
to come here but Sister isn't…' She tailed off, not sure
what to say next, anxious to be gone even though her
heart was beating a tattoo at the sight of him.

'No, she isn't,' agreed the doctor calmly. 'Come in,
Daisy.'

He got up from the chair behind the desk, closed the
door behind her. 'Do sit down,' he said and when she
shook her head came to stand so close to her that all
she could see was an expanse of dark grey superfine
wool waistcoat. She counted the buttons and lifted her

gaze sufficiently to study his tie—a very fine one, silk and vaguely striped. Italian, no doubt. Higher than that she refused to look while she strove to remember the speech she had rehearsed so carefully.

'I had no idea,' said the doctor at last, 'that courting a young lady could be fraught with so many difficulties. Why is it, I wonder, that I'm able to diagnose acute anterior poliomyelitis, measles, hydrocephalus, intersusception, inflamed adenoids, the common cold… and yet I find myself unable to find the right words?'

He was smiling down at her and she said with a little gasp, 'Oh, do be careful what you're saying; you might regret it—I dare say you're very tired or something.' She added urgently, 'I'm the orderly…'

His laughter rumbled. 'Oh, no, you're not, you're Daisy, my Daisy, the most darling girl in the world and so hard to pin down. I'm in love with you, my darling, have been since the first moment I set eyes on you…'

She looked up into his face then. 'But you never…' she began.

'You'd made up your mind that we didn't like each other, hadn't you? You are, my dearest heart, pigheaded at times.' He made that sound like a compliment. 'It seemed that I needed to be circumspect.' He wrapped great arms around her. 'You called me Valentine,' he reminded her, 'and you wanted to stay with me. You looked at me with those lovely grey eyes and I knew then that whatever you said it would make no difference, that you loved me too.'

'But I'm an…' began Daisy, and then added, 'Yes, I do love you.'

She didn't finish because he kissed her then. Presently he said, 'You'll marry me, my little love? And soon.'

She lifted her face from his shoulder. 'I have to give a week's notice.'

'Rubbish. I'll deal with that at once.'

'But you can't...'

'Oh, yes, I can and I will. You'll leave this evening.' He kissed her gently, 'My love, leave everything to me.'

She smiled mistily. 'I must go, Valentine—the milk-mugs...'

He kissed her once more and opened the door for her. 'I can't believe it's true,' she told him. 'What will everyone say?'

He caught her hand and held it for a moment. 'We'll ask them at our wedding. I'll be waiting outside for you this evening, my darling.' He smiled. 'The end of my waiting.'

Daisy nodded, her head full of glimpses of a delightful future. She stood on tiptoe and kissed his cheek and whisked herself away, back to her tray of mugs. But not for long.

* * * * *

THE AWAKENED HEART

Chapter 1

The dull October afternoon was fast becoming a damp evening, its drizzling rain soaking those hurrying home from work. The pavements were crowded; the whole-sale dress shops, the shabby second-hand-furniture emporiums, the small businesses carried on behind dirty shop windows were all closing for the day. There were still one or two street barrows doing a desultory trade, but the street, overshadowed by the great bulk of St Agnes's hospital, in an hour or so's time would be almost empty. Just at the moment it was alive with those intent on getting home, with the exception of one person: a tall girl, standing still, a look of deep concen-tration on her face, oblivious of the impatient jostling her splendid person was receiving from passers-by.

Unnoticed by those jostling her, she was none the less attracting the attention of a man standing at the

window of the committee-room of the hospital overlooking the street. He watched her for several minutes,
at first idly and then with a faint frown, and presently,
since he had nothing better to do for the moment, he
made his way out of the hospital across the forecourt
and into the street.

The girl was on the opposite pavement and he
crossed the road without haste, a giant of a man with
wide shoulders, making light of the crowds around
him. His 'Can I be of help?' was asked in a quiet, deep
voice, and the girl looked at him with relief.

'So silly,' she said in a matter-of-fact voice. 'The
heel of my shoe is wedged in a gutter and my hands
are full. If you would be so kind as to hold these...'

She handed him two plastic shopping-bags. 'They're
lace-ups,' she explained. 'I can't get my foot out.'

The size of him had caused passers-by to make a
little detour around them. He handed back the bags.
'Allow me?' he begged her and crouched down, un-
laced her shoe, and when she had got her foot out of
it carefully worked the heel free, held it while she put
her foot back in, and tied the laces tidily.

She thanked him then, smiling up into his handsome face, to be taken aback by the frosty blue of his
eyes and his air of cool detachment, rather as though
he had been called upon to do something which he had
found tiresome. Well, perhaps it had been tiresome, but
surely he didn't have to look at her like that? He was
smiling now too, a small smile which just touched his
firm mouth and gave her the nasty feeling that he knew
just what she was thinking. She removed the smile,
flashed him a look from beautiful dark eyes, wished

him goodbye, and joined the hurrying crowd around her. He had ruffled her feelings, although she wasn't sure why. She dismissed him from her mind and turned into a side-street lined with old-fashioned houses with basements guarded by iron railings badly in need of paint; the houses were slightly down at heel too and the variety of curtains at their windows bore testimony to the fact that subletting was the norm.

Halfway down the street she mounted the steps of a house rather better kept than its neighbours and unlocked the door. The hall was narrow and rather dark and redolent of several kinds of cooking. The girl wrinkled her beautiful nose and started up the stairs, to be stopped by a voice from a nearby room.

'Is that you, Sister Blount? There was a phone call for you...'

A middle-aged face, crowned by a youthful blonde wig, appeared round the door. 'Your dear mother, wishing to speak to you. I was so bold as to tell her that you would be home at six o'clock.'

The girl paused on the stairs. 'Thank you, Miss Phipps. I'll phone as soon as I've been to my room.'

Miss Phipps frowned and then decided to be playfully rebuking. 'Your flatlet, Sister, dear. I flatter myself that my tenants are worthy of something better than bed-sitting-rooms.'

The girl murmured and smiled and went up two flights of stairs to the top floor and unlocked the only door on the small landing. It was an attic room with the advantage of a window overlooking the street as well as a smaller one which gave a depressing view of back yards and strings of washing, but there was a

tree by it where sparrows sat, waiting for the crumbs
on the window sill. It had a wash-basin in one corner
and a small gas stove in an alcove by the blocked-up
fireplace. There was a small gas fire too, and these,
according to Miss Phipps, added up to mod cons and
a flatlet. The bathroom was shared too by the two flat-
lets on the floor below, but since she was on night duty
and everyone else worked during the day that was no
problem. She dumped her shopping on the small table
under the window, took off her coat, kicked off her
shoes, stuck her feet into slippers and bent to pick up
the small tabby cat which had uncurled itself from the
end of the divan bed against one wall.

'Mabel, hello. I'll be back in a moment to get your
supper…'

The phone was in the hall and to hold a private conversation on it was impossible, for Miss Phipps rarely
shut her door. She fed the machine some ten-pence
pieces and dialled her home.

'Sophie?' her mother's voice answered at once. 'Darling, it isn't anything important; I just wanted to know
how you were and when you're coming home for a
day or two.'

'I was coming at the end of the week, but Sister Symonds is ill again. She should be back by the end of
next week, though, and I'll take two lots of nights off
at once—almost a week…'

'Oh, good. Let us know which train and someone
will pick you up at the station. You're busy?'

'Yes, off and on—not too bad.' Sophie always said
that. She was always busy; Casualty and the accident
room took no account of time of day or night. She knew

that her mother thought of her as sitting for a great part of the night at the tidy desk, giving advice and from time to time checking on a more serious case, and Sophie hadn't enlightened her. On really busy nights she hardly saw her desk at all, but, sleeves rolled up and plastic apron tied around her slim waist, she worked wherever she was most needed.

'Is that Miss Phipps listening?'

'Of course…'

'What would happen if you brought a man back for supper?' Her mother chuckled.

'When do I ever get the time?' asked Sophie and allowed her thoughts to dwell just for a moment on the man with the cold blue eyes. The sight of her flatlet would trigger off the little smile; she had no doubt of that. Probably he had never seen anything like it in his life.

They didn't talk for long; conversation wasn't easy with Miss Phipps's wig just visible in the crack of her door. Sophie hung up and went upstairs, fed Mabel and opened the window which gave on to a railed-off ledge so that the little beast could air herself, and put away her shopping. What with one thing and another, there was barely time for her to get a meal before she went on duty. She made a pot of tea, opened a tin of beans, poached an egg, and did her face and hair again. Her face, she reflected, staring at it in the old-fashioned looking-glass on the wall above the basin, looked tired. 'I shall have wrinkles and lines before I know where I am,' said Sophie to Mabel, watching her from the bed.

Nonsense, of course; she was blessed with a lovely face: wide dark eyes, a delightful nose above a gentle, generous mouth, and long, curling lashes as dark as her hair, long and thick and worn in a complicated arrangement which took quite a time to do but which stayed tidy however busy she was.

She stooped to drop a kiss on the cat's head, picked up her roomy shoulder-bag, and let herself out of the room, a tall girl with a splendid figure and beautiful legs.

Her flatlet might lack the refinements of home, but it was only five minutes' walk from the hospital. She crossed the courtyard with five minutes to spare, watched, if she did but know, by the man who had retrieved her shoe for her—in the committee-room again, exchanging a desultory conversation with those of his colleagues who were lingering after their meeting. To-morrow would be a busy day, for he had come over to England especially to operate on a cerebral tumour; brain surgery was something on which he was an acknowledged expert, so that a good deal of his work was international. Already famous in his own country, he was fast attaining the highest rung of the ladder.

He stood now, looking from the window, studying Sophie's splendid person as she crossed the forecourt.

'Who is that?' he asked Dr Wells, the anaesthetist who would be working with him in the morning and an old friend.

'That's our Sophie, Night Sister in Casualty and the accident room, worth her not inconsiderable weight in gold too. Pretty girl…'

They parted company presently and Professor Rijk van Taak ter Wijsma made his way without haste down to the entrance. He was stopped before he reached it by the surgical registrar who was to assist him in the morning, so that they were both deep in talk when the first of the ambulances flashed past on its way to the accident room entrance.

They were still discussing the morning's work when the registrar's bleep interrupted them.

He listened for a minute and said, 'There's a head injury in, Professor—contusion and laceration with evidence of coning. Mr Bellamy had planned a weekend off...'

His companion took his phone from him and dialled a number. 'Hello, John? Rijk here. Peter Small is here with me; they want him in the accident room—there's a head injury just in. As I'm here, shall I take a look? I know you're not on call...' He listened for a moment. 'Good, we'll go along and have a look.'

He gave the phone back. 'You wouldn't mind if I took a look? There might be something I could suggest...'

'That's very good of you, sir; you don't mind?'

'Not in the least.'

The accident room was busy, but then it almost always was. Sophie, with a practised glance at the patient, sent the junior sister to deal with the less urgent cases with the aid of two student nurses, taking the third nurse with her as the paramedics wheeled the patient into an empty cubicle. The casualty officer was already there; while he phoned the registrar they began connecting up the various monitoring tubes and checked the oxygen flow, working methodically and with the sure speed of long practice. All the same, she could see that the man on the stretcher was in a bad way.

She was trying to count an almost imperceptible pulse when she became conscious of someone standing just behind her and then edging her gently to one side while a large, well kept hand gently lifted the dressing on the battered head.

'Tut, tut,' said the professor. 'What do we know, Sister?'

'A fall from a sixth-floor window on to a concrete pavement. Thready pulse, irregular and slow, cerebro-spinal fluid from left ear, epistaxis…'

Her taxing training was standing her in good stead; she answered him promptly and with few words, while a small part of her mind registered the fact that the man beside her had tied her shoelaces for her not two hours since.

What a small world, she reflected, and allowed her-self a second's pleasure at seeing him again. But only a second; she was already busy adjusting tubes and knobs at the registrar's low-voiced instructions.

The two men bent over the unconscious patient while she took a frighteningly high blood-pressure and the casualty officer looked for other injuries and broken bones.

Presently the professor straightened up. 'Anterior fossa—depressed fracture. Let's have an X-ray and get him up to Theatre.' He took a look at Peter Small. 'You agree? There's a good chance…' He glanced at Sophie. 'If you would warn Theatre, Sister? Thank you.'

He gave her a brief look; he didn't recognise her, thought Sophie, but then why should he? She was in uniform now, the old-fashioned dark blue dress and frilly cap which St Agnes's management committee refused to exchange for nylon and paper.

The men went away, leaving her to organise the patient's removal to the theatre block, warn Night Theatre Sister, Intensive Care and the men's surgical ward, and, that done, there was the business of his identity, his address, his family... It was going to be a busy night, Sophie decided, writing and telephoning, dealing with everything and the police, and at the same time keeping an eye on the incoming patients. Nothing too serious from a medical point of view, although bad enough for the owners of sprained ankles, cut heads, fractured arms and legs, but they all needed attention—X-rays, cleaning and stitching and bandaging, and sometimes admitting to a ward.

It was two o'clock in the morning, and she had just wolfed down a sandwich and drunk a reviving mug of tea since there had been no chance of getting down to the canteen, when a girl was brought in, a small toddler screaming her head off in her mother's arms, who thrust her at Sophie. ''Ere, take a look at 'er, will yer? Fell down the stairs, been bawling 'er 'ead off ever since.'

Sophie laid the grubby scrap gently on to one of the couches. 'How long ago was this?'

The woman shrugged. 'Dunno. Me neighbour told me when I got 'ome—nine o'clock, I suppose.'

Sophie was examining the little girl gently. 'She had got out of her bed?'

'Bed? She don't go ter bed till I'm 'ome.'

Sophie sent a nurse to see if she could fetch the casualty officer and, when she found him and he arrived, left the nurse with him and ushered the mother into her office.

'I shall want your name and address and the little girl's name. How was she able to get to the stairs? Is it a high-rise block of flats?' She glanced at the address again. 'At the end of Montrose Street, isn't it?'

'S'right, fifth floor. I leave the door, see, so's me neighbour can take a look at Tracey…'

'She is left alone during the day?'

'Well, off and on, you might say, and sometimes of an evening—just when I go to the pub evenings.'

'Well, shall we see what the doctor says? Perhaps it may be necessary to keep Tracey in the hospital for a day or two.'

'Suits me—driving me mad with that howling, she is.'

Tracey had stopped crying; only an occasional snivel betrayed her misery. Sophie said briskly, 'You'd like her admitted for observation, Dr Wright?' and at the same time bestowed a warning frown on him; Jeff Wright and she had been friends for ages, and he understood the frown.

'Oh, definitely, Sister, if you would arrange it. This is the mother?' He bent an earnest gaze upon the woman, who said at once,

'It ain't my fault. I've got ter 'ave a bit of fun, 'aven't I? Me 'usband left me, see?'

Sophie thought that he might have good reason. The woman was dirty, and although she was wearing make-up and cheap fashionable clothes the child was in a smelly dress and vest and no nappy. 'You may visit when you like,' she told her. 'Would you like to stay until she is settled in?'

'No, thanks. I gotta get some sleep, haven't I?'

She nodded to the child. 'Bye for now, night all.'

'Be an angel and right away get the children's ward,' said Sophie. 'I'll wrap this scrap up in a blanket and take her up—a pity we can't clean her up first, but I can't spare the nurses.'

All the same, she wiped the small grubby face and peeled off the outer layer of garments before cuddling Tracey into a blanket and picking her up carefully. There were no bones broken, luckily, but a great deal of bruising, and in the morning the paediatrician would go over the small body and make sure that no great harm had been done.

She took the lift and got out at the third floor and walked straight into the professor's vast person. He was alone and still in his theatre gear.

'Having a busy night, Sister?' he asked, in a far too cheerful voice for the small hours.

Her 'Yes, sir' was terse, and he smiled.

'Hardly the best of times in which to renew an acquaintance, is it?' He stood on one side so that she might pass. 'We must hope for a more fortunate meeting.'

Sophie hoisted the sleeping toddler a little higher against her shoulder. She was tired and wanted a cup of tea and a chance to sit down for ten minutes; she was certainly not in a mood for polite conversation.

'Unlikely,' she observed crossly. She had gone several steps when she paused and turned to look at him.

'That man—you've operated?'

'Yes; given a modicum of luck and some good nursing, he should recover.'

'Oh, I'm so glad.' She nodded and went on her way, her busy night somehow worth while at the news.

The senior sister, when she came on duty in the morning, was full of complaints. She was on the wrong side of forty and an habitual grumbler; Sophie, listening with inward impatience to peevish criticisms about the weather, breakfast, the rudeness of student nurses and the impossibility of finding the shoes she wanted, choked back a yawn and presently took herself thankfully off duty.

Breakfast was always a cheerful meal, despite the fact that they were all tired; Sophie poured herself a cup of tea, collected a substantial plateful of food, and sat down with the other night sisters. There was quite a tableful, and despite the fact that they were all weary the conversation was lively.

Theatre Sister held the attention of the whole table almost at once. 'We scrubbed at nine o'clock and didn't finish until after two in the morning. There was this super man operating—Professor something or other. He's from Holland—a pal of Mr Bellamy's—and over here to demonstrate some new technique. He made a marvellous job of this poor chap too.'

She beamed round the table, a small waif of a girl with big blue eyes and fair hair. 'He's a smasher—my dears, you should just see him. Enormous and very tall, blue eyes and very fair hair, nicely grey at the sides. He's operating again at ten o'clock and when Sister Tucker heard about him she said she'd scrub...'

There was a ripple of laughter; Sister Tucker was getting on a bit and as theatre superintendent very seldom took a case. 'Bet you wish you were on duty, Gill,' said someone and then, 'What about you, Sophie? Did you see this marvellous man?'

Sophie bit into her toast. 'Yes, he came into the accident room with Peter Small—I believe he's just arrived here.' She took another bite and her companions asked impatiently,

'Well, what's he like? Did you take a good look...?'

'Not really; he's tall and large...' She glanced round her. 'There wasn't much chance...'

'Oh, hard luck, and you're not likely to see him again—Gill's the lucky one.'

'Who's got nights off?' someone asked.

The lucky ones were quick to say, and someone said, 'And you, Sophie? Aren't you due this weekend?'

'Yes, but Ida Symonds is ill again, so I'll have to do her weekend. Never mind, I shall take a whole week when she comes back.' She put up a shapely hand to cover a yawn. 'I'm for bed.'

They left the table in twos and threes and went along to the changing-room and presently went their various ways. The professor, on the point of getting out of the silver-grey Bentley he had parked in the forecourt, watched Sophie come out of the entrance, reach the street and cross over before he got out of the car and made his unhurried way to the theatre, where Sister Tucker awaited him.

Sophie, in her flatlet, making a cup of tea and seeing to Mabel's breakfast, found herself thinking about the professor; she was unwilling to admit it, but she would like to meet him again. Perhaps, she thought guiltily, she had been a bit rude when they had met on her way to the children's ward. And why had he said that he hoped for a more fortunate meeting?

She wasn't a conceited girl, but she knew that she was nice-looking—she was too big to be called pretty and, though she was, she had never thought of herself as beautiful. She never lacked invitations to go out with the house doctors, something she occasionally did, but she was heart-whole and content to stay as she was until the right man came along. Only just lately she had had one or two uneasy twinges about that; she had had several proposals and refused them in the nicest possible way, waiting for the vague and unknown dream man who would sweep her off her feet and leave no room for doubts...

Presently she went to bed with Mabel for company and slept at once, ignoring the good advice offered by her landlady, who considered that a brisk walk before bed was the correct thing to do for those who were on night duty. That she had never been on night duty in her life and had no idea what that entailed was beside the point. Besides, the East End of London was hardly conducive to a walk, especially when there was still a faint drizzle left over from the day before.

Sophie wakened refreshed, took a bath, attended to Mabel, and, still in her dressing-gown, made a pot of tea and sat down by the gas fire to enjoy it. She had taken the first delicious sip when someone knocked at the door.

Sophie put down her cup and muttered crossly at Mabel, who muttered back. Miss Phipps, a deeply suspicious person, collected her rent weekly, and it was Friday. Sophie picked up her purse and opened the door.

Only it wasn't Miss Phipps; it was Professor van Taak ter Wijsma.

She opened her mouth, but before she could utter a squeak he laid a finger upon it.

'Your good landlady,' said the professor in a voice strong enough to be heard by that lady lurking at the bottom of the stairs, 'has kindly allowed me to visit you on a matter of some importance.' As he spoke he pushed her gently back into the room and closed the door behind them both…

'Well,' said Sophie with a good deal of heat, 'what in heaven's name are you doing here? Go away at once.' She remembered that she was still in her dressing-gown, a rather fetching affair in quilted rose-pink satin. 'I'm not dressed…'

'I had noticed, but let me assure you that since I have five sisters girls in dressing-gowns hold no surprises for me.' He added thoughtfully, 'Although I must admit that this one becomes you very well.'

'What's so important?' snapped Sophie. 'I can't imagine what it can be.'

'No, no, how could you?' He spoke soothingly. 'I am going to Liverpool tomorrow and I shall be back on Wednesday. I thought that a drive into the country when you come off duty might do you good—fresh air, you know… I'll have to have you back here by one o'clock and you can go straight to bed.'

He was strolling around the room, looking at everything. 'Why do you live in this terrible room with that even more terrible woman who is your landlady?'

'Because it's close to the hospital and I can't afford

anything better.' She added, 'Oh, do go away. I can't think why you came.'

'Why, to tell you that I will pick you up on Wednesday morning—from here?—and take you for an airing. Your temper will be improved by a peaceful drive.'

She stood in front of him, trying to find the right words, so that she could tell him just what she thought of him, but she couldn't think of them. He said gently, 'I'll be here at half-past nine.' He had picked up Mabel, who had settled her small furry head against his shoulder, purring with pleasure.

Sophie had the outrageous thought that the shoulder would be very nice to lean against; she had the feeling that she was standing in a strong wind and being blown somewhere. She heard herself saying, 'Oh, all right, but I can't think why. And do go; I'm on duty in half an hour...'

'I'll be downstairs waiting for you; we can walk back together. Don't be long, for I think that I shall find Miss Phipps a trying conversationalist.'

He let himself out, leaving her to dress rapidly, do her hair and face, and make suitable arrangements for Mabel's comfort during the night, and while she did that she thought about the professor. An arrogant type, she told herself, used to having influence and his own way and doubtless having his every whim pandered to. Just because he had happened to be there when she'd needed help with that wretched shoe didn't mean that he could scrape acquaintance with her. 'I shall tell him that I have changed my mind,' she told Mabel. 'There is absolutely no reason why I should go out with him.'

She put the little cat in her basket, picked up her shoulder-bag, and went downstairs.

Miss Phipps, pink-cheeked and wig slightly askew, was talking animatedly to the professor, describing with a wealth of detail just how painful were her bunions. The professor, who had had nothing to do with bunions for years, listened courteously, and gravely advised a visit to her own doctor. Then he bade her an equally courteous goodnight and swept Sophie out into the damp darkness.

'I dislike this road,' he observed, taking her arm.

For some reason his arm worried her. She said, knowing that she was being rude, 'Well, you don't have to live in it, do you?'

His answer brought her up short. 'My poor girl, you should be living in the country—open fields and hedgerows...'

'Well, I do,' she said waspishly. 'My home is in the country.'

'You do not wish to work near your home?' The question was put so casually that she answered without thinking.

'Well, that would be splendid, but it's miles from anywhere. Besides, I can get there easily enough from here.'

He didn't comment on her unconscious contradiction, and since they were already in the forecourt of St Agnes's he made some remark about the hospital and, once inside its doors, bade her a civil goodnight and went away in the direction of the consultant's room.

In the changing-room, full of night sisters getting into their uniforms, she heard Gill's voice from the further end. 'He's been operating for most of the day,' she was saying. 'I dare say he'll have a look at his patients this evening—men's surgical. I shall make an excuse to go down there to borrow something. Kitty—' Kitty was the night sister there '—give me a ring when he does. He's going away tomorrow, did you know?' She addressed her companions at large. 'But he'll be back.'

'How do you know?' someone asked.

'Oh, I phoned Theatre Sister earlier this evening—had a little gossip…'

They all laughed, and although Sophie laughed too she felt a bit guilty, but somehow she couldn't bring herself to tell them about her unexpected visitor that evening, nor the conversation she had had with him. She didn't think anyone would believe her anyway. She wasn't sure if she believed it herself.

Several busy nights brought her to Wednesday morning and the realisation that since she hadn't seen the professor she hadn't been able to refuse to go out with him. 'I shall do so if and when he comes,' she told Mabel, who went on cleaning her whiskers, quite unconcerned.

Sophie had had far too busy a night and she pottered rather grumpily around her room, not sure whether to have her bath first or a soothing cup of tea. She had neither. Miss Phipps, possibly scenting romance, climbed the stairs to tell her that she was wanted on the phone. 'That nice gentleman,' she giggled, 'said I was to get you out of the bath if necessary.' She caught Sophie's fulminating eye and added hastily, 'Just his little joke; gentlemen do like their little jokes…'

Sophie choked back a rude answer and went downstairs, closely followed by her landlady, who, although she went into her room, took care to leave the door slightly open.

'Hello,' said Sophie in her haughtiest voice.

'As cross as two sticks,' answered the professor's placid voice. 'I shall be with you in exactly ten minutes.'

He hung up before she could utter a word. She put the receiver back and the phone rang again and when she picked it up he said, 'If you aren't at the door I shall come up for you. Don't worry, I'll bring Miss Phipps with me as a chaperon.'

Sophie thumped down the receiver once more, ignored Miss Phipps's inquisitive face peering round her door, and took herself back to her room. 'I don't want to go out,' she told Mabel. 'It's the very last thing I want to do.'

All the same, she did things to her face and hair and put on her coat, assured Mabel that she wouldn't be away for long, and went downstairs again with a minute to spare.

The professor was already there, exchanging small talk with Miss Phipps, who gave Sophie an awfully sickening roguish look and said something rather muddled about pretty girls not needing beauty sleep if there was something better to do. Sophie cast her a look of outrage and bade the professor a frosty good morning, leaving him to make his polite goodbyes to her landlady, before she was swept out into the chilly morning and into the Bentley's welcoming warmth.

It was disconcerting when he remained silent, driving the car out of London on the A12 and, once clear of the straggling suburbs, turning off on to a side-road into the Essex countryside, presently turning off again on to an even smaller road, apparently leading to nowhere.

'Feeling better?' he asked her.

'Yes,' said Sophie, and added, 'Thank you.'

'Do you know this part of the world?' His voice was quiet.

'No, at least not the side-roads; it's not as quick…' She stopped just in time.

'I suppose it's quicker for you to turn off at Romford and go through Chipping Ongar?'

She turned to look at him, but he was gazing ahead, his profile calm.

'How did you know where I live?' She had been comfortably somnolent, but now she was wide awake.

'I asked Peter Small; do you mind?'

'Mind? I don't know; I can't think why you should want to know. Were you just being curious?'

'No, no, I never give way to idle curiosity. Now if I'm right there's a nice little pub in the next village— we might get coffee there.'

The pub was charming, clean and rather bare, with not a fruit machine in sight. There was a log fire smouldering in the vast stone fireplace, with an elderly dog stretched out before it, and the landlord, pleased to have custom before the noonday locals arrived, offered a plate of hot buttered toast to devour with the coffee.

Biting into her third slice, Sophie asked, 'Why did you want to know?' Mellowed by the toast and the coffee, she felt strangely friendly towards her companion.

'I'm not sure if you would believe me if I told you.

Shall I say that, despite a rather unsettled start, I feel that we might become friends?'

'What would be the point? I mean, we don't move in the same circles, do we? You live in Holland—don't you?—and I live here. Besides, we don't know anything about each other.'

'Exactly. It behoves us to remedy that, does it not? You have nights off at the weekend? I'll drive you home.'

'Drive me home,' repeated Sophie, parrot-fashion. 'But what am I to say to Mother...?'

'My dear girl, don't tell me that you haven't been taken home by any number of young men...'

'Well, yes, but you're different.'

'Older?' He smiled suddenly and she discovered that she liked him more than she had thought. 'Confess that you feel better, Sophie; you need some male companionship—nothing serious, just a few pleasant hours from time to time. After all, as you said, I live in Holland.'

'Are you married?'

He laughed gently. 'No, Sophie—and you?'

She shook her head and smiled dazzlingly. 'It would be nice to have a casual friend... I'm not sure how I feel. Do we know each other well enough for me to go to sleep on the way back?'

Chapter 2

So Sophie slept, her mouth slightly open, her head loll-ing on the professor's shoulder, to be gently roused at Miss Phipps's door, eased out of the car, still not wholly awake, and ushered into the house.

'Thank you very much,' said Sophie. 'That was a very nice ride.' She stared up at him, her eyes huge in her tired face.

'Is ten o'clock too early for you on Saturday?'

'No. Mabel has to come too...'

'Of course. Sleep well, Sophie.'

He propelled her gently to the stairs and watched her climb them and was in turn watched by Miss Phipps through her half-open door. When he heard Sophie's door shut he wished a slightly flustered Miss Phipps good morning and took himself off.

Sophie told herself that it was a change of scene

which had made her feel so pleased with life. She woke up with the pleasant feeling that something nice had happened. True, the professor had made some rather strange remarks, and perhaps she had said rather more than she had intended, but her memory was a little hazy, for she had been very tired, and there was no use worrying about that now. It would be delightful to be driven home on Saturday...

Casualty was busy when she went on duty that evening, but there was nothing very serious and nothing at all in the accident room; she went to her midnight meal so punctually that various of her friends commented upon it.

'What's happened to you, Sophie?' asked Gill. 'You look as though you've won the pools.'

'Or fallen in love,' said someone from the other side of the table. 'Who is it, Sophie?'

'Neither—I had a good sleep, and it's a quiet night, thank heaven.'

'If you say so,' said Gill. 'I haven't won the pools—something much more exciting. That lovely man is operating at eight o'clock tomorrow morning. I have offered to lay up for Sister Tucker—' there was a burst of laughter '—just so that everything would be ready for him, and I shan't mind if I'm a few minutes late off duty.' She smiled widely. 'Especially if I should happen to bump into him.'

Joan Middleton, in charge of men's medical, the only one of them who was married and therefore not particularly interested, observed in her matter-of-fact way, 'Probably he's married with half a dozen children—he's not all that young, is he?'

'He's not even middle-aged,' said Gill sharply. 'Sophie, you've seen him. He's still quite young—in his thirties, wouldn't you think?'

Sophie looked vague. 'Probably.' She took another piece of toast and reached for the marmalade.

Gill said happily, 'Well, I dare say he falls for little wistful women, like me...' And although Sophie laughed with the rest of them, she didn't feel too sure about that. No, that wouldn't do at all, she reflected. Just because he had taken her for a drive didn't mean that he had any interest in her; indeed, it might be a cunning way of covering his real interest in Gill, who, after all, was exactly the type of girl a man would fall for. Never mind that she was the soul of efficiency in Theatre; once out of uniform, she became helpless, wistful and someone to be cherished. Helplessness and wistfulness didn't sit happily on Sophie.

Sophie saw nothing of the professor for the few nights left before she was due for nights off. She heard a good deal about him, though, for Gill had contrived to waylay him in Theatre before she went off duty and was full of his good looks and charm; moreover, when she went on duty the following night there had been an emergency operation and he was still in Theatre, giving her yet another chance to exchange a few words with him.

'I wonder where he goes for his weekends?' said Gill, looking round the breakfast-table.

Sophie, who could have told her, remained silent; instead she observed that she was off home just as soon as she could get changed, bade everyone goodbye, and took herself off.

She showered and changed into a rather nice multi-check jacket in a dark red with its matching skirt, tucked a cream silk scarf in the neck, stuck her feet into low-heeled black shoes, and, with her face carefully made-up and her hair in its complicated coil, took herself to the long mirror inside the old-fashioned wardrobe and had an appraising look.

'Not too bad,' she remarked to Mabel as she popped her into her travel basket, slung her simple weekend bag over her shoulder, and went down to the front door. It was ten o'clock, and she didn't allow herself to think what she would do if he wasn't there…

He was, sitting in his magnificent car, reading a newspaper. He got out as she opened the door, rather hampered by Miss Phipps, who was quite unnecessarily holding it open for her, bade her good morning, took Mabel, who was grumbling to herself in her basket, wished Miss Phipps good day, and stowed both Sophie and Mabel into his car without further ado. He achieved this with a courteous speed which rather took Sophie's breath, but as he drove away she said severely, 'Good morning, Professor.'

'I suspect that you are put out at my businesslike greeting. That can be improved upon later. I felt it necessary to get away quickly before that tiresome woman began a conversation; I find her exhausting.'

An honest girl, Sophie said at once, 'I'm not put out; at least, I wasn't quite sure that you would be here. As for Miss Phipps, I expect she's lonely.'

'That I find hard to believe; what I find even harder to believe is that you doubted my word.' He glanced sideways at her. 'I told you that I would be outside your lodgings at ten o'clock.'

'I don't think I doubted you,' she said slowly. 'I think I wasn't quite sure why you were giving me a lift—I mean it's out of your way, isn't it?'

'I make a point of seeing as much of the English countryside as possible when I am over here.'

She wasn't sure whether that was a gentle snub or not; in any case she wasn't sure how to answer it, so she made a remark about the weather and he replied suitably and they lapsed into a silence broken only by Mabel's gentle grumbling from the back seat.

Sophie, left to her thoughts, wondered what would be the best thing to do when they arrived at her home. Should she ask him in for coffee or merely thank him for the lift and allow him to go to wherever he was going? She had phoned her mother on the previous evening and told her that she was getting a lift home, but she hadn't said much else...

'Would you like to stop for coffee or do you suppose your mother would be kind enough to have it ready for us?'

It was as though he had known just what she had been thinking. 'I'm sure she will expect us in time for coffee—that is, if you would like to stop...'

'I should like to meet your parents.' He sounded friendly, and she was emboldened to ask, 'How long will you be in England?'

'I shall go back to Holland in a couple of weeks.'

A remark which left her feeling strangely forlorn.

They were clear of the eastern suburbs by now and he turned off on to the road to Chipping Ongar. The countryside was surprisingly rural once they left the main road and when he took a small side-road before they reached that town she said in surprise, 'Oh, you know this part of the country?'

'Only from my map. I find it delightful that one can leave the main roads so easily and get comfortably lost in country lanes.'

'Can't you do that in Holland?'

'Not easily. The country is flat, so that there is always a town or a village on the horizon.' He added to surprise her, 'What do you intend to do with your life, Sophie?'

'Me?' The question was so unexpected that she hadn't a ready answer. 'Well, I've a good job at St Agnes's...'

'No boyfriend, no thought of marriage?'

'No.'

'And it's none of my business...' he laughed. 'Tell me, is it quicker to go through Cooksmill Green or take the road on the left at the next crossroads?'

'If you were on your own it would be best to go through Cooksmill Green, but since I'm here to show you the way go left; there aren't any villages until we get to Shellow Roding.'

It really was rural now, with wide fields on either side of the road bordered by trees and thick hedges, and presently the spire of the village church came into view and the first of the cottages, their ochre or white walls crowned by thatch, thickening into clusters on either side of the green with the church at one side of it, the village pub opposite and a row of small neat shops.

'Charming,' observed the professor and, obedient

to Sophie's instruction, turned the car down a narrow lane beside the church.

Her home was a few hundred yards beyond. The house was old and bore the mark of several periods, its colour-washed walls pierced by a variety of windows. A stone wall, crumbling in places, surrounded the garden, and an open gate to the short drive led them to the front door.

The professor brought the car to a silent halt, and got out to open Sophie's door and reach on to the back seat for Mabel's basket, and at the same time the door opened and Sophie's mother came out to meet them. She was a tall woman, as splendidly built as her daughter, her dark hair streaked with grey, her face still beautiful. Two dogs followed her, a Jack Russell and a whippet, both barking and cruising round Sophie.

'Darling,' said Mrs Blount, 'how lovely to see you.' She gave Sophie a kiss and turned to the professor, smiling.

'Mother, this is Professor van Taak ter Wijsma, who has kindly given me a lift. My mother, Professor.'

'A professor,' observed Mrs Blount. 'I dare say you're frightfully clever?' She smiled at him, liking what she saw. Really, thought Sophie, he had only to smile like that and everyone fell for him. But not me, she added, silently careless of grammar; we're just friends...

Mrs Blount led the way indoors. 'A pity the boys aren't at home; they'd have loved your big motor car.'

'Perhaps another time,' murmured the professor. He somehow conveyed the impression that he knew the entire family well—was an old friend, in fact. Sophie let

Mabel out of her basket, feeling put out, although she had no idea why. There was no time to dwell on that, however. The dogs, Montgomery and Mercury, recognising Mabel as a well established visitor, were intent on a game, and by the time Sophie had quietened them down everyone had settled down in the kitchen, a large, cosy room, warm from the Aga, the vast dresser loaded with a variety of dishes and plates, the large table in its centre ringed by old-fashioned wooden chairs. There was a bowl of apples on it and a plate of scones, and a coffee-pot, equally old-fashioned, sat on the Aga.

'So much warmer in the kitchen,' observed Mrs Blount breezily, 'though if I had known who you were I would have had the best china out in the drawing-room.'

'Professors are ten a penny,' he assured her, 'and this is a delightful room.'

Sophie had taken off her coat and come to sit at the table. 'Do you work together at St Agnes's?' asked her mother.

'Our paths cross from time to time, do they not, Sophie?'

'I'm on night duty,' said Sophie quite unnecessarily. She passed him the scones, and since they were both looking at her she added, 'If there's a case—Professor van Taak ter Wijsma is a brain surgeon.'

'You don't live here, do you?' asked Mrs Blount as she refilled his coffee-mug.

'No, no, my home is normally in Holland, but I travel around a good deal.'

'A pity your father isn't at home, Sophie; he would

have enjoyed meeting Professor van Taak…' She paused. 'I've forgotten the rest of it; I am sorry.'

'Please call me Rijk; it is so much easier. Perhaps I shall have the pleasure of meeting your husband at some time, Mrs Blount.'

'Oh, I do hope so. He's a vet, you know; he has a surgery here in the village and is senior partner at the veterinary centre in Chipping Ongar. He's always busy…'

Sophie drank her coffee, not saying much. The professor had wormed his way into her family with ease, she reflected crossly. It was all very well, all his talk about being friends, but she wasn't going to be rushed into anything, not even the casual friendship he had spoken of.

He got up to go presently, shook Mrs Blount's hand, dropped a casual kiss on Sophie's cheek with the remark that he would call for her on Sunday next week about eight o'clock, and got into his car and drove away. He left Sophie red in the face and speechless and her mother thoughtful.

'What a nice young man,' she remarked artlessly.

'He's not all that young, Mother…'

'Young for a professor, surely. Don't you like him, darling?'

'I hardly know him; he offered me a lift. I believe he's a very good surgeon in his own field.'

Mrs Blount studied her daughter's heightened colour. 'Tom will be home for half-term in a couple of weeks' time; I suppose you won't be able to come while he's here. George and Paul will be here too.'

'I'll do my best—Ida's just back from sick leave; she

might not mind doing my weekend if I do hers on the following week. I'll see what she says and phone you.'

It was lovely being home; she helped her father with the small animals, drove him around to farms needing his help, and helped her mother around the house, catching up on the village gossip with Mrs Broom, who came twice a week to oblige. She was a small round woman who knew everyone's business and passed it on to anyone who would listen, but, since she wasn't malicious, no one minded. It didn't surprise Sophie in the least to hear that the professor had been seen, looked at closely and approved, although she had to squash Mrs Broom's assumption that she and he had a romantic attachment.

'Oh, well,' said Mrs Broom, 'it's early days—you never know.' She added severely, 'Time you was married, Miss Sophie.'

The week passed quickly; the days weren't long enough and now that the evenings were closing in there were delightful hours to spend round the drawing-room fire, reading and talking and just sitting doing nothing at all. She missed the professor, not only his company but the fact that he was close by even though she might not see him for days on end. His suggestion of friendship, which she hadn't taken seriously, became something to be considered. But perhaps he hadn't been serious—hadn't he said 'Nothing serious'? She would, she decided, be a little cool when next they met.

He came just before eight o'clock on Sunday evening and all her plans to be cool were instantly wrecked. He got out of the car and when she opened the door and went to meet him, he flung a great arm around her shoulders and kissed her cheek, and that in full view of her mother and father. She had no chance to express her feelings about that, for his cheerful greeting overrode the indignant words she would have uttered. He was behaving like a family friend of long standing and at the same time combining it with beautiful manners; she could see that her parents were delighted with him.

This is the last time, reflected Sophie, going indoors again. All that nonsense about casual friends and needing male companionship; he's no better than a steamroller.

Anything less like that cumbersome machine would have been hard to imagine. The professor's manners were impeccable and after his unexpected embrace of her person he became the man she imagined him to be: rather quiet, making no attempt to draw attention to himself, and presently, over the coffee Mrs Blount offered, becoming engrossed in a conversation concerning the rearing of farm animals with his host. Sophie drank her coffee too hot and burnt her tongue and pretended to herself that she wasn't listening to his voice, deep and unhurried and somehow soothing. She didn't want to be soothed; she was annoyed.

It was the best part of an hour before the professor asked her if she was ready to leave; she bit back the tart reply that she had been ready ever since he had arrived and, with a murmur about putting Mabel into her basket, took herself out of the room. Five minutes later she reappeared, the imprisoned Mabel in one hand, her shoulder-bag swinging, kissed her parents, and, accompanied by the professor, now bearing the cat basket, went out to the car.

The professor wasn't a man to prolong goodbyes; she had time to wave to her mother and father standing in the porch before the Bentley slipped out of the drive and into the lane.

'Do I detect a coolness? What have I done? I could feel you seething for the last hour.'

'Kissing me like that,' said Sophie peevishly. 'Whatever next?' Before she could elaborate he said smoothly,

'But we are friends, are we not, Sophie? Besides, you looked pleased to see me.'

A truthful girl, she had to admit to that.

'There you are, then,' said the professor and eased a large well shod foot down so that the Bentley sped through the lanes and presently on to the main road.

'When do you have nights off?' he wanted to know.

'Oh, not until Tuesday and Wednesday of next week…'

'I'll take you out some time.'

'That would be very nice,' said Sophie cautiously, 'but don't you have to go back to Holland?'

'Not until the middle of next week. Let us make hay while the sun shines.'

'Your English is very good.'

'So it should be. I had—we all had—an English dragon for a nanny.'

'You have brothers and sisters?'

'Two brothers, five sisters.' He sent the Bentley smoothly round a slow-moving Ford driven by a man in a cloth cap. 'I am the eldest.'

'Like me,' said Sophie. 'What I mean is, like I.'

'We have much in common,' observed the professor. 'What a pity that I have to operate in the morning; we might have had lunch together.'

Sophie felt regret but she said nothing. The professor, she felt, was taking over far too rapidly; they hardly knew each other. She almost jumped out of her seat when he said placidly, 'We have got to get to know each other as quickly as possible.'

She said faintly, 'Oh, do we? Why?'

He didn't answer that but made some trivial remark about their surroundings. He was sometimes a tiresome man, reflected Sophie.

When they arrived at her lodgings he carried Mabel's basket up to her room under the interested eye of Miss Phipps, but he didn't go into it. His goodbye was casually friendly and he said nothing about seeing her again. She worried about that as she got ready for bed, but in the chilly light of morning common sense prevailed. He was just being polite, uttering one of those meaningless remarks which weren't supposed to be taken seriously.

She spent the morning cleaning her room, washing her smalls and buying her household necessities from the corner shop at the end of the street. In the afternoon she washed her hair and did her nails, turned up the gas fire until the room was really warm, made a pot of tea, and sat with Mabel on her lap, reading a novel one of her friends had lent her; but after the first few pages she decided that it was boring her and turned to her own thoughts instead. They didn't bore her at all, for they were of the professor, only brought to an end when she dozed off for a while. Then it was time to get ready to go on duty, give Mabel a final hug and walk the short distance to St Agnes's. It was a horrid evening, damp, dark and chilly, and she hoped as she entered the hospital doors that it would be a quiet night.

It was a busy one; the day sister handed over thankfully, leaving two patients to be admitted and a short line of damp and depressed people with septic fingers, sprained ankles and minor cuts to be dealt with. Sophie saw with satisfaction that she had Staff Nurse Pitt to support her and three students, two of them quite senior, the third a rather timid-looking girl. She'll faint if we get anything really nasty in, thought Sophie, and handed her over to the care of Jean Pitt, who was a motherly soul with a vast patience. She did a swift round of the patients then, making sure that there was nothing that the casualty officer couldn't handle without the need of X-rays or further help. And, the row of small injuries dealt with and Tim Bailey, on duty for the first time, soothed with coffee and left in the office to write up his notes, she sent the nurses in turn to the little kitchen beside the office to have their own coffee. It was early yet and for the moment the place was empty.

Not for long, though; the real work of the night began then with the first of the ambulances; a street accident, a car crash, a small child fallen from an open window—they followed each other in quick succession. It was after two o'clock in the morning when Sophie paused long enough to gobble a sandwich and swallow a mug of coffee. Going to the midnight meal had been out of the question; she had been right about the most junior of the students, who had fainted as they cut the clothes off an elderly woman who had been mugged; she had been beaten and kicked and slashed with a knife, and Sophie, even though she saw such sights frequently, was full of sympathy for the girl; she had been put in one of the empty cubicles with a mug of tea and told to stay there until she felt better, but it had made one pair of hands less...

She went off duty in a blur of tiredness, ate her breakfast without knowing what she was eating, and took herself off to her flatlet, and even Miss Phipps refrained from gossiping, but allowed her to mount the stairs in peace. Once there, it took no time at all to see to Mabel, have her bath and fall into bed.

That night set the pattern for her week. Usually there was a comparatively quiet night from time to time, but each night seemed busier than the last, and at the weekend, always worse than the weekdays, there was no respite, and even with the addition of a young male nurse to take over when one of the student nurses had nights off it was still back-breaking work. On Monday night, after a long session with a cardiac failure, Tim Bailey observed tiredly, 'I don't know how you stick it, Sophie, night after night...'

'I do sometimes wonder myself. But I've nights off—only two, though, because Ida isn't well again.'

'You'll go home?'

She nodded tiredly. 'It will be heaven, sleep and eat and then sleep and eat. What about you?'

'Two more nights, a couple of days off and back to day duty.' He put down his mug. 'And there's the ambulance again...'

Sophie ate her breakfast in a dream, but a happy one; she would go home just as soon as she could throw a few things into a bag and get Mabel into her basket. Lunch—eaten in the warmth of the kitchen—and then bed until suppertime and then bed again. She went out to the entrance in a happy daze, straight into the professor's waistcoat.

'You're still here?' she asked him owlishly. 'I thought you'd gone.'

'No, no.' He urged her into the Bentley. 'I'll drive you home, but first to your room.'

She was too tired to argue; ten minutes later she was in her flatlet, bundling things into her overnight bag, showering and dressing, not bothering with her face or hair, and then hurrying down to the door again in case he had changed his mind and gone. Her beautiful, anxious face, bereft of make-up, had never looked lovelier. The professor schooled his handsome features into placid friendliness, stowed her into the car, settled Mabel on the back seat, and drove away, not forgetting to wave in a civil manner to Miss Phipps.

Sophie tossed her mane of hair, tied with a bit of ribbon, over her shoulder. 'You're very kind,' she muttered. 'I hope I'm not taking you out of your way.' She closed her eyes and slept peacefully for half an hour and woke refreshed to find that they were well on the way to her home.

She said belatedly, 'I told Mother I'd be home about one o'clock.'

'I phoned. Don't fuss, Sophie.'

'Fuss? Fuss? I'm not—anyway, you come along and change all my plans without so much as a by your leave… I'm sorry, I'm truly sorry, I didn't mean a word of that; I'm tired and so I say silly things. I'm so grateful.'

When he didn't answer she said, 'Really I am—don't be annoyed…'

'When you know me better, Sophie, you will know that I seldom get annoyed—angry, impatient… certainly, but I think never any of these with you.' He gave her a brief smile. 'Why have you only two nights off after such a gruelling eight nights?'

'The other night sister—Ida Symonds—is ill again.'

'There is no one to take her place?'

'Not for the moment. The junior night sister on the surgical wards is taking over while I'm away.'

They were almost there when he said casually, 'I'm going back to Holland tomorrow.'

'Not for good?'

Her voice was sharp, and he asked lightly, 'Will you miss me? I hope so.'

She stared out at the wintry countryside. 'Yes.'

'We haven't had that lunch yet, have we? Perhaps we can arrange that when I come again.'

'Will you be back soon?'

'Oh, yes. I have to go to Birmingham and then Leeds and then on to Edinburgh.'

'But not here, in London?'

'Probably.' He sounded vague and she decided that he was just being civil again.

'I expect you'll be glad to be home again?'

'Yes.' He didn't add anything to that, and a few moments later they had reached her home and were greeted by her mother at the door before the car had even stopped, smiling a warm welcome. Not a very satisfactory conversation, reflected Sophie, in fact hardly a conversation at all. She swiftly returned her mother's hug and went indoors with the professor and Mabel's basket hard on her heels. He put the basket down, unbuttoned her coat, took it off, tossed it on to a chair and followed it with his own, and then gave her a gentle shove towards the warmth of the kitchen. Montgomery and Mercury had come to meet them and he let Mabel out of her basket to join them as Mrs Blount set the coffee on the table.

'Will you stay for lunch?' she asked hopefully.

'I would have liked that, but I've still some work to clear up before I return to Holland.'

'You'll be back?' He hid a smile at the look of disappointment on her face.

'Oh, yes, quite soon, I hope.' He glanced at Sophie. 'Sophie is tired out. I won't stay for long, for I'm sure she is longing for her bed.'

He was as good as his word, saying all the right things to his hostess, with the hope that he would see her again before very long, and then bidding Sophie goodbye with the advice that she should sleep the clock round if possible and then get out in the fresh air. 'We are sure to meet when I get back to England,' he observed, and she murmured politely. He hadn't said how long that would be, she thought peevishly, and he need not think that she was at his beck and call every time he felt like her company. She was, of course, overlooking the fact that her company had been a poor thing that morning and if he had expected anything different he must have been very disappointed. All the same, she saw him go with regret.

The two days went in a flash, a comforting medley of eating, sleeping and pottering in the large, rather untidy garden, tying things up, digging things out of the ground before it became hard with frost, and cutting back the roses. By the time she had to return to the hospital she was her old self again, and her mother, looking at her lovely face, wished that the professor had been there to see her daughter. She comforted herself with the thought that he had said that he would be back and it seemed to her that he was a man whose word could be relied on. He and Sophie were only friends at the moment, but given time and opportunity... She sighed. She didn't want her Sophie to be hurt as she had been hurt all those years ago.

It was November now, casting a gloom over the shabby streets around the hospital. Even on a bright summer's day they weren't much to look at; now they were depressing, littered with empty cans of Coca Cola, fish and chip papers and the more lurid pages of the tabloid Press. Sophie, picking her way towards her own front door a few hours before she was due on duty again, thought of the street cleaners who so patiently swept and tidied only to have the same rubbish waiting for them next time they came around. Rather like us, I suppose, she reflected. We get rid of one lot of patients and there's the next lot waiting.

Miss Phipps was hovering as she started up the stairs. 'Had a nice little holiday?' she wanted to know. 'Came back by train, did you?'

Sophie said that yes, she had, and if she didn't hurry she would be late for work, which wasn't quite true, but got her safely up the rest of the stairs and to her room, where she released Mabel, fed her, made herself a cup of tea, and loaded her shoulder-bag with everything she might need during the night. She seldom had the chance to open it, but it was nice to think that everything was there.

The accident room was quiet when she went on duty, but Casualty was still teeming with patients. She took over from the day sister, ran her eye down the list of patients already seen, checked with her Staff and phoned for Tim Bailey to come as soon as possible and cast his eye over what she suspected was a Pott's fracture, and began on the task of applying dressings to the patients who needed them.

Tim arrived five minutes later. 'I've seen this lot,' he said snappily. 'They only need dressings and injections; surely you—?'

'Yes, I know and of course we'll see to those… This man's just come in—I think he's a Pott's, and if you say so I'll get him to X-ray if you'd like to sign the form.'

She gave him a charming smile and she had sounded almost motherly, so that he laughed. 'Sorry—I didn't mean to snap. Let's look at this chap.'

She had been right; he signed the form and told her, 'Give me a ring and I'll put on a plaster, but give me time to eat my dinner, will you?'

'You'll have time for two dinners by the time I've got hold of X-ray; it's Miss Short and she is always as cross as two sticks.'

The man with the Pott's fracture was followed by more broken bones, a stab wound and a crushed hand; a normal night, reflected Sophie, going sleepily to her bed, and so were the ensuing nights, including the usual Saturday night's spate of street fights and road accidents. The following week bid fair to be the same, so that by the time she was due for nights off again she was more than a little tired. All the same, she thought as she coaxed Mabel into her basket and started on her journey home, it would have been nice to find the professor waiting for her outside the door.

Wishful thinking; there was no sign of him.

Chapter 3

Home for Sophie was bliss after the cold greyness of the East End. The quiet countryside, bare now that it was almost winter, was a much needed change from the crowded streets around the hospital. She spent her days visiting the surrounding farms with her father and pottering around the house, and her nights in undisturbed sleep. She was happy—though perhaps not perfectly happy, for the professor had a bothersome way of intruding into her thoughts, and none of the sensible reasons for forgetting him seemed adequate. If she had been given an opportunity she would have talked about him to her mother, but that lady never mentioned him.

She went back to the hospital half hoping that she would see him—not that she wished to particularly, she reminded herself, but he had said that he would return...

There was no news of him, although there was plenty of gossip around the breakfast-table after her first night's duty, most of it wild guessing and Gill's half-serious plans as to what she would do and say when she next saw him. 'For I'll be the lucky one, won't I?' She grinned round the table. 'If he's operating I can always think up a good reason for being in Theatre during the day...' There was a burst of laughter at this and she added, 'You may well laugh, but I'll be the first one to see him.'

As it turned out, she was wrong.

Sophie, bent on keeping a young man with terrible head injuries alive, working desperately at it, obeying Tim's quick instructions with all the skill she could muster, stood a little on one side to allow the surgical registrar to reach the patient, and at the same time realised that there was someone with him. She knew who it was even before she saw him, and although her heart gave a joyful little leap she didn't let it interfere with her work. He came from behind and bent his height to examine the poor crushed head, echoing Peter Small's cheerful 'Hello, Sophie' with a staid 'Good evening, Sister'.

She muttered a reply, intent on what she was doing, and for the next half an hour was far too busy to give him a thought, listening to the two men and doing as she was bid, taking blood for cross-matching, summoning X-ray and the portable machine, and warning Theatre that the professor would be operating within the hour. She heard Gill's delighted chuckle when she told her.

At breakfast Gill gave everyone a blow-by-blow account of the professor's activities. He had done a marvellous bit of surgery, she assured them, and afterwards he had had a mug of tea in her office. 'He was rather quiet,' she explained, 'but he had only been here for a couple of hours, discussing some cases with Peter; he must have been tired...' She brightened. 'There are sure to be some more cases during the night,' she added pensively. 'I've got nights off in two days' time. He's on the theatre list to do two brain tumours tomorrow; probably he'll be free after that.'

She called across the table, 'Hey, Sophie, didn't he go to the accident room? Did he say anything to you?'

'He said, "Good evening, Sister", and asked me where the man came from.'

Gill said happily, not meaning to be unkind, 'I dare say he likes small, fragile-looking girls like me.'

They got up to go then and Sophie changed out of her uniform and made for the entrance. It was raining again, which was probably why she felt depressed.

The professor was lounging against a wall, studying the notice-board. He straightened up when he saw her and walked towards her. When he was near enough he said, 'Hello, Sophie,' and smiled. It was a smile to warm her, and she smiled back from a tired unmade-up face.

'I'm glad you were there,' she said. 'Will he do?'

'I believe so—it's early days yet, but he's got a chance.' He fell in beside her, walking to the door. 'Are you glad because I was there to deal with the patient or were you glad to see me, Sophie?'

She stopped to look at him. 'Both.'

He tucked a hand under her elbow. 'Good, still

friends? I'm not operating until this afternoon and we both need some fresh air. Come along.'

She was whizzed through the door, by no means willingly. 'I have no wish for fresh air,' she told him, peevish after a long night's work. 'I'm going to bed.'

'Well, of course you are, but not just yet. We'll go to Epping Forest, have a brisk walk and a cup of coffee, and be back here by midday.'

'Mabel,' said Sophie feebly.

'We'll go there first. I shall come up with you, otherwise you might forget me and go to sleep.'

'No, no. You mustn't come up. I won't be more than five minutes or so.'

He stuffed her into the car and got in beside her and a few minutes later got out to open her door and usher her across the pavement and in through the shabby front door. 'Five minutes,' he reminded her and turned to engage in conversation with Miss Phipps, who had darted out, her wig askew, intent on a chat.

Mabel's wants attended to, her face made up after a fashion and her hair tidied, Sophie went back downstairs and was forced to admire the way in which the professor drew his conversation with her landlady to its conclusion in such a way that the lady was under the impression that it was she who had brought it to a close.

'Anyone would think that you liked her,' said Sophie waspishly. She wished suddenly that she hadn't come; thinking about it, she couldn't remember saying that she would in the first place.

'No, no, nothing of the sort, but if she should take a dislike to me she might show me the door, and then we would have to meet in the street or a park—all very well in the summer, but this is no weather for dallying around the East End.'

Sophie drew a deep breath. 'What do you mean— "have to meet"? We don't have to do anything of the sort.'

'My dear girl, use your tired wits. How are we to get to know each other unless we spend time in each other's company?'

'Why do we have to get to know each other? You don't even live here.'

She realised what a silly remark that was as soon as it was uttered.

'A powerful argument for our frequent meetings when I am,' he told her placidly. 'You have been home since I saw you last?'

His gentle conversation soothed her. She was tired but no longer edgy and by the time they reached the comparative quiet of the forest she was ready enough to walk its paths with him. Indeed, when presently he suggested that they should go in search of coffee she felt reluctant to leave, not sure whether it was the peace and quiet around them or his company which she was loath to give up.

They had been in the car five minutes or so when she pointed out that he had left the road back.

He reassured her. 'I thought we might have our coffee at Ingatestone; there's rather a nice place on the Roman Road.'

The nice place was a fifteenth-century hotel, quite beautifully restored. It would be busy in the evenings, she judged, but now there were few people there. They sat in a lovely room by a pleasant fire and drank their coffee, but Sophie wasn't allowed to stay for long. 'If we sit here much longer,' observed the professor, 'you'll fall asleep and I shall be forced to carry you upstairs to that room of yours, and all my efforts to keep Miss Phipps sweet would be useless.'

Sophie, warm and content, laughed at that.

Back once more, he saw her very correctly to the front door, bade her a brief goodbye, and drove away, leaving Sophie to fend off Miss Phipps's curiosity with the observation that she was almost too sleepy to get to her room...

She didn't see him during the next night. For once it was fairly quiet and all the night sisters were in the canteen at the same time for their midnight meal. It was Gill who mentioned him first. 'He operated at one o'clock,' she grumbled. 'I simply couldn't get up in the middle of the day, and besides, I couldn't think of a good excuse to turn up in Theatre. But luck is on my side, girls; he's operating at half-past eight this morning, so I shall forget something and go back to Theatre and chat him up.'

'I must say, you're keen,' said someone. 'Don't any of us get a look-in?'

Gill beamed round the table. 'Let's face it, I'm just his type; big men like little women.'

Sophie, her mouth full of scrambled egg, said nothing.

She saw the Bentley parked in the consultant's parking space as she left the hospital. He would be operating by now and doubtless Gill had found an excuse to go back to Theatre on some pretext or other. It was probably true, reflected Sophie, walking back to her flatlet in the teeth of a nasty little wind, that big men liked small girls. If so, why did he bother to see her? To go to the trouble of meeting her mother and father, take her for brisk walks for her health's sake? She pondered the problem and she couldn't find an answer. A conceited girl might have concluded that it was her strikingly pretty person which attracted him, but she wasn't conceited; three brothers had seen to that. She bade Miss Phipps an absent-minded good morning and gained the solitude of her room to find Mabel waiting for her with impatience. She fed her, had a bath, made herself a mug of cocoa, and went to bed trying not to think how pleasant a brisk walk in Epping Forest would have been. Tomorrow, she told herself sleepily, she would take a bus and tramp round Hyde Park even if it poured with rain. She closed her eyes and, lulled by Mabel's gentle purr, she slept.

A disgruntled Gill told her as they sat at their midnight meal that although she had gone back to the theatre with some excuse the professor had already started to operate and hadn't finished until the early afternoon. 'And on top of that,' she went on, 'he's gone to France—a last-chance op on a little girl with a brain tumour. There are several more cases lined up for him here, so he's bound to come back.' Her blue eyes were screwed up with annoyance. 'I wish I were on day duty. On the other hand, I'd see more of him at night.'

'Only if some poor unfortunate came in with severe head injuries, and who would want that?' Sophie had spoken tartly, and Gill gave her a searching look.

'Well, no, of course not. Sophie, I do believe that you haven't a spark of romance in you. If you weren't so large yourself you'd have the men falling about to get at you.'

There was a burst of laughter; 'large' hardly described Sophie's magnificent shape, and several voices pointed this out, while she, unperturbed, spooned her milk pudding, aware that a gratifying number of men had proposed to her and professed themselves in love with her. She had liked them all, but not enough to marry them—the only one she had felt differently about was a dim memory now, and she wasn't sure if she believed in love any more... Her thoughts were interrupted by her bleep and she sped away to deal with a very drunk man who had fallen through a glass door. His injuries weren't serious but needed a good deal of stitching, and it took some time to get his address and get his wife to come and fetch him home. It was the worst hour of the long night by now—almost four o'clock, when the desire to sleep was strong, to be countered by cups of tea and the hopeful tidying-up of the accident room and Casualty, although Sophie couldn't remember a morning when there hadn't been at least two patients arriving just as everything was pristine and ready for the day staff.

True to the promise she had made herself, she spent an hour in Hyde Park that morning, walking at a good pace and actually rather enjoying it. The weather had improved too and the air there was fresh, and the Serpentine gave an illusion of the country. She took a bus back to her lodgings, made her cocoa, had a bath, and fell into bed to sleep at once and not wake until Mabel, impatient for her food, roused her with an urgent paw.

Three more days, thought Sophie, diving into her clothes while the kettle boiled, and it's nights off again.

The night ahead of her, did she but know it, was going to be a very busy one, and at the end of it she was too tired to eat her breakfast; she pushed corn-flakes round her plate, drank several cups of tea, and got up from the table.

'You've had a busy night,' observed the men's medical ward sister, who hadn't. 'You must be dying for your bed.'

'It was rather much—luckily it isn't like that every night. There was this rally about something or other, and they always end up in a fight...'

'Nights off soon?' asked someone.

'Three more nights, and I've been promised a male student nurse; as long as Ida doesn't go off sick again, the future looks rosy. Bye for now.'

She went along to change, flinging her clothes on anyhow, something she would never dream of doing normally, but now all she wanted was her bed.

The professor was just outside the door as she went through it. He took her arm and marched her across the forecourt, opened the Bentley's door, and urged her inside. Only when they were sitting side by side did he say, 'Good morning, Sophie, only I see that it isn't for you. You've had a bad night?'

She found her voice, indignant but squeaky with tiredness. 'Yes, and if you don't mind I want to go home and go to bed—now.' She added as an after-thought, 'Good morning, Professor.'

'So you shall. Did you eat your breakfast?'

'I'm not hungry.' As she spoke she was aware that if

she went to bed without a meal she would wake after an hour or two and not sleep again, but that, she considered, was her business.

The professor edged the car out into the street. 'First we will see to Mabel, then we will go together and have breakfast, and then you shall go to bed.'

'I don't want—' began Sophie.

'No, of course you don't, but just be a good girl and do as I say.' He had stopped before her door and was already helping her out. 'I'm coming up with you.'

She stood where she was. 'Indeed you're not. Miss Phipps—'

'Sophie, I beg you to stop fussing; just leave everything to me.'

He opened the street door and pushed her ahead of him. 'Go on up,' he told her and turned to Miss Phipps, already with her head round the door.

Sophie did as she was told, vaguely listening to his deep voice. He sounded serious and she could hear Miss Phipps making sympathetic noises. She wondered what he had said to earn that lady's concern as she unlocked her own door, flung her bag on the divan, and went to get Mabel's breakfast. She was spooning the cat food into a saucer when the professor knocked and came in. The room was cold and he lit the gas fire, took the tin from her to finish the job, and told her to wash her face and comb her hair. 'And no hanging about, I beg you; I'm famished.'

She paused with a towel over her arm on the way to the bathroom. 'Don't they give you breakfast at St Agnes's?'

'Oh, yes, if I asked for it. I came over on a night ferry and came straight to the hospital.'

'An emergency?'

'If you are an emergency, then yes. Go and wash your face, Sophie.'

She went through the door and then poked her head back round it. 'Haven't you been to bed?'

'No, I drove down to Calais.'

Her dark eyes, huge with a lack of sleep, stared across the room at him. 'But why...?' she began, only to be told at once to do something to her face. 'For I refuse to take you out looking "like patience on a monument".'

'"Smiling at grief",' muttered Sophie, hurrying down the stairs.

She returned five minutes later, her face washed and made-up after a fashion. She had brushed her hair too, so that it was tidy in front, although the coil at the back was in need of attention.

'Take the pins out and tie it back,' sighed the professor, which she did, finding a bit of ribbon in her work basket and making a neat bow.

He settled Mabel in her basket, switched off the fire, and opened the door. 'You shouldn't hide your hair,' he said as she went past him.

She looked at him in astonishment. 'I couldn't possibly go on duty with it hanging down my back.'

He only smiled down at her, and, for some reason feeling awkward, she added, 'I don't always bother to put it up when I'm at home.'

'Oh, good,' said the professor, pressing his vast person against the wall so that she might pass him.

He whisked her past Miss Phipps with a brief, 'We shall be back presently, Miss Phipps,' before that lady could so much as open her mouth, and gently bundled Sophie into the car.

Catching her breath as he drove away, she asked, 'Where are we going?'

'To my house to eat breakfast; it should be ready and waiting for us.'

'Your house? I thought you lived in Holland...'

'I do.' He didn't offer any more information and somehow she didn't like to ask and sat silent while he drove across the city, but as he threaded his way through the one-way streets in the West End she ventured, 'You live in London?'

He turned the car into one of the narrow fashionable streets of Belgravia. 'Oh, yes.' He slowed the car and stopped before a terrace of Regency houses. 'Here we are.'

The houses were tall and narrow with bay windows and important doors gleaming with paint and highly polished doorknockers. He urged her across the narrow pavement, fished out a bunch of keys, and opened his door.

The hall was long and narrow, and as they went in a man came to meet them.

'Mornin', guv,' he said cheerfully. 'There's a nice bit of breakfast all ready for you and the lady.'

He was youngish, with nondescript hair and a round face in which a pair of small blue eyes twinkled, and he was most decidedly a Cockney.

The professor returned his greeting affably. 'This

is Percy, who runs the place for me together with Mrs Wiffen. This is Miss Blount, as famished as I am.'

'Okey-doke, guv, leave it to me. Pleased to meet you, miss, I'm sure.'

His little eyes surveyed her and he smiled. 'You go right to the table and I'll bring in the food.'

He took Sophie's coat and opened a door. 'Gotta lotta post, guv,' he observed. 'It's in yer study.'

The professor thanked him. 'Later, Percy—let me know if there are any phone calls.'

The room they entered was at the front of the house, not over-large but furnished with great taste, its mulberry-red walls contrasting with the maple-wood furniture. The table was circular, decked with a white damask cloth, with shining silver and blue and white china, and the coffee-pot Percy was setting on the table was silver, very plain save for a coat of arms on one side. Sophie took the seat offered by the professor and cast a quick look round her. She came from a family in comfortable circumstances, but this was more than comfort, it was luxury, albeit understated. There was a bracket clock on the mantelpiece which she was sure was eighteenth-century, perhaps earlier; it suited the room exactly, so did the draped brocade curtains at the bow window and the fine carpet, almost thread-bare with age, on the floor. The professor interrupted her inspection.

'Pour the coffee, will you, Sophie? Do you want to talk about your night or shall we lay plans for our next meeting?'

A remark which rather took her breath. She had it back by the time Percy had served them with a splendid breakfast and then gone away again. 'Are we going to meet again?'

He handed her the toast rack. 'Of course we are; what a silly remark. When do you have your nights off?'

'I have three more nights to work.'

'Good. I'll drive you home, but shall we see if we can spend a little time together first? Could you manage to spend the afternoon with me before we go? Go to bed for a few hours and I'll fetch you about one o'clock; we can have lunch somewhere and walk for a while.'

She speared a mushroom and ate it thoughtfully. She was feeling quite wide awake now and eyed him uncertainly. 'Well, yes, I could, but why?'

'Because some exercise will do you good and Epping Forest is on our way to your home.' Which didn't really answer her question.

She crunched a morsel of perfectly cooked bacon. 'Well, all right. It's very kind of you. I'd like to be home by suppertime, though.' She paused, looking at him. 'Perhaps you would like to have supper with us before you drive back here?'

'That,' said the professor gravely, 'would be most kind if your mother has no objection.'

'No. She'll be delighted. She likes you,' said Sophie matter-of-factly, not seeing the gleam in her companion's eyes. She applied herself to her breakfast with unselfconscious pleasure while they talked about nothing much, undemanding chat which was very soothing. It was a lovely house, she thought, welcoming and warm—one could live very happily in it…

She could have lingered there, uncaring of sleep,

but the silvery chimes of the clock reminded her of her bed and she glanced at the professor, who nodded his handsome head just as though she had spoken.

'I'm going to take you back now,' he told her. 'Go to bed and sleep, Sophie, ready for another night.'

Percy came then to help her with her coat, and she thanked him for her breakfast. 'I hope it didn't give you too much extra work.'

'Lor' no, miss. Nice ter 'ave a bit of company. Me and Mrs Wiffen and the cat get lonely when the guv's away.'

In the car she asked, 'Why does Percy call you guv? I mean, it's a bit unusual, isn't it? He's the houseman or valet or something, isn't he?'

'Ah, but Percy is unusual. I removed a tumour from his brain some five years ago and at the time he said that he would look after my interests until either he or I should die. I took him at his word and he is splendid at his job and always cheerful. As far as I'm concerned, he may call me what he likes. Did you like him?'

'Yes—I imagine you could trust him completely.'

'Indeed I do. There isn't much he can't do or arrange even at a moment's notice. I can go to and from Holland knowing that he will look after things for me.'

He had stopped the car outside Miss Phipps's house, and for a moment Sophie compared it with the house they had just left. A foolish thing to do, she reminded herself bracingly, and got out as the professor opened the door for her. Nothing could have been brisker than his manner as he saw her to the door and bade her goodbye.

'I suppose that was his good deed for the day,' said Sophie to an inattentive Mabel.

During the next three nights she heard a good deal about the professor. He was operating each day and Gill reported faithfully what he did and said to her and what she had said to him and thought about later; none of it amounted to much. There was no sign of him, though, and she went home to the flat at the end of her last night's duty feeling uncertain. True, he had said that he would drive her home, true also that he was calling for her at one o'clock and taking her out to lunch, but supposing he had forgotten or, worse, had issued a vague invitation, not meaning a word of it?

Common sense told her that that was unlikely; she went to bed as soon as she got to her room, with rather a nice tweed skirt and needlecord jacket with a washed-silk blouse to go under it lying ready to get into when she got up.

She set her alarm for half-past twelve, got up rather reluctantly, dressed, and, with her face nicely made-up and her hair in its smooth, intricate coils, urged Mabel into her basket, swung her shoulder-bag over her arm, and went downstairs.

The Bentley was outside with the professor at the wheel, reading a newspaper. He got out as she opened the door, dealt with the bag and Mabel, and settled her beside him.

'Lunch first?' he asked. 'I've booked a table at that place at Ingatestone.'

They talked in a desultory fashion as he drove, pleasant talk which required no effort on her part, and over their lunch he kept their conversation easygoing and rambling, not touching on any topic that was personal. Sophie, refreshed by her short sleep, agreed readily to a dish of hors-d'oeuvres, grilled Dover sole and sherry trifle and enjoyed them with an appetite somewhat sharpened by a week or more of solid hospital cooking and snatched sandwiches.

'That was delicious,' she observed, pouring their coffee.

'Splendid. We have time for an hour's walk before we need drive on to your home.'

A short drive brought them to Epping Forest. He parked the car and they started along one of the well marked paths running between the trees and dense shrubbery, almost leafless now, quiet and sheltered, winding away out of sight. Presently they came to a small clearing with an old crumbling wall overlooking a stretch of open country, and by common consent paused to lean against it and admire the view. The professor said quietly, 'May I take it that we are now good, firm friends, Sophie?'

She had had a sleep and a delicious lunch and the quiet trees around her were soothing. She smiled up at him; he was safe and solid and a good companion. 'Oh, yes.'

'Then perhaps you know what I am going to say next. Will you marry me, Sophie?'

Her smile melted into a look of utter surprise. 'Marry you? Why? Whatever for?'

He smiled at that. 'We are good friends; have we not just agreed about that? We enjoy doing the same things, laughing at the same things… I want someone to share my life, Sophie, a companion, someone to make my house a home, someone to be friends with my friends.'

She met his intent look honestly, although her cheeks were pink. 'But we don't—that is, shouldn't there be love as well?'

'Have you ever been in love, Sophie?' He wasn't looking at her now, but at the view before them.

She took a long time to answer, but he showed no impatience. Presently she said, 'Yes, I have. Oh, it was years ago; I was nineteen and I loved him so much. He threw me over for an older woman, a young widow. She was small and pretty and beautifully dressed and had money; I felt like a clumsy beanpole beside her. I would have given anything to have been five feet tall and slim... It's funny, but I can't remember what he looked like any more, but I'll never forget how I felt. I never want to feel like that again—it was like the end of the world.'

He still didn't look at her, but he flung a great arm across her shoulders and she felt comforted by it.

'You never think of him?'

'No. No, not for a long time now. It wasn't love—the kind of love that swallows up everything else—was it?'

'One is very vulnerable at nineteen, and had you thought that, if you had married this man on a flood of infatuation, by now, eight years later, you would be bitterly regretting it? One changes, you know.'

She turned to look at him. It wasn't just his good looks; he was so sure about things, so dependable and, underneath his rather austere manner, very kind.

'You haven't answered my question.'

'You answered it yourself, didn't you? You were hurt

badly once; for that to happen a second time is something you will never allow. My dear, marriage isn't all a matter of falling in love and living happily ever after. Liking is as important as loving in its way; feeling comfortable with each other is important too—and friendship. Add these things up and you have the kind of love which makes a happy marriage.'

'What about Romeo and Juliet, or Abelard and Héloïse? They loved—'

'Ah—that is something which only a few people are fortunate enough to share.'

His arm was still around her, but he made no attempt to draw her closer. 'I think that we may be happy together, Sophie. We do not know each other very well yet, but we have so little opportunity to meet. Would you consider marrying me and getting to know me after? I am quite sure that we can be happy; but let us take our time learning about each other, gaining each other's affection. We will live as friends if you like until we are used to the idea of being man and wife; I'll not hurry you...'

'I don't know where you live—do you have parents?'

'Oh, yes. My father's a retired surgeon; he and my mother live in Friesland. I live there too; so do two of my sisters. The other three live in den Haag.'

'All in one house?' The idea appalled her.

He laughed. 'No, no. We all have homes of our own. Have you any leave due, Sophie?'

'A week, that's all.'

'Long enough. Can you manage to get free by the end of next week? I've nothing over here after that;

I'll take you to Holland and you can make up your mind then.'

'I'm not sure, but I think this is a very funny kind of proposal,' said Sophie.

'Is it? I've not proposed marriage before, so I'm not qualified to give an opinion. Shall I start again and you tell me what to say?'

She laughed then and said, 'Don't be ridiculous,' and saw that he was smiling too, but she didn't see the gleam in his eye.

'I don't think that I can get a week off at such short notice,' Sophie said regretfully.

'Perhaps if I had a word… Apply to whoever it is who deals with such things when you get back on duty and see what happens.'

'All right, but I'm not certain…'

He said in a soothing voice, 'No, no, of course you're not. You would prefer to say nothing, I expect, for the time being.'

'Perhaps not at all,' said Sophie soberly.

'That seems to be a splendid idea.' He was all of a sudden brisk. 'Shall we go back to the car? Your mother doesn't expect us before the early evening, does she? Then let us find somewhere where we can have tea.'

It was obvious after a while that he wasn't going to refer to the matter again; she would dearly have liked to question him about his home in Holland, but she wasn't sure how to set about it. She liked him—there was no question about that—but she sensed that penetrating his reserve was something best left until she knew more about him. Sitting beside him as he drove away from the woods, she reflected that the idea of marrying him was beginning to take firm root in her head, which, considering she had never addressed him as other than professor or sir, seemed absurd.

Chapter 4

Sophie and the professor stopped at the Post House in Epping for their tea and, over buttered muffins and several cups of that reviving beverage, discussed everything under the sun but themselves. Sophie, ever hopeful, made several efforts to talk about her companion's life, but it was of no use; he gave her no encouragement at all. She gave up presently, feeling annoyed and trying not to show it, suspecting that he knew that and was secretly amused.

Her mother and father welcomed them with carefully restrained curiosity; the professor was becoming a fairly frequent visitor and, naturally enough, they were beginning to wonder why. It was after a leisurely supper, sitting in the comfortable drawing-room round the log fire, that he enlightened them.

'I am going back to Holland tomorrow for two days,'

he told them in his calm, unhurried way, 'but I hope
that I will see you again shortly.' He looked at Sophie.
'You won't mind, my dear, if I tell your parents that I
have asked you to marry me?'

It was too late to say that yes, she did mind, anyway. Not that she did; she had been wondering all the
evening what exactly she should say to her mother and
father. Before they could say anything he went on, 'I
shall be here for a week or so, which will give her time
to decide if she will marry me or not. If she agrees,
then I hope to take her to Holland with me so that she
may meet my family and see my home. If she should
refuse me I hope that she and I will remain friends and
that I shall see you from time to time.'

Sophie found three pairs of eyes looking at her.
'I thought I'd like to think about it,' she said a little
breathlessly. 'Just to be sure, you know.'

Her father said, 'Sensible girl,' and her mother observed,

'I would be delighted to see the pair of you married,
but Sophie's quite right to think it over; love is for a
lifetime.' She nodded her head in satisfaction. 'You're
well suited,' she added.

They were content to leave it at that; the talk was
of his journey the next day, Sophie's busy week and
the various countries he visited from time to time, and
presently he took his leave, and Sophie, feeling that it
was expected of her, went with him to the door.

'When will you be back in England?' asked Sophie,
once they were in the hall.

'In three days' time. I have to give a series of lectures.' He was standing close to her, but not touching her. 'Will you give me your answer then?'

She looked up into his face. He was smiling a little, friendly and relaxed and most reassuringly calm. 'I shall miss you.'

'And I you—that augurs well for our future, does it not?'

She said hesitantly, 'Well, yes, I suppose it does. I'll—I'll tell you when I see you.'

He bent his head and kissed her, a brief, comforting kiss, before he opened the door and got into his car, and drove away without looking back.

Tom, home from school while Sophie had nights off, declared himself delighted with the idea of her getting married. 'Splendid,' he crowed. 'Now I'll have somewhere to go for my holidays—'

'Don't count your chickens,' said Sophie severely. 'I haven't said I want to marry yet; we're not even engaged.'

'He's a prime fellow, Sophie, and he's got a Bentley.'

'Which is no reason for marrying anyone,' said Sophie firmly.

What would the reasons be if she did marry him? she wondered. He had been quite right; they got on well together and they liked each other. Liking someone that you were going to live with for the rest of your life was important. She would be a suitable wife to him too, since, being a nurse, she understood the kind of life he led and would make allowances for it. She wasn't a young girl either; she would be prepared to take over the duties of his household and cope with any special social life that he might have. She could see that from his point of view she was eminently suitable.

The thought depressed her, while at the same time she acknowledged his good sense in seeking a wife to suit his lifestyle. As for herself, she had no wish to fall in love again, with the chance of breaking her heart for the second time. On second thoughts, she acknowledged to herself that her heart couldn't have been broken, otherwise she wouldn't be considering the idea of marrying the professor. Rijk—she must remember to call him that.

Her parents had made no attempt to advise her, although they made it plain that they liked the professor; they also made it plain that she was old enough to make up her own mind, and George and Paul, when appraised of the situation, had given their opinions over the phone that he sounded a decent chap, and wasn't it about time she married anyway?

Sophie went back to St Agnes's with her mind very nearly, but not quite, made up, which was a good thing, because several busy nights in a row made it difficult for her to think of anything but her work and her bed.

Three days went by and there was no sign of the professor. There was no reason, she thought peevishly, why he couldn't have sent her a note at least, and surely he could have phoned her? She flounced out of the hospital with a cross, tired face, although she still managed to look beautiful.

The Bentley came smoothly into the forecourt as she crossed over, and the professor parked neatly and got out and strolled towards her.

His 'Good morning, Sophie' was cheerful, but she saw that he was tired.

She asked suspiciously, 'Have you just got here?' and then, remembering her manners, she said, 'Good morning, Rijk.'

'That is a most convenient ferry from Calais; even with delays on the motorway it still allows me time to reach you before you go to bed.'

He had a hand on her shoulder, urging her back to the car. 'We will go and attend to Mabel and then we will breakfast together.'

'Yes, well—all right.' She got into the car with the pleasant feeling that she wouldn't need to bother about anything any more. Common sense warned her that this was a piece of nonsense, but she was too tired to argue with herself. She asked, 'Have you been to bed?'

'No.' He smiled suddenly at her, and all the tired lines vanished. 'I had too much to think about.'

He stopped outside Miss Phipps's house and got out to open her door. 'Ten minutes? I don't feel up to your landlady; I'll wait here.'

'I'll be quick…'

It was a chilly morning and Mabel most obligingly wasted no time on the tiny balcony but nipped back smartly to eat her breakfast.

'I'll be back quite soon,' Sophie promised. Without bothering to do anything to her face or hair, she hurried back to the car.

The professor was asleep, his face as calm and placid as a child's, and she went round the bonnet and stealthily opened her door. Without opening his eyes he said, 'You have been quick,' and was all at once alert and wide awake.

'I didn't mean to wake you,' said Sophie. 'Are you sure you wouldn't like to go to your house and go straight to bed?'

'We are going straight to my house. As for bed, that will come later. Breakfast first.'

Percy flung the door wide as they got out of the car and greeted them with a cheerful, 'Morning, guv, morning, miss. Mrs Wiffen's got a smashing breakfast laid on. 'Ad a good trip, 'ave you?'

The professor replied that indeed he had and took Sophie's coat and tossed it to Percy, who caught it and hung it tidily away in the hall closet.

'There's a pile of letters in the study, but you'll eat first, eh?'

'Yes, thank you, Percy. As soon as you can get the breakfast on the table.'

'Watch me,' said Percy, and whizzed away as the professor urged Sophie into the dining-room.

There was a bright fire burning and the table was laid invitingly with patterned china, gleaming silver and a blue bowl of oranges as its centre-piece. As they sat down Percy came in with a tray, coffee and tea and covered silver dishes which he arranged on the sideboard, and then made a second journey with the toast rack.

'Thank you, Percy,' said the professor. 'We'll ring if we want anything.' He got up to serve Sophie. 'Bacon? Eggs? A mushroom or two? A grilled tomato?'

Sophie, her mouth watering, said yes to everything,

and, feeling that she should do her share, asked, 'Coffee or tea?'

'Coffee, please...'

She poured tea for herself and they sat in companionable silence, eating the good food, but when Percy appeared to take away their plates and bring fresh toast the professor said, 'Not too tired to talk?'

Sophie piled butter and marmalade on to a corner of toast. 'No, that was a lovely breakfast, thank you very much.'

He sat back in his chair, his eyes on her face. 'And are we to share our breakfasts together, Sophie? You have had several days in which to decide. Bear in mind that I am impatient and like my own way, bad-tempered at times, too, although I have learnt to control it...'

'Are you trying to put me off?' asked Sophie. 'If you are it's too late, because I think I'd like to marry you.' She added diffidently, 'That's if you haven't changed your mind?'

He smiled at her across the table. 'No, Sophie, I made up my mind to marry you when I first saw you standing there in the middle of the pavement...'

She opened her eyes at that. 'You did? How could you possibly decide something like that so quickly?'

'I realised that I had at last found a girl who matched me in height and so I decided to snap you up.'

She looked at him uncertainly. 'You're joking, aren't you?'

He didn't answer, but got up and went and pulled her gently from her chair. 'I believe that we shall have a most satisfactory marriage,' he told her, and bent to kiss her—a quick, gentle kiss, so that she really didn't have time to enjoy it.

'I'll take you back now. I'm operating in the morning tomorrow; could you get up in time for tea? We can have it together; we have a great deal to talk about. When do you get nights off?'

'In four nights' time.'

'I may be in Bristol, but I'll come and see you at your home if your mother does not mind.' He thought for a moment. 'I shall be able to drive you home before I go.'

'There's no need,' began Sophie, and stopped when he said quietly,

'But I should like to, Sophie.'

He saw her to her door, remarking that he was unlikely to see her until her nights off, and drove away, leaving her to parry Miss Phipps's avid questions before she escaped upstairs to her room and Mabel's undemanding company.

Curled up in bed presently, nicely drowsy after her splendid breakfast, she admitted that she had been glad to see Rijk again. She thought it very likely that they might not see eye to eye about a number of things, but they weren't things which mattered. She looked forward to a well ordered and contented future, free from the anguish of falling in love and being rejected. She and Rijk were sensible, level-headed people prepared to make a success of a marriage based on friendship and a high regard for each other.

Upon which lofty and erroneous thoughts she went happily to sleep.

Two mornings later, when she was on her way to

breakfast, she was asked to go to the office. She might leave, Matron told her graciously. Professor van Taak ter Wijsma had asked that the usual formalities of leaving might be overlooked, since he had to return to Holland shortly and was desirous of taking Sophie with him. Matron's features relaxed into a rare smile. 'I hope you will be very happy, Sister. The professor is a splendid man and very well liked here. He comes here frequently, as you know, so I hope that we shall see something of you from time to time.'

Sophie murmured suitably and got herself out of the room and started on the rambling passages which would take her to the canteen and breakfast. She didn't hurry; she had too much to think about, strolling along, contemplating her shoes while she viewed the future. Which meant that she didn't see Rijk until he stopped in front of her.

'Good morning, Sophie.' He appeared to be in no hurry. 'Have you been to the office yet?'

She nodded. 'Yes, just this minute. Matron was very nice; she said that I might leave whenever it was convenient for you...'

'And you,' he pointed out gravely. 'I shall be going back in five days' time; will you come with me and see what you think of Holland and my home? And if you feel you want to change your mind, no hard feelings, Sophie.'

He smiled then. 'You're on your way to breakfast, aren't you? And I'm expected in Theatre. I'll be outside on the day you leave. *Tot ziens.*'

She watched his vast back disappear down the corridor and hoped that *tot ziens* meant something nice like 'lovely to see you'. He had been rather businesslike, but probably he had his mind on his work...

She sat down at the breakfast-table, her mind full of all the things she had to do before she left, and the first one was to tell everyone at the table...

'I'm leaving in four days' time,' she announced during a pause in the talk, and, when they all looked at her in astonishment, hurried on, 'I didn't know until just now—it's been arranged specially. I'm going to marry Professor van Taak ter Wijsma and I'm going over to Holland to meet his family.'

The chorus of ohs and aahs was very gratifying; she was well liked, and only Gill looked disappointed, although she brightened presently. 'When you're married you can invite me to stay; there must be lots of people like him out there.'

Everyone laughed and then fell to congratulating Sophie and asking questions. She had to say that she didn't know to most of them. She wasn't even sure where Rijk was, only that he would be waiting for her when he had said.

There was so much to arrange; Mabel would have to be taken home while she was away, and she supposed that she would go home herself when they came back from visiting Rijk's home in Holland, and that would mean telling Miss Phipps. Unable to face that lady's curiosity, she stopped at a phone box on the way back to her flatlet and rang her mother.

Her parent's voice sounded pleased. 'I—your father too—think that you will be very happy; is there anything that you want me to do? It's rather short notice.'

'My passport—and would you just be a dear and

look after Mabel? I've no idea where Rijk is, only that he said he'd see me on the day I leave. I'm leaving in four days' time. It's all a bit sudden, but he seems to have arranged things.'

'You're happy, love?'

'Yes, Mother. I'm a bit scared of meeting his family—all those sisters… Supposing they don't like me?'

'You're marrying Rijk, love, not his sisters. I'm sure it will be all right.'

Her mother's voice was reassuring.

She had very little time to make plans; the junior night sister was to take over from her and Staff Nurse Pitt was to be made junior night sister in her place. The three of them had been working together for a year or two, so there was little need to explain things to them. Sophie rushed through an inventory with one of the office sisters, staying behind after breakfast and going back to her room long after she should have been in bed, to find an indignant Mabel waiting for her and an inquisitive Miss Phipps, still unaware of her impending departure. Sophie, falling into bed, stayed awake long enough to decide that since Rijk was arranging everything with such speed he could deal with her landlady too.

He was waiting for her after her last night on duty. She had been and paid a last visit to Matron's office, said goodbye to her friends and also to Peter Small and Tim and the porters, and now, burdened by various farewell gifts, she went through the hospital doors for the last time.

The professor got out of his car and came to meet

her. He took her packages and put them in the car and asked, 'What do you want to do first? We will be going over on the night ferry tomorrow; would it be a good idea if we go to your room and, while you collect Mabel and whatever you need, I'll see to Miss Phipps? I'll keep your room for a week or so so that when we get back you can come and pack up the rest of your things. That will give you the rest of today to sleep and put a few things in a case. I'll come for you tomorrow about six o'clock; we're going from Harwich…'

'You've thought of everything… How long will we be in Holland?'

'A week—I have to go to Leeds for a couple of days and then Athens. I'll bring you back here first; you'll want to be home for Christmas. I'm not sure how long I shall be there, but I'll come as soon as I can…'

'You'll be there for Christmas?'

'I rather think so.' He popped her into the car. 'But let us get you settled first before we discuss that.'

He was as good as his word and so Sophie, coming downstairs half an hour later with a hastily packed case and Mabel in her basket, found Miss Phipps waiting in the hall. The professor took her case from her and went out to the car and Miss Phipps said excitedly, 'Oh, my goodness, Sister, dear, what a romantic surprise— whoever would have thought it? Though I must say I did wonder… And don't worry about your flatlet; I'll keep it locked until you come back to get the rest of your things.' Her wig slipped a little to one side in her excitement. 'I don't know when I've had such a thrill.'

Sophie murmured suitably, assured her landlady

that she would be back within a week or so, and bade her goodbye.

'You'll make a lovely bride,' breathed Miss Phipps as Sophie went out to the car.

The professor was leaning against the gate, looking relaxed. He was a man, Sophie reflected, who seemed to make himself comfortable wherever he was. He looked as though he hadn't an anxiety in the world. The thought reminded her that she hadn't either. She got into the car and he shut the door and got in beside her, glancing at his watch. 'Your mother said she would have coffee ready at eleven o'clock.' He turned to smile at her then and she thought how pleasant it was to feel so at ease with someone. At the same time it struck her that she was being swept along by his well laid plans even though never once had they caused her inconvenience or given her reason to grumble.

'Have you been up all night again?' she asked him sharply.

He slowed the Bentley at the traffic lights and glanced at her, smiling a little. 'You sound very wifely. I slept on the ferry.'

'I didn't mean to nag...'

'If that is nagging I rather liked it.'

Her mother was waiting for them, with coffee on the table and a large newly baked cake, and ten minutes later with Mabel sitting between the dogs, Mercury and Montgomery, before the Aga, they were sitting around the kitchen table.

'You'll stay for lunch?' asked Mrs Blount.

'I've one or two things to see to, Mrs Blount. I'll be here tomorrow evening to fetch Sophie—we're going over on the Harwich ferry and that will give me all day…'

'You couldn't spend Christmas with us?'

'I would have liked that. I shall be in Greece, although I shall do my best to get back to my home even if only for a day.'

'You poor man,' said Mrs Blount, and meant it.

He went presently, saying all the right things to her and giving Sophie a quick, almost brotherly kiss as he went.

'You are happy about marrying Rijk?' asked her mother as they went back indoors.

'We're not in love or anything like that, Mother. It's just that we… He wants a wife and we get on very well together and I do like him very much.' Sophie gave her mother a worried look. 'Rijk says that a good marriage depends on friendship and liking and that just falling in love isn't enough.' She filled their coffee-mugs again and sat down at the table. 'I've been afraid of falling in love ever since…'

'Yes, dear, I understand. As long as you aren't still in love—it is a long time ago.'

'I told Rijk I can't remember his face or anything about him, but I remember how I felt. I've been so careful to avoid getting too friendly with any of the men I've met. Somehow Rijk is different… I'm not explaining very well, am I?'

'No need, Sophie, dear. It seems to me that you are ideally suited to each other. Rijk is old and wise enough to know what he wants and so are you. I am quite sure that you will be happy together.'

Mrs Blount gave her daughter a loving look. The

dear girl had no idea; it was a good thing that the professor was a man of patience and determination and that he had the ability to hide his feelings so successfully. Once they were married he would doubtless set about the task of making Sophie fall in love with him. She nodded her head and smiled, and Sophie, looking up, asked what was amusing her.

'I was thinking about a really splendid hat for your wedding, dear,' said her mother guilelessly. 'And, talking of hats, if you are not too tired, shall we go upstairs and look through your wardrobe? Pick out what you want to take with you and I'll get it pressed.'

A good deal of the rest of the day was taken up with the knotty problem of what to wear. Her Jaeger suit, Sophie decided; she could travel in it and it would look right during the day with a handful of blouses. A short dress for the evening—a rich mulberry silk, very plain with long sleeves and a straight skirt. And upon due reflection she added a midnight-blue velvet dress with a long skirt, very full, tiny sleeves and a low neckline.

'Take that jersey dress as well,' suggested her mother, so she added still another garment, dark green this time with a cowl neckline and a pleated skirt.

'It's bound to rain or snow or something,' said Sophie, and folded a quilted jacket with a hood, adding sensible shoes, thick gloves and a woolly cap, with the vague idea that Friesland sounded as though it might be cold in winter.

'I'll pack tomorrow,' she told her mother. 'Will Father be home for lunch?'

'Yes, dear, and this afternoon shouldn't you have a nap?'

She wasn't at all sleepy, Sophie decided, obediently curling up on her bed that afternoon; there was so much to think about. The next thing she knew was her mother's hand on her shoulder.

'A cup of tea, love, and supper will be about half an hour.'

She went to bed rather early, her hair washed, her face anointed with a cream guaranteed to erase all lines and wrinkles, determined to look her best for Rijk's family. It was to be hoped, she thought sleepily, that not all the five sisters would be there. And his brothers—would they be there too?

She fell asleep uneasily, suddenly beset by doubts.

There was no time for doubts the next day; there was the packing to do, the dogs to take for a walk, a last-minute anxious inspection of her handbag, and her father to drive to a nearby farm to attend a cow calving with difficulty. They got back home in time for tea and then it was time for her to go upstairs and dress for the journey. Rijk had said that he would come in the early evening, and she knew that the ferry sailed before midnight. The drive to Harwich wouldn't take much more than an hour, and her mother had supper ready.

He arrived while she was still in her room, studying her lovely face in the looking-glass, anxious that she should look her best, and, hearing the car and the murmur of voices in the hall, she hurried downstairs to find him, his overcoat off, sitting with her father. He got up as she went into the room and came to take her hand and give her a light kiss.

'I see that you are ready,' he observed. 'Your mother

has kindly invited me to share your supper—we don't need to leave for an hour or so.'

'I'll go and help her,' said Sophie, suddenly anxious to be gone when only a few moments earlier she had been equally anxious to see him again. It was silly to feel shy with him; she supposed it was because she was excited about going to Holland. She joined her mother in the kitchen and carried plates of hot sausage rolls, jacket potatoes, mince pies and toasted sandwiches into the dining-room. There was coffee too and beer for the men, although the professor shook his head regretfully over that, at the same time embarking on a discussion with Mr Blount concerning the merits of various beers. Sophie, while glad that her father and Rijk got on so well together, couldn't help feeling a faint resentment at the professor's matter-of-fact manner towards her. After all, they were going to be married, weren't they? Surely he could show a little more interest in his future wife? Upon reflection, she had to admit that their marriage wasn't quite the romantic affair everyone, even Matron, had envisaged, and Rijk wasn't a man to pretend...

They left after a leisurely meal and the promise on Sophie's part that she would let her mother know that they had arrived safely.

'You can phone,' said the professor, 'during the morning.' He smiled at Mrs Blount. 'I'll take good care of her, Mrs Blount.'

Her mother leaned through the car window and kissed his cheek. 'I know that. Have a good trip and a happy week together.'

The ferry was half empty; they had more coffee

and then parted for the night. 'I've told the stewardess to bring you tea and toast at six o'clock,' said Rijk. 'Sleep well, Sophie.'

It was rough on the crossing and, although she didn't feel seasick, she lay and worried, wishing that she had never agreed to meet his family, never agreed to marry him, for that matter, never allowed him to foster their friendship in the first place...

She drank her tea and ate the toast and dressed, somewhat restored in her spirits in the light of a grey overcast morning. She was looking out of the porthole when there was a knock on the door and the professor came in. He took a look at her face and flung an arm round her shoulders. 'You've been awake all night wishing you had never met me, never said that probably you will marry me, never agreed to come home with me.'

He gave her a sudden kiss, not at all like the swift kisses he had given her, but hard and warm, and her spirits rose with it. 'Haven't you any doubts at all?' she asked him.

'Not one. We're about to dock. Come along, you'll feel better once we're on dry land.'

Strangely enough she did, relieved that her vague disquiet had melted away; she felt comfortable with him again, asking questions about the country that they were passing through.

'We'll stop for coffee,' he told her. 'It's about a hundred and forty miles to my home; we should be there soon after eleven o'clock. We shall be on the motorway for most of the time—not very interesting, I'm afraid, but quick.'

The road ahead was straight with no hills in sight,

bypassing the towns and villages. Holland was exactly as she had pictured it: flat and green with a wide sky and far more built-up than she had expected.

'This is the busiest corner of the country,' Rijk explained. 'The further north we go, the fewer towns and factories. I think that you will like Friesland.'

They stopped for their coffee before they crossed the Afsluitdijk and by now, although it wasn't raining, there was a strong wind blowing, so that the water looked grey and cold.

The country had changed. They were across the *dijk* now and Rijk had taken a right-hand fork on to a motorway, passing Bolsward and circumventing Sneek before turning on to a country road. Villages were few and far between in the rolling countryside, but there were a few farmhouses, backed by huge barns, standing well apart from each other. In the distance a glimpse of water was visible.

'The sea?' asked Sophie, vague as to their direction.

'The lakes; Friesland is riddled with them. In the summer they're crowded with boats. That's Sneeker Meer you can see now. Presently we will go through a small town called Grouw, past more lakes. I live in a village well away from everywhere. We're going there first. Later we will go to my parents' home in Leeuwarden; that's only twelve miles or so.'

She was thankful to hear that. 'Will they be there? All your family?'

He gave her clasped hands on her lap a brief comforting squeeze.

'They will like you and you will like them.'

'Oh, I do so hope so. Is this Grouw?'

It was really a very large village on the edge of a small lake and with a small harbour. In the summer it would be delightful, she thought; even now on this grey day it was picturesque and the small houses looked cosy. There were a few shops too and a hotel by the harbour. She craned her neck to see as much as possible before the professor drove into a narrow road with another lake on one side and a canal on the other, to cross a narrow spit of land and turn north and presently back towards the shore of a much larger lake.

'This is the Prinsenhof lake—the village is called Eernewoude; I live just the other side of it. Very quiet in winter, but watersports in summer.'

'There aren't any hospitals near—doesn't it take you a long time to reach them?'

'We're still only twelve miles from Leeuwarden, where I have beds, and Groningen is less than thirty miles—I have beds there too. I can reach the motorway to the south easily—Amsterdam is only a hundred miles and the Belgian-Dutch border another sixty miles or so.'

'Do you go abroad a lot? Other than England?'

'Fairly frequently.' They were driving slowly through the village—a handful of houses, a church, a small shop, and then a narrow brick road, the water on one side, a brick wall on the other, with great wrought-iron gates halfway along its length. They were open and a drive curved away, bordered by dense bushes and bare trees. The house was at the end of the curve and when Sophie saw it she took a sharp breath at the sight of it. She hadn't known what to expect, certainly not this imposing house of red brick and sandstone with its steep tiled roof, tall chimneys and square central tower surmounted by more tiles and an onion dome. It sheltered the vast door. The windows were long and narrow with painted shutters and to one side of the house there was what she took to be a moat.

The professor had stopped before his door and got out, opened her door and taken her arm.

He said in a comforting kind of voice, 'It's quite cosy inside.'

Sophie looked up at him. 'It's beautiful—I had no idea. I am longing to go in; I can't wait—and there's a dog barking...'

He smiled down at her excited face. 'Come inside and meet Matt.'

Chapter 5

Sophie and Rijk climbed the shallow steps to the door together and it was opened as they reached it to allow a large shaggy dog to launch itself at the professor. Sophie prudently took a step back, for the animal was large and looked ferocious as well. The professor bore the onslaught with equanimity, bade the beast calm down, and drew Sophie forward.

'This is Matt. A bouvier. He'll be your companion, your devoted friend, and die for you if he has to.'

Sophie took off her glove and offered a balled fist and the beast sniffed at it and then rasped it with a great tongue. He had small yellow eyes and enormous teeth, but she had the impression that he was smiling at her. Indeed, he offered his head for a friendly scratch.

The man who had opened the door was as unlike Percy as it was possible to be, a powerfully built man with a slight stoop, grey hair and a round, weather-beaten face. The professor shook hands with him and clapped him on the shoulder and introduced him.

'This is Rauke, who looks after the house. His wife, Tyske, housekeeps and cooks; here she comes.'

Sophie shook hands with Rauke and then with the elderly woman who had joined them in the porch. She was as tall as Sophie, with a long face and grey hair and clear blue eyes. Her handshake was firm and she said something with a smile which Sophie hoped was a welcome.

The porch opened into a vestibule which in turn opened into the hall, square and white-walled, with a staircase facing the door, lighted by a long window on its half-landing. The ceiling was lofty and from it hung a brass chandelier, simple in design and, thought Sophie, very old. There was an elaborately carved side-table too and two great chairs arranged on either side of it. It was exactly like a Dutch interior, even to the black and white marble floor. Still gazing around her, she was led away by Tyske to a cloakroom under the staircase, equipped with every modern comfort. She had time to think while she did her face and tidied her hair, and back in the hall she said at once, 'You might have told me, Rijk.'

'What should I have told you?' He looked amused.

'Why, that you had such a grand house. I don't know what I expected, but it wasn't this.'

'It is my home,' he said simply, 'and it isn't grand—on the large side, perhaps, but I use all the rooms—not all the time, of course, but I live here, Sophie. Come and have a cup of coffee and presently we will go over it together.'

He ushered her through a double door into a room with windows overlooking the grounds at the back of the house. It was light by reason of the lofty ceiling and was furnished with sofas and easy-chairs arranged around the hooded fireplace, in which a fire burned briskly. The walls were panelled and hung with faded red silk and there were a great many paintings on them, mostly portraits. There were glass-fronted cabinets against the walls, filled with porcelain and silver, and a handsome Stoel clock hanging above the fireplace, and scattered around, with a nice regard for the convenience of the room's occupants, were small tables with elegant table lamps.

Matt came to meet them as they crossed to the fire and once they were seated facing each other he stretched out between them, breathing gusty sighs of content, one eye on the coffee-tray and the plate of biscuits beside it.

They drank their coffee in companionable silence broken only by the crunching of the biscuits the professor offered to Matt.

'He must miss you,' said Sophie.

'Oh, yes. He goes with me to Leeuwarden and Groningen, though. He will be delighted to have your company while I'm away.'

'You don't have to go away?'

The dismay on her face made him say at once, 'No, no. I was talking of when we are married.' He put down his coffee-cup and sat back at his ease. 'We have a whole week to be together, Sophie.'

And at the uncertain look on her face, 'My mother and father will come back here and stay with us for a week. They have many friends living around here; they will be out every day.' He grinned suddenly. 'You see how careful I am to observe the proprieties— unnecessary in this day and age, but we're a strait-laced lot in Friesland.'

Sophie, with a slightly heightened colour, looked him in the eye. 'I'm strait-laced too.'

'Which strengthens my argument that we are very well suited.'

He got up and Matt got up with him. 'Would you like to see the house?'

They crossed the hall with Matt keeping pace with them, and the professor opened a door on its opposite side. 'The dining-room,' he told her, 'but when I'm on my own I use a smaller room at the back of the house. I have asked Rauke to set lunch there for us.'

It was a splendid room; she could imagine a dinner party sitting around the rectangular table, decked no doubt with silver and crystal, and with the wall sconces sending a flattering glow on the women guests. There was a sideboard along one wall with flanking pedestal cupboards surmounted by urns and several large oil-paintings hung on the walls; a second door led to a smaller room—a kind of ante-room, she supposed. In turn it opened into a room at the back of the house with doors opening on to the terrace from which steps led to wide lawns and flowerbeds. It was a charming room, furnished with easy-chairs and a circular table; there was a television set in one corner and bookshelves and a dear little writing-table in another corner. There was a bright fire burning here and the professor declared, 'This is one of my favourite rooms—we shall lunch here, just the two of us.'

He opened a door beside the windows. 'This is the library.' It was a splendid room with enormous desks at each end of it, leather chairs arranged around small tables, and shelves of books.

'One more room,' he observed and led her through a door into the hall again and opened a door close to the staircase. 'My study.'

It was austerely furnished with a partners' desk, a vast leather chair behind it, a couple of smaller chairs facing it and again shelves of books. There was a computer, too, an electric typewriter and an answering machine all arranged on a smaller table under the two long windows.

'I have a secretary who comes three or four times a week and sees to my letters.' He flipped over the pile of correspondence on his desk. 'Let us go upstairs.'

The staircase was of oak with a wrought-iron balustrade with a half-landing from where it branched to the gallery above. It was quiet there, their footsteps deadened by the thick carpet as he led her to the front of the house. There were a pair of rather grand double doors here and he opened them on to a beautiful room, the vast bed and furniture of satin wood, the curtains and bedspread of ivory and rose brocade. Sophie rotated slowly, looking her fill.

'What a beautiful room. You have a lovely home, Rijk—it's a bit big, but it's so—lived-in.'

'I'm glad you like it. Come this way.' He opened a

door to a bathroom which led in turn to a smaller bedroom and then into the corridor.

There were passages leading to the back of the house and he led her down each one in turn, opening doors so that she might look at each room before going up a smaller flight of stairs to the floor above.

The rooms were smaller here but just as comfortably furnished, and right at the end of one passage there was a large, airy room with bars at the windows and a high fireguard before the big stove. There was a rocking-horse under the windows and a doll's house on one of the numerous shelves. Sophie wondered what toys the closed cupboards held.

'Your nanny must have had a busy time,' she observed. 'You and your brothers and sisters...'

'She stood no nonsense and we all loved her dearly. You shall meet her later on—she has her own rooms in my parents' house. The night nurseries are through there as well as a room for Nanny and a little kitchen. We spent a great deal of time with my mother and father— we all had a very happy childhood.'

They were back in the passage with Matt, breathing heavily with pleasure, at their heels when a gong sounded from below. 'Lunch,' said the professor. 'There's still another floor, but we can look at that later on.'

They talked about nothing much as they ate; the professor steadfastly refused to allow Sophie to ask questions of a personal nature and since she was hungry and the leek soup, bacon fritters and assortment of vegetables were very much to her taste she didn't much mind.

It was like being in a dream, she reflected, pouring coffee for them both; any minute she would wake up and find herself back in the accident room at St Agnes's…

They got into the car presently with Matt crouching in the back, poking his great head between them from time to time and giving great gusty sighs.

'Does he like cats?' asked Sophie.

'I have been told over and over again by well meaning people that he would kill any cat he saw. He takes no notice of them at all; indeed, he is on the best of terms with Tyske's Miep and her kittens, and Miep doesn't care tuppence for him.'

They were on the motorway now, racing towards Leeuwarden, and Sophie stared out of the window, a bundle of nerves.

Without looking at her, the professor began a rambling conversation about Matt which needed no replies and which lasted until he slowed the car to drive through the heart of Leeuwarden. The afternoon was darkening already and the shops were lighted, decked for Christmas, and the pavements were thronged with shoppers, but she didn't have much chance to look around her for Rijk turned away from the main streets and drove through narrow ways lined with tall old houses and then into a brick street beside a canal with a line of great gabled houses facing it. He stopped before one of them.

'Here we are,' he told her.

The man who opened the door to them was elderly, tall and thin, but very upright. He greeted the professor with a dignified, 'A pleasure to see you, Mr Rijk, sir,' and Rijk shook his hand and clapped him on the shoulder.

'How are you, Clerkie? Sophie, this is Clerk, who runs this place for my father and mother—has done for as long as I can remember—taught me to fish and swim and ride a bike—taught us all, in fact.'

Sophie put out a hand and he went on, 'Miss Sophie Blount, my guest for a week. Anyone at home?'

Clerk's calm features broke into a smile. 'Everyone, sir.' He gave Sophie a fatherly look. 'Shall I take Miss Blount's coat? And would she wish to arrange her hair and so forth?'

The professor turned to study her. 'Not a hair out of place and the face looks much as usual. You'll do, Sophie.' He took her arm and crossed the square hall with Clerk's figure slightly ahead to open the door on one side of it.

The room was large, with a high ceiling and enormous windows stretching from ceiling to floor; it was also full of people, children and dogs.

As they went in the loud murmurs of conversation stopped and there was a surge towards them with cries of 'Rijk' and a babble of talk Sophie couldn't understand, but the next minute she found herself face to face with the professor's parents, his arm tucked comfortably under hers.

At first glance Mevrouw van Taak ter Wijsma looked formidable, but that was by reason of her height and well corseted stoutness. A second glance was more reassuring; her blue eyes, on a level with Sophie's, were kind and the smile on her still handsome face was sweet. She was dressed elegantly, her grey hair swept into an old-fashioned coil on top of her head, her twin set and skirt very much in the same style as that of Sophie's mother. It was silly that such a small thing should have put Sophie at her ease.

The professor's father was still a very handsome man with white hair and dark eyes. He kissed Sophie's cheek and welcomed her with a warmth she hadn't expected, before Rijk led her around the room. His five sisters were there, and so were their husbands, their children and a variety of dogs; moreover, his two brothers were there too. She shook hands and smiled and forgot all their names the moment they were said, but that didn't seem to matter in such an atmosphere of friendliness. As for the children, they clung to their uncle, offered small hands and cheeks for a kiss and took her for granted. So did the dogs—two Labradors, a Jack Russell and a small whiskery creature with melting eyes. His name was Friday, she was told, and when she asked why one of the older children said in English, 'That was the day Daddy found him.' They asked, 'We have cats; do you?'

'Well, yes, I have a cat of my own; she's called Mabel.'

'Good, you will bring her here when you marry Uncle Rijk?'

'Well, yes. You speak very good English...'

'We have a nanny. When you and Oom Rijk have babies you will also have a nanny.'

The conversation was getting rather out of hand; she looked round for Rijk and caught his eye and he broke off the conversation with his father and made his way to her. 'Is Timon practising his English? He's Tiele's eldest son—she's the one in the green dress. Three boys so far, but they'd like a daughter… Come and talk to Loewert. He's at Leiden in his last year.'

He was a younger edition of Rijk and brimming over with the wish to be friendly. He obligingly took her round the room once more and told her all the names once again so that by the time they had all settled round the room drinking tea and eating fragile little biscuits she could pick out various members of the family for herself. Rijk's mother, sitting beside her on one of the massive sofas, was carrying on the kind of conversation which didn't need much thought, telling her little snippets of information about the family.

'We are such a large family,' she observed, 'and I am sure that Rijk quite forgot to tell you about us. He is immersed in his work—too much so, I consider.' She smiled at Sophie. 'You will alter that, I hope, my dear.'

Sophie, watching him talking to his brothers at the other end of the room, wondered if she would. It seemed unlikely.

Presently they got up to go. Rijk's parents went away to get their hats and coats, Matt was coaxed away from the garden where he had been romping with the other dogs, and Sophie began a round of goodbyes. She hadn't known about the Dutch kissing three times; by the time she had bidden goodbye to everyone in the room she felt quite giddy. She must remember to ask Rijk about it; he had never kissed her three times. Indeed, his kisses had been few and far between and then brief…

The elders of the party got into the back of the Bentley with Matt, and Sophie found herself sitting by Rijk, and really, she thought a little crossly, I've hardly seen him all afternoon.

He seemed unaware of her coolness, though, talking about his family in a desultory way until they reached his house and once they were there seeing to his parents' comfort, handing them over to Rauke, and then walking her off to the small sitting-room at the back of the house.

'There's half an hour before we need to change,' he told her. 'Come and have a drink and tell me what you think of my family.'

'They are very nice,' said Sophie inadequately. 'I haven't quite sorted them out yet...'

'Time enough to do that,' he said cheerfully. 'Would you like a glass of sherry? We'll meet in the drawing-room just before dinner, but I think you deserve a drink; the family like you.'

'Supposing they hadn't liked me?'

He shrugged huge shoulders. 'That would make no difference as far as I'm concerned.'

He turned away to pour the sherry and she said on impulse, 'Have you ever been in love, Rijk?'

He put the drink down beside her and settled into a chair opposite hers.

'Several times! If you mean the fleeting romances we are all prone to from time to time. But if you are doubtful as to any future entanglements of that nature on my part, I can assure you that I have long outgrown them.'

Once started she persisted. 'But you do believe in people falling in love and—and loving each other?'

'Certainly I do. For those fortunate enough to do both.' He added softly, 'Cold feet, Sophie?'

'No, no.' She blushed a little under his amused gaze. 'I was just being curious; I didn't mean to pry.'

'I'm glad we're good friends enough to be able to ask each other such questions.'

'Yes, well, so am I. I think I'd better go up and change…'

'I must take a quick turn in the garden with Matt. We'll meet again in the drawing-room.'

He got up with her and opened the door and stood watching her as she crossed the hall and started up the staircase. Sophie, aware of that, felt self-conscious, which wasn't like her at all.

She wore the mulberry silk; it suited her well and, studying her reflection in the pier glass, she felt tolerably satisfied with her appearance. She hadn't been quite sure what to wear, but somehow Rijk's mother looked the kind of lady to follow the conventions of her younger days. She was glad that she had decided to wear it when she entered the drawing-room, for Mevrouw van Taak ter Wijsma was in black crêpe, cut with great elegance, and a fitting background for the double row of pearls she was wearing. As for the men, they wore dark grey suits and ties of subdued splendour, so that Sophie felt that she was dressed exactly as she ought to be and heaved a small sigh of relief, noticed with the ghost of a smile by Rijk.

The evening was pleasant; the dinner was superb: mushrooms in garlic, roast duck with an orange sauce, lemon syllabub and a *bombe glacée* to finish.

Getting up from the table, Sophie wondered if the

meal was a sample of the week ahead. If so, she would have to take long walks or do exercises in her room each morning.

She didn't have to worry about the exercises; the next morning Rijk took her walking and she was glad of the sensible shoes and a thick woolly under the Jaeger jacket, for the weather was cold and the sky grey with a wind which hinted at snow later on. He took her briskly round the grounds and then down to the village beyond, with Matt prancing along beside them. As they walked he talked about his home and the life he led.

'I am away a good deal,' he told her, 'you know that already, but I come home whenever I can. Of course, if you wish you can accompany me to England when I go and visit your parents while I am working. You won't be lonely if you stay here; the family will see to that, and besides, you will soon make friends.'

It seemed to her that he was making it clear that he didn't want her with him while he travelled away from home. Reasonable enough, she supposed, it wasn't as though he was head over heels in love with her; theirs was to be a placid, well mannered marriage with no strong feelings, and she supposed that was what she wanted. She had told him that, hadn't she? He had taken her at her word, no doubt content to have found a woman who had the same attitude to marriage as he had.

They walked until lunchtime and had that meal together, for his mother and father had gone to visit neighbouring friends and wouldn't be back until the evening. When they had finished Rijk asked her if she would like to go with him to his study while he looked over the notes on several cases he had been asked to deal with. She was surprised, but settled down in a comfortable leather chair by the window with a pile of magazines, while Matt got under the desk at his master's feet.

The room was pleasantly warm and very quiet and she took care not to speak, even when she glanced out of the window and saw the first snowflakes falling, and presently she had her reward, for the professor closed his case papers and leaned back in his chair. 'How restful you are, Sophie; I'm sure you were longing to tell me that it was snowing...'

'Well, yes, I was, but I know how annoying it is when you're studying something or writing a report and someone keeps talking in hushed tones or sighing.'

'I can see we're ideally suited. Come and have tea; you deserve a whole pot to yourself.'

His parents came back presently and they dined and spent the rest of the evening sitting in the drawing-room. Mevrouw van Taak ter Wijsma made no bones about questioning Sophie, in the nicest possible way, about her life and home. Sophie answered readily enough; if she were a mother, even if her son were an adult well able to look after his own interests, she felt sure that she would want to know as much as possible about a future daughter-in-law.

Rijk followed her out into the hall when she and his mother went to bed. 'Shall we walk again in the morning?' he asked her. 'I'm going to Leeuwarden after lunch; perhaps you would like to come with me? You can look around the shops while I am at the hospital.'

She agreed readily, and presently, in bed and half

asleep, began on a list of presents she would take home with her. She was asleep before it was even half finished.

They walked away from the village in the morning, taking a narrow cart track which wound round the shores of the lake, and Sophie, muffled in her coat and with her head swathed in a cashmere scarf of Rijk's, was glad of them, for the wind was cutting and the snow, long ceased, had frozen on the ground. Looking around her, she had to admit that the scenery was bleak, and yet she liked it. Which, she conceded silently, was a good thing if she were to marry Rijk. She hadn't made up her mind yet, she reminded herself, despite his cool assumption that their marriage was a foregone conclusion.

Even while she thought about it, she knew in her heart of hearts that she would marry him; he would be a good husband, kind and considerate and undemanding, and more than anything else she wanted the security and contentment which he had offered her. Romance, she had decided wistfully, wasn't for her. Her only taste of it had turned sour; far better settle for a comfortable relationship.

He drove her to Leeuwarden in the afternoon, set her down in the centre of the shopping centre, close to the ancient Weigh House, told her that he would wait there for her at four o'clock, and drove himself off to the hospital.

Left to herself, Sophie studied the shop windows and presently made a few purchases. Cigars for her father, a Delft blue vase for her mother, a thick slab of chocolate for Tom and, after a lengthy search, a book on Friesland for George, who was a bookworm, and a pen and pencil set for Paul. She could have bought that in England, but at least it was in a Dutch box and the description was in that language, which made it rather different.

By then it was getting on for four o'clock and she made her way back to the Weigh House and found Rijk waiting. He took her parcels from her, settled her in the car and got in beside her. 'You found shopping easy enough?' he wanted to know.

'Well, yes; once or twice I got a bit muddled, but almost everyone speaks English. Did you have a busy afternoon?'

'An unusual case...' He began to tell her about it and she listened with intelligence and real interest, so that he observed, 'How delightful it is to discuss my work with someone who knows what I'm talking about and is really interested.'

Which gave Sophie a gentle glow of pleasure.

The next day he put her in the car and took her on a sightseeing tour of Friesland. North first, to Dokkum, where they had coffee at a nice old-fashioned hotel by the canal, and then on to the coast and the Wadden-zee, bleak and cold, with a distant view of the islands, looking lonely beyond the dull grey sea.

'Do people live there?' asked Sophie.

'Good heavens, yes. In summer they swarm with holiday-makers. They're very peaceful out of season; there are bird sanctuaries and beautiful beaches. We will go in early spring and you shall see for yourself.'

He drove south again along narrow brick roads built on their dikes, bypassed Leeuwarden, and stopped in

Franeker, where they had a lunch of *erwtensoep*, a thick pea soup, rich with pieces of sausage and pork, followed by smoked eel on toast—the kind of food, Rijk assured Sophie, which kept the sometimes very cold winter at bay.

They sat over their coffee until a watery sun decided him that it would be worth going down the coast to Hindeloopen and Staveren before turning for home.

Even on a winter's day, Hindeloopen was charming. They walked along the sea wall before driving on to Staveren, which disappointed her so much that Rijk drove inland to Sloten; the sixteenth-century charm of the tiny town more than made up for the unattractiveness of Staveren.

It was dusk as they arrived back at the house, and the windows glowed with light. The professor got out and opened Sophie's door as Rauke, already on the porch, stood back to allow Matt to hurl himself at his master, and she stood quietly, looking around her.

In the fast-gathering dark the house looked beautiful and a little awe-inspiring. There was already a touch of frost on the lawn before it and the trees surrounding it were rustling and sighing. She wondered how long they had been standing there, guarding the house. After her happy and contented day she felt suddenly uncertain; if it hadn't been for Rauke standing there in the cold waiting for them to go inside she would have unburdened herself to Rijk there and then; as it was she went into the house and allowed Rijk to take her coat before she went to her room to tidy her hair and do things to her face. It glowed with the cold air and her eyes sparkled, but it didn't mirror her feelings. She went down to the sitting-room, where the professor was waiting for her, the tea-tray with its shining silver and delicate china already on the sofa table.

Much though she wanted a cup of tea, she had made up her mind to say what she had to say first. She began at once. 'Rijk…'

He looked up from the letters he was glancing through and studied her face. 'Something is worrying you, Sophie?'

'Yes, how did you know?'

He said quietly, 'We are friends—close friends—are we not, my dear?'

'Yes, oh, yes, we are. I'm a bit worried. You see, I didn't know about all this.' She waved a hand around her at the understated comfort and luxury around them. 'I knew you were a very successful man; I supposed that you would have a nice house in Holland and be— well, comfortably off. But this is different. Are you very rich?'

His firm mouth twitched. 'I'm afraid so. I can only plead that a good deal of my wealth is the result of no doubt ill gotten gains from my merchant ancestors.'

She nodded like a child, glad to have had something explained. 'Yes, I see. You don't think that I am marrying you for your money, Rijk?'

He said gently, 'No, Sophie, I don't think that.'

'Because I'm not. Money's nice to have, isn't it? But it isn't as important as other things. If—if I say I'll marry you it wouldn't make any difference to me if you were on the dole.'

He crossed the room to where she was still standing and took both her hands in his, bent his head, and kissed her. A gentle kiss, as gentle as his voice had been. It reassured her so that she said, 'Well, that's all right, then, isn't it?'

'Perfectly all right. Come and pour the tea and I'll tell you what I have to do tomorrow.'

He was going to Brussels to examine some highly connected man with a suspected brain tumour. 'I shall be away all day. Mother and Father would like you to go with them on a visit to my grandmother—she lives in Heerenveen—for lunch and tea. I hope to be back in time for dinner.'

'You aren't going to drive all that way there and back?' She sounded, did she but know it, like an anxious wife, and he smiled.

'No, I shall fly. I have a light plane I use from time to time.'

'You can fly as well?'

'It saves a great deal of time. Do you drive a car, Sophie?'

'Oh, yes. I take Father round when I'm home; my brothers taught me.'

'Good; we are a little isolated here, but if you have a car you will be able to go where and when you like.' And at her anxious look, he added, 'When I am not at home.'

In bed that night, reviewing her day, she knew that she would marry Rijk. He had, of course, all this time behaved as though she had already agreed to do so, although she was aware that he was prepared to wait for her answer when they got back to England. Her mind made up, there was no point in staying awake; she slept dreamlessly and never heard the plane's engines from a nearby field as Rijk flew off to Brussels.

She was disappointed to find him gone when she went down to breakfast, but, his parents being at the table too, she had no time to brood over that. Bidden to be ready by ten o'clock, she took Matt for a walk in the grounds and joined them in the hall. Rijk's father drove an elderly, beautifully maintained Daimler, and Sophie had expected to be taken at a gentle speed to Heerenveen, but the elderly doctor drove with a speed sometimes alarming on the narrow roads, and since his wife, sitting with Sophie in the back, appeared to find this quite normal, Sophie said nothing, but watched the rolling countryside and made suitable replies to her companions' friendly talk.

Heerenveen was rather nice, she decided as their driver at last slowed down to go through the town and take a narrow road which presently revealed a small lake. Old Mevrouw van Taak ter Wijsma lived in a fair-sized square house close to the water, with a sprinkling of small houses along the road, cared for by several devoted servants. She went out seldom, but kept a sharp eye on her numerous family. She was a tall old lady, very thin, with a high bridged nose and bright blue eyes, dressed in black with a great many gold chains, and she received them in a room overlooking the lake, furnished with old-fashioned heavy furniture, its small tables covered by photos in silver frames, and great cabinets along its walls loaded with beautiful porcelain. She offered a cheek to her son and daughter-in-law and then studied Sophie at some length.

'So you're the girl that Rijk intends to marry. At

least you match him with height. Nice-looking too. You'll make him a good wife, no doubt.'

Sophie murmured suitably; there seemed no point in explaining that she hadn't actually said that she would marry Rijk and didn't intend to until he asked her if her mind was made up. She was told to sit by the old lady and spent the next hour making the right replies to that lady's questions.

Lunch was a solemn, long-drawn-out meal and afterwards, their hostess retiring for a brief nap, Sophie was invited to look round the house with Rijk's mother, and by the time they had peered into a great many rather gloomy rooms it was time to join the old lady for milkless tea and very small biscuits.

Presently they drove back to Rijk's home, his father, doubtless pleased at having been able to leave before it was quite dark, driving with a carefree speed which set Sophie's neat head of hair on end.

Rijk was home and came to help his mother and Sophie out of the car while Matt got in everyone's way. As they went indoors he took Sophie's arm.

'And did you like Granny?' he asked. She nodded. 'She's a darling…'

He paused in the hall so that for a moment they were alone. 'She phoned just now; she says you're a darling too.'

For a moment Sophie thought that he would kiss her, but he didn't; he only smiled.

Chapter 6

There were only two days left. Sophie went down to breakfast in the morning wondering if Rijk had any plans.

He had: a walk down to the village to meet the dominie and look round the church and then, since it was a clear, cold day, a walk along the lakeside to an outlying farm which he owned. 'And in the afternoon, if you would like, we will drive to Groningen and take a look round—there's a rather splendid church and the university.'

On the way to the village presently he told her that they would go back to his parents' house on the following day, lunch there, and then come back and have an early dinner before driving down to the Hoek to catch the night ferry.

Sophie agreed cheerfully, thankful that she had

bought her presents when they had gone to Leeuwarden. 'Do phone your people if you would like to,' went on Rijk. 'We should be back around nine o'clock.'

'Would you like to stay? There's plenty of room—Mother will expect you for lunch, I'm sure.'

'Lunch, by all means, but I've a consultation in the afternoon and I'm operating on the following day and then going to Leeds for a couple of days...'

'But it's almost Christmas...'

'Which I shall have to spend away from home—I did tell you.'

'I forgot. So we can't see each other for a while?'

'No.' He tucked a hand under her elbow. 'May I come and see you on my way home?' He smiled at her. 'Life is one long rush, isn't it?'

'In four days' time? You want to know...'

She paused and he said easily, 'Yes, please, Sophie.'

The dominie was a bearded giant of a man. His wife, fair-haired and blue-eyed, offered coffee and took Sophie to see the youngest of their children, a calmly sleeping baby. 'The other three are at school. You like children?'

'Yes,' said Sophie and blushed when her companion said cheerfully,

'Of course, Rijk will want a family.'

They went round the church when they had had coffee, a severely plain edifice with whitewashed walls and small latticed windows. A number of Rijk's ancestors were buried beneath its flagstoned floor and even more in the small churchyard. His family had lived there for a very long time—centuries.

Presently they said goodbye to the dominie and his

wife and took a rough little lane skirting the lake. It was very quiet there and they walked briskly, arm in arm, stopping now and then while he pointed out some thing of interest, telling her about the people and the country round them. Presently they came to the farm, a flat dwelling with a tiled and thatched roof, its huge barn at its back. 'The cows live there throughout the winter,' explained Rijk. 'Come inside with me and meet Wendel and Sierou.'

The farmer was middle-aged and powerfully built and his wife was almost as stoutly built as he was. After the first polite greetings, Rijk murmured an apology and carried on the conversation in Friese. Dutch is bad enough, reflected Sophie, Friese is far worse; but she enjoyed sitting there in the vast kitchen, drinking more coffee and listening to Rijk's quiet voice and the farmer's rumbling replies.

They got up to go presently and walked back the way they had come, and over lunch presently the talk had been of a variety of matters, none of them personal. Rijk's parents had been out too and lunched with them, but they didn't linger over the meal since they were to drive to Groningen.

Rijk cut through to the motorway from Drachten to Groningen, a journey of twenty-five miles or so, which, while quick, missed a good deal of the smaller villages. 'We shall come home through the side-roads,' he promised her.

The city delighted her. The old houses lining the canals were picturesque and the fifteenth-century old St Martinkerk was magnificent. 'A pity the tower is closed for the winter,' observed the professor. 'It is three hundred and fifteen feet high; a splendid climb.'

'I don't like heights,' said Sophie baldly.

The university was a fairly modern building, its thousands of students each wearing a coloured cap to denote his or her faculty, and since the professor knew several of the lecturers there they were allowed to wander around while he patiently answered Sophie's questions.

Presently he took her to a restaurant on the Gedempte Zuiderdiep and, while they drank their coffee, explained the layout of the city to her. 'Of course you can see very little of it in such a short time, but we will come again.'

She let that pass. 'Do you come to the hospitals here as well?'

'From time to time, but of course Leeuwarden is my home territory.'

Since they had finished their coffee he took her to the Prinsenhof Gardens, which even in winter were beautiful.

True to his promise, they drove back along country roads, taking a roundabout route which went through several small villages. It was already dusk but the sky was clear and there were still a few golden rays from the setting sun. The villages looked cosy and there were lighted windows in the farms they passed. There was little traffic, but they were held up from time to time by slow-moving farm carts, drawn by heavy horses. 'I like this,' said Sophie.

'So do I; this is Friesland, how I think of it when I'm away.'

Rauke, without being asked, brought in the tea-tray

as soon as Sophie joined Rijk in the drawing-room. It was already five o'clock, well past the normal tea hour, but all the professor said was, 'We will dine later—there is no hurry this evening.' He said something to Rauke, who murmured a reply and went soft-footed from the room.

The tea was hot and quite strong. Sophie, when she had first arrived, had expected Earl Grey or orange pekoe—it was that kind of a house, she had decided—so it was delightful to find that the tea in the lovely old silver pot was the finest Assam. It hadn't occurred to her that the professor—a perfectionist in all he did—had taken the trouble to find out her preference. There were tiny sandwiches too and fairy cakes and a plate of biscuits which Matt was allowed to enjoy, leaning his furry bulk against his master, delighted to have them home again.

'He will miss you,' observed Sophie, sinking her nice white teeth into a fairy cake.

'Indeed, as I shall miss him. And you, Sophie, will you miss me?'

He was watching her intently and she wished that she knew how to give him a light-hearted answer which promised nothing. After all, he might be joking…

A quick glance at his impassive face made it clear that he wasn't joking; she said simply, 'Yes, I shall. I like being with you, Rijk.'

When he smiled she went on impulsively, 'And there is no need to wait…'

The door opened and his mother came into the room and Rijk got up, to all intents and purposes delighted to see her. Sophie, on the very brink of telling him that she would marry him, wondered if it was a sign of some sort to make her change her mind at the last minute.

As for the professor, there was nothing in his manner to indicate whether he regretted the interruption; his mother sat down, declaring that they had had a cup of tea an hour or more ago. 'I am very fond of your aunt Kinske, but she serves a poor cup of tea; she should speak to her cook.' She turned to Sophie. 'You enjoyed your afternoon, Sophie?'

Sophie said that yes, she had and added that she liked the villages they had driven through.

'Not at all like your own countryside, though,' Rijk's mother commented. 'I shall enjoy looking around me when we come to your wedding.'

Sophie opened her mouth to speak, caught Rijk's eye, and closed it again. He wasn't smiling, but she knew that he was amused. She went rather red and Mevrouw van Taak ter Wijsma, thinking that she was blushing for quite another reason, nodded her head in a satisfied manner.

Really, thought Sophie, they all take it for granted and I haven't even said... She remembered what she had been on the point of saying only a short time ago and made some trivial remark about the English countryside without mentioning a wedding. The professor's lips twitched and his mother thought what a nice girl Sophie was, and so exactly right for her eldest son.

The rest of the day passed pleasantly enough, but Sophie had no opportunity to speak to Rijk alone, even if she had wanted to, and, as she told herself in bed later on, she hadn't wanted to. What a good thing his mother had joined them when she had, although it would have been interesting to see what he would have done or said. He wouldn't do anything, she reflected peevishly, probably shake hands—wasn't that what friends did when they agreed to do something together? She bounced over in bed and thumped the big square pillow, feeling put out and not sure why.

She felt better in the morning; after all, she was doing what she wanted: marrying someone who shared her ideas of married life as well as a mistrust of romantic nonsense, which led only to unhappiness. She went down to breakfast with a cheerful face.

They drove to Leeuwarden later in the morning, to be joined by all five of Rijk's sisters at his parents' house, although, rather to Sophie's relief, the husbands and the children were absent. As were his brothers.

'You will see them all at the wedding,' said Mevrouw van Taak ter Wijsma in a consoling voice. She didn't appear to expect an answer, which was a good thing, for Sophie hadn't been able to think of one.

They sat over lunch; the talk was all of Christmas and the New Year and there was a good deal of sympathy for Rijk, although Tiele said, 'Next year will be different, Rijk. We'll have a marvellous family house party at your place; we can come over for the day and you can put up the rest of us.' She glanced at Sophie, 'You have brothers, haven't you, Sophie? And parents. What a splendid time we'll have...'

Sophie smiled and the professor sat back in his chair, saying nothing and looking wicked. He had put her in a very awkward position, fumed Sophie, and she would make no bones about telling him so.

Her chance came as they drove back to his home.

The goodbyes had been protracted and affectionate; she had been thoroughly kissed and warmly hugged and Rijk's father had taken her hands in his and told her that Rijk would make her happy. 'I shouldn't boast of my own children, but I am sure that you will suit each other very well, and that,' he had added deliberately, 'is just as important as loving someone.'

She remembered that now, peeping at Rijk's calm profile. 'Your family seem to have made up their minds that we are to marry...'

He said easily, 'Yes, indeed. What did you think of Nanny?'

It was a successful red herring. 'Oh, she's an old darling, isn't she? A bit peppery but I can quite see why you have such an affection for her.' She paused, remembering her brief visit to the old lady, sitting cosily in the sitting-room leading from the kitchen, surrounded by dozens of photos of her charges. The room had been most comfortably furnished and Sophie had seen the bedroom leading from it.

'She wanted to be there,' explained Rijk, 'within sound of the kitchen, and of course people are popping in and out all the time so that it never gets lonely. Mother quite often has coffee with her.'

Sophie remembered that she was annoyed with him. 'You could have explained—' she began.

'No need.' He sounded placid. 'If you should decide against marrying me, then that is time enough to explain.'

'Will you be annoyed if I do that?'

'Annoyed?' He considered the question. 'Why? I thought I had made it clear that you were free to make up your mind; you are surely old and wise enough to do that.'

That nettled her. 'How well you put it,' she said peevishly.

He ignored the peevishness. 'Will you mind having your tea on your own? I still have some work to clear and we must dine early. We need to leave here around half-past seven—if we dine at half-past six? Will that suit you?'

'Yes, of course. I've only a few things left to pack.' Her ill humour had vanished; indeed, upon reflection, she wasn't quite sure why she had felt so cross in the first place.

They went on board the ferry with little time to spare, but that, she realised, was what Rijk had intended, taking Matt for a last-minute romp in the dark, cold grounds, bidding Rauke and Tyske a leisurely goodbye, and then racing smoothly through the dark evening, over the Afsluitdijk and down the motorway until they reached the Hoek with just sufficient time to go on board before the ferry sailed.

Sophie, who had watched the clock worriedly for the last fifteen minutes or so, realised that she had been anxious about nothing. Rijk was a man who knew exactly what he was doing, and she had no need to fuss. The thought was reassuring as she curled up in her bunk and went to sleep.

Her mother was waiting for them as they stopped outside her home the next morning. The door was flung wide to allow Monty and Mercury to rush out to greet them, closely followed by the lady of the house. They drank their coffee in a flurry of talk, although the professor said little.

'You must be tired,' said Mrs Blount. 'Are you sure you can't stay?'

'Quite sure, I'm afraid. I must go to St Agnes's this afternoon, but I'll come in four—no, three—days, if I may.'

'You're always welcome.' Mrs Blount gave his massive shoulder a motherly pat. 'Arthur will be back presently. You can have a nice chat while you unpack, Sophie, and I can get on with lunch.'

So Sophie had little chance to be alone with Rijk, and she wasn't sure if she was glad about that or not; certainly he gave no sign of annoyance at the lack of opportunity to be with her and presently, after lunch, when he took his leave, his placid, 'I'll see you in three days, Sophie,' and the peck she received on her cheek hardly stood for any eagerness on his part to have more of her company.

The car was barely out of sight when her mother asked, 'What have you decided, darling?' She glanced at her beautiful daughter's face. 'Perhaps you still aren't quite sure...'

Sophie sat down on the edge of the kitchen table. 'I'm sure—I think I was sure before we even went to Holland. You see, Mother, he thinks as I do; we both want a sensible, secure marriage. We like each other and we like the same things and we do get on well together. There won't be any violent feelings or quarrels. Rijk has had his share of falling in love and so have I. We shall be very happy together.'

Mrs Blount listened to this speech with an expressionless face. It sounded to her as though her dear daughter was reassuring herself, and all that nonsense about being sensible and secure. That was well enough, but no use at all without love. A good thing that Rijk loved Sophie so much that he was willing to put up with her ideas. Indeed, she suspected that he might even be encouraging them for his own ends, whatever they might be.

She said comfortably, 'Now just sit there and tell me what his home is like.'

'It's beautiful and rather grand, a long way from everywhere, although there's a village ten minutes' walk away. There's a lake close by. Mother, Rijk's a rich man—I didn't know that. Oh, I knew he was comfortably well off—I mean, he's well known internationally for his brain surgery—but I had no idea. There's a butler and a housekeeper and two maids, only he doesn't seem to be rich, because he never mentions money or his possessions. His parents have a large house in Leeuwarden and of course he has his house in London.' She cast a worried glance at her parent. 'Do you suppose it will be all right? I do like him, he's become a dear friend, and I don't care tuppence if he's without a shilling.'

'Money is nice to have, love, and I'm sure it won't make any difference to you—you're too sensible and well brought up—and someone like Rijk who has been born into it and been taught its proper place in life isn't likely to let it interfere with his way of life.' She became all at once brisk. 'I suppose you will marry quite soon? After Christmas? You will need clothes...'

'Yes, but I won't do anything until I see Rijk.'

'Of course not, dear. Now come upstairs. The boys will be home tomorrow and I've still any number of presents to tie up; do come and help me.'

The three days went quickly; there were the preparations to make for Christmas, last-minute shopping, friends calling, and the last Christmas cards to send. Sophie was in the kitchen making mince pies when Rijk arrived. She saw that he was tired and put down her rolling-pin at once and came across the kitchen to meet him.

'You've been working hard?' And then she added, 'It's nice to see you, Rijk.' She put a hand on his sleeve. 'You'll stay for lunch?'

He put a hand over hers. 'No. I must get back to the hospital as quickly as possible; I've an out-patients clinic this afternoon and a consultation. I mustn't miss the evening ferry.'

'At least have a cup of coffee—it's here, on the Aga.'

'That would be nice.' He sat down at the table and ate a mince pie, still warm from the oven. 'You're ready for Christmas?'

'Yes.' She put a mug of coffee before him and went to sit down opposite him. He took another mince pie. 'I've come for my answer, Sophie.'

'I'll marry you, Rijk, and I'll try to be a good wife— I hope I'll be able to cope...'

'Of course you will. I'll get a special licence. You would like to marry here?'

'Yes, please, and would you mind if we had a quiet wedding?'

'I should like that myself. My mother and father and Bellamy for my best man—I was his...'

'When will you be back here?'

'In two weeks' time.' He thought for a moment. 'Any day after the seventeenth of January will be fine.' He smiled suddenly at her. 'The eighteenth or nineteenth?' And when she nodded, 'I'll try to come over before then so that we can see your rector.' He put down his mug. 'I must go…'

'Where have you come from?'

'Leeds.'

'That's miles away; you must be worn out.'

'Not a bit of it.'

He came round the table and put his hands on her shoulders. 'We shall be happy, Sophie.' He bent and kissed her gently. 'And here is a token of our happiness.' He fished a small box from his pocket and opened it. The ring inside was exquisite; sapphires and diamonds in an old-fashioned gold setting. 'My grandmother's ring; she had it from her husband's grandmother.'

He slipped it on her finger and then kissed her hand.

'Were you so sure?' asked Sophie.

'Oh, yes. *Tot ziens*, Sophie.' He had gone as unfussily as he had come, leaving her looking at the ring on her finger and wondering if other girls arranged their weddings in such a businesslike way, and all in the space of a few minutes. Of course neither she nor Rijk were hampered by sentimental ideas about getting married. She heaved a sigh and began cutting rounds of pastry and when her mother came into the kitchen she said soberly, 'He'd driven down from Leeds and he's got a full afternoon's work…'

Her mother, who had seen the professor getting into his car and been the pleased recipient of a warm hug, said cheerfully, 'Yes, dear, but I should imagine that he knows just how much he can do before he needs to rest. He's a very strong man.' She admired the ring and noted with satisfaction that Sophie was still fretting about Rijk.

'When you are married I dare say you will be able to persuade him to work a little less hard, dear. Have you fixed a date for the wedding?'

When Sophie told her she said, 'You might go and see the rector tomorrow before he gets tied up with Christmas. A quiet wedding?'

'Yes. We would both like that. Just you and Father and the boys and Rijk's mother and father and the best man—Mr Bellamy from St Anne's—they've been friends for years.'

'His sisters and brothers?' prompted Mrs Blount.

'I don't know, but I dare say they'll come—they're a close family.'

'How nice. What will you wear?'

They finished the mince pies together, arguing the merits of a winter-white outfit or a pale grey dress and jacket. It was bound to be cold and probably a grey day to boot. 'Directly Christmas is over you must go shopping.' She frowned. 'Of course the sales will be on, but you might find something.'

The boys came home presently, wished her well with brotherly affection, stated their intention of being at her wedding, and demanded to know every detail of her holiday.

'It sounds super,' commented Paul. 'We'll all come and stay and you can be the gracious lady of the house.'

'Why not?' said Sophie placidly. 'There's heaps of

room and I dare say there'll be ice-skating if it gets cold enough.'

'You won't want us to visit you as soon as that,' declared Tom. 'You'll need a few weeks to be all soppy with each other.'

Sophie laughed, knowing it was expected of her. She couldn't imagine Rijk being soppy. For that matter, she had no intention of being soppy either.

She went out the next morning and bought a Dutch grammar; she must do her small best to make their marriage a success, and a good start would be to speak at least a few words of Rijk's language. There was very little time to do more than glance through its pages, what with helping around the house and helping to cook the nourishing meals her brothers constantly needed, besides entertaining various friends and acquaintances who popped in for a drink and to admire the ring. It was amazing how quickly the news had spread through the village; it wasn't until she picked up the *Telegraph* and saw the announcement of their engagement that she discovered why.

There had been no message from Rijk and although she hadn't expected one she had hoped that he might find time to phone before he left. He would be back at his home. She corrected herself; he wasn't going home, he was going straight to Schiphol. He would be in Greece now, bringing his skill to bear upon a patient with no thought of Christmas and certainly not of her.

She was mistaken. On Christmas Eve a basket of red roses, magnificent enough for a prima donna, was delivered and the card with it was in his handwriting too. He wished her a happy Christmas and was hers, Rijk.

She placed it in a prominent position in the drawing-room and looked at it every time she went into the room. He had thought of her even though he was so busy. Her lovely face took on an added sparkle and she bore her brothers' teasing remarks about red roses for love with good humour. Of course, that hadn't been Rijk's meaning; red was, after all, the colour for Christmas. It was only much later, going to bed after going to midnight service with her family, that Sophie allowed the thought which had been nagging her to be faced. Surely Rijk could have written to her or telephoned? She had made all kinds of excuses for him, but she found it hard to believe that he couldn't have scribbled a post-card before he got on the plane. The roses had been a lovely surprise, of course, but if he had had time to arrange for those he surely could have phoned her too? She lay awake wondering about it and when, at length, she slept she dreamt of him.

She hadn't been home for Christmas for several years and, despite her uneasy thoughts, she found herself soothed and reassured by the ritual of giving and receiving presents, lighting the tree, going to church again and helping her mother serve up a dinner which never varied from year to year. As she ate her turkey and Christmas pudding she wondered where she would be in a year's time—here with Rijk or in Friesland, sharing Christmas with him and his family.

'Such a pity Rijk isn't here,' observed her mother. 'I wonder what kind of a Christmas he is having?'

The professor wasn't having Christmas at all; he was undertaking a tricky piece of surgery on his patient's brain and, being a man with plenty of will-power, he hadn't allowed his thoughts to stray from this difficult task. Even when the long and complicated operation was over, he stayed within call, for the next day or two were crucial. On New Year's Eve, flying back to his home, satisfied that his work had been successful, he allowed himself to think of Sophie. He had swept her into a promise of marriage to him, but that, he was only too well aware, was only the beginning.

Rauke was waiting for him at Schiphol with an ecstatic Matt on the back seat, and he drove through the early evening back to his home, to change his clothes, wish his household a happy New Year, and then get back into his car again and drive to his parents' house, where the entire family were celebrating. He was a tired man, but no one looking at him would have seen that; he joined in the final round of drinks before midnight, piled his plate with the delicious food, and on the stroke of midnight toasted the New Year with champagne. The ceremony of kissing everyone, shaking hands and exchanging good wishes over, the professor slipped away to his father's study, and picked up the phone to dial a number.

Sophie and her family were still sitting round the fire, drinking the last of the port her father had brought up from the cellar and making sleepy plans to go to bed, when the phone rang and, since Sophie was nearest to it, she got up to answer it. Rijk's quiet voice, wishing her a happy New Year, sent a pleasant little thrill through her person; she had hoped that he might phone, but she hadn't been sure about it. She said fervently, 'Oh, Rijk,' and then, 'A happy New Year to you too. Where are you?'

'In Leeuwarden. I got back a few hours ago. I'll be with you the day after tomorrow—I'm not sure when. You'll be at home?'

'Yes, oh, yes.'

'I'll see you then. *Tot ziens*, Sophie.' He rang off and she felt vague disappointment at the brevity of his call, but it was quickly swamped at the thought of seeing him again. It surprised her that she had missed him so much.

She was in the kitchen washing her mother's best china when Mrs Broom put her head round the door.

'Yer young man's at the door, love.' She beamed at Sophie. 'Ere, give me them plates and wipe yer 'ands, mustn't keep 'im awaiting.'

Sophie thrust a valuable Wedgwood plate at Mrs Broom and dashed out of the kitchen, wiping wet, soapy hands on her pinny as she went. It was a deplorable garment, kept hanging behind the kitchen door and worn by anyone who needed it, regardless of size, but she had forgotten that.

The professor was in the hall talking to her mother, towering over her, immaculate in his cashmere overcoat and tweeds. He looked as though he might have come fresh from his valet's hands, and Sophie slithered to a halt, suddenly conscious of the apron and the fact that she hadn't bothered with her hair but tied it back with a ribbon.

The knowledge that she wasn't looking her best made her say crossly, 'I didn't expect you so soon,' and then, 'It's lovely to see you, Rijk.'

She rubbed her still wet hands on the apron. 'I was just washing the best china…'

The professor's eyes gleamed beneath their lids. 'I like the hair,' he said and bent to kiss her. 'Shall I come and help you with the plates?'

'No, of course not.' She smiled, her good humour restored, feeling comfortable with him just as friends should with each other. 'I'll fetch the coffee—did you come over on the night ferry?'

'Yes. I've a case this afternoon at St Agnes's but I wondered if we might go and see your parson this morning? I'll come back this evening and we'll go out to dinner; there is a good deal to discuss.'

She nodded. 'Yes. Are you going to be in England for a while?'

'I'm afraid not. Two or three days. I've a good deal of work waiting for me and I'd like to get it done before the wedding.'

'Yes, of course.' They went into the sitting-room, where her mother had prudently retired, and presently, over coffee which that lady brought, the conversation turned to the wedding.

'A quiet one?' her mother asked and went on, 'Just a handful of people—we can all come back here for lunch afterwards if you would like that. I dare say you'll want to be off somewhere or other.'

'We shall catch the night ferry to Holland; I can spare only a couple of days.'

'Well, let me know what you arrange between you,' said Mrs Blount comfortably, 'and I'll fit in.' She spoke cheerfully; like all mothers she would have liked to see her beautiful daughter swanning down the aisle in white satin and her own wedding veil, which she had kept so carefully for just such an occasion; it might have comforted her if she had known that Sophie had had a fleeting regret that the white satin and veil weren't for her. Only for a moment, however; a romantic wedding would have been ridiculous in their case. All the same, she would find something suitable for a bride, however modest the wedding...

Her father and Tom came in presently and she slipped away to take great pains with her face and hair and present herself in a quilted jacket and woolly gloves, ready to go to the rectory with Rijk.

They walked there, talking idly about this and that, very much at ease with each other, and when they reached the rectory the professor, while giving the appearance of asking Sophie's opinion about dates and times, had everything arranged exactly as he had planned it. The wedding was to be at eleven o'clock in the morning in two weeks' time by special licence; it was to be a quiet ceremony. As they would be leaving for Holland that same day they were both most grateful to the rector for arranging to marry them at rather short notice.

'Delighted, delighted,' observed the old man, 'and I trust that I may have the happy task of christening your children.'

Sophie smiled, murmured and avoided Rijk's eye, and was a little surprised to hear his agreement, uttered in a grave voice, although she felt he meant it. Of course, she told herself, he didn't want to hurt the rector's feelings. That was the one doubt she had about their marriage; she liked children and she rather thought that Rijk did too, but if they kept to their agreement and lived the life he had envisaged there wouldn't be any. Of course, perhaps later on... In the meantime, she told herself, they would share a very pleasant life together without heartbreak and the pitfalls of falling in love. She walked back with Rijk, quite content with her future.

He left shortly after they got back with the reminder that he would be back in the early evening. As he got into the car he asked her, 'Have you any preference as to where we should go?'

'Must it be a restaurant?' she asked diffidently. 'Would it be a bother to Percy and Mrs Wiffen if we dined at your house?'

She was rewarded by his pleased look. 'No bother at all; they're all agog at the idea of a wedding and I'm sure they're longing to see the bride again.' He kissed her cheek lightly, got into the car, and drove off, leaving her to go into the house and go through her wardrobe for something suitable to wear. The brown velvet skirt and ivory silk blouse with the frilled collar would do nicely...

The evening was a great success; Percy and Mrs Wiffen had presented them with a delicious meal and afterwards they had sat in the drawing-room by the fire, talking. Waking in the night, Sophie had been unable to remember what they had talked about, only the satisfying memory of it. It was only when she woke again just as it was getting light that she knew without any doubt at all that she had fallen in love with Rijk.

Chapter 7

Sophie got up and dressed, although it was still early; to lie in bed was quite impossible. She dragged on an old raincoat, tied a scarf over her hair, pulled on her wellies, and went quietly out of the house.

Montgomery and Mercury, delighted at the prospect of a walk so early in the day, slid through the back door after her, and she was glad of their company.

It was drizzling with a cold rain and the wind was bitter, but she really hadn't noticed either. 'Now I'm in a pickle, aren't I?' she asked them. 'Must I say that I've changed my mind or shall I go ahead and marry him and then pretend for the rest of my days that I've nothing but friendly feelings towards him?'

Mercury gave a sympathetic yelp and Montgomery huffed deep in his throat.

'The thing is,' went on Sophie, intent on getting

things straight in her head, 'is it better never to see him again or marry him and never let him know that I love him?' She added in a shaky little voice, 'He's the one, you see. I know that now; I can't think why I didn't discover it earlier. No one else really matters. He does like me, we get on so well together—like old friends, if you see what I mean—and I don't think I could bear never to see him again…'

She stopped in the middle of the muddy lane and the dogs stopped with her, looking at her with sympathetic eyes. 'I'm going to marry him,' she told them briskly. 'Half a loaf is very much better than no bread.'

She turned for home, her mind made up, and feeling relieved, so that when, over breakfast, her mother broached the subject of buying clothes she agreed that the sooner she did some shopping the better.

'And I wonder how many of Rijk's family are coming to the wedding?' her mother mused. 'Should I invite them?' She didn't wait for an answer. 'I'll write a note to his mother and invite any member of the family who might wish to come.' She began to reckon on her fingers. 'There will be nine of them if they all come, and I haven't counted the husbands…'

'They won't come to the wedding,' said Sophie. 'Just his mother and father and perhaps a brother or sister. He told me that there will be a big family gathering when we get back to Friesland.'

'Then I'll cater for about twenty to be on the safe side. I must see about the wedding-cake this morning. When will you go shopping, love?'

'Tomorrow; I don't need much…'

'No, dear, perhaps not, but one or two good outfits besides your wedding clothes.'

Sophie gave her mother a dreamy look, her head full of Rijk. 'Winter-white if I can find it, a coat and dress, and I'll have to buy a hat.'

Her mother gave her a thoughtful look; if she hadn't known better she would have said that the dear girl was in love, her head in the clouds and her wits addled.

'That would be very nice,' she said in a matter-of-fact voice. 'Will you be seeing Rijk before the wedding?'

'No, he goes back to Holland tomorrow. He wants to clear up as much as possible before we are married.'

She went up to London the next morning. Her father drove her into Chipping Ongar and put her on the London train with instructions to spend the cheque he had given her, and if she needed more money she had only to ask for it. There was money in her own bank account too; if she wanted to she could be wildly extravagant. Why not? she reflected. It was her wedding and she wanted Rijk to be proud of her.

She avoided the big stores where the sales were in full swing; there were several boutiques where, even if they had sales, they would have something to suit her tucked away.

By late afternoon she was tired, hungry and triumphant. She also had a charming outfit for the wedding, a winter-white dress and long loose coat to match it in a fine woollen material. Even with a few pounds taken off as a concession to the sales, the price had been horrific, but, as the owner of the boutique had said, it was an outfit which could be worn repeatedly and not lose its chic. There was a hat to go with it too, a confection of velvet and feathers, faintly pink-tipped.

'A wedding outfit?' murmured the saleslady, who had seen Sophie's ring.

'Well, yes—a very quiet wedding…'

'Exactly suitable and very elegant. You have a splendid figure, if I may say so, madam. I expect you have already bought a good deal, but I do have a jersey suit—so suitable for this time of year. It is your size and I would be pleased to make a reduction on its price.'

A jersey suit would be useful, Sophie had reflected, and, since it was a perfect fit and a mixture of blues and greens which suited her dark hair and eyes, she bought that too.

She had snatched a hasty lunch then before going in search of something for the evening. Rijk lived in some style; certainly there would be at least one dance or dinner. This time she found exactly what she wanted— a dress with a full long skirt, the bodice square-necked and with tiny sleeves. It was in almond-pink chiffon and suitable, she hoped, for an eminent surgeon's wife, and since she still had some money in her purse she bought a brown and gold brocade top, high-necked and long-sleeved; it would go well with her brown velvet skirt… Marks and Spencer provided her with new undies and, well pleased with her purchases, she went back home.

It had been a lovely day and beneath the excitement of buying new clothes was the knowledge that she loved Rijk, and that was exciting too, so that when

he phoned later that evening she was for the moment
bereft of words.

In answer to his quiet 'Sophie?' she said breathlessly, 'Rijk, where are you?'

'At Eernewoude. What have you done with your day?'

'I bought a wedding-dress... Will you be there until
you come back here?'

'No, four or five days here and then a quick trip
to Brussels to see a patient and then here again until
I leave for England. You may not hear from me for a
day or two...'

'That's all right,' said Sophie. She wanted him to
phone her every day—twice a day if possible—just to
hear his voice, but on no account must he ever know
that. 'You don't need to bother; we'll see to everything.'

She wasn't sure, but it sounded as though he had
laughed before he said goodbye.

There was plenty to keep her occupied at home;
her mother had sent invitations to Rijk's family and
was happily immersed in preparations for the wedding
breakfast. 'Something simple,' she declared, 'if you
have to leave for the ferry.' She paused. 'But doesn't
that go at night? Rijk said he would want to leave directly after we have had lunch.'

'Perhaps he wants to call at his London house,' suggested Sophie.

'Probably.' Her mother frowned. 'Smoked salmon
and those little cheese puffs, baby sausage rolls and
tiny quiches—the kind you can hold in your hand without them going crumbly—and the cake, of course...'

Sophie said, 'Yes, Mother,' in a dreamy voice. As far
as she was concerned they could chew cardboard just

as long as she and Rijk were safely married. It would take time, she reflected, to get him to fall in love with her. She knew that she was a lovely girl and, while not in the least bit conceited, she knew that it was an asset. Rijk thought of her as a friend; all she had to do was to get him to see her in a different light…as an attractive woman as well as a practical young woman who understood his work and was prepared to take second place to it in his life.

She thought about it a good deal during the next few days. The thing was to make him see her in a new light. She still hadn't planned a course of action by the time he returned, and it was hard to behave as she always had done, to greet him with the friendly pleasure he expected and answer his questions about their wedding in a matter-of-fact voice.

His parents and two of his sisters had travelled over at the same time, driven their own car, and gone straight to his London home; only he had driven on to see her and make sure that everything was in train for the next day.

'Loewert and Iwert are flying over this evening— Bellamy will bring them down in the morning. That makes seven on my side. How many have you?'

They were sitting in the kitchen drinking coffee, and she tried not to look at him too often; just having him there, close to her, was sending her heart thumping at her ribs. She told herself silently not to be silly. 'Well, there's Mother and Father and the boys—that's five—and me, of course, and you… That's fourteen. The rector and his wife will come to lunch—it's a buffet.' She cast him a quick look. 'We weren't sure when you would want to leave.'

'I thought we might have dinner at home, just the two of us, before we go to the ferry.'

She nodded agreement. 'Mother would love everyone to stay for tea and supper; it would be nice if everyone got to know everyone else.' She added, 'I forgot Mr Bellamy...'

'He'll have to go back soon after we leave.'

The professor got up from his chair opposite her and came and sat on the corner of the table, close to her. 'No doubts?' he asked softly.

She gave him a direct look. 'None at all,' she told him clearly.

He bent and kissed her. 'Nor I. Shall we go for a walk? I'm going back after lunch; I'm sure you want to wash your hair or whatever women do before they get married.'

Sophie laughed. 'Well, as a matter of fact, I do have to do that—however did you know?'

'Remember that I have five sisters.' He pulled her to her feet. 'Get a coat and I'll find your mother.' He glanced at his watch. 'Is lunch at one o'clock? Then we have all of two hours.'

It was a cold morning, but there was a watery sun and they walked briskly.

'Tell me about your trip to Greece,' said Sophie. 'Was the op successful?'

She listened with real interest, understanding what he was talking about and asking sensible questions from time to time, and the professor paused in the middle of a particularly complicated explanation to say, 'What a pleasure it is to be able to talk about my work to someone who understands me. It is said that one shouldn't take one's work home with one, but how satisfactory it will be to come home and mull over my work without fear of boring you.'

'You would never bore me,' said Sophie and went bright pink because she had sounded a bit too fervent. She wasn't looking at him and didn't see his slow smile. She added quickly, 'Don't forget that I've been nursing for a long time.'

'Shall you miss it?' he asked casually. 'Life at Eernewoude is quiet...'

'I shall like that and there will be so much to keep me busy—I must learn to speak Dutch and understand it, and there's Matt and getting to know everyone in the village and your family.'

'We shall entertain too, Sophie. I have many friends and there is a surprisingly brisk social life. And when we are married I suspect it will be even brisker.'

'You will like that?'

'Not very much. I shall rely on you to fend off all but my closest friends.'

'You'll have to give me a list,' said Sophie, 'and I'll do my best.'

The professor went again after lunch, but not before he had given Sophie his wedding gift—diamond and sapphire earrings, the sapphires surrounded by diamonds, hanging from diamond-studded pendants. She put them on, struck dumb with their beauty. 'They're magnificent,' she told him. 'Thank you, Rijk, I'll wear them tomorrow...' She reached up to kiss his cheek. 'I

can't give you diamonds and sapphires, can I? Only a
wedding-ring…'

'Which I shall wear with pride.'

Sophie was up early on her wedding-day; she had
slept well, but once awake there was no point in lying
in bed—she was too excited. She was happy too and at
the same time apprehensive. It would be heaven to be
with Rijk each and every day, but supposing, just supposing he found her boring or, worse, fell in love with
another woman? A beautiful face wasn't enough; she
knew that… She crept down to the kitchen and made
herself some tea and sat drinking it by the Aga with the
dogs on either side of her. Soothed by the warmth and
the ordinary action, she went back upstairs to bath and
presently have an early breakfast in her dressing-gown.

Even if she had wanted to brood she had no chance;
her brothers saw to that until her mother bustled her
back to her room to dress.

'Mother, there's heaps of time,' she protested.

'You must dress and then sit quietly and compose
yourself,' said her parent. 'Anyhow, I want everyone out
of the way. Mrs Broom will be here with her daughter
in a few minutes and I must make sure that everything
is ready in the drawing-room.'

So Sophie dressed and went to sit in her window;
she could see the church spire above the trees. In less
than an hour she would be beneath it, getting married.
She wondered what Rijk was doing; supposing he got
held up on the way—an accident, roads up for repair,
a puncture? She was glad when her mother came in
to ask her advice as to the exact angle of her new hat.

They studied it together in the looking-glass. 'Very mother-of-the-bride,' said Sophie. 'You do look nice, Mother, dear.'

'Will Rijk's mother look nice too?'

'I'm sure she will—she looks a bit fierce but she isn't. I think you'll like each other.'

The house was quiet once her mother and brothers had gone; she sat in the drawing-room with her father, waiting for the hired limousine to take them to the church. In a few hours she would have left home, she reflected, and took comfort from the thought that Rijk had said that she might come over to England whenever he did and see her family. He was a kind man, she mused, as well as a close friend. And, of course, a husband.

The car came and they got in and were driven the short distance to the church, and, Sophie being Sophie, there was no nonsense about being late—it was striking eleven o'clock as, holding the small, exquisite bouquet Rijk had sent her, and her arm tucked in her father's, she walked down the aisle.

For a quiet wedding the church was remarkably full. The village, delighted to have a dull winter day enlivened by such an event, had turned out in force, crowding the pews behind Sophie's family and Rijk's parents, two of his sisters and his brothers, sitting on the other side of the aisle. But she barely glanced at them; Rijk was there, waiting for her, his massive bulk reassuring even though he didn't turn to look at her. Only when they were standing beside him did he turn and smile into her eyes for a moment before the service began.

She became aware then that there was music and

the choir and flowers. She wondered who had arranged
that and then made herself listen to the rector's old
voice and presently, obediently following his quaver-
ing tones, promising to love, honour and obey...

They went out of the church arm in arm and she
smiled vaguely from side to side, feeling as though she
were in a dream, and at the church door they had to
pause for a moment while someone took photos, and
then everyone else crowded round them and she was
being kissed and everyone was talking at once.

In the Bentley, beside Rijk, she asked, 'Who arranged for the choir and the organ and all those lovely
flowers?'

'I did. I wanted you to have a fitting background,
Sophie.'

'Thank you, it was all so—so... I don't know the
right word, but do you know what I mean?'

'Yes. I think I do. You look very beautiful, my dear.'

'Oh, thank you.' She glanced sideways at him; his
grey suit was magnificently cut, his tie a rich silk in a
darker shade, a white carnation in his buttonhole; he
was the epitome of a well dressed man. 'You look awfully nice yourself.'

He dropped a hand on her knee. 'A well suited couple, are we not?'

The wedding breakfast was a triumph. Mrs Blount
glowed with pride. She had had to get caterers in, of
course, but a good deal of it she had seen to herself. She
beamed around her; Sophie looked marvellous, so did
Rijk, and she and his mother had taken to each other
immediately. She had found his father a little daunting to start with, but then she had seen the twinkle in

his eyes—the same eyes as his son. After all, he was only an older edition of Rijk. His sisters and brothers were friendly too and there was no worry about understanding them; their English was as good as hers. She went and sat down by Rijk's mother and that lady patted her arm. 'This is a delightful occasion—we can be proud of our new son and daughter, can we not? As soon as they are settled in you must all come over and stay with us—we have plenty of room for the boys and even if we hadn't there are so many of us that there is always a room for anyone who cares to come and stay.'

'You're very kind,' said Mrs Blount and added, 'I'm very fond of Rijk—we all are. He—he just sort of fitted in from the moment he came to see us.' The two ladies smiled mistily at each other and Mrs Blount said, 'I think it is time to cut the cake; they want to be off by two o'clock.'

They drove away in a shower of confetti, still in their wedding clothes, for they were to change at the London house.

'Warm enough?' asked Rijk.

'Yes, thank you. Won't your family want to come to the London house this evening?'

'After we have gone—Father has arranged for everyone to dine at Ingatestone…'

'The Heybridge Moat House?'

'That's the one. They can discuss the wedding at their ease; it won't matter how late they are. He's arranged for a car for Loewert and Iwert and he'll drive Mother and the girls back himself. He phoned your father this morning…'

'How very kind and thoughtful of him.' She looked

out of the window at the wintry fields. 'What time do we have to leave London?'

'About eight o'clock; we'll dine first.' He smiled down at her. 'I enjoyed our wedding, did you?'

She realised with some surprise that she had. She had expected it to be a kind of dream in which she wouldn't feel quite real, but it had been real enough and she had felt happy... 'Yes, I did. I've heard people say that they couldn't remember their wedding clearly, but I can remember every word.'

She didn't say any more; the wish to tell him that she loved him was so strong that she had to clench her teeth, and presently he asked, 'Tired? We'll soon be home.'

She hurried to tell him that she wasn't in the least tired, that it was excitement. 'So much has happened today—it was so nice having your people here, and our mothers took to each other at once, didn't they?'

She embarked on a rather pointless conversation about the wedding and felt relief when they reached the outskirts of London and he was forced to slow down and give his whole attention to the traffic.

Percy opened the door with a flourish as the professor stopped before his house. 'Heartiest congrats, guv, and you, madam. All the best and lots of little 'uns. This is an 'appy day and no mistake.'

'Why, thank you, Percy.' The professor sounded at his most placid and Sophie, doing her best to follow his example, shook Percy's hand and thanked him.

'Well, now. There's champagne in the drawing-room and Mrs Wiffen 'as bust her stays over yer dinner.' Percy beamed at them as he took Sophie's coat.

'If I may say so, madam, you look smashing. I'll fetch in the luggage in half a mo'—you'll want to change before you leave.'

He urged them into the drawing-room, softly lighted and decked with enough flowers to stock a florist's shop. 'Me and Mrs Wiffen thought as 'ow it'd be nice ter 'ave a few flowers,' explained Percy, and something in his voice sent Sophie across the room to take his hand in hers.

'Percy, how kind of you both, and the room looks beautiful. It's such a lovely surprise; how I wish we could take them all with us to Holland.'

'Well, there is that... P'raps yer could take a small bunch wiv yer?'

'I most certainly shall. I've never seen such a wonderful display. Thank you and Mrs Wiffen; you couldn't have pleased us more, could they, Rijk?'

The professor, thus addressed, made haste to add his appreciation to Sophie's, and Percy, looking pleased with himself, went away, back to the kitchen to tell Mrs Wiffen that the newly wed pair looked a treat and no mistake. 'A bit of all right is the missus and that's for sure,' he pronounced.

Sophie sat by the fire in the steel grate and drank the champagne which Rijk had poured for her. Rijk sat down and with a word of excuse became immersed in a pile of letters beside his chair.

'It looks as though I shall have to come back here in about six weeks' time.' He glanced at her, smiling. 'You might come too if you wish to see your parents. I shall have to go to Denmark too very shortly, just to operate; I dare say you will find plenty to do at home...'

She saw that she wasn't to be allowed to interfere with his work in any way. She agreed serenely and drank her champagne.

Mrs Wiffen had excelled herself: crab mousse, surrounded by a sauce of her own invention, followed by grilled Dover sole with tiny potatoes and braised celery in a cheese sauce and rounded off by a confection of fresh pineapple and meringue. They drank their coffee at the table and Sophie said, diffidently, 'Would you mind if I went to the kitchen and thanked Mrs Wiffen? She has gone to a great deal of trouble…'

Rijk got up as she did. 'I'll come with you.'

Mrs Wiffen, treated to a sight of the bride's outfit, was almost tearful. 'I'm sure we so wish you happiness, madam, and you, sir. I 'opes you'll be back soon to sample some more of my cooking.'

'I look forward to that,' said Sophie. 'The professor often comes here and I shall come with him.'

She went upstairs presently to a charming bedroom, its satinwood furniture gleaming in the soft pink glow of the shaded lamps, the bedspread and curtains in quilted pastel chintz. Someone had unpacked her case and her travelling clothes were lying ready. She got out of her wedding outfit, folded it carefully in tissue paper, and packed it. There was really no point in taking it with her, but to leave it behind was unthinkable…

Presently, dressed for the journey, she went downstairs again in the jersey suit and her winter coat. It was a cold night and it might be even colder in Holland; she had prudently stuffed a scarf and thick gloves in her pockets.

Rijk, in tweeds and his cashmere overcoat, was

waiting for her in the hall, talking to Mrs Wiffen and Percy.

'Oh, have I kept you waiting?' Sophie hurried forward to be reassured by Rijk's placid,

'Not at all, my dear! You are most punctual and we have plenty of time.'

She made her goodbyes, taking the little bouquet of flowers which Percy offered her. 'I'll put them in water the moment we arrive,' she told him, 'to remind me of your beautiful decorations for us this evening.'

'Be seein' you,' said Percy cheerfully, and he and Mrs Wiffen waved from the door as Rijk drove away.

It had been cold in London; it seemed to Sophie as they drove away from the Hoek the next morning very early that it was a great deal colder in Holland. The Bentley was warm, though, and they stopped presently for coffee at a small café by the motorway.

Sophie bit into a *kaas broodje*. 'How long a holiday have you got?' she asked.

'I've several patients to see in two days' time, then I shall be in Amsterdam for a few days; after that I shall be home for some time...'

He spoke casually, but his eyes were on her face.

Sophie summoned an interested smile. 'Oh, yes, you must have a marvellous secretary keeping tabs on your appointments.' She reflected that it was only what she had expected after all. He was no lovesick bridegroom and she must take care not to dwindle into a lovesick bride. If she hadn't fallen in love with him she would have been quite content with his answer.

They drove on presently, going north along the east

side of the Ijsselmeer, skirting Utrecht and then on to Meppel and Drachten. The short day was drawing to its close as they turned in between the gates of his home. They had stopped a few miles before Zwolle and had their lunch at a small restaurant tucked away from the main road. They had had the typical Dutch lunch— *koffietafel*—omelette, a basket of rolls and bread, cheese and cold meats and as much coffee as they could drink. The restaurant was fairly full and pleasantly warm and Sophie left it reluctantly to go back outside into the grey day, but once she was in the car beside Rijk her spirits rose again. They were starting this, their married life, together and she had every intention of making a success of it—and that was the least of it; surely, with a little encouragement on her part, he might, in time, fall in love with her...

They received a warm welcome, with Matt racing out of the house to lean against them, and Rauke, Tyske and the two maids were waiting in the porch despite the cold.

There was tea waiting for them, and Sophie, bidden to hurry down from her room as quickly as possible, did so to find Rijk sitting in his great wing-chair by the fire, sorting through a pile of letters. He got up as she went in and put the letters down, and she said at once, 'Do read your post; there may be something important,' and sat down beside the tea-tray and poured the tea, feeling unreasonably hurt when he did so. It was, after all, only yesterday that they had married.

She drank her tea and ate the little cakes Tyske had made and tried to look as relaxed as Rijk, sitting there going through his correspondence as though they had

been married for years… Presently she went back to
her lovely room to find that her things had been unpacked and put away in the wall closet and the tallboy
drawers. There was nothing for her to do but bathe and
change into the brown velvet skirt and one of the silk
tops to go with it. That done, she went and sat by the
window and looked out on to the dark grounds around
the house, the darkness pierced by the light streaming
from its many windows. She could hear Matt barking and presently saw him dashing across the lawns
below, followed by Rijk, who looked up and, when he
saw her, waved.

She went downstairs then and found him waiting
for her. 'I dare say you're tired,' he observed kindly. 'I
usually dine at eight o'clock when I'm here, but I asked
Rauke to serve us earlier this evening. Come and sit
down and have a drink first. Is your room quite comfortable? If there is anything that you need you have
only to ask.'

She had the strange feeling that she was a guest in
his house as she assured him that she had everything
that she could possibly want, glad of Matt's attentions
as she sat down and then took the glass offered to her.
Presently, she felt better; Rijk was completely at ease,
much as though they had been married for years and
sitting there chatting over drinks was something they
had done forever…

However matter-of-fact Rijk was over their homecoming, Rauke and Tyske had seen to it that it should
be marked in an appropriate manner. The dining-table,
decked with white damask, gleamed with silver and
crystal, and the arrangement of flowers at its centre

was decidedly bridal: white roses and freesias, pale pink tulips and lilies of the valley and blue hyacinths; they smelled delicious. The professor, who had conferred with Rauke over this, their first dinner as a married couple in their own home, watched Sophie's face and was content at the look of surprised delight upon it.

The dinner itself was delicious: watercress soup, lobster thermidor with a potato salad and dishes of vegetables followed by a lemon sorbet and a spectacular *bombe glacée*. They ate unhurriedly and Sophie found her initial vague disappointment melting under her husband's undemanding conversation, and presently, when they went back to the drawing-room to have their coffee by the fire, she said, 'What a nice homecoming, and how beautifully Rauke and Tyske look after you.'

'They will look after you just as well, Sophie. In a few days, when you feel at your ease here, Tyske will take you round the house—she is most anxious to inspect the household linen and the kitchen cupboards with you. Rauke will translate for you, but I'm sure that within a short time you'll be able to manage on your own. I dare say you would like some Dutch lessons? I'll see to that for you. Tomorrow we will go and see those of the family who were not at the wedding, and if you like to come to Leeuwarden with me on the following day...? I'll show you where the hospital is and you had better meet the head porter so that if you should need me they can arrange for you to see me at once.'

She agreed quietly; life was going to be strange for a time, but she would learn quickly. She suspected that he expected her to have her own interests when he was away, and she would have to be careful not to infringe upon his life but just to be there when he wanted her company. That would all be altered, she told herself, but it might take time. He had got what he wanted, the kind of wife and marriage he wanted—it was up to her to change his mind for him.

She glanced across at him, loving very much every line of his face, longing to shout her feelings out loud; instead, after a suitable time had elapsed, she wished him a friendly goodnight and took herself off to bed. He had opened the door for her and kissed the top of her head as she passed him, an action she treasured as she lay in bed, considering the future.

They were to have lunch with his three sisters who hadn't been at the wedding. Siska, the eldest of them, welcomed them to her house and Sophie found all three of them there. They hugged Rijk and kissed her with warmth and wanted to know everything there was to tell about the wedding. 'We would have loved to have come,' said Siska, 'but you knew about the measles, didn't you? When Mother and Father are back and the rest of us as well, we shall have a family party. There are many uncles and aunts and cousins all wishing to meet you.'

Sophie, having assured her sisters-in-law that she had had the measles, was taken to visit her spotty little nephews and nieces. Later, going back home with Rijk, she said, 'What a nice family you have, Rijk; I do like them.'

'They like you too. You will see a good deal of them, you know.'

Breakfast was to be early in the morning since Rijk was due at the hospital by nine o'clock. Sophie, well wrapped against the chilly morning, drove with him to Leeuwarden, was shown where the hospital was, told at what time to be there in the afternoon, given a roll of notes, and told to go and enjoy herself, which, rather to her surprise, she did. There was plenty to see and she spent a long time choosing wool. Knitting was something she had never had much time for; but now there was the chance to get expert at it. She bought canvas and tapestry wools too and several paperbacks as well as a notebook and a useful book entitled *A guide to Dutch for the tourist*. Even a smattering of that language would be useful.

Rijk went to Amsterdam the following day, leaving while it was still dark, and, since he wouldn't be home again until early evening, Sophie filled the hours by inspecting cupboards of linen—enough to last forever, she considered—and more vast cupboards in the kitchen and the pantry, filled with china and glass, and then, lastly, she was shown the safe where the family silver was kept. By the time Rijk got home she was beginning to feel that she was a married woman with a home to run.

The next day she went to the kitchen and sat down at the table there with Tyske while Rauke translated his wife's detailed account of just how the house was run. She enjoyed that; it was a lived-in room and something on the massive Aga smelled delicious. There was a cat and kittens too in a basket before the stove and Matt sitting beside her, watching her lovingly with his yellow eyes.

Rijk was tired when he got home, but not too tired to tell her of his day, and she made a good listener, sitting there with her knitting, asking all the right questions in a quiet voice. Halfway through an account of a patient's treatment he paused to say, 'Did I ever tell you what a restful girl you are, Sophie? I enjoy coming home and finding you here, knowing that I can talk to you and that you will listen intelligently and we are good friends enough for you to tell me when I begin to bore you.'

'Oh, I'll do that,' she assured him, making her voice briskly friendly, 'but it's not likely.'

'I must arrange for you to meet some of my friends so that they may be your friends too, and you must come to the hospital...' He smiled suddenly. 'No one expects us to be very social for a week or two.'

She summoned a smile in return. She hoped it looked like an understanding smile between friends.

Rijk finished at Amsterdam and, although he went to Leeuwarden or Groningen each day, she saw more of him. They walked together in the early mornings with Matt and, although he spent most of the evening in his study, at least he was in the house. Sophie began to feel cautiously happy.

It was several days after he had come back from Amsterdam that she decided to go to Leeuwarden. Rauke was taking the Land Rover in to fetch groceries and she went with him, assuring him that she would go to the hospital and return home with the professor. She spent the early afternoon searching for the extra wools and needles she would need for her tapestry and then made her way to the hospital, nicely in time to meet Rijk.

She was opposite the hospital forecourt, waiting for

a lull in the traffic, when she saw him coming out of the entrance. He wasn't alone; a tall, slender woman was beside him, laughing up at him, and he was holding her arm as they walked towards the Bentley. Sophie shut her eyes and then opened them again; they hadn't deceived her. The pair of them were in the car and Rijk swiftly drove it out of the forecourt; moreover, he was going in the opposite direction from his home...

Chapter 8

Sophie watched the tail-lights of the Bentley disappear, oblivious of the impatient people jostling her as they hurried past her. Who was the woman Rijk was with and where were they going? It was plain that they knew each other. Rijk had been laughing... Sophie ground her splendid teeth and looked around for a policeman.

Yes, he told her, holding up the traffic while he explained where the bus depot was, there would certainly be a bus to Grouw, but she would need to hurry. She thanked him nicely from a white face and hurried through the streets and found the bus, already full, on the point of leaving. Once on it, jammed between two old men with baskets of eels and smelling strongly of fish, she pondered what she would do when she got to Grouw. Eernewoude was still some miles further at the end of a secondary road which meandered round the lake. She would have to hire a taxi… One of the old men spoke to her and she dredged up her few words of Dutch—'*Ik ben Engels*'—and gave him a smile, and he broke into instant speech. Not even Dutch, she thought despairingly, but Friese, which sounded even more unintelligible than Dutch. There was a stirring in the bus, for he had a loud voice, and someone said, 'English— Professor van Taak ter Wijsma's wife, yes?'

'Yes,' said Sophie, feeling awkward.

'On a bus?' said the same voice. 'You have no car? You are alone?' The owner of the voice sounded quite shocked. 'The professor is not allowing that?'

Of course, in this sparsely populated part of Friesland, he would be known, at least by name. She said clearly, 'I was to go home with him, but I have missed him in Leeuwarden. He will fetch me in Grouw.

'That's not likely,' she murmured to herself, listening to the satisfied chat around her.

The bus stopped frequently, presumably to suit the wishes of the passengers getting on and off in the dark night. There were few villages, for the bus was travelling along a country lane, away from the main road, but there would be farms. Indeed, when she bent to peer out of a window she could see a light here and there away from the road. It looked lonely country and she wished that she was at home, sitting by the fire, working away at her tapestry. The two old men were still on either side of her, talking across her as though she weren't there, and she allowed her thoughts to wander. Where was Rijk? she wondered. And if she asked him when she got home would he tell her?

The bus rattled to a halt in Grouw and she got out last of all, her ears ringing with the chorus of '*Dag*' from her companions on the journey. Now to find a taxi… She turned round to get her bearings and found Rijk right behind her.

Surprise took her breath, but only for a moment. She said in a rush, 'I went into Leeuwarden with Rauke and I meant to meet you at the hospital, but they said you'd already left, so I caught a bus…'

He had a hand on her arm. 'I left early. I'm sorry you had this long, cold ride.' He was walking her across to the Bentley.

'I enjoyed it. Everyone talked and I didn't understand any of it. How did you know that I would be on the bus?'

'Rauke had expected you to be with me. You're a sensible girl; I knew you would get yourself back, and this was the last bus to Grouw. I got back into the car and drove over.'

'I was going to get a taxi.'

The car was blissfully warm and Matt's breath was hot on the back of her neck. Seated comfortably, she was waiting for him to tell her why he had left with that girl, but it was evident that he wasn't going to, even though she stayed silent so that he had the chance to do so. Instead he observed casually that the following week there was to be a reception at the hospital in their honour. 'And Mother phoned today; they are back and there is to be a family dinner within the next week or so. You will enjoy that, will you not, Sophie? Perhaps life is a little dull for you here.'

'Dull? Certainly not. The days aren't long enough—not that I do anything useful, but I'm always busy.'

'I'm glad you are happy here. I hear that cold weather is expected, with snow, which means that we shall be able to skate.'

'I can't...'

He stopped the car in front of the house and turned to look at her. 'I'll teach you; it's splendid exercise—the children have days off from school and they light up the canals.'

She forced herself to answer with a show of enthusiasm, hoping against hope that he would explain. He didn't, however. They reached home and he got out and helped her from the car and over the icy steps to the door. He nodded to Rauke as they went inside but made no move to take off his coat.

'I've a meeting in Leeuwarden this evening; shall you mind dining alone? I shall probably be back late.'

She minded very much but she wasn't going to say so. 'What about your dinner?'

'Oh, we have sandwiches and coffee and Rauke will leave something for me in the kitchen. Don't wait up, my dear.' He dropped a casual kiss on her cheek. 'I'll see you in the morning.'

He took Matt with him so that she had no company as she dined and afterwards, sitting by the fire, savagely poking her needle in and out of her tapestry work.

She went to bed early because he had made it clear that he didn't expect to see her when he got home, and she lay awake until she heard the car whisper to a halt below her window and presently his quiet footsteps in the house.

'I've made a mess of things,' muttered Sophie, weeping into her pillow.

In the morning at the breakfast-table she was bright and brisk, making a brief reference to his meeting without waiting for an answer. He asked her then what she was going to do with her day, and she told him that she intended to explore the attics, take Matt for a walk, and be home in time for Loewert, who had phoned to say that he would call.

'I dare say he'll stay for dinner,' she observed, and Rijk looked surprised.

'By all means; I should be home in good time this evening.'

'How nice,' said Sophie sweetly. She met his thoughtful look with a smile. 'Do you suppose it will snow today?'

'Very likely. Don't go near the lake; it's beginning to freeze over, but it won't be safe for several days.' He got up from the table and offered her a handful of envelopes. 'Invitations—will you look through them? And we'll decide what to do about them.'

'Yes, of course.' She gave him an overbright smile. 'Don't do too much.'

Loewert arrived just before lunch. 'I'm playing truant,' he told her happily. 'I've exams at the end of the week and I thought a day away from my books might help.'

'What exams are they?' She led him into the drawing-room and they sat down before the fire with the coffee-tray between them.

'Ear, nose and throat and gynae.'

She passed him his cup and watched him spoon sugar with a lavish hand.

'You think you'll pass?'

He grinned and she thought with a little leap of her heart that Rijk must have looked like that when he was younger. 'I hope I will. With old Rijk as an example, what else can I do? He's the one with the brains, of course, though he'd give me a good thump if he heard me saying that.'

He looked at Sophie, quite serious for a moment. 'He's a splendid fellow, you know—but of course you do; you're married to him.' He passed his cup for more coffee and took another biscuit. 'We were beginning to think that he would never find himself a wife, and then you turned up, an answer to our prayers—a beautiful angel and a darling...'

'You'll turn my head,' said Sophie and laughed gently, 'but that's kind; thank you for the compliment.'

'You get enough of those from Rijk,' said Loewert and grinned again so that she blushed a little, remembering the things he had said to her before they married; nothing romantic, of course, but nice all the same. It was a pity that he hadn't found it necessary to repeat any of them now that they were married. It was as though they had slipped at once into a comfortable state of middle-aged marriage, and that within weeks...

She listened to Loewert's cheerful talk and wondered what she should do about it. She supposed that if she hadn't fallen in love with Rijk she would have been quite content to let their relationship dwindle into the state he seemed to want: pleasant companionship, a hostess for his table and complete lack of interest in his life. She loved him, though, which made it an entirely different matter. So something had to be done to remedy the matter, and she would do it…

'You do look fierce,' said Loewert. 'Have you got a headache?'

'No, no. I was trying to remember if Matt had his breakfast before he went with Rijk. So sorry; I was listening… You were telling me about the blonde nurse in Out-patients. Is she very pretty?'

The description of this blue-eyed paragon took some time. 'But of course I'm not serious,' he told her firmly. 'Time enough for all that when I've qualified and got established. I mean, look at old Rijk; plenty of girlfriends, mind you, but he never lost sight of the fact that he intended to be on top of the ladder before he settled down for good.' He sighed. 'If I'm half as good as he is when I'm as old, I'll be very satisfied.'

'Rijk isn't old,' protested Sophie.

'No, no, I know that—he's twelve years older than I am and eight years older than Iwert, who's doing quite well for himself. I suppose Rijk's the goal we are both aiming for.' He beamed at her confidingly. 'He's made a name for himself.'

'I'm sure you'll succeed. Are you going to specialise?'

He plunged into a rose-coloured version of his future. 'Though I'll never be as good at it as Rijk.' He smiled rather shyly. 'But I hope I meet someone as beautiful as you and marry her.'

'Why, thank you, Loewert—she'll be a lucky girl.' She got to her feet. 'Shall we have a short walk before lunch? Rijk says it will snow…'

They took the lane down to the lake and stood looking at its grey, cold water. 'It's certainly going to snow,' said Loewert. 'Look at those clouds.'

They were massing on the horizon, a nasty grey with a yellowish tinge sweeping towards them, driven by a mean wind.

They didn't stay out long but went back to the house and had lunch together on the best of terms.

They were playing draughts on the discarded tea-tray beside Sophie's chair when Rijk got home. She looked up and smiled as he came into the room, and he bent to kiss her cheek before greeting his brother.

'I've had a wonderful day,' said Loewert. 'I had no idea that a sister-in-law could be such fun. I hope I'll be invited again…'

'Any time you like,' said Rijk. 'Stay to dinner?'

'I promised Mother that I'd go home. I'd better go now or she may think I've forgotten.'

Sophie got up too and he kissed her with obvious pleasure. 'Next time I'll stay for dinner if you'll have me,' he told her.

'I've enjoyed our day together; pass your exams and we'll have a celebration dinner.'

Rijk went out of the room with him and she sat down again and picked up her knitting, presenting a picture of serene domesticity to Rijk when he came back to the room.

He said quietly, 'I'm glad you enjoyed your day; Loewert is great fun. Did you have time to look through the invitations?'

'Yes, I did, and there is a note from your mother asking us to go to dinner next week.'

'The entire family will be there—aunts and uncles and cousins, and, of course, Grandmother. Which reminds me—I've opened an account for you at my bank; maybe you will want to buy clothes.' He gave her a cheque-book and she turned it over slowly and then looked inside. It was very like her own cheque-book, save for the sum of money written on its first stub.

'Your quarterly allowance,' said Rijk, watching her. 'If you need more money you have only to ask.'

'That's a fortune.' She raised troubled eyes to his.

'You will need every cent of it; it won't do for you to be seen too often in the same dress. You dress charmingly, Sophie, but I can't have my friends saying that I don't give you enough pin money.' He smiled at her. 'Do you want to shop in London or den Haag? I'll make some time to go with you.'

'No, no, there are some lovely shops in Leeuwarden. I'll have a good look round. I have brought one or two dresses with me, but perhaps they aren't grand enough.'

He crossed the room and took her hands in his. 'They don't have to be grand, my dear, but there will be tea-parties and coffee-parties and several dinner parties we cannot refuse. You don't like dressing up?'

'I've never had much chance to do that.' She smiled up into his face. 'But I think I shall enjoy it as long as it's not too often.'

'I'll promise you that. I'm not very social myself, only, now that I have a wife, friends and acquaintances are going to invite us.'

Rauke came in then to take away the tray, and Matt, who had been having his supper in the kitchen, came with him, delighted to see Sophie again, rolling his yellow eyes at the prospect of his evening walk.

'I'll come with you,' said Sophie and, wrapped in an elderly loden cloak kept in the hall closet, went out into the dark evening. The cold hit her like a blow, and Rijk took her arm.

'I said that it would snow,' he said with satisfaction as the first feathery flakes fell.

They walked fast down towards the lake and back again while Matt, impervious to the cold in his thick coat, dashed to and fro, barking. He had a deep, very loud bark.

They went back indoors presently to eat their dinner and discuss which of the invitations they should accept. Afterwards, back in the drawing-room, leafing through them once again, Sophie asked, 'Who is Irena van Moeren? She's written a little note at the bottom, but I don't know what it means.'

'Irena? A very old friend; we must certainly accept.' He stretched out a hand for the card. 'She writes at the bottom, "You must come for old times' sake".' He glanced at the date. 'I must make a point of being free—you'll like her.'

Sophie murmured a gentle reply; she would hate her. Old times' sake, indeed... And what if she turned out to be the woman she had seen Rijk with?

She sat, the picture of tranquillity, stitching away at her tapestry, not looking at him. If she had done so she would have been surprised to see the look on his face as he watched her.

It was snowing hard when she got up the next morning, and there was already a thick layer covering the lawn and shrubs. She went down to breakfast presently and was met in the hall by Rauke.

His 'Good morning' was grave and fatherly. 'The professor left early, *mevrouw*; he was called to an urgent case at four o'clock this morning.'

'He is operating this morning too; the list starts at nine o'clock. I do hope he gets some breakfast...'

'I'm sure that he will be looked after, *mevrouw*. I'll bring the coffee; you must have your breakfast.'

As he set the pot before her Sophie asked, 'Rauke, you speak such good English—have you been there?'

'No, *mevrouw*. I was with the professor's father during the occupation—underground, of course; we had a good deal to do with escaped prisoners and Secret Service personnel.'

She put out an impulsive hand. 'Oh, Rauke, I'm proud to know you.'

He took her hand gravely. 'Thank you, *mevrouw*. Would you care for a boiled egg?'

She was finishing breakfast with Matt in loving attendance when Rijk telephoned.

'Good morning, Sophie; you slept well?'

'Me? Slept? Oh, yes, thank you.' Ungrammatical and incoherent; she must do better. 'Are you tired? Was the op a success?'

'Yes, I think so; the next forty-eight hours will determine that.'

'Have you had breakfast?'

'Oh, yes.' She fancied that he was laughing. 'I'm going to scrub in a few minutes. If you go out, be careful, wear wellies—there are several pairs in the outer kitchen—and do take Matt with you.'

'Well, yes, I will. Will you be home in time for tea?' She did her best to make her voice sound brisk and friendly.

'Doubtful; I'll let you know later.' He rang off and she put the receiver down slowly. It was ridiculous to want to cry about nothing. She gave a sniff and blew her beautiful nose and went along to the kitchen to start the difficult but interesting business of deciding what to eat for the rest of the day.

It started to snow while she was out with Matt and she was glad of the wellies, for it was freezing now and the ground was icy. She walked down to the lake and took the track running beside it, which would lead her eventually to the village. The water, grey and sullen, reflected heavy cloud which covered the skies, and here and there there were great patches of ice forming.

'A winter's day and no mistake,' said Sophie to Matt, 'and I rather like it; it's like being in a Bruegel painting.'

In the village she bought stamps and a bar of chocolate in the small, crowded shop, exchanging greetings in her awkward Dutch, wishing she knew more words and making do with smiles and nods. The shop's owner was an old woman dressed severely in black, her hair dragged back in a severe bun, bright blue eyes almost hidden in her wrinkled face. She chattered away, not minding that Sophie understood one word in twenty, but she was friendly and when other customers came into the shop they all had a few words to say. Sophie went on her way feeling as though she belonged, munching chocolate. Matt munched too, keeping close to her as they took the narrow road to the house.

Rijk phoned late in the afternoon. It was snowing hard now and Rauke had drawn the heavy curtains across the windows, shutting out the dark early evening. Sophie, conning her Dutch phrase book, snatched the phone from its cradle. 'Rijk, when will you be home?'

He sounded placid. 'Very late, I'm afraid. I may have to operate again shortly. I'll get something to eat here. Don't wait up. What have you done with your day?'

'Well, I went for a long walk with Matt by the lake and then to the village and this afternoon I wrote letters and knitted.'

How dull it sounded; she was fast turning into an idle woman, and he would get bored with her. She said urgently, 'I should like to start Dutch lessons...'

'I'll see about it—I know the very person to teach you. What are you knitting?'

He sounded so kind that she felt the tears pricking her eyelids.

'A sweater for you,' she mumbled.

'That's the best thing I've heard all day,' he observed and with a brief '*Tot ziens*' rang off.

He was already sitting at the table when she went down to breakfast the next morning. His 'Good morning' was cheerful as he stood up and pulled out the chair opposite his.

Sophie sat down and poured her coffee. 'Were you very late?' she asked. She had waited until she had heard his footsteps soon after eleven o'clock, but she wasn't going to say so.

'Later than I had intended; the snow is piling up in

the country roads, although the main roads are clear for the moment.'

'Oh—is it going to snow still?'

'Yes, and the temperature has dropped; we shall be skating by the end of the week.' He passed his cup for more coffee. 'Don't attempt to go on the lake, Sophie. The ice looks solid enough, but it isn't safe yet.'

'Will you be home for dinner this evening?' She added quickly, 'I only want to know so that Tyske can plan her cooking.'

'I should be home around six o'clock, so tell Tyske to go ahead. You should receive a phone call some time this afternoon from Mevrouw Smit, who will give you lessons in Dutch.'

'Oh, good, thank you, Rijk. Will she come here or shall I go to her?'

'You can arrange that between you. There will be a car for you in a few days, although I suggest that you wait for the weather to improve before you drive yourself; the roads are very bad at the moment.'

He dropped a hand on her shoulder as he went, but he didn't kiss her. Sophie gave Matt the rest of her toast and went along to the kitchen. To keep busy was important. She would answer their invitations during the morning and take Matt for a walk after lunch. There was the family dinner party to think about too...

The snow stopped during the morning and after lunch she wrapped herself in her top coat, tugged a woolly cap over her head, put on the thick gloves she had prudently bought in Leeuwarden, and began to walk briskly towards the village with Matt. It was slippery underfoot and very cold but the air was exhilarating and when she reached the village the few shops had their lights on and those people she saw called a greeting to her. There were lights on in the one hotel too; she supposed that if there was a good deal of skating, they would have plenty of custom. It was a sports centre, even if it was a small one.

Matt expected chocolate; she bought a bar and, since it was still reasonably light, decided to walk back along the track by the lake.

The water had become ice overnight; it looked solid enough but she remembered what Rijk had said. Once it was pronounced safe she supposed the whole lake would be crowded with skaters; he had told her that she would find it easy to skate, but she felt doubtful about that. The lake looked cold and vast and very lonely in the gathering gloom.

The track curved away from the water for a short distance and then turned back to the lake, and now she could see the lights from the house; in a few minutes she would go through the little wooden gate which led to the grounds. There would be tea waiting and perhaps a phone call from Rijk…

High-pitched shrieks brought her to an abrupt halt; there were children ahead of her, standing dangerously near the edge of the lake and screaming; they sounded excited until one of them darted on to the ice and started to run.

Sophie ran too; she had reached them when the ice cracked and the small figure disappeared. The children were silent now, dumb with shock, and she turned to the nearest. 'Help!' she shouted, and then, gathering her sparse vocabulary together, added urgently in Dutch, 'Go and get help! Quick!'

The child, a small boy of six or seven, gave her a frightened look and ran off and the others followed him as she took off her coat and boots and started across the lake; it gave at once under her weight, and Matt, slithering and slipping beside her, sent up great splashes of icy water. The child was standing now, the water up to his chest, shrieking his head off and not moving, and when she reached him he stopped his screams, his small face bluish with cold and his teeth rattling. She put an arm, heavy with freezing water, around him. 'Come on.' She tried to smile from a face rigid with cold. 'We can get back easily.'

He didn't move, however, and she realised that in a few minutes she would be in like case; the numbness was already creeping into her legs and in a very short time she wouldn't be able to use them.

Matt had kept close to her, uncertain but willing, and now she said, 'Fetch the master, Matt. Hurry—the master.'

He didn't like to leave her, but he went, plunging through the broken ice and racing away, jumping the gate and tearing up to the house. She watched him go, and then, fighting the bitter cold, she took a deep breath and started to scream for help. It was a quiet evening and surely someone would hear her.

Rijk had just stopped in front of his door when Matt reached him and he said sharply, 'You're soaked—you've been in the lake.' He put out a hand, but Matt shook it off, barking furiously and then turning and running back round the house, to appear a moment later, still barking, dancing impatiently round Rijk, then running off again.

The professor was a fit man despite his vast size; he ran as fast as Matt, vaulted the gate, and came to a halt by the lake in time to hear Sophie's shouts. Matt was already in the water; Rijk tossed off his coat and waded in after him. The water was already freezing over...

It wasn't far but it was hard going, for the ground was a slithering mud. When he reached her he put an arm round her. 'All right, my darling, we'll be out of here in no time...'

'Legs,' said Sophie through chattering teeth.

'I know. I'm going to put an arm round you both. Hold on to the child; it's only a few yards.'

They were halfway there when the first of the men arrived with torches and ropes. They waded into the water and, while one of them took the boy in his arms, the other one took Sophie's arm and between them he and Rijk half carried Sophie in to the bank.

The professor said something to the men, picked Sophie up and started towards the house, the man and the child with him, Matt panting beside him, while the second man ran ahead.

The door leading to the kitchen was open, light streaming from it and Rauke waiting there. The professor spoke to him and he went away to return within minutes with an armful of blankets. Moments later the child was being undressed by Tyske and one of the men and rolled into a blanket and Sophie, her sodden person swathed in yet more blankets, was laid carefully in one of the old-fashioned basket chairs by the Aga.

Rijk hadn't spoken; he went over to the child and

Tyske took his place, taking off Sophie's stockings and rubbing her feet and legs with a towel. She talked soothingly as she did so and Sophie bit her lip, trying not to cry as life began to return to them.

She turned her head to see where the boy was and asked, '*De kind*? Is OK?' Tyske nodded and smiled and went on rubbing.

The kitchen seemed full of people; the boy's mother had been fetched and the child was sitting up now, drinking warm milk, still shaking and crying. The professor had been telephoning from a corner of the kitchen and the boy was sitting on his father's knee now, still crying.

Sophie looked up at Rijk as he came over to her. 'He's all right?'

'He's fine. I'm sending him to the cottage hospital at Grouw for the night—he can have a check-up there. His father can borrow the Land Rover.'

He smiled at her. 'I'm going to carry you up to your room and Tyske will help you have a warm bath and get to bed. One of the maids is getting you a warm drink.' His eyes searched her face. 'You'll feel better after a good night's sleep.'

'But you—you're cold and wet too.'

He stooped and dropped a kiss on to her wet head. 'All in good time.'

'Matt's all right?'

'Rauke's giving him a good rub down and a warm meal. He can come and see you presently.'

He scooped her up then and carried her upstairs, with Tyske trotting in front to open the door and throw a blanket over the bed.

'I'll be back,' he told her and went away.

Half an hour later she was in bed, blissfully warm once more, her newly washed hair tied back, sipping warm milk which Tyske brought her before she bustled round the room collecting discarded clothes and tidying up.

When Rijk knocked on the door Matt came in with him, coming to lean against the bed and stare at her, his tongue hanging out with pleasure.

'You splendid brave fellow,' said Sophie and rubbed his rough head in the way he liked best, glad of something to do, because she felt shy of Rijk, who had come to sit on the bed.

He took her hand, but only to feel her pulse, his manner impersonal but friendly. 'Feeling better?' he asked.

'I'm fine really. I feel a fraud lying here in bed.' She sat up straighter. 'Thank you, Rijk, for saving us—you were so quick. We really couldn't move, you know.'

He was still holding her hand. 'Cold, wasn't it?' He smiled at her.

'Very. You've changed? You're all right? And the boy?'

'Gone to Grouw to the hospital there for the night. His mother and father asked me to tell you that they would be indebted to you for the rest of their lives.'

'I was so frightened…'

'Which makes you doubly brave.' He laid her hand on the coverlet. 'You'll eat your supper in bed and then go to sleep.' He got up, towering over her. 'I'll look in later just to make sure that you are asleep.'

'You don't have to go anywhere? You'll be here?'

'I'll be here.' He went quietly, with Matt crowding at his heels.

Anneke, one of the housemaids, brought her supper presently: soup, creamed chicken, potatoes whipped to an unbelievable lightness and a *crème brûlée* to finish off. She ate the lot with a splendid appetite and drank the glass of hock accompanying it and when Anneke came for the tray told her in awkward Dutch that she wanted nothing more.

The house was very quiet and the room pleasantly warm; the curtains drawn across the windows shut out the cold dark outside. Sophie closed her eyes and slept. Rijk, coming to see how she fared around midnight, stood for several minutes, looking down at her. She lay curled up in bed, her hands pillowing her cheek, her lovely mouth slightly open, so that there was no mistaking the faintest of snores. He bent and dropped a kiss on her head and then went away.

She was young and strong and healthy; she got up the next morning feeling none the worse for her ducking. She was halfway down the staircase on her way to breakfast when Rijk's voice stopped her. His study door was half open and he was on the phone and, hearing her own name, she stopped and listened.

He was speaking Dutch, but she understood a word here and there, enough to know that he was saying something about the accident at the lake. It was when he said, laughing, 'Oh, Irena,' that she stiffened. He had a rather slow, clear voice and she could pick out more words now. Something about this evening and dinner… He stopped speaking and she nipped smartly upstairs again, and then, as he came from his study and crossed the hall, she started down again. He looked up and saw her and they went into breakfast together.

'You're feeling perfectly fit?' he wanted to know. 'It might be a good idea if you stayed indoors today. I've a busy day ahead of me and, alas, I shan't be home for dinner, so have something and go to bed early.'

'Very well. Surely you aren't operating this evening?' She was pleased at her casual tone.

'No.' He stared at her across the table. 'An evening engagement with an old patient that I prefer not to put off. I can, of course, do so if you want me at home, but since you are looking quite yourself and it is a matter of some importance I should like to go.'

'No, no, of course you don't have to come home. I've so much to keep me occupied; the days are never long enough. Besides, Tiele is coming to tea.'

She gave him a dazzling smile. 'It would be silly of me to ask you to drive carefully, wouldn't it?'

He got up, ready to leave. 'Very silly, but rather nice too.' He touched her lightly as he went. 'Don't wait up,' he said casually as he went through the door.

Chapter 9

Sophie sat at the table after Rijk had gone, feeding Matt pieces of toast while she thought. It had been wrong of her to eavesdrop, she knew that, but if she hadn't she wouldn't have known, would she? She wasn't sure what she did know, but it seemed likely that Rijk was still seeing someone—a woman—whom he had known and perhaps loved or been in love with before he met her and decided that she would fill the empty space he had allocated for a suitable wife. 'The heartless brute,' said Sophie in a stony little voice and, since she loved him with all her heart, not meaning a word of it.

She had told Rijk that she would stay indoors, but Matt had to go out; she put on the woolly cap and the loden cloak, stuck her feet into wellies, and took him for a brisk run in the grounds. The sky was still grey and the wind bitter, but the snow had stopped. When she got back to the house Rauke told her that tomorrow everyone would be skating.

Tiele came after lunch, bringing with her another young woman, a friend with whom she had been lunching and who had professed a keen desire to meet Rijk's bride. She was older than Tiele, tall and fair and with cold blue eyes, quite beautifully dressed. Sophie didn't like her and knew that she wasn't liked either, but on the surface at least they appeared good friends, and Tiele—kind, warm-hearted Tiele—noticed nothing, and there was plenty to talk about—the children, the family dinner party, only two days away now, and finally Elisabeth Willenstra's engagement.

'I shall have a big wedding,' she told Sophie, 'for we have so many friends, Wim and I. You and Rijk must come, of course—it will be in two months' time. Such a pity that I shall be away for your party, but we're sure to meet again—Rijk has so many friends.' She gave Sophie a sharp glance. 'I expect you have met Irena—Irena van Moeren—by now? One of his oldest friends.'

Sophie busied herself with the teapot. 'We haven't met yet; there has hardly been time. We had an invitation—'

'I'm sure Rijk will have found time.'

There was so much spite in Elisabeth's voice that Tiele looked up. 'If he has, it must have been by chance,' she said, 'and I'm sure Sophie knows about her, anyway, don't you, Sophie?'

'Oh, yes, of course,' said Sophie. It was surprising how easily the lie tripped off her tongue. It was in a good cause, she decided, for Elisabeth looked disappointed.

Alone again, she allowed herself half an hour's worry about the tiresome Irena. Elisabeth had been trying to needle her; all the same, this Irena van Moeren was someone to reckon with. Sophie decided that she would feel much better if she met the woman...

Rijk was late home, which was a good thing, for Sophie was in a bad temper and ripe for a quarrel.

The same bad temper prevented her from going to Leeuwarden to look for a dress for the family party. She would wear the pink she had bought in London. What did it matter what she wore? she reflected pettishly, wallowing in a gloomy self-pity; no one would notice. And of course by no one she meant Rijk.

She had tried hard to forget Elisabeth Willenstra's sly remarks. All the same, she hadn't been very successful; Irena van Moeren was beginning to loom very large on her horizon, and she wished with all her heart that she didn't need to go to the family gathering.

There was to be a family dinner first before the guests arrived, and Rijk had come home early and spent half a hour with her in the drawing-room before they'd parted to dress, and now she was on the point of going downstairs.

The pink dress had lifted her spirits; it was pretty without being too girlish and flattered her splendid person. She had done her hair in its usual complicated coil, hooked in the diamond earrings, and fastened the pearl necklace; now she took a last look at her reflection in the pier-glass in her room and, catching up the mohair wrap to keep her warm on their journey, she went downstairs.

Rijk was in the drawing-room, standing by the open

French window while Matt pranced around in the snow. Sophie, coming quietly into the room, thought that he was the handsomest man she had ever set eyes on; certainly a dinner-jacket, superbly cut, set off his massive proportions to the very best advantage.

He turned round at the soft sound of her skirt's rustle and studied her at his leisure. 'You look beautiful,' he said quietly.

She thanked him just as quietly; she had very little conceit, but she knew that she was looking her best. If only her best would match up to Irena van Moeren...

Matt came bounding in to stand obediently and have his great paws wiped clean before going to his basket, and Rijk said, 'If you are ready, I think we had better be on our way.'

He was perfectly at ease as they drove to Leeuwarden, telling her about his day's work, asking her what she had been doing, promising that since he was free on the following day he would take her on to the lake and give her her first skating lesson. She answered suitably in a voice so unlike her open manner that he asked her if she was nervous.

'You don't need to be,' he assured her. 'The family may be overpowering but they love you and, as for the guests, I'll be there to hold your hand.'

She said, 'You have so many friends, haven't you? I shan't remember any names, and will they all speak English?'

'Oh, yes. Although I expect Grandmother will make a point of addressing you in Dutch—she can be very contrary—although I have it from Mother that she approves of you, largely because you look as a woman should look.'

'You mean my clothes?'

'No, Sophie, your person. Your curves are generous and in the right places; she considers that a woman should look like one, not like a beanpole.' He glanced sideways at her in the dimness of the car. 'And I do agree with her, I certainly do.'

Her face flamed and she was glad that he couldn't see that. Her 'Thank you' was uttered in a prim voice which made him smile.

The whole family were waiting for them as they entered the drawing-room, and she was glad that she had worn the pink dress; she felt comfortable in it and it matched the other dresses there in elegance. Rijk had taken her hand, going from one person to another after they had greeted his parents, reminding her of names. Aunts and uncles, cousins and the older nieces and nephews, there seemed to be no end to them, but presently, after they had drunk their champagne and spoken to everyone, she found herself at the dinner-table, sitting on the right of her father-in-law, and thankfully Loewert was on her other side. Rijk was at the other end of the table, sitting beside his mother, and the meal was conducted in a formal manner since it was, as her host assured her, a most important occasion in the family.

Dinner was lengthy and delicious and, between father and son, Sophie began to enjoy herself. By the time they rose and made their way back to the drawing-room she felt quite at ease, and when Rijk joined her and slipped an arm round her waist she smiled up at him, momentarily forgetful of her worries, only to have them all crowding back into her head as the guests began to arrive and her foreboding was realised.

Irena van Moeren was one of the first to arrive and she was indeed the woman Sophie had seen with Rijk; moreover, she was a strikingly handsome one, not young any more, but beautifully turned out in a black gown of utter simplicity.

That she knew everyone there was obvious and when she reached Rijk and Sophie she lifted her face for his kiss in a way which made it plain that she had done it many times before. She kissed Sophie too, and held her hand, telling her how delighted she was to meet her. 'We must become friends,' she said, and sounded as though she really meant it.

If Rijk was in love with her, reflected Sophie, agreeing with false enthusiasm, then she couldn't blame him; Irena was charming and obviously kind and warm-hearted. If Sophie hadn't hated her so thoroughly, she would have liked her. There was no sign of her husband and she must either be married or a widow, for she wore a ring. Perhaps, thought Sophie, allowing her thoughts to wander, Rijk had been unable to marry her when her husband was alive, and, now that he was dead, he was married himself.

She became aware that Irena was saying something to her. 'Rijk has asked me to spend an afternoon with you both, skating on the lake.'

'I don't skate,' said Sophie bleakly. She would have to stand and watch the two of them executing compli-cated figures together...

'You'll learn in no time, Rijk on one side of you and me on the other.'

Rijk hadn't spoken; she summoned up an enthusiasm she didn't feel and said heartily, 'Oh, that sounds wonderful. Do come.' She glanced at Rijk. 'I'm not sure when you're free, but if you could bring Irena for lunch one day soon?'

He didn't remind her that he had already told her that he was free on the following day. 'Tomorrow? I'll fetch you, Irena; we'll have an early lunch so that we can get the best of the afternoon.'

'Oh, yes,' Sophie added, 'and stay for dinner; I shall look forward to it.'

They were joined by several other guests then and it wasn't until the end of the evening that Sophie spoke to Irena again. She had come over to say goodbye and Sophie said gaily, 'Don't forget tomorrow—I do look forward to it.'

They were the last to leave; the family had stayed for a little while after the last of the guests had gone, mulling over the evening and then going home, until only Rijk's brothers and parents were left.

'It was a perfectly lovely evening,' declared Sophie, kissing and being kissed. 'Thank you very much. I—I feel one of the family now and I hope you will let me be that.'

Mevrouw van Taak ter Wijsma embraced her with warmth. 'You dear child, you have been one of us since the moment we saw you. I look forward to a delightful future with my new daughter. You are so exactly right for Rijk.'

Sophie smiled; of course she was right for Rijk,

but did he think so too? Was she to be second best in his life? He would be good to her and care for her as his wife, but would he always be eating his heart out for Irena?

If he were, he showed no signs of it as they drove back home. It was a clear night with a bright moon, turning the snow-clad countryside to a fairytale beauty; he talked about their evening and the various people who had been there, apparently not noticing her silence. Only when they got home did he remark that it had been an exciting evening for her and that she must be tired. 'Go to bed, my dear,' he told her, 'and get some sleep. You have no need to get up for breakfast—I'll fetch Irena about midday and I'm sure that Tyske will cope with lunch.'

A remark which brought her out of her silence. 'It was a lovely evening and I am a little tired, but I don't want to stay in bed in the morning. Since you aren't going to the hospital in the morning perhaps we might have breakfast a little later, though?'

'Of course; tell Rauke before you go to bed. Would you like coffee or tea now?'

She shook her head, wished him goodnight, had a word with Rauke, and went to her room. She undressed slowly and got into bed and lay awake long after the house was quiet. The thought of the hours she must spend in Irena's company made her feel quite sick. She slept at last, to dream that Irena had come to the house, accompanied by piles of luggage, and that she herself was transported, in the way of dreams, on to an icy waste and told to skate back to England. It took her all of half an hour, using all her common sense, to face the grey light of early morning.

She got up thankfully and dressed carefully, wishing that she had gone to Leeuwarden as Rijk had suggested and bought some new clothes. She got into corduroy trousers and a heavy sweater and was rewarded by Rijk's genial, 'Ah, all ready to skate, I see.' He had given her face, pinched by worry and lack of sleep, a quick look. 'It should be excellent on the lake; there's not much wind. I've been down to have a look and there's plenty of hard, smooth ice, just right for you.' He added kindly, 'Of course, if you don't feel like it, you have no need to skate today—there will be ice for some time, I should think.'

She took a reviving sip of coffee. The idea of allowing him and Irena to spend half the day on the lake was sufficient to make her doubly keen to skate; jealousy was a great incentive, she had just discovered, although she despised herself for giving way to it. She said airily, 'Oh, but I'm longing to learn—I must be the only person living in Friesland who can't skate.'

He laughed then and began to talk about other things and presently went away to his study to emerge in time to take Matt for a walk before he went to fetch Irena.

Sophie, making sure that lunch was going to be ready by the time they returned, wondered how she was going to get through the day.

Standing at the window, she watched the car stop before the house and Irena and Rijk get out. Irena was laughing, obviously happy, and looking eye-catching in a scarlet anorak and stretch leggings, a scarf, tied with careless elegance, over her blonde hair.

Sophie went into the hall to meet them, the very picture of a smiling and delighted hostess, hurrying her guest away to take off her jacket and tidy herself, keeping up a flow of chat in a manner so unlike her that Rijk, getting drinks for them all, turned away to hide a smile, at the same time puzzled as to her manner…

With Matt in delighted attendance, they went down to the lake in the early afternoon and Rijk fastened skates on to Sophie's boots. They were broad and, she was assured, just right for a learner. He and Irena put on a quite different skate, specially used in Freisland and very fast.

Once on the ice Sophie did her best, held firmly on either side, sliding and slipping, until Rijk said, 'You're doing splendidly; lean forward a little and don't think about your feet. Irena is going to let go of you in a moment, but you won't fall; I have you safe.'

She didn't fall; the sight of Irena, skimming away with casual grace, inspired her to keep on her feet and presently she said, 'I believe I could go alone; may I try?'

She struck out bravely, letting out small screams of delight as she went forward. 'Look, look,' she called to Rijk. 'I'm skating; I can—'

The next moment she was tottering, waving her arms wildly in an effort to keep her balance as Rijk put a bracing arm around her and stood her upright again.

'That was splendid,' he observed, but Sophie, floundering around trying to regain her balance, could see Irena gliding gracefully back with an effortless ease which did nothing to improve Sophie's self-confidence.

'Sophie—but how splendid, you were skating alone.

Never mind that you lost your balance; in a few days you will be good. Rijk, I will stay with Sophie while you take a turn around the lake.'

Of course Rijk had every right to go off on his own, but did he need to go so willingly, with nothing but a nod and a smile for her? She watched him race away, his hands clasped behind his back, moving effortlessly.

'He's very good,' said Irena. 'He has taken part in our *Elfstedentocht* several times, and twice he has won. It is a great test for a skater, for they must skate on the canals and waterways between eleven towns in Friesland.'

'I suppose he was taught when he was a little boy.'

'Yes, we all skate almost as soon as we can walk; we all learned together, but he was always the best of us.' She put a firm arm under Sophie's elbow. 'Now let us continue... Strike out with your right foot, so. Good, now do it with your left foot, and again, faster... You know about Rijk and us...?'

She spoke very quietly and when Sophie shot her a glance she looked sad.

'Yes,' said Sophie; she looked to where Rijk was tearing back across the ice.

'Good, then we do not need to speak of it; it is for me very sad.' She became brisk once more. 'Now if you will go alone, and if you fall I shall pick you up.'

If only she could go somewhere quiet and have a good cry, thought Sophie despairingly, but she was quite unable to deal with her wretched skates, and anyway, what would be the use? How much easier it would be if she could hate Irena, even dislike her a little, but she liked her; she could quite see why Rijk loved her.

She plunged forward, not caring if she fell and broke a leg or an arm, and to her great surprise she kept on her feet for several yards until she was neatly fielded by Rijk, back again.

'You're an excellent pupil,' she was told, 'but that's enough for today; let us go home and have tea.'

'Wouldn't you and Irena like to skate together? I don't mind a bit; if you would take off my skates I'll go on ahead and make sure tea is ready.'

He gave her a quick look, his eyes thoughtful. 'We've had enough, haven't we, Irena? We'll have tea and then I'll take you back.'

'I thought Irena was staying for dinner?' Anyone would think, reflected Sophie, that I am enjoying this conversation.

'I did tell Rijk; I'm so sorry that I didn't tell you too—' Irena looked quite crestfallen '—but I have an appointment this evening and it is important that I should be there. Forgive me, Sophie.'

'Well, of course; you must come another time. We'll have tea round the fire…'

Which they did, with Matt crouching beside his master, accepting any morsel which might come his way, and the talk was all of skating and how well Sophie had done, and presently Irena said that she really must go.

Sophie, the hospitable hostess even though it was killing her, murmured regret and the wish that they might meet again soon, and waved them away from the porch, Matt beside her, puzzled as to why he wasn't going too. Sophie was puzzled as well; after all, Rijk was only driving into Leeuwarden and back again.

The pair of them went back to the fireside, Matt to snooze and she to sit and worry. It had been a horrendous day; she had been hopelessly outclassed on the ice and Irena's calm acceptance of the situation had left her uncertain and unhappy. She was deeply hurt too that Rijk hadn't talked to her about it. After all, it could happen to anyone, and she was fair enough to realise that to have been in love, perhaps for years, with each other with no hope of marrying and then to find the way clear, only for Rijk to have married someone else in the meantime, must be a terrible thing to happen. Was Irena's husband dead, she wondered, or were they divorced? When Rijk came home she would ask him; after all, they were the best of friends and should be able to discuss the problem without rancour.

She gave a great sigh and Matt opened his eyes and grunted worriedly. 'I think my heart is broken,' said Sophie. 'It would be so simple if only I didn't love him.'

Matt got up and laid his great head on her lap and presently, when she went upstairs to change her dress, even went with her. He wasn't allowed in the bedrooms, but she sensed that he was disobeying out of kindness. She put on one of her prettiest dresses, took pains with her face and hair, and went downstairs to wait for Rijk.

Only he didn't come. It was only a few minutes to dinner when the phone rang.

'Sophie.' Rijk's voice sounded urgently in her ear. 'I shall be delayed. Don't wait dinner and don't wait up.'

'Yes,' said Sophie and hung up. It had been an inadequate answer; she might have said, 'I quite understand,' or even, 'Very well.'

She dined alone with Rauke serving her and taking

away the almost uneaten plates of food with a worried air. She saw the look and said hastily, 'I'm not hungry, Rauke; it must be all that skating. If the professor isn't back by eleven o'clock will you lock up, please, and leave the door for him and something in the kitchen? He may be cold and hungry. He didn't say when he would be home, but it sounded urgent.'

She added that last bit to make it sound convincing, even though in her mind's eye she could see Rijk and Irena spending the evening together. With a mythical headache as an excuse, she went to bed early.

She didn't sleep; it was almost two o'clock when she heard Rijk's quiet tread on the stairs. Only then did she fall into a troubled sleep.

He was already at the table when she went down to breakfast in the morning.

'Don't get up,' she told him sharply. 'I dare say you're tired after your short night.' Then, because she was beside herself with lack of sleep and unhappiness and worry, she allowed her tongue to say things she had never meant to utter.

'I'm only surprised that you bothered to come home, but of course you weren't to know that I know all about it.'

She stopped then, otherwise she might have burst into tears, and poured herself a cup of coffee with a shaking hand. After a heartening sip, she added, 'You might have told me.'

The professor sat back in his chair, watching her. He was bone-weary, after operating for hours, but his voice was placid enough as he asked, 'And why should I not come home, Sophie? I live here.'

Sophie mauled the slice of toast on her plate. 'Bah.' Her voice shook. 'I've just told you, I know about you and Irena…'

The professor didn't move. 'And?' he asked in an encouraging voice.

'Well, are we supposed to go on like this for the rest of our lives? Elisabeth Willenstra said—'

'Ah—Elisabeth.' His voice was quiet, but his blue eyes were hard.

'Well, that you and Irena were old friends… She didn't say anything in so many words, but I can take a hint. Besides—' she gulped back tears and went on steadily '—that evening I came back by bus—I had gone to the hospital to go home with you. It was as I was waiting to cross the street opposite the entrance that I saw you both coming out together. She looked so happy and you were smiling at her and holding her arm and…yesterday Irena asked if I knew about you… Those were her words—"You know about Rijk and us?"—and of course I said yes.' She could hear her voice getting louder and shrill, but she couldn't stop now. 'And you stayed out almost all night and she was coming to dinner but then she said she had to go back and went with her.'

The professor still hadn't moved. 'You believe that I would do this to you?'

Something in his calm voice made her mumble, 'You can't help falling in love, can you? I mean, when you do it matters more than anything else, doesn't it?'

'Indeed it does. I see no point in continuing this conversation at the moment. I shall be late home; don't wait up.'

He was at the door when she asked in a small voice, 'Are you very angry, Rijk?'

He turned to look at her. He wasn't just tired, he was white with anger, his eyes blazing.

'Dangerously so, Sophie,' he said and went away, closing the door softly behind him.

She wished with all her heart that she had held her tongue.

She took Matt for a walk presently, in the cold stillness of the icy morning, and she was able to think clearly. She would have to apologise, of course, and ask to be forgiven, although it was she who should be doing the forgiving, and she would insist on a sensible discussion. They had always been good friends, able to talk easily and communicate with each other. It was a great pity that she had fallen in love with him; it was a complication she hadn't envisaged.

She went back home and made a pretence of eating the lunch Rauke had ready for her and then wandered around the house, unable to settle to anything. She was in the small sitting-room, looking unseeingly out of the window, when Rauke announced Irena.

Sophie pinned a smile on her face and turned to welcome her guest. Rijk would have seen her, of course, and she had come to explain...

Irena came in with an outstretched hand. 'Sophie, I am on my way back to Leeuwarden and I thought I would come and see you. You don't mind?'

Sophie took the hand. 'Of course not. I expect you've seen Rijk?'

Irena looked puzzled. 'Rijk?' She frowned. 'No.' She looked suddenly anxious. 'He has telephoned here?

He would like to speak to me urgently?' She had gone quite white. 'Jerre—he is not so well... I must telephone... He was improving; what can have happened?'

She sounded distraught and Sophie said, 'Who is Jerre?'

'My husband—you knew? You said that you did. He had a brain tumour and Rijk saved his life, but we told no one because Jerre is director of a big business concern and if it were known that he was so very ill it would have caused much panic and shareholders would have lost money...but I must telephone.'

'It's all right, Irena, I'm sure your husband is all right. It's just that I thought that you might have seen Rijk. It's just that I didn't know about your husband.'

Irena was no fool. 'Oh, my poor dear, you thought Rijk and I... He is Jerre's best friend; we all grew up together. Why should you think that of us?'

'Someone called Elisabeth...'

'That woman... She pretends to be everyone's friend, but she is spiteful; she likes to make trouble. Nothing of what she said to you is true; you must believe me.'

'I do, only I've quarrelled with Rijk, and, you see, I'm in love with him and he doesn't know that. I can't explain...'

'No, no,' said Irena soothingly, 'a waste of time. Get your coat and hat and come to Leeuwarden with me. He will be at the hospital; you must find him there and explain to him. He is angry, yes? He has a nasty temper, but he controls it. Tell him you love him.'

Sophie shook her head. 'I can't do that; if I do I shall have to leave him...'

'You must do what you think is best, but I do beg you, get your coat.'

Irena dropped her off outside the hospital, kissed her warmly, and waited in the car until she saw Sophie through the doors.

The porter was in his little box. Seeing Sophie, he shook his head. 'The professor is not here, *mevrouw*.' His English was surprisingly good. 'He is gone.'

'But his car is outside.'

'He holds his clinic five minutes away from here; he walks.'

'Will you tell me where the clinic is?'

The directions were complicated and she wasn't sure if she had them right, but she had wasted enough time already. She thanked him and he said, 'The clinic lasts until five o'clock; you should hurry, *mevrouw*.'

She hurried, trying to remember his directions, but after five minutes' walking she knew that she had gone wrong; the street she was in was narrow, lined with old houses and run-down shops, and it didn't appear to have a name. A matronly woman was coming towards her and Sophie stopped her, gathered together the best of her Dutch, and asked the way. Precious moments were lost while she repeated everything under the woman's beady eyes.

'*Engelse*?' she wanted to know, and, when Sophie nodded, broke into a flood of talk, not a word of which Sophie understood. She was wasting time. When the woman paused for breath, Sophie thanked her politely and hurried on. There was a crossroads ahead, not a main street, but it might lead somewhere where she could ask again. She was in a quite nasty temper by now; she was lost and unhappy and she was never going to find Rijk, and that was more important than anything else in the world. She shot round a corner head first into a broad expanse of cashmere overcoat.

'What a delightful surprise,' said Rijk, wrapping both arms around her.

'So there you are,' said Sophie in a very cross voice. 'I've been looking for you.' And she burst into tears.

Rijk stood patiently, rock-solid, while she sniffed and wept and muttered into his huge shoulder. Presently he took a very large white handkerchief from a pocket, still holding her close with his other arm, and mopped her face gently.

'Have a good blow and stop crying and tell me why you were looking for me.'

'I didn't mean a word of it,' said Sophie wildly. 'I've been mean and jealous and silly and I'm so ashamed and I can't skate and you only want us to be friends—' she gave a great sniff '—but I can't because I've fallen in love with you and I'll have to go away; I really can't go on like this.'

'My darling wife, I have been waiting patiently to hear you say that.' He smiled in the darkness. 'Ever since the moment I first saw you standing on the pavement outside St Agnes's and fell in love with you.'

'Then why didn't you say so?'

'My dear love, you weren't even sure if you liked me.'

She thought this over. 'But you do love me? You were so angry this morning that I didn't know what to do, but Irena came to see me and told me about Jerre and I came to say that I was sorry.'

'What a delightfully brave wife I have. Have you any idea where you are?'

'No, the porter told me where to go, but I couldn't understand him.'

He gave a rumble of laughter. 'However, you found me.' He bent his head and kissed her soundly. 'I shall always take care of you, my darling love.'

He did kiss her again, and an old man, shuffling past, shouted something and laughed.

'What did he say?' asked Sophie.

Rijk said gravely, 'Translated into polite English, he begged me to kiss and hug you.'

Sophie lifted her face to his. 'Well, hadn't you better take his advice?'

* * * * *

*"Brenda Harlen writes couples with such great
chemistry and characters to root for."*
—New York Times *bestselling author Linda Lael Miller*

*The story of committed bachelor Liam Gilmore,
rancher turned innkeeper, and his brand-new manager,
Macy Clayton. She's clearly off-limits, but Liam can't
resist being pulled into her family of adorable triplets!
Is Liam suddenly dreaming of forever after with the
single mom?*

*Read on for a sneak preview of
the next great book in the* Match Made in Haven
miniseries, Claiming the Cowboy's Heart
by Brenda Harlen.

"You kissed me," he reminded her.

"The first time," she acknowledged.

"You kissed me back the second time."

"Has any woman ever *not* kissed you back?" she
wondered.

"I'm not interested in any other woman right now," he
told her. "I'm only interested in you."

The intensity of his gaze made her belly flutter. "I've
got three kids," she reminded him.

"That's not what's been holding me back."

"What's holding you back?"

"I'm trying to respect our working relationship."

"Yeah, that complicates things," she agreed. Then she finished the wine in her glass and pushed away from the table. "Will you excuse me for a minute? I just want to give my mom a call to check on the kids."

"Of course," he agreed. "But I can't promise the rest of that tart will be there when you get back."

She gave one last, lingering glance at the pastry before she said, "You can finish the tart."

He was tempted by the dessert, but he managed to resist. He didn't know how much longer he could hold out against his attraction to Macy—or if she wanted him to.

Had he crossed a line by flirting with her? She hadn't reacted in a way that suggested she was upset or offended, but she hadn't exactly flirted back, either.

"Is everything okay?" he asked when she returned to the table several minutes later.

She nodded. "I got caught in the middle of an argument."

"With your mom?"

"With myself."

His brows lifted. "Did you win?"

"I hope so," she said.

Then she set an antique key on the table and slid it toward him.

Don't miss
Claiming the Cowboy's Heart *by Brenda Harlen,*
available February 2019 wherever
Harlequin® Special Edition books and ebooks are sold.

www.Harlequin.com